WHEN A SPARROW FALLS

WHEN A SPARROW FALLS

A Novel

AUBREY AND ROGER MORRIS

Library of Congress Control Number: 2015900211
ISBN: Hardcover   978-1-5035-3249-6
               Softcover   978-1-5035-3250-2
               eBook   978-1-5035-3251-9

Scripture quotations marked *KJV* are from the Holy Bible, King James Version (Authorized Version), first published in 1611. Quoted from the KJV Classic Reference Bible, © 1983 by the Zondervan Corporation

This is a work of fiction. Names, characters, places and incidents either are the product of the author's imagination or are used fictitiously, and any resemblance to any actual persons, living or dead, events, or locales is entirely coincidental.

Any people depicted in stock imagery provided by Thinkstock are models, and such images are being used for illustrative purposes only.
Certain stock imagery © Thinkstock.

This book was printed in the United States of America.

Rev. date: 01/07/2015

To order additional copies of this book, contact:
Xlibris
1-888-795-4274
www.Xlibris.com
Orders@Xlibris.com
701957

CONTENTS

PART ONE
Shadow Of Death

Chapter 1 —Shenandoah—...13
Chapter 2 —The Recruits— 19
Chapter 3 —Front Royal—..25
Chapter 4 —In Harm's Way— 29

PART TWO
Enemy At The Gates

Chapter 5 —The Message— 39
Chapter 6 —Chimborazo Hospital— 46
Chapter 7 —Pandemonium in the Streets—...................................54
Chapter 8 —Mayo's Toll Bridge—...66
Chapter 9 —A Ragged Rabble— 70
Chapter 10 —Wings as Eagles— 75
Chapter 11 —High Bridge—..80
Chapter 12 —Farmville— 83
Chapter 13 —Toward Appomattox— 89
Chapter 14 —Federal Pickets—..93
Chapter 15 —Swords into Plowshares—.......................................105
Chapter 16 —Elsie—...109
Chapter 17 —Roving Scallywags—...117
Chapter 18 —Shadow of Death—...125
Chapter 19 —The Decision— 129

PART THREE
Unto The Hills

Chapter 20 —Foothill Country— 141
Chapter 21 —A Persuasive Way— 146
Chapter 22 —Edgewood—.. 152
Chapter 23 —Strange and Mysterious Ways— 156
Chapter 24 —Heaven and Earth—..................................... 163
Chapter 25 —Lyle Doolin— 168
Chapter 26 —The Mountaineers— 173
Chapter 27 —The Laborers Are Few— 185
Chapter 28 —The Deputy— 194
Chapter 29 —A Passing Storm—....................................... 198
Chapter 30 —The Teacher—...202
Chapter 31 —The Bell Tolls— 209
Chapter 32 —Any Man's Life— 213
Chapter 33 —Confrontation—...220
Chapter 34 —The Race— 226
Chapter 35 —The Shooters—..232

PART FOUR
A Time To Die

Chapter 36 —Lilly—...245
Chapter 37 —Murder— 250
Chapter 38 —April's Cross— 256
Chapter 39 —The Sly Fox—...260
Chapter 40 —A Hanging Mood—....................................... 271
Chapter 41 —The Gifts— 277
Chapter 42 —A Bit Early—..280
Chapter 43 —The Lord Will Provide—.................................284
Chapter 44 —The Throne of God— 292
Chapter 45 —A Time to Wed—...296

—PREFACE—

In midseventeen hundred the Scottish Irish—after years of battle with the Irish population over land, embittered with the British, and with devastating crop failures—began a mass migration from Northern Ireland to America. Over two hundred and fifty thousand of these impoverished and uneducated immigrants poured into Philadelphia and other Delaware River ports. Met with harsh resentment, considered uncouth and ignorant, these Scottish Irish migrants found themselves shunned by the English, Dutch, and German populace.

With their distilling equipment and centuries-old recipes many of these independent-minded settlers pushed on through the valleys to the Blue Ridge and Appalachian Mountains.

The undulating foothill country east of the Blue Ridge—already gobbled up by huge land grants to prominent English families before the Revolutionary War and recent settlers from the East—left them little choice. In almost total isolation, these hardy immigrants and their descendants scratched out a hardscrabble living on their little, rock-infested mountainside farms.

In the nineteenth century a few preachers, some barely able to read, came into the mountains and began Christian services wherever they were able to gather small groups to listen. Some of these services occurred at harvest time, at corn shucking gatherings in late summer and pig butchering in November. But these roving preachers soon realized that weekend fiddling and dancing was the magnet to draw in far-flung mountaineers.

Most young backwoodsmen ignored the American Civil War, or War of Northern Aggression, as defined by most Southerners, but a few adventurous souls "jined up"—some with the Federals and some with the Confederates.

Both armies soon discovered these lean, tough, untrained mountain men to be superb marksmen and used many as snipers.

Near the end of the war, a few of these Confederate sharpshooters found themselves five miles west of Petersburg in serpentine, mud-infested lines of trench warfare—now manned by ever-thinning ranks of ragged, starving Confederate soldiers.

*

PART ONE
SHADOW OF DEATH

Yea, though I walk through the valley of the shadow of death, I will fear no evil; for thou art with me; thy rod and thy staff they comfort me.

—Psalms 23:4

CHAPTER 1

—SHENANDOAH—

"WHOA," A VOICE sounded from the velvety darkness. Trace chains jangled, and as the rumble of turning wheels died away, a voice boomed urgently. "It's gettin' late, Davie! I 'spect we ought t' get a-goin'. We need to be in Staunton by noontime."

The tall nineteen-year-old lad noisily slurped two quick, tongue-burning swallows of black coffee and deposited the large half-empty cup on the heavy-legged kitchen table. "I'll be there in a minute or two," he responded loudly. "Uncle Ben sure manages to concoct a bitter brew," David Spence muttered. He scooped up the smoky, foul-smelling lantern, strode to the open door, looked out into the early morning darkness, and half-smiled. "Late. It's over an hour until daybreak," he muttered again as the weak yellow lantern glow found the old gray haversack by the woodbox. He slipped the haversack strap over his shoulder and lifted the long-barreled Enfield rifle from the rack above the door. He cut an encompassing glance back to the table. And in the dying rays from the lantern's weak glow, he saw his mother's black Bible. The tall lad paused again, shrugged, and stepped out into the predawn darkness. He turned back, latched the door, and struck out on long-striding legs toward the heavy-laden wagon, looming darkly in the chilly, starlit night.

David Spence hung the flickering lantern on a sideboard hook and held the rifle up to his barrel-chested uncle, sitting stockily on his yellow feather-stuffed cushion. And using the wheel hub as a step, he climbed onto the planked seat beside his uncle.

With a firm giddyup and a flick of lines against his big, well-matched draft horses' haunches, Benjamin Roberts put the big two-horse wagon into motion toward the Staunton railhead, some fourteen miles away.

Behind the seat, the crated hog squealed a mild protest, but neither Ben nor David spoke as the wagon jostled along the narrow, rutted road, cutting through Ben's wide, lush pastures.

Finally, after ten minutes or so, the stocky sixty-year-old man grunted, leaned left, spat a tobacco chaw into the darkness, and raised his eyes to the high moon in a star-canopied sky.

"Now, Davie, I ain't . . ." Ben Robert's voice trailed off. A few silent seconds and he went on cautiously. "Now, Davie, I ain't telling you what t' do, but maybe you ought not quit your schooling and join up with Ol' Tom Jackson's army jus' yet. You've done promised your mama you'd finish studying t' be a preacher and not get yourself caught up in thu fighting. May is planting time, and I'll be needing all thu help I can get. You can spend thu summer with me and go on back to Richmond to finish your schooling. It's a pity you've done got this far along not to finish."

"I appreciate your advice, Uncle Ben, but I've made up my mind," young Spence responded quietly. He had already decided that God, if He exists at all, was a cruel and vengeful God. He shrugged, sighed, and went on, his voice low and hoarse now. "That yellow fever epidemic in fifty-five took Papa, and now that Mother's gone, I'm . . . well, I'm not sure I believe anymore."

"You . . . you ain't believing anymore!" Ben Roberts exclaimed loudly, jerking his head around to face David. "You see them stars and that moon up there?" He lifted his dark eyes and pointed a thick finger skyward. "Now, Davie, there ain't no way they could get up there by accident. It was God that flung them up there. Somewhere in scriptures it says:

> When I consider thy heavens, the work of
> Thy fingers, the moon and the stars,
> which Thou hast ordained; what is man,
> that thou art mindful of Him?

With a sincere Amen, Ben cut an under-brow glance at the lad. In the moon glow he detected a slight frown.

Uncle Ben is well acquainted with scripture, David admitted silently. He tilted his head and frowned at the starlit sky. God, why did you let my mother die? I prayed over her for over a month. It did no good—no good at all.

Ben dug a tobacco twist from a sagging coat pocket and bit off a good-size chunk. "Seems t' me you're still peeved at God for taking your mama," he said in a low, thoughtful tone and leaned from the wagon to spit.

David, casting an under-brow glance at his uncle, said nothing.

Ben turned his eyes skyward again, sighed, and went on earnestly. "Well, I have t' admit t' being a bit peeved at God for a while, but I finally got into thu scriptures and found my way." He slipped a big hand in his coat pocket, pulled out a small dog-eared testament, nudged the lad's arm, and went on softly, casting a puzzled glance at his young nephew. "Now, Davie, if'n you're planning t' join up with Jackson's army, you might as well take this little testament on with you. Since you forgot t' bring your Bible, I 'spect you'll be a-needing it . . . sooner or later."

David shrugged imperceptibly. And without comment, he took the testament and stuffed it in his coat pocket.

The mist-shrouded orange sun had climbed above the Blue Ridge Mountains when the wagon topped a low knoll. Ben Roberts pulled lines, and the big horses, rather anxious to cooperate, brought the heavy wagon to a grinding halt.

"Need t' let thu horses blow awhile," David's uncle explained quietly as he looped the lines around the brake handle. "Think I'll stretch my legs a bit," he mumbled and heaved his bovine body from the wagon.

Several long strides and Ben was at the hillcrest, shading his eyes with a wide hand. "Well, I do declare, now ain't that a sight for sore eyes?" he muttered. "Now ain't that a sight?" he repeated to his nephew, now at his side. Ben laid a long, heavy arm across the lad's wide shoulders. There was a long silence as they gazed into the undulated Shenandoah Valley washed in streaks of orange glow from the rising sun and framed by the tree-crested mountain.

Finally Benjamin sighed deeply and spoke up reverently. "Davie, m'lad, I believe that's what heaven might look like . . . or oughtta look like." With that he smiled, chuckled lightly, cleared his throat, and raised his deep voice, singing an old favorite ballad:

> Oh, Shenandoah, I long to see you.
> Away you rolling river.
> Oh, Shenandoah, I long to see you.
> Away, I'm bound away,
> 'Cross thu wide Missouri . . .

David Spence had to smile.

*

The warm sun was high in the sky as the big wagon rumbled through the outskirts of Staunton and on down Main Street to the center of town.

A loud "Whoa" and Ben drew the two plodding draft horses to a chain-jangling stop at the entrance to Harry Jenkins's Butcher Shop. He turned to his nephew, threw a thumb over his shoulder, and smiled. "That hog oughtta bring a goodly price. Ol' Tom Jackson's army will be needing all thu meat they can get their hands on."

"Where is his army?" young Spence asked wonderingly. "All I saw was a few men in a pasture back there, nailing targets to trees."

"Could be they're down at thu Virginia Central railhead," Uncle Ben surmised as he looped the lines around the whip socket and gruntingly rose from the flattened cushion.

"Well now, Ben," a short, massive man at the door spoke up, "I see you've done brought me another corn-fed shoat."

Ben Roberts chuckled politely as he climbed from the wagon. "Nothing but thu best for you, Harry—nothing but thu best," he repeated as he turned, looked into the butcher's dark, wide-set eyes and grasped his plump, outstretched hand.

Harry Jenkins released Ben's callused hand, pulled a bloodstained apron from his elephantine girth, and cut a sharp, penetrating gaze to David, who was still on the wagon. "I reckon that lad to be your nephew."

The big farmer started to speak, but Jenkins went on.

"Must be that young'un you've been bragging about bein' a crack shot . . . an' all." The butcher chuckled comfortably, and the stripling lad reddened.

Ben glanced at his nephew and responded in a low voice, imbedded with a slight tone of pride. "His name's David Spence, my sister's son. He's done dropped outta Bible school to join Tom Jackson's army. He'll be using his shooting skills t' fight Federal blue jackets. I reckon it's his keen eyes. I figured he'd make a good shooter when I found out he could see a fly on thu wall that nobody else could see—God-given, it is."

Jenkins grunted, shook his huge graying head, and spoke up thoughtfully. "I believe he's all that, but don't reckon he'll be signing up with Ol' Tom Jackson's army any time soon. They've done pulled up stakes and moved on somewhere up round Harrisonburg, I heard."

"Around Harrisonburg," David echoed from the wagon, disappointment in his voice.

"I'm reckonin' they'll be back in a few days," his uncle temporized, stroking his graying chin whiskers. You can join up then. That is, if'n you still have a mind to."

Harry Jenkins grunted a brief chuckle and nodded significantly. "Well, lad, I ain't seeing a need to rush into thu war. I 'spect it'll be with us fur a good while. I'm thinking it to be . . ." He paused a moment to reflect. "Since we thrashed them up 'round Manassas, then went an' let 'um off thu hook, I 'spect it might take nigh on another year or so to whip them bluecoats."

"I'd say a year," Ben agreed judiciously, nodding. "I reckon round this time next year t' be about right."

With obvious apprehension, David frowned, turned on the wagon seat, and pointed. "Well, what about those men back there? They seemed to be preparing for target shooting."

The butcher shook his big head slowly and spoke up in a tone that seemed somewhat apologetic. "I clear forgot about them. Saw them heading out that away 'bout an hour ago, reckon it was. Word is, they joined up late an' have to prove their shooting skills before leaving with thu supply wagons t' join up with General Jackson's army, wherever it might be."

Ben's nephew grasped the Enfield, vaulted from the wagon, turned to his uncle, and put on a thin smile. "I'll go to see if they can use another man with . . . with shooting skills." He saw a deep frown crawling across Ben's wide brow and his little smile disappeared.

Suddenly, a distant volley of rifle fire reached their ears.

"Well, it seems they've started," David said hastily, turning to his uncle. "If I'm not able to join up, I'll wait for you out there."

Benjamin Roberts grasped his nephew's arm and forced a thin smile. "Well, if'n you can't join up," he murmured, "I'll be on in 'bout two hours or so and we . . . we'll talk."

His tall nephew nodded and opened his mouth to speak. But finding nothing to say, he forced a thin smile, slung the haversack strap over his shoulder, firmly held the long-barreled rifle in his right hand, and trotted away.

For a few seconds the two men watched the tall, wide-shouldered lad moving at a fast trot up the dusty street. Finally, Ben sighed, threw a heavy arm across the butcher's round shoulders, and said softly, "I shore hope that boy don't get shot up by some Federal soldier. He's more liken a son than a nephew t' me." He pulled a red handkerchief from a back pocket and blew his nose.

And then, squealing in urgent protest, the crated hog caught their attention.

CHAPTER 2

—THE RECRUITS—

A HALF MILE or so beyond the state asylum, the tiring lad drew back to a brisk walk alongside a split-rail fence. Off to his right, intermittent rifle fire caught his attention. He saw powder smoke climbing skyward. He turned his eyes to the grassy meadow beyond the fence and saw a ragged line of men—about twenty, he reckoned—biting at paper cartridges and rodding them into rifle barrels. "They seem to be in some sort of competition," David Spence muttered, breathing hard.

He stopped and leaned against the top fence rail to observe the motley-dressed men, some seventy yards away, kneeling and hefting their assortment of long-barreled weapons. He shifted the Enfield to his left hand, vaulted over the rail fence, and struck out on long, swift strides across the wide pasture. As David drew nearer, he noticed a heavy youth in a well-fitting uniform. The gray-clad lad was a Virginia Military Institute student, young Spence realized.

The stocky cadet raised a long polished sword. It arched downward. The blade flashed in the bright sunlight, and he yelled in a high voice, "Fire!" With loud echoing explosions of black powder, flame and smoke jetted from nineteen recoiling rifles. A cloud of acrid powder smoke enveloped the stocky cadet. But in a light breeze, the pale smoke slowly dissipated.

And David, with some curiosity, watched the men, all but one, rise to their feet and rush out to retrieve their targets. After a few seconds, he turned his eyes back to the young cadet, now busily and rather clumsily sheathing his long sword. "He's about my age," Spence guessed. "Do I report—?" he started but stopped. The cadet was hurrying toward one of the recruits, now on his feet and fumbling with his long-barreled rifled musket that had failed to fire. The tall gray-whiskered man's age, young Spence figured, was well beyond sixty.

"Mr. Ramsey," the cadet said seriously, grasping the old man's arm, "I'm sorry. I can't sign you up today. Maybe. . . perhaps next time you will qualify," he went on gently.

The man's chin dropped, his countenance reflecting obvious disappointment as tears filled his eyes. He quietly shouldered his antiquated weapon and reluctantly trudged away.

The young cadet turned his brown eyes on David and closed the eight strides between them. He stopped, cleared his throat, extended his right hand, and introduced himself in a surprisingly high-pitched voice. "My name is Albert—Albert Simpson. Did you come to join General Jackson's army or to be an onlooker?"

David shifted the Enfield to his left hand, nodded, and took the offered hand briefly. "I'm David Spence. I would like to join, if I can qualify."

Simpson sighed lightly and pointed. "As soon as those recruits retrieve their targets, you'll have three timed shots at Mr. Ramsey's target—one standing, one kneeling, and one from the prone position. If you hit the target in the allotted time and are able-bodied, you will qualify."

David glanced over the cadet's shoulder. He saw the approaching recruits examining their targets. And several, he noticed, were adroitly punching holes in the flimsy paper.

"Some of those men—"

"Get three cartridges from that box while I examine those targets," the chubby cadet said in a high voice, pointing again. And David detected a knowing smile on his round face.

As young Spence plucked three cartridges from the nearly empty ammunition box, he heard the cadet announce pleasantly, "Well, except Mr. Ramsey, it seems some of you seem to be expert marksmen. After the late arrival attempts to qualify, we'll march to the railhead and have Dr. Adams examine you."

All eyes turned to David, now standing about ten paces off to the left. He felt somewhat embarrassed.

And the cadet, holding back a smile, cut his brown eyes to David and went on. "If you are able to walk, able to talk, and have enough teeth to chew, he'll turn you over to Sergeant Baker. And then"—he paused for effect—"you can sign enlistment papers or make your mark if you're unable to write or print your name." A weak cheer rose from the nineteen recruits.

The chubby cadet turned to David and pulled a silver-plated, stem-winding watch from his uniform pocket. He lifted a brow and half-smiled at the tall lad. "Are you ready Mr. . . . ?"

"My name is David Spence," Ben's nephew repeated brusquely, somewhat annoyed by the tone in Simpson's voice.

The cadet opened the watch cover, looked at David, and smiled. "All right, Spence, when I give the order, you'll have fifteen seconds to load and fire. From the standing position."

David nodded. *Simpson's tone seems somewhat friendly now*, he thought as he stuffed two cartridges in a trouser pocket and clasped the remaining paper cartridge between his teeth. He tilted the rifle and stole a sideways glance at the clump of recruits, who were now watching intently.

"Go!" the high-pitched voice yelled.

David bit into the paper cartridge. And with the sour taste of black powder, he stuffed it in the rifle barrel and jerked the ramrod from the Enfield. And with a motion almost too fast to see, he rammed the cartridge down the long barrel. And without hesitation, he thumbed the hammer to half cock, capped the nipple, and raised the rifle to his shoulder. As the front and rear sights aligned with the target, some seventy yards away, he brought the hammer to full cock and squeezed the trigger.

Before the powder smoke cleared, the young cadet was frowning admonishingly. "That was a quick shot, Spence. Too quick. How do you expect to qualify if you don't take time to aim?"

David cocked his head and chuckled mirthlessly. "Well, when shooting birds on the wing, you have to aim quickly or you're just wasting powder and shot. I believe hitting a fixed target to be a little easier than downing a partridge in full flight."

"We'll see about that, after you finish shooting," Cadet Simpson muttered and pointed a plump finger at the trampled ground. He turned his eyes back to his big silver-plated watch and ordered in his squeaky voice, "Take the kneeling position."

Five minutes later David was striding sprightly across the weedy pasture. With the trailing recruits chiding at his back, every long stride toward the trees raised his pounding heart a beat or two.

"Thu young shooter seems t' know what he's a-doin'," a lanky, clean-shaven man offered with a light chuckle. "I'm willing t' bet a dollar he got at least one hit—maybe more'n one."

That brought on a round of ribald laughter, followed by a caustic response from a long-bearded, slack-jawed recruit. "I'd be willin' t' take that bet if'n I had a dollar, or could borrow one." He shook his balding head. "An' I'm reckonin' there ain't a single dollar t' be found among this whole bunch."

The recruits fell silent and strained to see the growing target on the bullet-scarred maple tree. They crowded in as Spence, with the oppressive odor of unwashed bodies in his nostrils, reached for the paper target and managed to jerk it from the tree before they could see. And with the murmur of halfhearted complaints in his ears, David folded the target, shrugged his shoulders, and spoke up. "Cadet Simpson should see the target first. Maybe he'll let you take a look," he added, hiding a smile.

"I'll see it now." The cadet's high voice silenced their protestations. The recruits parted and he stepped forward, hand extended.

A faint smile and a little flourish and Spence handed Simpson the paper target. He stepped aside as the motley recruits flooded in and surrounded the young cadet.

Except for the rustle of paper and a couple of inaudible comments, there was silence for a few seconds. And then the long-bearded man's voice rose above the motley group. "Dang! One looks t' be dead center an' thu other two t' be off by no more'n au hair. Beats anything I ever seed. That young fellow's a-fixin' t' be thu deadliest shot in this whole bunch. Could just be thu deadliest shot in thu whole army, I'm a-thankin'."

With wide smiles and laudatory comments, the recruits turned to the uncomfortable lad and administered several congratulatory back slaps and firm handshakes.

The round-faced cadet stepped forward, pulled out his watch, and spoke up sharply, trying to force authority in his high tone. "All right, men, we must hurry to the railhead and help load the supply wagons. They are scheduled to move out about three o'clock, if the supply train arrives on time."

"Will I have time to bid my uncle farewell?" David asked seriously. "I believe he's still in town."

A discernible twinkle came into the young cadet's dark-brown eyes. He extended a pudgy hand and responded through a spreading grin. "How can I refuse the request of a sharpshooter?" Still lightly grasping David's strong hand, he went on in a low, sincere tone. "You must be at the railhead well before three o'clock, though." The cadet paused. After a thoughtful moment he went on. "I'll say good-bye now and wish you Godspeed." He released Spence's hand and nodded slightly. "After I escort these recruits to the railhead, I'll be leaving for VMI."

Somewhat surprised by Simpson's friendly comments, David hesitated, searching for an adequate response. "Well, well, maybe we'll meet again. . . someday soon," he finally managed quietly.

*

It was nearing five o'clock when the seven-car train with a long wail of its whistle and clashing of colliding metal chugged away from the Stanton railhead and trundled northward, down the Shenandoah Valley.

Perched on a high wagon seat with the odor of woodsmoke from the little locomotives firebox still in his nostrils, young David Spence turned to the tall, lanky man at his side and asked seriously, "Where are we going?"

The long-boned teamster, chafing over the delay, eyed the youth sourly and disdainfully spat a brown stream of tobacco juice on a wagon wheel. "Well, young fellow," he answered solemnly, "I ain't thu one t' be asked 'bout that." He pulled a sullied hand across his tobacco-stained whiskers and asked roughly, "What name you go by, boy?"

To cover his resentment of the word *boy*, Ben's nephew cleared his throat, forced a wan smile, and answered evenly. "I'm David Spence. And what is your name?" He thought to add *old man* but changed his mind.

"Simon—Simon Gordon," the teamster said, smiled thinly, and cut a pale, mischievous eye to the gangly lad. "Except rifle and pouch, you didn't bother to bring a blanket nor gear—that I can see," the older man added.

David frowned. "Well, I thought, except for underclothes and rifle, the army would supply my needs."

A low grunt, followed by a little shrug, and Simon reached down to pull a long braided leather whip from the wagon bed. "When we make camp tonight, I'll dig out a blanket or two. After all"—Simon chuckled lightly—"this here's an supply wagon."

Young Spence looked beyond the scrawny mules. Some fifty yards ahead, he saw a tall, frustrated captain astride a big bay stallion, waving the long line of wagons into motion.

Loud giddyaps and cracking whips sent twenty-two heavy-laden, canvas-covered army wagons, followed by three captured howitzers, rumbling away from the Virginia Central Railroad and turning northward on the rough, dusty valley turnpike.

Chapter 3

—FRONT ROYAL—

FOUR DAYS LATER, after traversing a narrow, twisting mountain road from the Shenandoah, they finally found General Jackson's worn army bivouacked in the Luray Valley, near Bentonville, a hamlet about ten miles south of Front Royal.

In drizzling rain, David turned to Gordon and asked, "When do you think we'll stop?" The balding teamster opened his mouth to answer, but Private Spence went on. "It's turning dark and these wet mules seem mighty worn."

"With thu little I can see, them wagons look t' be pullin' off into that field up yonder a ways," Simon Gordon submitted sagely, spitting and shifting his chaw. He expertly reined through a gap in the split-rail fence into the long, grassy field and reined the jaded mules to a snorting stop.

Out of twilight's darkening shadows, Sergeant Baker—a tall, muscular man, thirty years of age or thereabouts—appeared beside the wagon. "No fires tonight, Gordon," he ordered firmly. "Hitch the mules and be ready to move out by five in the morning." He paused to pull a small black notebook from beneath his slicker. "Are you Spence?" the bearded sergeant asked, lifting a squinty gaze from the little notebook to David.

"Yes. I . . . I'm Spence. Private Spence, sir," the recruit answered hesitantly.

In the growing darkness Sergeant Baker smiled tiredly. "Don't call me sir. I'm not an officer . . . yet." He turned and pointed to a large oak tree about twenty yards away. "All right, sharpshooter, report to me at that tree, no later than ten minutes till five in the morning, for assignment."

In quiet apprehension, David nodded.

*

Dawn's first light was rimming the Blue Ridge as David made his way past the line of wagons toward the widespread oak. Up ahead, silhouetted darkly under the tree, he spotted a group of murmuring men. "I might be a little late," he muttered and lengthened his stride. As he approached the mumbling men, he heard a friendly chuckle. "Well, here comes thu sharpshooter."

David recognized the voice. It was a voice that carried the unique cadence of the tall, slim, clean-shaven man he had seen at target shooting.

With a narrow smile on his face, the slender man stepped forward, right hand extended. "I'm Joseph Meeks. Word has it that we'll be split up for replacements. I'm thinking, if'n you and me line up side by side, we might stay together. That is, if it's all right with you," he went on in a low voice of confidentiality.

"Well, well, that's fine with me," David responded halfheartedly. Somewhat bewildered, he nodded and took the man's extended hand.

"Form a line over here," Sergeant Baker's loud, authoritative voice sounded.

And a ragged line it was. David Spence found himself dangling at the left end with the men at his right, shuffling back and forth, trying to form up. It was all to no avail.

With a disgusted look on his sun-browned face, the tall sergeant pulled out his little notebook. "Stop shifting about and listen up," he ordered in a firm military tone, his sharp, penetrating eyes sweeping along the ragged line of recruits and coming to rest on David. "You men . . ." He paused and frowned. "You recruits will be split up and assigned a regiment. Lest you forget, I'll give each of you a slip of paper naming your assigned regiment. If you can't read it, find someone who can." He tore a page from his notebook and walked purposefully toward Private Spence, standing stiffly on the end of the ragged line at what he supposed was an attitude of attention.

*

In the warming midmorning sun the three Confederates, striding at a hurried pace along the Luray Road, finally overtook the rear elements of the First Maryland Regiment.

Sergeant Baker gestured and said tiredly, "It looks like them Marylanders are taking the lead and swinging eastward at that little church." He adjusted his haversack and went on. "I believe they—"

Private Meeks cleared his throat. "It looks like they're turning up that lane at Asbury Chapel and climbing the high ridge to Gooney Manor Road. Might be hard pullin' t' get them wagons up that hillside, I'm thinkin'."

Baker raised a thick brow and chuckled lightly. "You seem to have some knowledge of the area."

"I was born n' raised back yonder a ways," the slender private said, waving his hand back toward the little town.

For a few seconds they watched the two long columns, now torturously winding their way at a snail's pace up the treelined, serpentine trail.

"Do you know where we're going?" David Spence asked thoughtfully as they trudged on.

Meeks replied matter-of-factly, "Like as not, they're heading to Front Royal. It's 'bout four or five miles off to thu north," he added, conviction in his tone.

"Pick up the pace," the tall sergeant ordered. "We have to move on past the Marylanders and report to Colonel Johnson."

David detected a touch of urgency in the sergeant's voice.

*

On the Gooney Manor Road, about a mile from Front Royal, Sergeant Baker and the two dog-tired recruits finally reached the head of the long columns.

Baker gestured. "That's Colonel Johnson over there." He stopped, doffed his forage cap, pulled out a red handkerchief, and wiped his sweat-beaded brow. He adjusted his cap and ordered tiredly, "Wait here while I report to the colonel."

The two worn privates moved into the shade of a small oak, leaned on their long-barreled Enfield rifles, and watched the wide-shouldered sergeant quickstep over to the heavy officer at the fringe of the narrow road, astride his bay stallion.

With a booted leg hooked about the pommel of his McClellan saddle, the colonel seemed to be intently scrutinizing his bone-weary Marylanders trudging along the hilltop road in two raggedy lines.

Sergeant Baker drew himself up and threw the colonel a sharp salute, and Johnson responded with a wave of his mutilated cigar.

They conversed for about three or four minutes.

Finally, the big-boned Confederate officer smiled, leaned from the saddle, and handed his binoculars to the tall sergeant. Baker looped the strap over his shoulder, raised his right hand to his sweat-stained forage cap, and snapped a parting salute.

The colonel waved his chewed-down, slobber-soaked cigar, put foot to stirrup, clucked to his horse, and galloped away.

Still leaning on their rifles, the anxious recruits watched the sergeant approach. The expression on his face seemed to be somewhere between a smile and a frown.

"Well, we have our assignment," Baker informed them seriously. He adjusted the binocular strap and went on thoughtfully. "I believe I impressed Colonel Johnson somewhat more than intended, telling him about your shooting skills. He handed me his binoculars and said his skirmishers could use a few more sharpshooters."

"What . . . what are skirmishers?" David asked haltingly.

The sergeant thoughtfully stroked his dark chin whiskers awhile. "Well, I'd say they're the soldiers that scout out front." He glanced at the tired, ragged line of passing Marylanders and went on hastily. "I'll explain later. We need to hurry."

CHAPTER 4

—IN HARM'S WAY—

IT WAS SHORTLY after midday when the Confederate skirmishers, now well ahead of the main force, were moving stealthily across the crest of a tree-covered hill just southeast of Front Royal. They positioned themselves along a shallow depression at the fringe of the trees and scanned the weedy hillside toward the town.

On his knees, Sergeant Baker was looking through the colonel's binoculars. A swift survey and he lowered the glasses. "Well," he muttered, "I don't see any bluecoats near that redbrick house. Looks like we can . . ." and his voice trailed off. He peered through the binoculars again and went on, a touch of excitement in his voice. "We may be able to take that house without a fight."

At his elbow, Joseph Meeks muttered timorously. "Looks like General Jackson's done fooled them again."

"I certainly hope so," David put in, trying to keep his voice calm. He raised his head above the low embankment and cut a brief, encompassing look down the long, weed-infested slope. A thoughtful pause and he turned to the sergeant. "When do you think we'll attack?"

"Not long," Baker responded astutely, lowered the glasses, and glanced along the depression. He saw nearby Marylanders waiting anxiously and tossed a thumb off to the right. "Looks like General Jackson's gonna have our Confederate Marylanders attacking those Federal Marylanders," he went on calmly, spiting.

"I'm reckonin' we . . . we'll be in a tussle with them bluecoats soon," Meeks stumbled.

David heard fear in the private's voice and clutched his rifle firmly to calm a trembling hand.

Private Meeks cupped a hand near David's ear and almost whispered, "Are you as scared as I am?"

Private Spence muttered, "Yes. Well, I'm—"

"Skirmishers out!" echoed along the line. And simultaneously, it seemed to David, forty-two Confederates rose up, rushed out from the trees, and dogtrotted down the weedy slope toward the town.

They were halfway down the slope, when Sergeant Baker, now at the far left, threw up a hand and wheezed, "Stop, we've pulled ahead. Wait for the other skirmishers to close up."

And at Baker's right, the two privates sucking deep breaths into their burning lungs pulled up and looked back.

A slight headshake and Sergeant Baker explained. "We'll be tempting targets if we get too far ahead."

No sooner had the words left the sergeant's lips that Federal artillery fire erupted from somewhere beyond the town, sending a volley of shells streaking across the sky and plowing into the hillside about twenty yards behind the skirmishers.

"Take cover," Baker shouted, turned, and dived in a shallow depression. And already on their knees, the two privates were scrambling for cover. Meeks crawled in a rain-washed ditch, David behind him.

A pause, then Federal cannons sent another salvo of death-dealing shells and solid shot toward the hunkered-down skirmishers.

They have the range now, David thought.

Off to their right, a deafening blast filled the air with smoke and flying debris. The two privates felt the earth-shaking explosion, and almost simultaneously, debris and sod enveloped them.

Joseph Meeks blasphemed loudly, his heart pounding.

Dry-mouthed, David pressed his face in the high weeds and prayed silently.

Again, the cannons fell silent and Baker's voice rang out. "You can get up now. I reckon they've stopped for a while."

"That was close," Meeks muttered as he climbed to his feet.

"Very close," David agreed. He scanned the weedy, poke-marked slope and saw a dozen or so sprawled bodies. *Those dead men up there were close—close enough to be killed*, he thought.

"All right, let's move on," Baker ordered, tone muted.

Somewhere, a clamor of musketry fire erupted.

David and Sergeant Baker exchanged questioning glances.

"That's Federal rifle fire," Meeks cried, raising his Enfield to his shoulder. "It's down there." He pointed the weapon. They saw a pale of powder smoke drifting from behind the redbrick house, and the young privates tensed.

"They're not targeting us," Baker concluded calmly, glancing up the weedy slope. At the fringe of the tree-crested hilltop, he saw the main body of the First Maryland Brigade forming up.

Again, rifle fire flared and David called, pointing, "There's someone running up that ravine."

"It's a woman!" Meeks exclaimed angrily. "Looks like them bluecoats are targeting her."

Baffled, the three Confederates watched as lead rifle balls plucked up clumps of sod about the racing girl. Her white sunbonnet and apron presented prime targets, but the lithe figure was moving quickly and using the ravine to good effect.

Somewhere beyond the town a cannon boomed. A shell fuse traced a pale line across the Virginia sky, and gray smoke blossomed on the hillside about ten yards beyond the rushing girl.

Again, David's eyes turned to the slender woman, now noticeably tiring as she stumbled from the shallow ravine and dropped to the ground. He caught his breath. "She's wounded," he muttered.

At a fast trot the three Confederates approached the exhausted girl, now on her knees, head bowed and whispering a prayer.

"Are you—?" Sergeant Baker saw her praying and stopped. She raised her blue eyes and he asked hurriedly, deep concern in his voice, "Are you all right?" Still gasping for air, the young woman managed a shallow nod as Baker reached down and grasped a small arm. He gently helped the girl rise to her feet and said seriously, "Young lady, don't you realize you're in harm's way?"

"Goodness gracious!" the girl responded breathlessly, a hand over her heart. "I need a moment to recover my breath." About ten seconds passed. She sucked a deep breath and went on, urgency in her voice. "My name is Bell Boyd. I have information for General Jackson. I must—" The swift thud of galloping hooves stopped her.

A big Confederate officer reined his snorting horse. "Bell!" he exclaimed. "What are you doing here?"

"Henry, take me to General Jackson," she gasped anxiously, recognizing the major. "I have important information concerning Federal forces."

Off to their left, about twenty yards or so, a shell exploded, sending another geyser skyward, and Major Henry Douglas, with some difficulty, managed to jerk his nervous mare around. And with reins tight, he kicked a foot from the stirrup, turned his eyes on David, and ordered hastily, "Private, help Ms. Boyd up."

Spence nodded, handed Meeks his rifle, and quickly stepped forward. He clamped his big hands about the girl's slender waist and lifted her up. He guessed her age to be about seventeen or eighteen.

With no visible evidence of embarrassment, Bell Boyd put a foot to the empty stirrup and hiked her lace-fringed petticoats. And effortlessly, it seemed to David, she threw her willowy body astraddle the anxious horse behind the big officer. With slender arms firmly about the major's waist, she turned her blue eyes on David and cast him a brief smile.

Douglas slacked the reins and the anxious mare bolted away.

The three Confederates shifted their attention to the redbrick house and the unseen blue-coated soldiers they would, no doubt, encounter shortly.

"Spread out," the sergeant ordered firmly as they moved on down the slope. "Stay about ten feet apart," he went on calmly as they drew within fifty paces of the front porch. Baker ventured a glance over his shoulder. He saw the Maryland Brigade debouching from the hilltop trees and charging down the long slope. "Pick up the pace," he ordered hurriedly, sweeping his eyes back from the charging Confederates. "And watch the windows," he ordered again.

Fully focused on their assigned mission now, the three skirmishers moved cautiously toward the big two-story house.

A heavy bluecoat rounded the rear corner of the house. With quick surprise on his wide face, he stopped, nervously pulled the Winchester's hammer to half cock, and fumbled to cap the nipple.

Now separated by five or six paces, the two Confederate privates in unison raised their Enfield rifles and thumbed hammers to full cock. Meeks squeezed the trigger. A rush of emotion coursed through his veins. The hammer fell with a nauseating dull click. He had neglected to cap the nipple.

David's right eye looked down the long rifle barrel and saw the bluecoat's face and his rifle, the Federal still fumbling. With sour bile in his throat, he aligned the sights on the blue-clad chest, caught his breath, and tightened his finger against the trigger. "Shoot!" he heard Meeks's frantic voice call.

I . . . I must pull the trigger, David's mind cried desperately. *Think of a partridge in flight*, he told himself. Then another voice seemed to whisper in his ear: *Thou shalt not kill.* It was his mother's soft voice. The rifle barrel wavered. Sweat beaded the young recruit's brow. He clinched his jaw and forced his trigger finger. It refused to obey. The blue blouse seemed to morph into his mother's blue dress. He glanced at Meeks and saw magnified eyes, now rounded with fear, staring back at him.

Suddenly, somewhere ahead, a shot rang out. Time seemed too slow. A lead ball found Private Meeks's gray blouse, ripped a jagged hole in his chest, and flung him backward.

Petrified, David watched Joseph Meeks fall to the ground. He glanced up. Just beyond the private's bleeding body, he saw smoke and flame leap from Sergeant Baker's Enfield.

In the echo of Baker's rifle, about ten paces behind them, an ear-splitting explosion filled the atmosphere with dirt, smoke, and death-dealing shards of hot metal.

A shriek of pain came into Private Spence's ears. The sound seemed distant, but he knew it had risen from his own throat. He saw a blinding light that scattered into a thousand stars. His legs buckled. Dazed and blinded, he found himself on his back, enveloped with dirt and debris. Confused, David Spence struggled to rise but fell backward. "I . . . I can't feel my left leg," he moaned. "Oh Lord! I've—I think I've lost my leg."

"Lie still, Spence," a low voice responded evenly. "You ain't lost your leg," Baker went on softly and placed a restraining hand on David's shoulder. "I must stop the bleeding before you—" The big sergeant stopped abruptly. Hastily, he pulled the bayonet from his rifle and cut the tattered, blood-soaked trousers from Spence's leg.

"How . . . how does it look?" David moaned.

Baker muttered. "Oh, it ain't too bad, considering—"

"Considering!" David blurted, "What . . . what do you mean?"

"Well, looks like it missed the bone. It's still bleeding some, though. If gangrene don't set in, you'll be good as new in . . . in a few weeks."

Baker's remark was unconvincing.

Just then, with the overwhelming sound of rushing feet and bloodcurdling yells, a solid wave of gray-and-butternut-clad soldiers flooded on past and sprayed the retreating bluecoats back into the center of town.

The battle for Front Royal that had just begun seemed to be about over. The desultory Federal rifle fire slowed and then stopped altogether as the charging Confederates pushed them into a full-blown, chaotic retreat toward Winchester.

*

"This should slow the bleeding . . . somewhat," Sergeant Baker said calmly as he cinched the leather belt around David's leg, just above his knee.

Half-conscious, Private Spence opened his eyes and turned his blurred gaze to the body—prostrate in a pool of spreading blood. "Meeks is dead. I . . . I killed him," David moaned.

A little confused, Sergeant Baker cast a quizzical look at Spence and was silent a thoughtful moment. Finally, he said clearly, "That's not possible." Baker shook his head in disbelief. "You couldn't have killed him."

"I caused his death," David sobbed. "I could have shot that Federal soldier. I couldn't do it."

"Couldn't do it?" Baker echoed. "Did your rifle misfire?"

David Spence rose on his elbow and almost whispered. "I couldn't pull the trigger. I believe . . . I'm sure God stopped me."

"Well, He didn't stop me," the sergeant retorted firmly. "I spotted the bluecoat that shot Private Meeks and fired. Sadly, it was a bit late, but I got him."

"I could have shot that Federal when he rounded the corner of the house," David muttered.

"Rounded the corner!" the sergeant exclaimed dubiously, his dark eyes flashing. "The bluecoat at that upstairs window killed Meeks. I'm sure of that," he went on forcefully, pointing to the blue-clad body draped over a second floor window sill.

David was skeptical. "What happened to the Federal that rounded—?"

"He ran off," Baker answered the unfinished question and rose to his feet. "I'll help you onto the porch and go up the hill to find an ambulance wagon and, hopefully, a doctor," he said softly.

Sprawled on the front porch for about fifteen minutes, his left leg throbbing painfully, Private Spence reached under his blouse and pulled out Uncle Ben's pocket testament. He saw a jagged hole in the black leather cover. "What—?" he started, hastily opened the testament and found a buried thumbnail size, metal sliver. "This little testament probably saved my life," he muttered and thought of Uncle Ben as he slipped it in his coat pocket.

David could still hear distant, sporadic rifle fire as a wagon rattled to stop a few feet away. Steps creaked, footfalls approached, and Sergeant Baker spoke up, his tone compassionate. "I ran into the ambulance wagon up the hillside a ways but couldn't get the doctor. He was busy amp . . . treating the wounded. Two stretcher bearers were with the wagon. I made . . . convinced them to come along."

The two men tromped heavily onto the porch, carefully placed the wounded private on a canvas stretcher somewhat short for his frame, and carried him out to the wagon.

Baker vaulted aboard. A whip cracked and two bony mules jerked the iron-rimmed, canvas-covered wagon forward.

As they jolted up the rough hillside, the sergeant asked, trying to sound positive, "Do you plan to remain in the army after your leg heals?"

"No," David muttered, almost too low to hear. "A man that can't kill the enemy is no soldier. After my leg heals I'll probably return to divinity school."

"You studied religion?" Baker blurted incredulously.

The wounded private nodded his tousled, dust-ridden head. "I studied theology for two years, but it seems, since my mother's death, I've been dealing with the devil."

The sergeant put a hand to his chin and stroked his dark whiskers a long moment. Finally, he forced a small smile. "You ain't been dealing with the devil," he said sincerely. "It seems to me you've been wrestling the devil."

"Wrestling the devil," David Spence whispered drowsily, feeling in his coat pocket for Uncle Ben's little testament. "Maybe . . . well, maybe you are right. I'm sure now. God alone will determine my destiny." His eyes fluttered, then closed, and he fell into a fitful slumber.

PART TWO
ENEMY AT THE GATES

Our feet shall stand within the gates,
O Jerusalem.

—Psalm 122:2

CHAPTER 5

—THE MESSAGE—

IT WAS SUNDAY morning, the second day in April, and the twenty-two-year-old chaplain was squinting at the reflected image of his broad face in a small oval wall mirror. He shrugged his shoulders, pulled a long finger across his dark mustache, and his mind drifted back all the way back to the battle at Front Royal.

How long has it been since that battle? David Spence asked himself. "It's been almost three years," the tall Confederate chaplain confided to his reflection as he buttoned his clerical collar. "It seems a lifetime." *I believe the War Department has branded me a coward*, he ventured silently. *Ever since I graduated from divinity school, all my appeals to minister soldiers on the battlefield have been rejected.* He sighed deeply and thought on. *Well, maybe it's God's will that I minister to wounded soldiers in Richmond hospitals.*

"Rachel, would you look to see if Isaac has Nicie hitched?" the young chaplain called, his weighty voice carrying easily into the kitchen. "Today is communion Sunday at St. Paul's. I'm a little late."

As he slipped into his threadbare coat, a deep chuckle came from the kitchen, followed by a woman's friendly drawl. "Well, it ain't much doubt about being late. It's already ten thirty and looks like thu preaching's gonna be well along by thu time you get there." A brief pause to glance through the window and she went on. "I see Isaac bringing thu mare and buggy from out back."

David moved hastily into the kitchen and on toward the porch. At the door he stopped, noticed a frayed sleeve, and bit off the stray thread. "My Bible," he muttered and swung around.

As the long striding chaplain approached the bulky woman, a smile split her broad face. And chuckling lightly, she pulled a black dog-eared Bible from somewhere beneath her apron. "I didn't think you'd get far without your Bible."

"Thank you, Rachel," David said in a low voice that carried a tone of sincerity. He took the Bible, turned, and hurried out the kitchen door.

Rachel sighed. "He ain't hardly let that Bible outta his sight since his mama handed it to him as she lay abed dying. I reckon it's been nigh on four years since she went to be with thu Almighty. My, oh my, how time does fly," the big woman mumbled as she turned to the big cast-iron cook stove.

With frock tail flapping, David stepped down from the side porch and hurried toward the buggy, his limp barely discernible. "I'll go directly from St. Paul's Church up to Chimborazo Hospital," David murmured thoughtfully as he skirted a muddy puddle and climbed in the buggy. He looked down at Isaac, now stroking the docile mare's neck with a wide, toothy smile on his long, bewhiskered face, and said, "I hope Rachel can scrape up something for supper. It'll probably be dusk before I arrive with Willie Marshall. He's the wounded lad I spoke to you about," the chaplain added thoughtfully.

The tall, raw-boned sixty-three-year-old man's smile turned into a frown. He shook his graying head slightly. "Well, vittles are gettin' mighty hard t' come by these days." He pushed a long index finger under his stained straw-hat, scratched a few seconds, and went on unsurely. "I reckon we can scrape up a mouthful or two."

David nodded slightly. "I think . . . Well, Isaac, I'm sure you can." He flashed his even, white teeth, took up the lines, and clucked the bay mare into a respectable trot.

"I don't know how we're gonna feed another mouth," Isaac muttered, scratching under his hat again, as he watched the buggy splash through the mud and turn onto Fifth Street.

The peal of distant church bells reached David's ears. He jerked the whip from the socket and touched up Nicie's haunches, and the bay mare gated into a syncopated trot. Then mingling with the clatter of iron-rimmed buggy wheels and the clop of the mare's hooves on cobblestone, another sound came to him; it was the distant rumble of exploding cannon shells. *The firing seems ominous today,* he thought. It could be Confederate fire—more than likely to be Federal, though.

Across the street he saw yellow daffodils and dogwood trees robed in the blooming garb of spring. And then on beyond the city was a clear, blue sky. The trees are stirring a bit. *Maybe the breeze from the south is enhancing the rumble of the cannon fire,* he tried to convince himself.

David's thoughts turned to Chimborazo Hospital. It was shortly after dark last night, when thirty-one hollow-cheeked men arrived and a badly wounded old veteran, on the bunk across from Willie, whispered his prediction: "Them Federals done turned our flank over at Five Forks an' captured au passel of our soldiers. I'm a-thinkin' them t' be in Richmond by tomorrow, maybe 'fore daylight comes."

David turned the buggy onto Grace Street, shook his head slightly, and murmured, "Maybe this bloody war will end soon. A generation of young men have been wounded or killed. It's all madness . . . madness." He raised his eyes. In the distance, at the corner of Ninth Street, he saw St. Paul's Episcopal Church steeple protruding just above the trees.

As the old buggy drew near the church, he noticed a few late worshippers—men in their best shoes and long frock coats and women in their lightly bustled spring dresses—rushing up the wide stone steps and disappearing between large columns. The muffled sounds of exploding cannon shells, some twenty-five miles off toward Petersburg, did not worry them, it seemed to the young chaplain. It was a balmy spring day and after all the Federal siege had continued for almost nine months without disturbing Richmond.

David buttoned his frayed coat and muttered, "I'm a little late. I may not find a seat. Communion Sunday seems to swell a congregation considerably." *Just a few stragglers now,* he noticed as he drew the mare down to a walk and turned the rig onto Ninth Street. A pull of lines accompanied by a firm "Whoa" brought the old buggy to a creaking stop behind a black phaeton.

Chaplain Spence clambered down, lifted the horse-holding weight from the buggy box, and tethered it to the mare's halter. With the battered black Bible clutched firmly in his right hand, he struck out toward the wide steps.

In the vestibule, he saw the church sexton—a short, chubby Englishman named William Irving—standing by the sanctuary door.

As usual, he was dressed in a snug, threadbare blue suit with brass buttons and a starched white shirt with ruffled collar and sleeves. The long-time sexton, who seemed to have a touch of arrogance about him, was well past sixty, David guessed.

As he hurried toward the sanctuary, the pompous sexton shook his head and put a plump white-gloved index finger to his wide lips. "Just a minute," he whispered with obvious disapproval. "Wait for the hymn before you enter."

"I apologize for arriving late," Spence whispered back. "I was at Chimborazo Hospital until—"

The organ blaring "A Mighty Fortress Is Our God" stopped him.

Irving's frown evaporated. A nod of his balding head and he gestured toward the spacious sanctuary.

Quietly, David slipped into the large gray-walled room and stood several seconds, scanning for a vacant seat. He found the congregation to be mostly women, many in long black mourning dresses, mingled with well-clothed government officials and military officers in dress uniforms. A few worshippers were ambulatory wounded soldiers. Several, the chaplain noticed, were patients from Chimborazo Hospital.

There, eight rows from the rear, is a small space beside that woman wearing a feathered blue bonnet. *Maybe I can squeeze in*, he told himself as he made his way quietly and reverently down the aisle as the congregation sang "Jesus, Lover of My Soul." The young chaplain reached the pew and waited for the hymn to end.

And the tall, rail-thin woman, with a hidden glance at the big, handsome man standing in the aisle at her side, smiled and sang on.

A little off-key, David thought. But hearing her sing on, he changed his mind. *That thin woman is way off-key*, he decided.

The hymn concluded. And with the scrape of boots, a few light coughs, and rustling petticoats, the congregation sat down on the uncomfortable polished-oak pew seats. The long-removed plush cushions had been donated to Richmond hospitals.

A vague gesture and David forced a small smile. He leaned forward and whispered to the woman, "Would you mind . . . ?"

The forty-year-old spinster put on a thin-faced little smile, gave the young man a shallow nod, gathered her bustled skirts, and slipped over to make room. With another brief glance she noticed the chaplain's garb and her smile morphed into a frown. What kind of chaplain would be late for church service? The slender woman condemned him silently.

While easing his big body on the pew seat, David saw her thought, managed another small smile, and turned his attention to the pulpit where the pious rector, Dr. Charles Minnigerode—a bespectacled little German immigrant with thin lips and high forehead—was clearing his throat. The little rector adjusted his spectacles. And in his thickly accented voice, he launched into a well-rehearsed sermon. With the ominous rumble of distant cannon fire as a backdrop, the diminutive German droned on.

David struggled mightily to concentrate. He was determined to avoid the pitfalls that many visiting pastors fall into—of unintended evaluation and outright criticism.

*

A young courier galloped his underfed gray gelding noisily up the cobblestone street and reined in at St. Paul's. The gangly lad tossed the reins over the snorting horse's head, leaped from the worn Grimsley saddle, and hurried up the wide steps. With a mild jangle of spur rowels, he entered the vestibule and approached the corpulent sexton still standing by the sanctuary door. The young messenger saw the disapproving frown on the sexton's round face and forced himself back to a brisk stride, rowels still jangling.

It was about eleven thirty when he pulled up before the frowning sexton and cleared his throat. "I . . . I must deliver a very important message to President Davis," he whispered hoarsely.

"Dr. Minnigerode will be having prayer in a minute," Irving responded in a firm whisper. "You'll have to wait until he finishes."

"But—"

A gloved finger at the heavy sexton's lips stopped the lad. A few thoughtful seconds and the young messenger, mumbling incoherently, shifted his feet and pulled a folded note from his coat pocket. He pressed it in the Englishman's hand and whispered urgently, a touch of irritation in his voice. "President Davis must get this message immediately."

William Irving glanced at the folded note and read silently:

FOR PRESIDENT DAVIS'S EYES ONLY

His broad face paled. "I'll . . ." His voice faded away when he lifted his eyes and saw the slender lad hurrying toward the door.

As the rotund sexton's unsure feet carried him through the entrance to the sanctuary, he realized the little minister was well into the communion homily and paused. And with all the dignity he could muster, Irving sucked a deep, silent breath and strode down the aisle with the note in a gloved hand, extended just enough to attract the somnolent congregation's attention. Anxious eyes turned from the thin-faced German and followed the heavy sexton, now advancing down the aisle to pew sixty-three.

Irving stopped. And with some hesitation, he reached out and gently touched Davis's shoulder.

Startled slightly, the Confederate president jerked his head up to see the heavy sexton bow a bit stiffly. And with a mild flourish, he handed Davis the note and straightened to attention as best he could, his apprehensive eyes fixed on the president's skeletal face.

President Davis unfolded the slip of paper, and except for a barely perceptual movement of thin lips, there was no noticeable change of expression as he silently read the hastily scribed message:

> Gen. Lee telegraphs that our lines are broken.
> I advise you come to the office immediately
> and prepare to leave Richmond
>
> —Breckinridge

At David's side, the slender woman tilted her head to see. Her hat feather brushed his cheek. Instinctively, he drew his head back slightly and momentarily pulled his eyes from the president to see a tail feather. It was all the remains of a Dominic rooster that had long ago been sacrificed to the cook pot, he suspected. The chaplain shifted his gaze back to the president but failed to see his face.

The congregation seemed to hold its collective breath as the sallow-faced Confederate president stuffed the note in the pocket of his gray Prince Albert coat and retrieve his broad-brimmed hat from the pew seat. Silently he rose to his feet, gave Irving a slight nod, and strode at a deliberate pace up the aisle toward the vestibule.

All eyes seemed to follow him to the rear of the sanctuary, trying to find some solace in his expression. They saw none. As the skeletal president passed, all Chaplain Spence could discern was his stern expression and possibly more pallor in his face.

Minnigerode continued the service, sensed the increasing restiveness of the congregation, and hurried on, his tone rising slightly, his German accent more pronounced.

He was busily preparing for communion as the heavy sexton, perspiring profusely and breathing heavily, returned hurriedly to escort government officials from the room.

David turned, glanced over his shoulder, and saw a few nervous whispering back-pew members moving stealthy toward the doors. But most of the congregants remained seated, he noticed, as he swept his eyes back to the pulpit.

Several minutes later the diminutive rector ended the service. A brief prayer and he daubed at his sweat-beaded brow with a white handkerchief. And the congregation—except for a dozen or so, dawdling to converse in lowered tones—silently filed out.

Chaplain Spence paused briefly in the vestibule to shake Dr. Minnigerode's limp, bony hand, forced a thin smile, and made his way on out into the bright, warm sunlight. At the steps he stopped, shaded his eyes with a hand, and squinted across to the mingling congregations from St. James's and St. Paul's in Capitol Square, near the bronze equestrian statue of Washington.

His eyes adjusted to the light and he glanced down Grace Street. At the Central Hotel, now serving as a government building, flame and blowing smoke caught his attention. Clerks with boxes of documents were rushing from the hotel to the street and dumping them on blazing piles of flaring papers, sending hot tendrils of rising smoke into the sunlit April sky.

After a minute or so, David sighed deeply and descended the steps. With respectful nods and several brief handshakes, he moved on through the inquiring throng. He saw rising despair in the congregants' pale faces as they shook hands with tear-filled eyes.

"What should we do? Will Federal soldiers burn Richmond? Should we evacuate or stay in our homes?" David heard strained voices asking more than once. Confused and afraid of what the future would hold, they slowly dispersed.

The young chaplain too was contemplating the immediate future as he moved with long strides to his buggy.

CHAPTER 6

—CHIMBORAZO HOSPITAL—

WITH THE CLATTER of buggy wheels and clop of Nicie's hooves on cobblestone, the thoughtful trek up Taylor Street to Chimborazo Hospital was taking much longer than expected.

The direful tidings had spread like wildfire and sudden panic sent the populace—with baggage, bundles, and trunks—scrambling down the clogging streets. And mingling with the fleeing tide of pedestrians, David saw many overloaded carts, wagons, and buggies.

Finally, after struggling through the heavy traffic for over an hour, he topped Chimborazo Hill and reined the winded mare near the entrance to one of the long, whitewashed hospital buildings with a faded number 12 painted upon it. He stepped down and greeted the wounded men—fifteen or so, he guessed—seated on several long, rough benches, soaking up the warm April sun.

David smiled down at the twenty-year-old thin-faced, redheaded man with a heavily bandaged left arm supported by a dirty makeshift sling. "Hello, James," he said softly and gestured. "I pray your arm is better today."

James J. Parker responded, squinting into the bright sunlight. "Well, Chaplain, tain't thu arm that's troublin' me much. But my missin' left hand's itching and thar ain't nowhere t' scratch." He raised his right hand to brush back a stray red curl from his forehead and smiled, exposing his yellow teeth.

David forced a chuckle and fished in his coat pocket. He pulled out a cigar, nodded toward the mare, and frowned. "James, would you watch that horse and buggy? It may not be a good day to leave a convenient means of transportation unattended."

"Don't reckon t' mind thu hoss an' buggy at all, but I don't smoke," Parker responded, still squinting in the bright sunlight. "I might jus' take a little chaw of tobacco, if'n you got any."

"I'd surely like a smoke myself," a raspy-voiced, rangy man on the bench beside James cut in.

Spence forced a smile and handed him the cigar. "Well, you're a fortunate man. That's my last cigar." He flared a match and held the flame to the cigar as the older man puffed vigorously.

The raw-boned man drew more smoke, pulled the cigar from his mouth, observed it a few seconds, and then shook his bandaged head. "Well, young fellow, I didn't aim t' take thu last one." He chuckled lightly, inserted the cigar, and puffed again.

David forced another smile. "I must confess. I've never smoked. I use cigars as an opportunity to acquaint myself with my fellow man and impart a few verses from the Gospel." He raised his Bible and ran his blue eyes across the emaciated men lining the benches. "If you gentlemen don't mind, I'll read a few verses of scripture."

As he thumbed through the Bible, James nodded approvingly. But the older man, now shrouded in a haze of tobacco smoke, glanced at him uncertainly, pulled the saliva-soaked cigar from his mouth, and swept a dirty finger across his wispy mustache. "I reckon it t' be all right if'n ain't too long." He chucked lightly and scratched at his right ear. "Anyhow, ye done trapped me with this here cigar."

David smiled tolerantly. He cleared his throat, and in resonant tones, he read,

Thou shalt not be afraid for the terror by night,
nor for the arrow that flieth by in day.
Nor for the pestilence that walketh in darkness;
nor for the destruction that wasteth at noonday.
A thousand shall fall at thy side,
and ten thousand at thy right hand;
but it shall not come nigh thee.

"Amen." David looked up and saw a pitiful cluster of ragged, dirty Confederates—tears streaming down their skeletal faces. He tried to speak, but the words caught in his throat. He wiped away a tear, turned, and mounted the two rickety steps to building 12.

The young chaplain, anticipating the putrid odor, unconsciously caught his breath as he stepped across the narrow porch and on through the open doorway into the dingy hospital room. In the dimness, David released the pent-up breath, coughed, and resisted the urge to raise a hand to stifle the sickening stench.

He paused a few seconds. And behind him a soft voice said, "Hello, Chaplain Spence."

David recognized the voice and swung about to face the stout Surgeon Moore leaning heavily on a large polished cane. With intelligent gray eyes and jutting full-bearded chin, he was about fifty years old, David guessed.

The surgeon, a former captain in the Forty-Second Virginia Regiment, was wounded early in the war. After six months, his leg had healed and he was eager to resume his medical practice.

Dr. Moore switched the cane to his left hand, extended his right, and flashed a tired smile. "Well, David, did you get a good night's rest?"

Spence furrowed his brow and took the doctor's hand. "Much more than you, I'm sure."

"Oh." Moore nodded. "I had to help sort out the wounded, poor souls, who were able to walk and send them off with the Home Guard. Fortunately I managed a catnap just before daybreak."

"Will Marshall—" Stopping, David drew a deep breath. "Did they take Willie?" he asked seriously.

"Well, he wanted to go," the doctor responded with a slight headshake, "but he could barely stand without his crutches. Anyway," he added forcefully, "I wouldn't have permitted him to go." He paused a thoughtful moment, sighed, and went on. "That knee is not his only problem."

"Well, maybe—"

"Maybe I was wrong," the surgeon interrupted. He frowned and stroked his graying whiskers. "I told William there was nothing to be done about his knee, that he would need a miracle to be able to bend his leg. He seems to have descended into a state of depression . . . self-pity."

The young chaplain spoke up. "Maybe, if I get him away from the hospital . . . hospital surroundings, he'll feel somewhat better."

"Yes. Well, a change of scenery could help." Moore's words carried little conviction. He gestured lightly. "I'll walk with you to William's cot." As they started down the long, dim room, he grasped David's arm and chuckled. "Since he has just turned twenty, he's decided Willie wouldn't be a fitting name for a man his age." Moore chuckled again. "He would like to be addressed as Will or William. I believe he will be impressed if you address him as such."

"I will." Spence nodded and scanned the row of narrow, wood-framed cots. "No more than half are occupied," he muttered.

"They took all the men and boys able to walk and heft a rifle," the surgeon answered, anticipating David's question.

As the two men approached William Marshall's narrow cot, they fell silent. He was on his back, vacantly staring at the ceiling.

"Hello, Willie—William," Chaplain Spence greeted the tall, rail-thin lad hesitantly and forced a brief smile. "Be prepared to leave later today. We have a comfortable bed and a good meal awaiting your arrival." *The meal could be problematic*, he thought.

The young Confederate soldier turned his dull eyes on the chaplain and remained silent.

Dr. Moore sighed. "Well, David, I'm a little late. I need to examine the exchanged prisoners that arrived this morning. It seems some Federals are deliberately starving our captured soldiers." He pulled a large silver-plated watch from his fob pocket, opened the lid, took a look, grunted, and went on. "I'll be in my office about four o'clock. Come by before you leave." With that, he limped away.

The chaplain turned his eyes back to Willie, now propped on an elbow, watching the retreating surgeon, brow furrowed.

"I reckon I'll be needing one of them canes too." Will Marshall sighed and settled back on the narrow cot.

"Maybe not, miracles do happen," David responded, trying to keep his tone positive.

Willie shrugged lightly, eyeing the dingy ceiling.

After a long minute, David looked across the aisle, saw the empty cot, and asked seriously, "What happened to the man I counseled last night?"

"Oh, he just—" Willie stopped, tears filling his eyes. The slender lad turned his head, swiped at the tears with the back of his hand, and went on. "He said he was going on up to heaven. I . . . I reckon he just faded away."

"I'm sure he's in heaven," David said softly.

Will Marshall turned his eyes back to the chaplain, wagged his head briefly, and said just above a whisper, "Well, I . . . I doubt I'll be going up there." He pointed a slender finger toward the soot-stained ceiling.

David reached out a sympathetic hand, grasped his arm, gazed into the boy's dark eyes, and forced a smile. "William, no one is faultless. We are all sinners, but if we pray with sincerity in our hearts, all our sins will be forgiven."

Willie shrugged his bony shoulders. "But I don't believe God hears my praying. Not bragging at all, but I've done killed off a dozen or so bluecoats. I joined up to be a soldier—a soldier like my pa was. He got shot dead by some Federal at Bull Run. When Captain Brunson made me a sharpshooter, I was out to kill off a passel of them bluecoats. He sent me on out every morning a while before daylight to wait in the woods for a bluecoat to come out of the trench. Once he got his britches down to use the straddle ditch, I'd pick him off. Sometimes, if I figured him to be an officer of some sort, I'd crawl out, grab up his handgun, and dig in his pockets for . . . things." Willie stopped and looked away. He sighed deeply, turned back to David, and rasped desperately, "Down at Five Forks, the day before I got my left knee hit, we shot up a passel of charging Federal riders." He rose on an elbow and gestured. "That's how I got them boots. With all the killing and such, I doubt God pays attention to me at all," Willie went on frowningly.

The chaplain glanced at the almost new Union cavalry boots. Standing against the scarred wall, he saw a rickety, cane-bottomed chair and sat down.

"Yes," David responded softly, leaning forward, "God knows you intimately. I have to confess, I was about your age when I became a sharpshooter."

"You . . . you was a sharpshooter?"

David heard skepticism in Willie's voice. He nodded soberly. "Who among us has not sinned? Fortunately, God had his hand on me. Through my mother's voice, He restrained my trigger finger with a Federal soldier in my sight."

"Can God do that?" There was still a touch of skepticism in Willie Marshall's voice.

David Spence nodded and half-smiled. "Yes, William, He can do that. God can do more than that . . . much more." He paused to thumb through his mother's Bible. A few seconds later David muttered, "Here it is." He cleared his throat and read,

> Are not two sparrows sold for a farthing?
> And one of them shall not fall on the ground without
>   your Father.
> But the very hairs of your head are all numbered.
> Fear ye not therefore, ye are of more value than many
>   sparrows.

The Confederate chaplain reverently closed the worn Bible and turned his eyes back to the slender lad. "You see, William, God knows when a sparrow falls. We are much more valuable to Him than a sparrow or anything else." With that he went meditatively silent.

After a long, thoughtful minute, William Marshall grimaced and spoke up hesitantly. "But I . . . I ain't been baptized. My ma says, if you ain't been baptized, you ain't saved."

David leaned forward again and forced a little smile. "Well, if you wish, I'll bring in a pan of water and baptize you."

Willie frowned. "My ma says, and I believe, for a proper baptizing, a body has to be dipped in a creek to wash away their sins. Ever since I fell off a log into Crooked Creek and about drowned, I've stayed outta creeks, unless I can see the bottom."

David reflected a long moment. Finally he nodded and said quietly, "All right, William, we'll wait until your knee heals." He took the lad's hand, looked into his brown eyes, and continued. "After that, I'll be pressing you."

Spence got to his feet, pulled out his father's old watch, and opened the lid. He observed it a moment, sighed, and pushed it back in a fob pocket. "I'll have to leave you for a while to visit Chaplain Snyder and some wounded patients," he explained cordially.

It was sunset when David returned to find Willie sleeping peacefully, a grime-ridden haversack on his chest and a beat-up Enfield rifle at his side. He smiled down at the tall, slender lad and laid a hand on his shoulder, a narrow, bony shoulder. "William," he said softly. Willie's dark eyes blinked open and Chaplain Spence went on apologetically. "I'm sorry you had to—"

"Oh, that ain't a problem. Matron Pember's done come by and got my things gathered up." William Marshall grinned, pushed the haversack aside, and swung his feet from the cot.

David swept up the haversack, looped the strap over his shoulder, and smiled good-humoredly. "I need to get you down to my house for a hardy meal before you starve." With little effort, he gathered up the hundred-nineteen-pound lad.

"My crutches . . . I need—"

"After I carry you to the buggy, I'll come back for the crutches and boots," David explained as he strode toward the distant doorways fading light.

It was turning dark when he saw Phoebe Pember on the little porch in a rickety old rocking chair, watching her patients—now in long, ragged lines—shuffling down Chimborazo Hill into the teeming city.

Phoebe spoke up cynically. "Well, Chaplain, it seems the halt, the lame, and the blind are cured."

"Maybe they . . . some could be leaving to follow General Lee's army," David responded cordially and glanced at the evolving turmoil in the city below.

She snorted and pulled her gray shawl around her neck. "I'm staying with my patients—what's left of them—come Federals or no Federals. And I bid you good-bye, Chaplain Spence," Phoebe went on, her tone turning friendly. "And you too, William." She half-smiled at the slim lad in the tall chaplain's arms.

David spoke quietly. "I'll be praying for you."

Phoebe pointed, "Those men are the ones that need prayer."

"Yes." The chaplain nodded again and sighed. "We all need prayer . . . sincere prayer." He turned, saw his mother's old buggy in the growing darkness, and breathed a deep sigh of relief. David descended the steps and strode on past the benches now empty.

"Who's that?" Willie asked softly, nodding toward the buggy where a dim figure waited asleep in the seat.

"That's James Parker," David muttered.

Startled awake, James jerked his head around. "That you, Chaplain?" he intoned just above a whisper, squinting into twilight's dim light at the tall man with a slender, long-legged lad in his arms, who seemed to be holding a rifle in his right hand.

David started to speak, but James, with sudden recognition, went on. "I figured you t' be here a bit sooner." He covered his mild criticism with a low chuckle and adjusted the begrimed sling on his left arm. He swung his skinny legs over the side and clambered down from the buggy. In the dim light he smiled and said lightly, "Well, since you got your hands full, I'll take thu haversack."

"Thank you, James," Spence responded with a tired smile as Parker grasped the strap with his right hand and, rather clumsily, lifted the haversack from the tall chaplain's shoulder.

A dozen or so strides carried David to the buggy, and he carefully deposited Willie on the cracked leather seat and eased his bandaged leg atop the dashboard. He turned to James and gestured. "While I go back inside for Will's crutches and boots, you can put the haversack in the buggy box and climb aboard."

A wide smile broadened Parker's narrow face. "I was a-hoping you'd say that."

David sighed lightly and smiled weakly. "The box will be somewhat uncomfortable, but it beats walking."

About ten minutes later Chaplain Spence handed the crutches and cavalry boots up to Willie, climbed in the buggy, took up the lines, and flicked the mare into a slow trot down Chimborazo Hill.

CHAPTER 7

—PANDEMONIUM IN
THE STREETS—

EXCEPT FOR PILES of burning paper, glowing dimly, and a few torches, they found the streets dark. And mingled with anxious pedestrians, heavy-laden vehicles were rushing down the crowded streets. Some were impatiently struggling toward the train depot, but most were urgently moving toward Mayo's Bridge.

"How far is it to your house?" Willie shouted above the din of the rowdy crowd. "My legs are aching mighty fierce."

David pulled off his well-worn coat and rolled it into a pillow. "This should help," he muttered as he lifted Willie's wounded leg and cushioned the dashboard. "We've just passed Twentieth Street," he informed Willie and James in a raised voice as the buggy, at an agonizingly slow pace, rattled over cobblestones down the crowded street. "I seriously doubt we'll reach my house before midnight," he guessed.

"Is that music I'm hearing?" Willie asked, turning to David.

"Might be a band playing," James put in, nodding. "It looks t' be coming from that street up ahead."

"Well, it seems our soldiers will soon flood the streets and converge on Mayo's Bridge to join the retreating forces," David speculated. "I believe that regimental band, blaring patriotic music, is an effort to conceal the loud rumble of caissons and supply wagons rolling over street cobbles."

He reined in the tiring mare, handed the lines to Willie, and twisted on the seat. "James, you move up here with William. I'll walk in front and lead the mare through the crowd." He stepped down and moved to Nicie as James climbed from the buggy box into the seat. David grasped the old mare's bridle firmly, glanced over his shoulder, saw James in the seat, and pushed on through the milling throng. As the crowd gave way and moved aside, he picked up the pace and guided the mare on down Cary Street.

About half an hour later, at Fifteenth Street, Willie called, pointing, "There's a bunch of soldiers lighting up torches in front of that big old building. You reckon they're fixing to set it afire?"

"That's Shockoe Tobacco Warehouse," David said worriedly. "I see no reason to burn a warehouse." He stopped the mare and hurried back to the buggy. "Wait here while I see what's going on." With that, he turned and shouldered his way through the crowd toward the warehouse, looming darkly, about thirty paces away.

In the flickering torchlight David spotted a heavyset Confederate captain, standing before the warehouse, who seemed to be in charge. He tapped the large officer's shoulder and nodded toward the nearby building where soldiers were rolling back the wide doors. He cleared his throat and spoke up in a pulpit voice. "Captain, do you realize burning that warehouse could put the entire city at risk?"

Captain William Timberlake clinched his jaws, whirled, and faced David squarely. "And who are you to advise me?" he responded brusquely.

Suddenly realizing he had removed his clerical collar and dark, frock-tail coat, the chaplain apologized softly. "I'm sorry, Captain. I was rude. My name is David Spence. I'm a Confederate chaplain."

"Well, Chaplain." Timberlake sighed deeply and responded worriedly. "I'm somewhat concerned as well. But as you well know, I must follow orders." He turned back to the soldiers standing at the entrance with flaming torches, impatiently waiting. The captain gestured and four fiery streams flew through the black rectangle into the warehouse filled with about ten thousand hogsheads of tobacco. Tongues of flame flared and licked at the walls. Billowing gray smoke rolled out the wide doorway, and like a tidal wave, pandemonium moved in the crowded street.

David turned and saw the panic-stricken throng fleeing from a growing pillow of smoke, laced with lengthening tongues of flame. With the pungent odor of burning tobacco in his nostrils, he forced his way through the unruly throng toward the stranded buggy.

The mare whinnied fearfully and backed the buggy. A wheel struck the narrow cobblestone walk, the jolt almost unseating Willie and James. Willie righted himself, jerked the whip from its socket, and lashed the mare's haunches. But Nicie, now frantic with fear, paid scant attention.

Somehow, Spence's strong hand managed to grasp the bridle. "James!" he called desperately. "Toss that coat to me."

James hesitated momentarily. Then he jerked the frockcoat from the dashboard, rose to his feet, and flung it toward the chaplain. The coat flared and landed atop the restless mare. And with some difficulty, David managed to hold the animal in check with his left hand and reach the dangling garment with his right. He struggled to drape the frayed coat over the mare's bobbing head.

Nicie snorted a complaint.

Finally, David managed to cover the mare's eyes and knot the coat sleeves around her neck. After several seconds his familiar soothing voice and stroking hand had calmed the blindfolded animal.

On the street at the Columbia Hotel entrance, David, with the horse in tow, encountered throngs of anxious women pouring out from the hotel, hiking long skirts to their knees, and rushing on past the slow-moving buggy.

The mare felt the heat, and so did the chaplain.

"Cover your face!" he shouted, firming his grip on the bridle.

And Nicie, surprised by the rough treatment, jerked the buggy forward, sending a young pedestrian sprawling. Before David could speak, the man was on his feet and melted into the teeming crowd.

As they rattled along the rough cobblestone street, David glanced over his shoulder. He saw boiling smoke and flaring tarpaper from the collapsing warehouse roof spreading, on a brisk breeze, to the adjacent flour mill and sending tendrils of burning debris to buildings across the street.

About two hundred yards beyond the burning buildings, David pulled the mare to a halt, loosened the knotted coat sleeves, and gently pulled the garment from the mare's head. He turned toward the buggy and stopped. "Where . . . where is James?" he asked, a puzzled frown on his face.

Willie shrugged his shoulders, turned, and pointed. "Oh . . . he just lit out that a-way. He said he was gonna cross the bridge and join General Lee's army."

"Join General Lee's army!" David exclaimed dubiously. "But with one hand how—?"

"James said he was getting hisself a gun and kill the first Federal he comes across," Willie said worriedly and stole a guilty look at the big chaplain.

"We must pray for his safety." David sighed significantly as he climbed in the buggy. He slipped the folded coat under the slender private's wounded leg and took up the lines. He slapped the mare into motion and the buggy rattled on toward Main Street.

"Look!" Willie spoke up hurriedly, tugging at David's sleeve. "There are some soldiers up ahead, busting kegs . . . of some sort."

In the dim light from piles of burning paper, the chaplain saw determined soldiers swinging axes into barrelheads, sending the gushing liquid into the street. As the pungent odor reached David's nostrils, he remarked frowningly, "They seem to be destroying the whiskey supply."

Lured by the potent scent, the crowd rushed to the gutters and hastily scooped up the flowing liquor with cupped hands, bottles, shoes, and any available liquid container. Some, they noticed, were prostrate on the cobblestone sucking up the fiery libation.

"There's no authority left!" David exclaimed as he reined the mare onto Main Street.

As they approached Miller and Tyler's Jewelry Store, he saw a squadron of cavalry, with drawn sabers, forcing their way through the milling crowd.

Suddenly, with pockets bulging and jewelry dangling from his hands, a short, lean man leaped out from the shattered store window.

A cavalry captain heeled his big stallion to the sidewalk and brought the barrel of his revolver to the fleeing thief's tousled head.

Now unconscious, the slender man tumbled to the street, scattering jewelry along the rough cobbles.

Captain Farinholt leaped from the horse and holstered his weapon as he moved hurriedly to the prostrate man. The young officer bent down, dug three watches from the thief's filthy gray coat, and gathered up the jewelry—all he could recover from the darkened street. He hurried to the shop, deposited them on the floor, slammed the door behind him, and rushed back to his stallion. He swung aboard the anxious horse and spurred him into a canter. The big captain met the buggy with a casual salute to the chaplain and rode on toward Mayo's Bridge.

"Where is the army going?" David called after the officer. But in the deafening melee, he realized it was impossible for Farinholt to hear him. With some frustration, the tired chaplain pulled out the whip and reluctantly lashed Nicie through the unruly crush of men, women, and children lighting their way with strips of burning paper.

In the growing tide of chaos, the pitifully few guards left to maintain order and restrain the criminal element were soon overwhelmed.

"Over there!" Willie exclaimed urgently, pointing in the smoky dimness. "It's a woman."

"I see her," David responded promptly, jerked the mare to a quick stop and bolted from the buggy. In the milling crowd he saw a plucky, buxom, black-robed woman, with gritty determination, hanging onto her purse strings and frantically kicking at a slender Confederate deserter. His attempt to jerk the purse from her gloved hands seemed to be a bit more difficult than he anticipated. The scruffy soldier drew back a grimy hand to strike the graying, well-dressed woman. "Give me that—"

A pair of big, long-fingered hands at his throat silenced the high voice. The hands lifted him onto his toes. A firm shove sent the soldier skidding across the rough, cobbled street. And the chaplain, regaining his composure, mumbled a short prayer:

Forgive me, Lord. I've failed you again.

He walked over to the gray-coated, somewhat-inebriated figure, now struggling to his knees. David extended a helping hand. "Are you hurt?" he asked seriously.

The young soldier retrieved his battered forage cap, cast an apprehensive eye at the chaplain, and mumbled, "Reckon I'll live."

He's young, about sixteen or seventeen, David suddenly realized as he pulled the scruffy lad to his feet. He looked at the young deserter's narrow face and apologized softly. "I'm sorry. I lost my temper." He glanced at the woman and thought she had a small smile on her face, but in flickering dimness, he wasn't sure.

"I reckon I'm the one who ought to be apologizing," the lad said quietly, so quietly that David barely heard what he said. "I . . . I forgot all civilized behavior in the trenches round Petersburg and took a swig from a whiskey jug—a big swig." He forced a thin grin.

David stared at the begrimed youth suspiciously for a long moment. Finally, he nodded, grasped the young deserter's upper arm firmly, and guided him back into the crowded street. "I believe you owe that lady over there by my buggy the apology."

As they approached the woman in black, still holding her little smile, the boy doffed his sullied forage cap. And with a shallow head bob, he apologized in a low voice. "I . . . I'm awful sorry 'bout what I done, ma'am." Nervously twisting his dirty cap, he cast another glance at the chaplain. "I reckon—"

"Young man," the buxom woman spoke up, shaking a black-gloved finger in his face, "the Bible says plainly, 'Thou shalt not steal.'"

"Yes, ma'am, I know." The lad nodded respectfully. A sudden grin and he continued. "The Bible also says, 'Judge not that ye be not judged.'"

He had heard this statement somewhere, but he wasn't sure it was scriptural.

She eyed him hard for a while. Finally, she nodded. "Come along with me, young man." Imbedded in her forceful tone, the skinny soldier knew, was an order he would be unable to resist.

He shot an under-brow glance at the muscular chaplain and started to speak, but the widow took his arm and smiled at him. "My son was fortunate enough to get a salt-cured ham from a government storehouse. You look like a young man who could consume a goodly portion. And . . . a good scrubbing seems to be in order as well." She sniffed. "My house is just half a block from here," David heard her say as they walked away, arm in arm, on through the rampaging mob, and quickly disappeared.

*

It was a few minutes after midnight when David turned the old buggy on Fifth Street. He cast a troubled glance over his shoulder at the raging firestorm, now only three or four blocks away. And on the dim street beyond the plodding mare, he glimpsed several roving gray jackets staggering along with half dozen or so drunken civilians—Confederate stragglers, he suspected.

The darkened houses seemed deserted, but an occasional narrow flash of yellow lamplight between shutters told a different story. The chaplain's terrified neighbors were cowering behind shuttered windows and locked doors, waiting for daylight and for the Federal army to appear.

Off to the left, looming darkly against the night sky, David's house came into view. As they approached the two-story building, the spent mare, sensing rest and fodder just ahead, surged into a fast trot and, without guidance, wheeled the dilapidated buggy in the rutted track just beyond the house.

As Willie drew the exhausted mare to a stop, the kitchen door squeaked open and a soft yellow glow pierced the darkness.

David stepped down from the buggy, turned, and saw Rachel on the porch, holding a lamp high to light the way. "It's about time you got home," she scolded worriedly. "Isaac's went out and got us a slab of side meat and a bucket of biscuit flour for supper."

David heard the worry in her tone and responded, his voice cheerful. "Thank you, Rachel. We'll be there after I stable Nicie."

"It's done got cold by now," she muttered to herself and turned toward the kitchen door.

"Come on in. I'll take care of the mare." A familiar voice sounded from the dim figure in a chair beside the door, with a double-barreled shotgun resting comfortably across his long legs. "I 'spect her t' be a bit . . ." Isaac's voice trailed away as he climbed to his feet and propped the old shotgun against the wall.

"I'll walk," Willie announced stubbornly as David lifted him from the buggy. "My legs got a bit cramped, long ride and all."

*

At his father's scarred desk, the tired chaplain placed a sheet of paper in the radius of the yellow lamplight, dipped the nib of his long pin in the inkwell, and scratched rapidly across the paper. He scratched on for about ten minutes. Finally, with a bold flourish, he signed the paper and waved it back and forth a few seconds to dry the ink, pushed the chair back, and rose to his feet. David crossed to the adjacent room, found the door open, and paused momentarily. He put on a thin smile and entered the dimly lit bedroom.

"William—"

"I'm already awake," Willie mumbled as he buttoned his blouse.

"William," David repeated gently, "I need your signature on a document."

"Me . . . sign a document?" Somewhat confused, Willie scratched his tousled head.

"Yes. I've composed a document for Rachel and Isaac to present Federal forces when they arrive—if necessary. I'll need a witness signature before I leave."

The slender lad rose up and looked at David in bewilderment. "Where . . . where're you going?"

Chaplain Spence moved to the bed, laid a sympathetic hand on Willie's narrow shoulder, and responded softly. "I don't know . . . but I must go with General Lee's army."

Will Marshall's lips tightened. "Well, what about—?"

A shotgun blast from somewhere outside and Isaac's menacing voice shouted, "Get away from that shed! Better be gettin' yourself away before I blow your head clean off."

David turned on a heel and sprinted past Rachel and on out the kitchen door into the night. A glass-shattering blast sent him to the porch floor. Dazed, he struggled to his feet. *Federal artillery*, he thought. Still wobbly, David stepped down to the yard and saw off toward the river a huge pillow of fire and smoke rolling heavenward. "That's not artillery fire, it's the arsenal!" he exclaimed as he watched a chain of exploding shells streaking across the dark sky.

Out of the smoky darkness a galloping horse appeared. "Whoa, Nicie," David called, as the walleyed mare rounded the corner into the front yard and slowed to a trot. With the odor of lush grass underfoot, the hungry mare decided to disregard the fear and stop to graze awhile.

Chaplain Spence rushed to the corner of the house and breathed a deep sigh of relief. Nicie was busily nipping at the tender, spring grass. And sensing his presence, the animal, with three feet of shredded halter rope dangling, raised her head and whined briefly.

Heavy footfalls and Isaac—wheezing loudly—pulled up. "Did you see thu mare?" he gasped. And before David could answer, he went on. "You reckon them Federals done blowed up something?"

The big chaplain shook his head, frowned and pointed toward the growing inferno. "No, Isaac. What you see down there is the destruction of the city and death of the Confederacy."

Somewhat perplexed, the tall, graying man thoughtfully scratched under his straw-hat. A few quiet seconds and he frowned—still scratching. "Well, what about thu mare?"

David responded thoughtfully. "I'll hobble Nicie and let her graze another hour or so before I leave. I must be across Mayo's Bridge by dawn. I think it will be destroyed by daylight . . . or shortly thereafter."

Isaac nodded decisively. "Don't you worry none. I'll be keeping a sharp eye on thu mare . . . and this old shotgun in hand." He drew a caressing hand across the weapon's walnut stock.

Spence walked away and Isaac breathed a troubled sigh, knowing that "the fat is in the fire," as he often said.

As David crunched across the glass-infested porch, Willie hobbled out from the kitchen, muttering, "It looks like old Richmond's getting torn apart."

The chaplain sighed deeply and raised his sad eyes to see the flash of exploding ammunition. After a few seconds he placed a long arm across the lad's bony shoulders and spoke up solemnly. "It seems the city prefers suicide rather than surrender to the Federals."

They entered the large kitchen and found Rachel standing before the wood-burning cast-iron stove, in a hot cloud of hanging grease smoke.

And trying to ignore the earth-shaking explosions, the heavy woman was humming softly as she gathered her long gray apron to insulate her hand. Without turning, she stopped humming and began forking slices of salt pork from a large iron skillet onto a tin platter.

"Rachel," David said, brow furrowed, "you're cooking much more than we can eat."

She faced him and smiled her knowing smile. "Well, I'm reckoning you and thu boy might need traveling vitals. I'm gonna whip up a batch of hoecakes with some of that biscuit flour too."

"That's being mighty thoughtful," Willie said smilingly. "I reckon we'll be going in about an hour or two, ain't we?" Unabashed, he stared directly at David and managed a thin smile.

A slight gesture toward the parlor door, and the frowning chaplain spoke up. "We should discuss this further . . . in there."

He followed Willie into the parlor and closed the door. He pulled out his father's old watch, opened the lid, and observed it thoughtfully as the slender private hobbled across to the high-backed rocker. David pulled his eyes from the watch and studied Willie a long moment. When he spoke, his voice was low, his tone soft. "William, you must be realistic. It would be foolhardy to carry you with me on such a dangerous and difficult journey."

"I'm thinking . . ." Willie's voice trailed off.

David went on, forcing his voice calm. "With your wounded knee we would have to use the buggy. And that old buggy, as well as the mare, will be able to endure those rough roads only two, maybe three days."

With a growing flush in his narrow face, Will Marshall gave him a hard look. "Well then, reckon I'll just be heading off to the Blue Ridge," he said sharply as he struggled to his feet and took up his crutches. "I ain't waiting for them Federal blue jackets."

David Spence pondered awhile.

*

It was well after five o'clock in the morning and daylight was riming the eastern sky, when Isaac hoisted the McClellan saddle into the buggy box. "Can't see why he's taking that stove-up boy on this old buggy," he mumbled as he scooped up cracked-corn—all he could recover from the shed floor in the dim glow from the smoky lantern. "I doubt it'll feed thu mare no more'n two days," he mumbled on as he stuffed the feed bag in the buggy box. Isaac turned, rounded the rear wheel, and gruntingly climbed onto the worn leather seat. He gathered the lines and flicked Nicie into a slow trot through the smoky darkness toward the house. "Well," Isaac muttered to the mare, "I'm reckoning, he's reckoning, this old rig might break down or he wouldn't be lugging thu saddle along."

On the side porch, pacing impatiently, David saw the buggy rattle through the dim glow from the kitchen window. Hastily, he gathered the bulging haversack from the porch floor and turned to Willie, now sitting, uncomfortably, in the slatted chair. "We must leave immediately if we are to reach Mayo's Bridge by sunrise . . . or shortly thereafter," he said, a tone of urgency in his voice.

A soft "Whoa" and Isaac reined in the mare.

David stepped down from the porch, moved quickly across the yard, and slung the haversack in the box atop the saddle.

Isaac turned on the buggy seat and extended the shredded rope. "I 'spect you oughtta tie them down," he suggested evenly. "The roads you'll be traveling I 'spect t' be mighty rough."

"I'm sure they will be rutted." David sighed, took the rope, knotted it to the buggy box, and went on. "My major concern is Willie." His face turned somber as he cast a glance at the dim figure on the porch, now climbing unsteadily to his feet.

At that moment, Rachel, mumbling incoherently, came out from the kitchen with a thick pillow and two rain slickers. A low grunt and the corpulent woman stepped to the ground and strode heavily across to the buggy. "You'll need these slickers," she said firmly, lifting her sharp eyes in the lantern's dim glow to the torn canvas top. "This pillow's for thu boy's leg and to lay his head on for a nap, if need be."

As she positioned the pillow on the seat, Spence responded quietly, his right hand moving to an inside coat pocket. "That's very thoughtful, Rachel." He pulled out a folded paper and pressed it in the big woman's rough hand. "This paper authorizes you and Isaac to remain in the house. When this bloody war is over, I'll deliver William to his home in the Blue Ridge and go from there to my uncle's farm near the Shenandoah Valley. If I fail to return within a year, this property will be yours."

For a long moment, Rachel gazed at the yellow paper, tears filling her eyes. "You mean—" She raised the hem of her apron and dabbed at flowing tears. "You're meaning, when them Federals show up, they won't bother us at all if'n we show them this here paper?"

"I doubt you will be harmed by Federal soldiers, but it would be wise to keep it in a safe place." David's voice carried some trepidation. He wrapped his long arms around her wide body and kissed her wet cheek.

Finally, he hoisted Willie in the buggy and handed him the Enfield rifle, which William Marshall believed would be indispensable. David Spence turned and shook Isaac's long, slender hand. And with the galling squeak of rusting springs, he climbed in the buggy, took up the lines, and looked down in the growing light to find Rachel and Isaac arm in arm—he with hat in hand and she with tears flowing profusely down her round face.

"Good-bye . . . and I pray God will keep you safe," David managed chokingly. He flicked Nicie lightly. And with the ominous roar of exploding shells at the armory and the glow from burning buildings, the old buggy rattled up the cobbled street into the smoky dimness.

CHAPTER 8

—MAYO'S TOLL BRIDGE—

As NICIE SALLIED along Main Street, the sun was above the eastern horizon, dimly glowing through a widespread pall of billowing gray smoke.

"You reckon we'll get to Mayo's Bridge before our boys set it afire?" Willie asked worriedly.

David answered thoughtfully. "Well, I believe they will wait until all our soldiers are across, or until Federal troops appear."

With the rhythmic clop of shod hooves, Will Marshall yawned and closed his eyes and the buggy rattled on.

Off to their right, a huge pillow of smoke and flame shot skyward. The nervous mare shied, wanting to run.

"Easy, Nicie," Chaplain Spence said, tightening the lines.

Jolted from a deep doze, Willie jerked his head up and exclaimed, "What's that?"

"I think it's the collapsing roof of Gallegos Flour Mill on Cana Street," Spence said worriedly. "It seems—"

"I'm hearing wagons . . . horses," William Marshall cut him short, a touch of apprehension in his tone.

In the smoke-choking atmosphere and smoldering buildings along Main Street blocking their view, David reined the mare in.

As the din of rumbling wheels and clatter of shod hooves grew closer, Willie went on in a lowered voice, his anxious eyes locked on the intersecting streets. "You reckon that to be Federal blue jackets?" He lifted the Enfield rifle to his lap.

"No." Chaplain Spence spoke up firmly, pulling the weapon from Willie's hands. "As far as we are concerned, the war is over."

"The war's over?" Willie questioned confusedly.

David scotched the rifle butt against the dashboard and responded quietly. "Yes. For us, it's over."

"Well," Willie muttered, "I ain't shooting any bluecoats, unless I have to."

"We must—" Spence started, but the rumble of heavy wagons and braying mules stopped him. He breathed a deep sigh of relief when a long line of mule-drawn Confederate wagons rattled out from the smoky dimness. He tapped the mare forward and sighed. "I believe they're heading to Mayo's Bridge."

At Fourteenth Street, he pulled lines again and watched the passing wagons. Drawn by underfed animals and guided by dejected teamsters, they rolled noisily toward Mayo's Bridge.

"I count twenty-seven," Willie drawled tiredly as the last supply wagon crossed Main Street.

David raised the lines to go on but paused when he saw a troop of Confederate cavalry trotting their worn horses a few yards behind the rear wagon.

As the horsemen reached the intersection a captain turned in his saddle, spotted the stranded buggy, waved a gauntleted hand and bellowed, "Get that old rig moving!"

And with a light flick of lines against the mare's haunches, David navigated onto Fourteenth Street. And as the buggy drew abreast the Confederate officer, he noticed David's chaplain garb and presented a sharp, apologetic salute.

The wagon caravan and horsemen moved on and David found the trailing buggy engulfed by roving pillagers, intermingled with pitiable burned-out families, flowing toward the bridge.

"Get out of the way," a loud, stern voice barked.

David leaned out, looked back, and saw the captain spurring his big roan stallion and busily scattering the howling looters with the flat of his saber. And with some difficulty, the big officer forced his nervous stallion through the mob to the stranded buggy. He sheathed his saber, cupped his left hand at his mouth, tightened the reins with his right, and called, "I'm Captain Clement Sulivane. The situation is . . . is somewhat chaotic at the moment," he understated, smoothed his mustache, and went on. "My troops should clear this street in a few minutes."

David leaned out again and called, "Is Mayo's Bridge intact?"

Sulivane responded loudly, half-smiling. "It should be. I'll be giving the order to destroy it. Good-bye and good luck," the captain called again and lifted the reins to turn the stallion.

Willie muttered, "Chaplain, I . . . I figured you'd ask that captain about General Lee's army."

"Captain," David called back, "Do you know the location of General Lee's army?"

Sulivane tightened the reins and answered loudly, "The rendezvous point will be at Amelia Courthouse—for the few that's left, I heard." The captain shook his head sadly. "It seems our army is melting away like a snowball in . . . in Hades." He spurred the big horse, unsheathed his saber, and prodded his way toward the bridge, about two hundred yards away.

A few minutes later, with shod hooves clattering on cobblestone and drawn sabers glittering in the morning sunlight, Sullivan's South Carolina troopers arrived. With little choice now, the sullen mob slowly melted away.

As the buggy approached the bridge abutment, Willie spotted Sulivane, afoot now and vigorously waving heavy-laden pedestrians and wheeled carts onto the smoldering structure.

William Marshall tugged at David's sleeve and spoke up worriedly. "It looks like the bridge is already afire."

Sulivane slapped the buggy with his saber. "Keep moving, Chaplain. That smoke is from a burning river barge wedged beneath the bridge." Captain Sulivane turned and gestured toward a dozen or so gaunt soldiers. "We have to wait until General Kershaw's troops are across before we set the bridge afire," he explained gravely.

David looked beyond Sulivane and saw seven men busily rolling barrels onto the bridge. And five others, with their anxious eyes locked on the captain, were impatiently waiting with unlit torches at the ready position.

A glance over his shoulder at the approaching South Carolina soldiers and Sulivane waved the old buggy toward the west bank of the James River. As the buggy rumbled ahead, he swung aboard his prancing stallion, nudged him onto the bridge, and waited.

As Kershaw's soldiers flooded across the bridge, Sulivane, standing in the stirrups, spotted the general at the tag end of his trotting ragtag soldiers. With a deep sigh, the big Confederate turned the nervous stallion, faced the five anxious gray-clad men, and ordered loudly, "All right, lads, light them up."

General Joe Kershaw trotted his horse past the waiting engineers, their torches burning. He looked back, tipped his hat, and yelled at the top of his voice, "All over, boys! Send it to hell!"

And with hasty efficiency, they did.

CHAPTER 9

—A RAGGED RABBLE—

THE DIM GLOW of sunlight was still shafting through swirling smoke as the old buggy rattled on past the little tollbooth standing over an island in the river.

David Spence looked back. His eyes came to rest on a line of soldiers with bayoneted rifles, quickly stepping ahead of a wall of flame. On the smoky street beyond the blazing abutments, as far as his eyes could reach, he saw terrified, homeless refugees struggling with bundles of salvaged household items. He saw, clinging to their mothers' soot-infested skirts, frightened, hungry, shoeless children at the cusp of total exhaustion and tears came into his eyes.

Chaplain Spence wiped the tears away with his sleeve, nudged the slumbering lad, and said hoarsely, "Will, look back, and you'll see what Armageddon might look like."

With some difficulty, Willie managed to turn on the buggy seat. "Well," he commented causally, "it looks like that captains got the fire going right smartly." He raised his gaze to the crowded street, shook his head slowly, and said sadly, "Seems like the whole world's falling apart."

"I pray this carnage will end soon . . . very soon." David sighed. "Maybe then we can live in peace." He nodded slightly, looked at Willie, and said softly, "Well, we'll leave it in God's hands."

"In God's hands," Willie echoed reverently with a slow affirmation nod. "That's where a thing ought to be, I reckon."

With the bridge burning behind them, David pulled lines and guided the mare from the slow-moving tide of desperate humanity.

And with a tired "Whoa, Nicie," he brought the buggy to a stop on Manchester Hill. "I'll let the mare rest awhile before we move on." He sighed.

Willie didn't hear. With the big feather-stuffed pillow behind his slumping head, he was peacefully asleep.

"Sleep on," Spence muttered. "I fear there will be little rest in the near future." He sighed deeply, stepped down, pulled the feed bag from the buggy box, and moved to the mare.

Nicie noticed the feed bag and lowered her head. David pulled the bit from the mare's mouth and slipped the strap over her ears. "Well, old girl," he almost whispered, caressing the mare's neck, "this may be your last meal for a while." Without hesitation, the mare crunched on.

The chaplain glanced at Willie and muttered. "He's still asleep." A momentary pause and David strode a dozen or so paces from the buggy. He stopped and looked down Manchester Hill. Mesmerized, he saw a kaleidoscope of devastation and chaos. Flaring ships and barges, floating down the James and billowing clouds of dark gray smoke, laced with tongues of yellow flame, engulfing the bridge.

"God save us all!" he exclaimed, doffed his hat, fell to his knees, and breathed a silent prayer.

"Chaplain Spence," Willie interrupted, "I 'spect we ought to be going on, if we're gonna catch up to General Lee's army."

David took a long breath and whispered an addendum to his silent prayer. "Precious Lord, give me more patience. Amen."

He put on his black hat, rose to his feet, and pulled the feed bag from the mare. "Well, Nicie," he said as he forced the bit in her mouth, "it seems you've managed to devour most of the corn." David deposited the feed bag atop the saddle and climbed in the buggy. He took up the lines and guided the mare through streaming Confederate stragglers and trudging civilians, struggling along the rutted road toward Amelia Courthouse. Many exhausted women, old men, and small children, he noticed, were seated on their bags and bundles along the roadside. And the older children in frantic desperation were rushing through the mud into the flowing stream of wagons, artillery pieces, and cavalry horses, searching for a crust of bread and sip of water.

"How much water do we have?" David asked Will quietly.

"Well, I reckon"—the slim lad reached under the seat, pulled out a canteen, and gave it a gentle shake"—this one's about half-gone. The canteen in the box is well-nigh full though."

Spence reined Nicie from the quagmire to the border of the roadside ditch, pulled her in, and stepped down. "We must help those emaciated children," he murmured feelingly as he delved into the buggy box and drew out the haversack.

Willie nodded solemnly and asked wonderingly, "Are you planning to hand out hoecakes to the children?"

"Yes. Well, I think—"

"Them children!" Willie gasped, pointing.

David looked up and caught his breath. He saw children dodging heavy-laden wagons and darting recklessly across the rutted, mud-infested road toward the old buggy.

"Stop!" he called desperately, and the mud spattered children—five boys and three girls—slowed momentarily but did not stop. Strung out somewhat, they rushed on to the buggy and gathered around David. He tried to smile as they stood silently with anticipatory eyes gazing up into his face. "All right . . ." Chaplain Spence's voice trailed off and tears flooded his eyes. A brief pause and he placed a comforting arm about a small straw-haired girl. "All right, children, we must bow our heads in prayer before we distribute the bread and water," he went on in a soft, gentle tone. And then, with an under-brow glance at the restless children, David pulled off his black hat, lowered his chin, and prayed,

> Oh, Lord, I place these children under Your protection,
> realizing that all humanity must come unto Thee as
>   little children.
> I pray You will always hold these little ones in the palm
>   of your hand.
> And we thank You for the food we are about to receive.

"Amen." David looked up and forced another smile. "Now, children, all together say 'Amen.'"

They echoed a weak "Amen."

He uncorked the canteen, handed it to the straw-haired girl, and said gently, "Take three swallows and pass it on." He shifted his eyes to

Willie and gestured. "After you drink, go around the buggy to Private Marshall for a biscuit."

Willie glanced at the haversack and muttered. "I surely hope there's enough biscuit bread to go around."

As the canteen passed from child to child, David noticed an older boy gulping five or six swallows but remained silent as the ragged lad, forcing a half smile, handed him the empty canteen.

Several minutes later the children had consumed the biscuit bread and quietly slipped away.

Suddenly, warning shouts filled the air and Spence turned his eyes to see the teeming traffic. Just ahead of fast approaching limbered artillery, drawn by four underfed horses, he saw a small girl on hands and knees in the churned mud. "My Lord!" he called frantically,

The gray-clad soldier, astraddle the left lead horse, jerked the bit hard. But it was too late—much too late.

In the flickering of an eye, a hand grasped the blue dress and sent the petrified child flying through the April atmosphere. The barefoot soldier slipped. Gray-clad legs flared momentarily and then disappeared under the galloping horses.

A heavy iron-rimmed wheel rolled over the prostrate soldier and buried the lifeless body in clinging mud. The rider spurred the snorting lead horse hard and the heavy caisson rolled on.

A large woman—the girl's mother, David guessed—grabbed up the sobbing, mud-infested child and held her close.

Two ragged Confederate soldiers waded through the muck to retrieve the mutilated body, and the big woman, still holding the sobbing girl firmly, disappeared in a knot of slow-flowing humanity.

David pulled lines, turned the buggy, and moved on with the remnants of General Lee's army—an endless flow of gaunt, ragged men—staggering along the muddy road toward Amelia Courthouse.

A few minutes of thoughtful silence and Willie spoke up worriedly. "I figure this here old war's gonna be done with . . . before long."

Chaplain Spence sighed deeply. "Yes. It looks like our Southern army is disintegrating into a ragged rabble with overwhelming numbers of well-equipped Federal soldiers nipping at their heels."

After jolting on about five miles, David Spence found a gap in the slow-moving ragtag ranks. He reined the mare into a fallow field, clambered down, pulled out his watch, and opened the lid.

And Will Marshall, who seemed to be dozing, cleared his throat, raised his head, and asked wearily, "You reckon we'll be making that church before dark sets in?"

David looked at his watch and sighed. "Well, it's past two o'clock now. I doubt we'll reach Tomahawk Church before nightfall. Nicie needs rest . . . at least half an hour's rest."

CHAPTER 10

—WINGS AS EAGLES—

IT WAS ABOUT two hours after sunset and the night had turned chilly, when David reined the mare on a strip of trampled grass between Tomahawk Church and its cemetery. He gathered up his big Bible, climbed down from the buggy, and raised his blue eyes to Willie. "Wait here," he said tiredly, gesturing. "I'll speak with those men by that campfire."

Half-asleep, Private Marshall roused himself and started to speak, but David was gone.

In the flickering glow, David saw a dozen or more exhausted Confederates lounging on the wet ground. In the deep darkness beyond the smoky fire, he heard the murmur of many voices filled with curses and mirthless laughter. David stepped into the firelight's dim glow, and in a resonant voice, he spoke up:

"Gentlemen, I'm Chaplain Spence. I'll be having service shortly. All who wish to hear our Lord's message are welcome."

A tall, big-boned man rose to his feet and pulled at his dark whiskers a long moment. Finally he smiled, thrust out a grimy hand, and drawled. "I'm Lieutenant Walter Dillon from down Carolina way. You'll have to make the message short. I have orders to move these men out at midnight—maybe a mite sooner."

"It's mighty good t' see a man of thu cloth," a private at the edge of the fire's flickering glow spoke up sincerely. "I reckon we'll be a-needin' a passel of prayin' afore this here fightin's all said an' done with."

"Yes, indeed," David affirmed with a shallow nod, "we all need prayer. Lieutenant," he went on hurriedly, cutting his eyes back to the tall officer, "if you and your fellow soldiers don't mind spreading the word, we'll gather at the church steps for a short service . . . and a hymn or two."

The Confederate officer smiled. "I would like that." After a long pause he said evenly, "I must remind you, Chaplain, it is imperative my men leave by midnight."

It was ten minutes after eleven o'clock when David climbed the three church steps. He opened his Bible and turned to see about fifty ragged figures standing silent in the weak moon glow, kepis and slouch hats in their hands, waiting.

A short prayer, then he opened the Bible, and in a robust, passionate voice, he read,

> Hast thou not known? Hast thou not heard,
> that the everlasting God, the LORD,
> the Creator of the ends of the earth, fainteth not,
> neither is he weary? There is no searching of his
>   understanding.
> He giveth power to the faint; and to them that have
>   no might
> he increaseth strength.
> Even the youths shall faint and be weary,
> and the young men shall utterly fall:
> But they that wait upon the LORD shall renew their
>   strength;
> they shall mount up with wings as eagles;
> they shall run, and not be weary;
> and they shall walk, and not faint.

"Amen." With forced exuberance, David said, "Well now, gentlemen, we'll sing until midnight . . . or until Lieutenant Dillon stops us."

"Can I play along with my harmonica?" a high voice drawled from the darkness.

David chuckled. "Come forward and play. I'll need all the help I can get." And in the dimness, the harmonica began the mournful strains of an old familiar hymn, and David's clear baritone voice soared well beyond the ragged soldiers:

> Rock of ages cleft for me,
> Let me hide myself in Thee;
> Let the water and the blood,
> from Thy riven side which flowed—

His voice choked and then stopped, but the harmonica played on and a multitude of voices rose into the night:

> Not the labors of my hands can fill
> Thy law's demands; could my zeal no rasped know,
> Could my tears forever flow.
> All for sin could not atone;
> Thou must save and Thou alone.

*

The morning of April fourth was well gone when David, after a strenuous jog of fifteen miles, guided the exhausted mare up a low wooded hill just outside Amelia Courthouse. He reined in near half dozen or so ragged Confederates squatting around a smoky cook fire crackling under a large blackened cast-iron pot normally used for boiling clothes and cooking hog fat into lard. The pilfered pot, now balanced rather precariously on fieldstones, David noticed, seemed to be about half-filled with steaming stew.

While roasting corn dodgers on ramrods, the hungry soldiers' eyes were darting hungrily between the browning dodgers and the bubbling pot.

David gathered his Bible from the buggy seat, gruntingly climbed down, and introduced himself. "I'm David Spence, a chaplain. If you don't mind I will read a few verses of scripture."

A rangy corporal climbed slowly to his feet, extended a long-fingered hand, and smilingly introduced himself. "I'm Walter Thompson . . . uh, chaplain. We're mighty proud t' have you stop by for a few minutes or so."

David took the offered hand and said sincerely, "It's good to meet you, Corporal Thompson. I hope you and these soldiers can find time for a short service."

Covetously, Walter glanced at the steaming pot.

"That is, after you finish your meal," David added.

"I ain't much account fur cookin', but thu stew's 'bout done," a stubby, balding man announced proudly, still stirring the bubbling concoction with a long rough-hewn paddle while occasionally shifting upwind to avoid the blowing smoke.

Walter raised his eyes from the pot to David, smiled crookedly, and sent a steam of tobacco juice into the crackling fire. "Well, Chaplain, you might's well come on an' sup with us. I 'spect you might be a bit hungry."

David's blue eyes swept the emaciated faces and then turned back to the corporal. "I have to admit I'm hungry, but I cannot accept your generous offer." He gestured. "That wounded soldier in the buggy needs nourishment."

"Are you meaning," Walter put in, chuckling, "he's hungry?" Before David could answer he went on. "Tell him to come on up. I reckon we can allow you and that wounded boy a cup, maybe two." He maneuvered the big chaw to the other side of his mouth and added, "We're a bit short on corn dodgers, though."

Five minutes later Willie was slurping loudly from a rusting tin cup. He drew his hand across his mouth, raised his eyes, smiled, and spoke up in a complementary way. "Thank you kindly. I've been hankering for a good meal. This here soup's mighty tasty, with that meat and all. I was about hungry enough to eat a horse."

The lounging men chuckled in unison and Walter spoke up. "Well, I reckon I ought t' tell you, you're already eating one. But it shore beats sour belly and parched corn," he added, chuckling.

The raised cup paused at William Marshall's open mouth. After a long, thoughtful moment, his hunger overwhelmed his nausea. And with furrowed brow, he swallowed the concoction—all of it.

Drawn by two plodding, bony mules, a canvas-covered forage wagon, creaking and rattling on mud-caked rims, turned from the rutted road and rumbled to a chain-jangling stop. The teamster, a smallish, long-bearded man, wrapped the long lines around the brake handle, raised his sullied, wide-brimmed hat, and scratched his tousled head.

Finally the little teamster climbed down, paused, and pulled a crumpled paper from a baggy coat pocket. A slight headshake and on muddy bare feet he moved toward the lounging men who had, up to that moment, paid him scant attention. He strode slowly toward the smoky fire, mumbling, the yellow note clutched tightly in his hand. He stopped, ran his dark eyes over the ragged Confederates, waved the note, and spoke up, frustration in his voice. "I've got this here paper signed by Gen'ral Lee hisself. I'm t' go out and haul in vittles t' feed our starvin' army. I've been all over this here countryside a-lookin' fur vittles an' ain't found a scrap." He stroked his long tobacco-stained beard, observed the black pot a long moment and sighed deeply. "Well," he went on, resignation in his tone, "I've done m'best. I 'spect thu Genrul's gonna be a bit peeved but—Where'd you boys find that stew beef?" he interrupted himself. "I figured birds a-flyin' over these here parts would starve t' death, less they were carrying their own vittles. 'Cept buzzards," he added and strained a mirthless chuckle.

The corporal raised his bushy brows and half-smiled. "There ain't no need to fret about that. There's plenty of meat. I 'spect, if you're starvin' enough, you'll have t' get ahead of the buzzards."

The corporal's comment came with slight sarcasm, David thought. He walked over to the little teamster, put his long arm across his thin shoulders, looked down into his long, bearded face, forced a small smile, and announced, "I'll be starting service in a few minutes and hope all will attend." David raised his eyes to meet Walter's guilty gaze and continued, "The subject of my sermon will be from Matthew, chapter eighteen—humility."

CHAPTER 11

—HIGH BRIDGE—

As DARKNESS GAVE way to the gray light of dawn, David, now afoot in a cold, drizzling rain, made his way through the clinging mud to the Appomattox River. He crossed the wagon bridge and followed the slow-moving buggy up the steep, rutted slope to the west end of High Bridge.

"The mare looks to be nigh tuckered out," Willie called over his shoulder as the buggy rattled across the railroad track.

"So am I," David responded breathlessly. "Pull Nicie off the road for a brief rest." He glanced across to the rain-soaked railroad bridge and saw several ragged figures desperately fanning small piles of smoky pine faggots with their soiled forage caps.

Suddenly, about seventy yards beyond the ragged Confederates, rifle fire erupted. Out of the cloud of powder smoke, a squad of yelling Federal soldiers appeared and rushed on, trying to reload and fire as they ran.

Surprised, the Confederates turned to run.

A slim figure, running full tilt, while frantically trying to pull his revolver, stumbled and fell on the rough crossties. He struggled to his feet and limped forward a few steps. Puffs of gray smoke leaped from Federal rifles and a lead ball overtook him. Slowly, the ragged private settled to his knees and the long-barreled revolver slipped from his fingers.

David caught his breath.

From the trees, off to his right, a rattle of Confederate musketry counter fire broke out, pouring hot lead toward the Federal skirmishers.

A desultory firing from the bluecoats and the brief flurry sputtered to a halt. With the sure knowledge that their overwhelming forces would soon prevail, the Federals hurriedly retreated, leaving a dozen or so dead and wounded blue-coated soldiers behind.

David turned his eyes back to the young man. With sick nausea in his throat, he watched in disbelief. On his knees, with the soft breath of a morning breeze brushing his burnished red curls, he saw James J. Parker struggling to retrieve his weapon. And with a prayer on his lips, he rushed out to the slender soldier and gathered him in his arms.

Near death, James heaved a deep breath, coughed, and whispered, "I don't reckon I'll be a-killin' no bluecoat after all. I reckon au bluecoats done killed me. If'n I don't make it on home, would you give this ol' Colt t' my pa? I'm thinkin' he might like t' have it."

The chaplain nodded, pulled the revolver from Parker's dying hand, and stuffed it in his coat pocket. "I'll pray for you," he said softly.

The ragged Confederate looked into David's face, a pale little smile stretching his mouth. "Chaplain, if'n I die, can you pray me into heaven . . . an' ask God t' give me a new hand?" James J. Parker coughed again and sucked a slow, shallow breath.

And the chaplain, losing his ability to answer, nodded. A brief pause and he finally managed, "Yes, I'll . . ." He paused again, raised his eyes heavenward and went on. "I believe . . . I'm sure you'll be whole when you walk through heaven's golden gate and touch the face of God."

David opened his mouth to pray, looked into the lad's face, and saw the light fade from his eyes.

"Is . . . is James dead?" Willie asked tremulously as Chaplain Spence, with the limp lad in his arms, approached the buggy.

David nodded somberly and gently laid the blood-soaked lad on the wet grass. He turned back to Willie and almost whispered, "When facing death, every man clings to that thin sliver of abiding hope. Then at the end, when crossing that threshold into a place where all hope is gone, he reaches for help beyond himself, to luck, to fate, or to God." And David Spence went to his knees.

He was still on his knees, praying silently, when a Confederate galloped his gray stallion out from the woods, reined him to a snorting stop, and said, his tone urgent, "Chaplain, you must move on. The Federals will be upon us in a few minutes."

David got to his feet, faced the Confederate officer on the big, prancing stallion, and asked sadly, "What about this young soldier and the other wounded and dead on the bridge?"

"We'll take care of him and the others as well, if we have time," the young lieutenant spoke up impatiently. "There are three hospital wagons just beyond those trees and a stretcher is on the way. There they are now," he went on, pointing.

Spence turned to look. About fifty yards away he saw two ragged, slender, barefoot Confederates, one with a folded canvas stretcher under his right arm, trotting toward them.

The two soldiers hastily laid James Parker on the stretcher and quickstepped down the rutted road, his limp arms dangling.

David reached in his coat for the revolver. He started to speak, but the impatient young rider was galloping away. The weary chaplain climbed in the buggy, handed the weapon to Willie, and sighed. "William, see if you can find somewhere to put this."

"Your slicker is a mite bloody. Maybe . . ." Willie's voice trailed away.

Quietly, David husked the blood-streaked slicker and folded it to cover the blood. "Wrap the Colt in this slicker and stuff it under the seat," he said softly. With a deep sigh, he took up the lines and put Nicie into a slow trot toward Farmville.

Chapter 12

—FARMVILLE—

It was nearing ten o'clock when the buggy rattled down a shallow slope into the outskirts of Farmville. Off to the left David noticed several large structures. Near the road stood a white sign embossed with black lettering. As the buggy drew closer, the words became clear:

FARMVILLE FEMALE COLLEGE
ESTABLISHED 1839

Willie spoke up wonderingly. "With them bluecoats pressing in from all sides, the females might've done gone on home."

"No, Will. Not all have gone home. Listen."

And then they head a chorus of mellifluous voices rising from a long second-floor porch. While waving their handkerchiefs to the trudging Confederates, the girls were singing a familiar Isaac Watts's hymn:

O God, our help in ages past,
our hope for years to come,
our shelters from the stormy blast
and our eternal home.

Near the side entrance to the building—almost overwhelmed by a long line of exhausted, ragged, starving Confederates—they saw four young women handing out dippers of water.

Spence gestured. "Will, pull the buggy into that grass. We'll let Nicie graze while we help those young ladies."

Willie flashed a grin, swung the buggy, and reined the mare onto the lawn.

Gruntingly, David swung down on the tender grass and admitted, "I'm a little stiff. Will, you need to get out and exercise your legs," he went on calmly. "I'll pull the bit from the mare's mouth to let her graze." He turned and nodded toward the growing line of thirsty Confederates. "We need to give those young ladies a helping hand."

Still lashing his galloping horse, a slender, gray-clad Confederate appeared and reined the smallish bay mare in before the line of thirsty men. While trying to hold back his anxious animal with his left hand, he spoke a few words, gestured toward the town with his right, dug spurs into the prancing mare's haunches, and bolted away.

Whooping and hollering, the men, seemingly exhausted a minute ago, were trotting down the slope toward the town.

"What . . . what you reckon's going on?" Willie was puzzled.

Somewhat puzzled himself, David shrugged and said, "I don't know. Well," he went on calmly, "I'm sure those young ladies heard the officer." He moved to the buggy, raised a big hand, and smiled. "Come on and we'll ask them." With a firm grip on Willie Marshall's arm, he helped the slender private from the buggy and on across the campus toward the large two-story brick building.

Suddenly, as they neared the building, a gush of water splashed at their feet. "I'm sorry." The red-faced girl dropped the bucket and apologized again. "I'm . . . I'm so sorry. I didn't see you."

David looked into her big brown eyes and smiled. "You should have aimed a little higher." He glanced at Willie. "We both could use a bath."

The private nodded and drawled, "I don't doubt that a bit."

The girl ran her sharp eyes across the tall man in the dingy, well-worn chaplain uniform, regained her composure, and the blush faded from her face. "Well, Chaplain, I doubt you need to be baptized," she said boldly.

"I don't," David confirmed, glanced at Willie, and smiled. "But hopefully, I'll baptize Private Marshall when we get to the Blue Ridge."

The young lady turned her eyes on Willie and flashed a smile, and the thin private blushed.

David raised a brow inquisitively. "Do you know why those soldiers hurried away?"

The girl's countenance turned serious. "Yes. I heard the Lieutenant say rations had arrived from Lynchburg and they should hurry to the Depot. He said they could hold off Grant's soldiers only a couple of hours before moving the train back to Lynchburg."

"Only a couple of hours," David echoed meditatively. "I'll let Nicie graze awhile before we leave." He glanced at the mare, grazing hungrily, still harnessed and still hitched.

From somewhere inside, a piano came to life.

A door squeaked open and a hasty, anxious female voice called, "Helen, Ms. Prichard wants you to come inside right away. She'll be starting practice in a few minutes." The girl stepped outside and went on in a lowered tone. "And, Helen, she said you could invite those two soldiers inside to rest awhile and listen to our choir."

Helen looked at the chaplain and smiled. "Would you—?"

"We would be honored," David answered before she finished. He smiled broadly, glanced at Willie, and found him grinning. Spence turned back to the girl and looked at her quizzically. "How did she—?"

The girl giggled lightly. "Oh, indeed, Ms. Prichard is very protective of her students. She was on the porch when you got out of the buggy."

David nodded. "I'm sure she is . . . protective."

Helen turned, led them inside, and walked slowly—to match Willie's hobbling gait—as they moved down a long corridor.

They went through the doorway, and David gave the gray-walled room an encompassing survey. Above the mantle, encasing a wide brick fireplace, he saw a large gold-framed oval mirror. On the wall across from the windows he scanned a long, tall bookcase fronted by four narrow tables. Near the back wall stood a heavy-legged concert piano. And in a semicircle, facing the piano, sat eleven young women quietly leafing through their songbooks.

And then his eyes moved to the young lady at the piano, nervously arranging her music. A sheet fluttered to the floor. She spun the swivel stool and reached down to retrieve the sheet music, and for a brief moment, her bright blue-green eyes met David's.

His heart leaped.

The instructress, Ms. Prichard, standing beside the girl, looked up and saw the two Confederates. A brief smile and she spoke up primly, a slight touch of authority in her tone. "Welcome, gentlemen. Introduce yourselves, have a seat, and sing along if you wish."

Willie's face reddened and the tall chaplain smiled. "I'm David Spence and this young man"—he turned his eyes to Willie, now forcing a smile through his deepening blush—"is Private William Marshall." David paused momentarily, stroking his dark, bristly three-day-old beard. "I apologize for our . . . condition."

Will Marshall sat silently, but Chaplain Spence, familiar with the hymn, could not restrain himself for long before he was humming, patting a foot, and finally singing along with the young women, his baritone voice filling the room:

> All hail the power of Jesus's name!
> Let angels' prostrate fall;
> bring forth the royal diadem,
> and crown Him Lord of all.

They were well into the fifth hymn, when Willie tugged at David's sleeve. "What time you reckon it to be?" he asked worriedly.

Spence smiled and pulled out his watch. "Well, we've been here only—" He opened the lid, glanced at the watch, and leaped to his feet. "We are late!" he exclaimed much louder than intended. "It's ten past twelve. We must leave immediately or—" He looked up and saw Bettie Prichard approaching on hurrying feet. David forced himself calm, took Ms. Prichard's slender hand lightly, half-bowed, and said sincerely, "I thank you and your students for your gracious hospitality." He swept his eyes across the smiling girls and brought them to rest momentarily on the young lady in the blue dress, still at the piano and looking back, a little smile dimpling her rosy cheeks.

David forced his eyes back to Ms. Prichard and went on poetically. "This brief interlude from the tides of war will dwell in my memory forever." With that, he took Willie's arm, flashed a good-bye wave, and hurried away.

At the buggy Chaplain Spence helped the lad onto the seat and moved to Nicie, still grazing hungrily. The reluctant mare snorted and turned somewhat mettlesome as he pulled her head up and forced the bit in her mouth. David climbed in the buggy, and touched up the mare with the lines. And with the crackle of distant rifle fire, the buggy rattled onto the road and turned down the shallow slope into the little town.

Immediately, they caught the sound of galloping hooves approaching from the rear. Willie turned his head and saw, about seventy yards away, a Confederate horseman lashing his stallion with the reins and spurring him onward at breakneck speed.

As he drew near the swaying buggy, the rider—a tall, slender sergeant—with a quick, anxious look over his shoulder, pulled the big, snorting horse back into a cantor and called loudly, urgency in his tone, "Union calvary's coming, and coming fast. You'd better put that horse into a fast gallop or . . ." His voice trailed off as he glanced over his shoulder again. He yanked the big bay past the trotting mare, viciously dug spur rowels into the horse's heaving flanks, and galloped away.

Almost simultaneously, David and Willie looked back and saw a troop of blue-clad horsemen, about three hundred yards away, charging down the muddy road.

David turned and lashed Nicie. The surprised mare lurched into a gallop. But William Marshall's sharp eyes could see the bluecoats rapidly closing the gap.

As the buggy rattled into the town, David realized Nicie was flagging badly and turned to Willie. "I'll have to—"

"Them bluecoats have done stopped," Willie cut in worriedly, still looking back.

"Stopped? I don't—" David didn't bother to finish. He saw gray-clad soldiers blocking the street ahead, their rifles at the ready position. Out front stood a howitzer, pointing up the street and loaded with grapeshot, he guessed.

As he pulled the winded mare back into a slow trot, a Confederate captain rode forward, touched his hat brim, reined his chestnut gelding near the buggy, and smiled. "Well, Chaplain, it looks like you're caught between two armies that seem determined to kill each other."

David nodded. "Yes, we were, but God has his hand—"

The captain glanced over his shoulder, gestured, and said hastily, "There's a rider coming in with a white flag." And in the approaching beat of galloping hooves, he nudged his horse just beyond the buggy and pulled reins.

The galloper, a Federal lieutenant, reined his lathered horse in near the Confederate's gelding and executed a waving salute. "I have a message for General Lee," he said, voice strained. "It's from General Grant."

Captain Myers's strong voice retorted firmly, ignoring the salute. "No. I will not deliver a message to the general, unless your troopers stay where they are."

"That's no problem. We'll wait until it's delivered," the lieutenant rejoined brusquely, handing Myers the folded note.

As the Federal lieutenant pulled the mud-spattered horse around and galloped away, Myers read the note, reined his gelding, swept his bright eyes across the two disheveled men in the buggy, and smiled. "Well, General Lee will finally get good news. His son Curtis is a prisoner, but he's alive and well."

"Is General Lee still in Farmville?" David asked quietly.

"He is. But he'll be leaving for Appomattox Courthouse within the hour. Chaplain," Myers went on, his tone turning serious, "I suggest you get that buggy across the river before it's too late."

A few minutes later, the buggy rattled on past the railroad station where hungry Confederates were frantically filling their pockets with anything eatable and rushing on toward the bridges spanning the Appomattox River.

CHAPTER 13

—TOWARD APPOMATTOX—

THE OLD BUGGY finally managed to cross the river, and once again, they found themselves trailing heavy-laden wagons, caissons, and exhausted, demoralized infantry moving slowly toward Appomattox Courthouse. Along the road, with sad eyes, they saw the stark evidence of a vanishing army, dead horses still in harness and still hitched to broken-down wagons, scattered ammunition, and occasionally a Confederate soldier—dead and unburied.

After an hour or so they came upon a downed bridge and a heavy wagon, on its side in a muddy, rain-swollen creek.

Willie pointed. "There's a little trail about a hundred strides up ahead, turning off to the left."

"Maybe we can bypass the blocked bridge." David sighed wistfully and reined Nicie on the weedy, narrow road forking to the southwest.

Willie nodded lightly. "I figure going this a-way we might come up on a patch of grass for the mare that ain't been chewed down to the ground."

The chaplain responded quietly. "Well, maybe we will."

The mare moved along the trail about half an hour. Finally, off to the left, fronting a grove of tall pine trees, a falling down, split-rail fence came into view. After jouncing on four or five hundred yards in the deepening twilight, the buggy splashed across a shallow stream and rolled with exasperating slowness toward a pale square of distant light. The light grew and became a window in a farmhouse. And sensing rest just ahead, Nicie gaited into a sustained, albeit feeble trot.

David reined the jaded mare in front of the old run-down house and climbed stiffly from the buggy. And in the dim moon glow, he made his way through the high weeds to the porch. He mounted the two rotting steps and glimpsed tatty window curtains part slightly. He crossed the porch on warped unpainted boards and rapped the door lightly.

The slow shuffle of heavy shoes and the door creaked open a few inches. A sliver of slanting yellow light spilled onto the porch, followed by a long-barreled shotgun.

Surprised, David stepped back and called hoarsely, "Hello, friend. I'm a Confederate chaplain with General Lee's army. I need water for my mare and a handful of corn, if you have any to spare." Then he thought, *I hope these people are Christians.*

From inside a weak voice croaked, "Whut name ye go by?"

"My name is David—David Spence. I'm a Confederate chaplain," he answered, forcing his voice calm.

"I'm au confirmed Presbyterian m'self," the man behind the door said, his tone combative. "Anyhow, ye sound like a Northerner . . . of sorts. How do I know you're who ye a-claimin' t' be?"

"Hold your lamp out the door to see my chaplain garb." David forced a light chuckle. "Only a chaplain would wear this garb."

On a low grunt from the house, the sagging door slowly scraped open and a pale yellow light shafted across the porch. And squinting into the glow, David saw a thin, stooped old man holding a smoky lamp high in one hand and a wavering shotgun in the other.

The old man gave him a long, frowning look. "A man jus' can't be too careful this day an' time," he finally croaked. "Them Federal thieves seem t' be a-trottin' all over thu countryside."

His croaking voice, David thought, seemed somewhat apologetic.

"I've been a-waitin' fer them t' show up so's I could blast them with this ol' shotgun," he went on, waving the weapon feebly.

"Yes, friend," David said, flashing his Bible with a slight headshake. "It is a sad situation we've gotten ourselves into, but the Lord will take care of His own."

The old man followed with a headshake of his own, his heavy, long-barreled weapon slowly sagging. Finally, abandoning the effort to point the old shotgun, he turned and propped it against the wall. "Maybe so, but I'm gonna be a-given Him all thu help I can." He laughed silently and went on, gesturing feebly. "Well, might's well come on in an' rest yo' weary bones awhile."

Nicie snorted.

The old farmer jerked his head up and looked out into the darkness. "Ye alone?" he asked, cutting his pale, squinty eyes back to the tall chaplain.

"I'm not alone," David responded patiently, throwing a thumb toward the rig. "There's a wounded soldier in that buggy. I don't believe I got your name," he continued in a friendly tone, holding out his hand.

"My name's a-bein' Thomas Turner, but most folks 'round these parts calls me Ol' Tom."

As they shook hands, the Confederate chaplain looked into the weathered, timeless face, whose age, he thought, could possibly be anywhere between sixty and ninety.

The old man turned his head, squirted a stream of tobacco juice onto the porch, swiped the back of his bony hand across his thin, bluish lips, and went on. "I might be able t' dig out an ear or two of left over corn fer yo' hoss." He turned and pointed a knurled arthritic finger. "I reckon you an' thu wounded boy t' be a bit hungry. All I got air two, maybe three pieces of left over corn pone," he mumbled thoughtfully.

David half-smiled. "Cold corn pone for us and one or two ears of corn for Nicie would be a feast."

Turner pulled at his straggly whiskers while allowing a thin smile to crawl across his wrinkled, stoic face. "Well, reckon I ain't never heard 'bout a hoss with a name such as that."

The chaplain explained softly. "My uncle gave the mare to my mother about twelve years ago. The filly was so gentle, so nice, she named her Nicie." David paused, his countenance suddenly serious. Finally he issued a deep sigh and asked quietly, "Have you seen any Federal soldiers pass this way?"

Ol' Tom shook his balding gray head. "I ain't seen nary a one, blue nor gray . . . yet." He scratched in his scraggly whiskers awhile. "Anyhow," he went on thoughtfully, "I live off thu main road a ways an' ain't seein' many passin' folks. Jed Lawson—a neighbor, I reckon him t' be—is livin' 'bout a mile off t' thu South. On his ol' gray mule, he stopped by an' said he'd seed a dozen or so bluecoats a-riding by his place. They seemed t' be scoutin', he figured. Well, don't reckon I got a thing more pressin' t' do right now. Come on in an' rest yo'selves?

I'd be willin' t' take yo' hoss an' buggy out t' thu barn. Reckon it t' be safe . . . fer thu night."

"I appreciate the offer, but I believe it's my duty to move on with the army." A short pause and David gestured. "Can you tell me where that little road goes?"

Thomas Turner stroked his gray, tobacco-stained whiskers awhile. "That thu road, I 'spect might jus' stay were 'tis." He issued a short chuckle and went on. "But it tracks on by Jed's place an' meanders a ways of t' thu west t' Pamplin City, which I'm a-guessin' t' be bought ten miles . . . as thu crow flies. I'm thinkin' it t' be a purdy rough ride, though." He shook his balding gray head briefly and smiled, exposing a wide gap between yellow, decaying teeth—upper and lower. "Well, I reckon I oughtta quit talkin' an' fetch thu corn pone afore ye starve."

Several minutes later David made his way through the tall, dew-wetted grass, climbed in the buggy, and handed Willie a thick corn pone and two ears of corn.

Thomas limped up.

Spence leaned from the buggy, reached down, took his bony hand, and forced a smile.

The old man hung on a long moment. Finally, he pulled his withered, arthritic hand away, raised the lantern, and turned his watery gaze to Willie. "Young fellow," he said, a serious tone in his croaky voice, "I'll be a-praying you'll be healing up 'fore long."

Willie bent forward and responded in a low, sincere drawl. "I'm much obliged for that, and thanking you for the bread and corn."

Ol' Tom stroked his beard and turned his pale, protuberant eyes back to David. "Preacher," he croaked, "there's a thing I oughtta be tellin' afore ye go on."

"What are you telling me?" David asked, creasing his brow.

A thin smile crawled across the wrinkled face. "Well, reckon I oughtta be a-tellin' you . . . that ol' shotgun ain't loaded."

"Not loaded?" Spence chuckled. He curbed the mare as she started forward and leaned from the buggy. "And I reckon I ought to tell you, it wasn't cocked either." He chuckled, gave the old man a waving salute, and flicked the mare with the lines. The buggy lurched and then began to roll slowly down the rutted trail.

Chapter 14

—FEDERAL PICKETS—

THE PALE MOON was high and a canopy of stars winked brightly in the sky as the old rig creaked its way up the narrow, dappled trail, winding through a grove of over-arching oaks and topped a low hill.

"Whoa!" Willie called urgently, jerking the lines from David's limp hands and reining the surprised mare to a halt.

"What—?" David started, raising his head from a nodding doze.

"Down there"—Willie gestured—"looks to be campfires in them tall pines."

Chaplain Spence looked down the dark slope. In a small clearing, about three hundred yards away, he saw the soft yellow glow of flickering, smoky campfires. "Yes. They're probably Federal pickets," he ventured worriedly. "Maybe we—"

"Where do you think you're going?" a deep voice boomed in the darkness.

David stiffened, shifting his gaze toward the sound. Several seconds passed, the rustle of leaves, and a dark figure emerged from behind a large oak into a stippled patch of moonlight.

"We—" Stopping, David squinted to recognize the figure's uniform.

"Put your hands on your heads and keep them there," the approaching figure demanded harshly. With his new Spencer lever-action rifle pointing toward the buggy, the big Federal stopped, half-turned, and called excitedly. "Jones, light up the lantern and come on out. It looks like we've caught us a couple of rebels."

Beyond the big soldier, in the deep darkness, a match flared and a cupped hand carried it down to the wick. The hand lowered the mantle and the glow from a coal oil lantern spread into a yellow circle. And casting its dim glow on the blue-coated figure just ahead, the bobbing light moved toward the buggy.

In the weak light, the two Confederates saw a tall, rather heavy, brutish-looking sergeant with thick reddish chin whiskers.

"Jones," the big blue-clad sergeant ordered, "hold the light up so we can see what we've caught up here."

"Sergeant," David intervened calmly, lowering his hands, "what you have here is a wounded soldier and a chaplain."

"A chaplain, are you?" the big soldier retorted gruffly. There was a mirthless smile on the sergeant's ruddy face as he ran his hard eyes across the two Confederates. He pointed toward the Enfield rifle propped against the buggy seat. "Seems like a weapon in your buggy. I've never seen a chaplain carrying a rifle before." A contemptuous laugh and he swung his large head to face the young blue-clad private. "Jones, you might as well get the rifle that's propped between them two rebels."

Instinctively, Willie reached for the rifle.

"No, Will!" David grasped the boy's slender arm.

The sergeant swept the Spencer up and the young Confederate found himself looking into the barrel of a repeating rifle. And Will Marshall slowly moved his empty hand back to his head, saying, "I was gonna—" He didn't finish the sentence. Wide-eyed, he looked into the sergeant's bearded face and, in the lantern's dim glow, he saw a maniacal little grin. Willie shuddered imperceptibly as the big soldier fingered the weapon suggestively. *That big Federal is mighty anxious to use that rifle*, he figured.

David noticed the sergeant's grin as well. And forcing his voice calm, he intervened again. "That old rifle is not loaded. This wounded soldier brought it along . . . too discourage thieves."

Now standing by the buggy with the lantern held high, the slender private leaned forward, reached a long arm across Willie's bandage-encased leg and pulled the Enfield from the footboard.

The private lowered the lantern to the ground, put on a crooked little grin, and pointed the long barrel skyward. Still eyeing Willie, he thumbed the weapon to full cock and squeezed the trigger. The hammer fell on the nipple with a dull click. Private Jones cut his eyes to the sergeant and chuckled. "That reb seems to be right. This old weapon ain't loaded."

"Well then, Jones," the big sergeant ordered with a touch of disappointment in his deep, raspy voice, "search the buggy and that skinny rebel."

Private Jones examined the contents of the buggy box, looked in the haversacks, and moved to Willie. And in the dim glow from the lantern, he grinned up at the frowning gray-clad lad sitting stiffly on the worn leather seat and ran a grimy hand over his pockets. "Sergeant, I didn't find weapons or vittles. All I found in the box was a saddle, au empty haversack, and au pair of boots. And looks like a big dog-eared book on the seat—seems to be a Bible."

Will Marshall relaxed. Private Jones had failed to discover the revolver. He shot David an under-brow glance and almost smiled. Then he thought, *I hope them Federals won't be taking a look come daylight.*

"Give me the lantern and stay on guard up here while I turn these rebels over to Captain Foster," the big sergeant ordered, caressing his thick red beard while running his squinty eyes over the two captives. He took the lantern and moved sprightly around the mud-spattered buggy. The big, bearded man thrust the foul-smelling lantern close to the chaplain's face. "You'd better not move another inch," he warned and put the rifle barrel at the tall chaplain's throat."

David managed a thin smile and spoke up, forcing a pulpit tone. "Well, Sergeant, it seems you are anxious to use your rifle."

The sergeant eyed him suspiciously.

Under David's unwavering gaze, the truculence faded from the red-bearded soldier's face and he pulled the rifle back. "Well, well, Chaplain," he sighed, "this has been a long war and a soldier that's been in quite a few battles—can get a bit edgy at times."

David nodded and settled back in the buggy seat.

The lantern sputtered several seconds, then it went dark. The heavy sergeant lowered the soot-infested lantern and gestured toward distant flickering campfires. "See if you can nudge your horse down to Captain Foster's bivouac. And keep that animal at a walk," the sergeant warned belatedly.

In the dappled glow from the high-hanging half-moon and the big sergeant striding at the rear, the old buggy wobbled down the long slope toward a dozen or so dying campfires glowing dimly within a piney grove.

"Password!" a voice rang out from the darkness.

"Is that you, Charley?" Woods asked, chuckling knowingly. "I guess you drew out the short straw."

"Password!" the sentry called again. "I know who you might be, but orders are orders. You ain't passing without saying it."

"The password is Abraham!" The big sergeant's deep voice growled as he strode past the buggy.

"Ought to say the password right off, seems to me," Charley mumbled to himself.

"Is the Captain up yet?" Sergeant Woods went on impatiently.

A demanding voice rose from the dark grove. "Sergeant, what is all the commotion about?"

The sentry and the big, wide-shouldered sergeant stiffened and halfheartedly saluted the approaching figure.

"Sir," Woods reported demurely, "I've captured a couple of rebels in a buggy. One's a chaplain, he says, and the skinny boy is a wounded private."

"You've captured a chaplain and—?"

With the galling rasp of rusting springs, David heaved himself from the buggy, cleared his throat, took a deep breath, and spoke up tiredly. "I'm David Spence, a Confederate chaplain." He gestured toward the silhouetted rig. "And that wounded young man in the buggy is Private Marshall."

The Union captain raised his lantern and considered a moment. And with an encompassing glance at Willie, he holstered his long-barreled revolver. The captain—a tall, slender thirty-year-old man with jet-black hair and a well-trimmed mustache—turned his dark eyes back to David, flashed a half smile, and extended his right hand. "My name is John—John Foster," he said in a Northeastern accent.

The captain's manner seemed friendly. And Spence, somewhat relieved, issued a shallow nod and took the offered hand briefly, raising an inquisitive brow. "Has the war ended?" he asked anxiously. "We've been out of touch for a day or two."

"Not yet," Captain Foster responded somberly as he thoughtfully fingered his neatly trimmed mustache. A slight headshake and he went on. "But I believe, after devastating losses at Sailor's Creek, General Lee will surrender soon . . . probably in two or three days."

"Yes," David agreed sadly. "I pray this carnage will end soon and the soldiers, all of them, can return to their families and live in peace. And, Captain," he went on sincerely, "I believe our God does not favor one army above another. He deals with us as individuals, not as an army . . . or a nation."

Foster was surprised. After a long, thoughtful moment, he smoothed his mustache and sighed. "Well, that's the way of war—young men kill, young men die, and those who remain grieve. But like you, Chaplain, I hope this war will end soon—very soon."

The Union captain glanced at Willie frowningly, turned back to Spence, and said seriously, "Take the boy to my tent. I'll get fresh bandages and be there shortly to dress the wound." He turned to the uncomfortable sergeant, held out his lantern and ordered calmly, "Light the way for the . . . prisoners to my tent and have one of your men unhitch and feed the chaplain's horse."

A casual salute and the big sergeant, with a weak gesture, guided the two Confederates through the piney woods to a clearing about fifty yards away. As they came out from the trees, they saw three tents standing starkly against the starlit sky.

Woods gestured and mumbled, "That's the captain's tent." With that, he turned and walked away, and the lantern's dim light disappeared in the piney grove.

David pulled the flap aside and Willie hobbled into the tent. In the weak glow from a ridgepole lantern, he dropped his crutches, threw his exhausted body on a worn canvas cot, and mumbled, "I hope that Captain don't take offence at me for being on his cot."

"I doubt he will," David responded with a tired sigh. He ducked into the tent and encountered the foul odor of coal oil from the sputtering lantern. He tossed William Marshall's Union boots under the cot and lowered himself onto a three-legged campstool.

Twenty minutes later Captain Foster bowed into the tent, deposited a black, leather satchel on the map table and turned to find Willie snoring peacefully on the cot.

And David, balanced precariously on the stool with his chin on his chest, seemed to be in a nodding doze. He jerked his head up and apologized. "I'm sorry, Captain."

Foster frowned at the sleepy-eyed chaplain, nodded, and said quietly, "It seems you've had very little sleep lately."

And trying to remember, David scratched his head. "Well, except for a few naps in the buggy, I think it's been two, maybe three nights. I'm not sure."

Another glance at the sleeping private and the captain opened the bag. "I'll examine the lad's leg and replace the bandage. After that, I'll have my orderly bring in another cot. And hopefully, you will get a couple of hours' sleep before dawn." Foster reached up to the ridgepole and adjusted the lantern wick and the tent brightened. He pulled a scalpel from his black satchel and gently shook Willie's arm.

"What?" Startled, Will Marshall struggled to rise. "What's going on?" With the captain's restraining hand on his chest, he settled on his back and noticed the poised scalpel, and his eyes widened in bewilderment.

Foster chuckled. "Don't worry, I'm not performing surgery. I need to slit your trousers to see how the wound is healing and replace the bandage. When were you wounded?" he asked softly as he efficiently slit the grimy trousers.

And trying to remember, Willie shrugged his thin shoulders. "I'd say it to be about six weeks ago. Could be a bit longer."

Captain Foster removed the dirty bandage, tossed the splints aside, and carefully examined the slender leg. He flashed a brief smile at Willie as he ran his long fingers over the lad's left knee. "Well, it seems to be healing well enough to discard the splints. I suspect there is a sliver of shrapnel lodged under your kneecap. You should have it removed if . . . when you find a competent surgeon." He turned to David and nodded. "Chaplain, hand me that roll of bandages."

David handed him the bandages and smiled. "Captain, I think you could become an excellent doctor."

Captain Foster forced a brief chuckle as he efficiently applied the bandage. "Well, before this bloody war, I was a country doctor in Maine. Young man, you need to exercise that leg as much as possible," he said sternly, his countenance serious. He turned his sharp brown eyes on David and sighed. "Have him discard the crutches when you think he can navigate without them."

"Captain, you reckon I'm gonna be able to bend my knee if I get a surgeon to cut out that piece of metal?" Willie asked.

Foster, glanced at David, and forced a thin smile. "Well, that depends upon what the surgeon finds. Maybe—" He paused thoughtfully. "Well, maybe, without the splints, you'll be able to wear those boots. Now"—he started to leave—"I'll have a cot brought in and let you rest until dawn. We'll break camp shortly after sunup."

*

The braying of a hungry mule brought David awake. Still half-asleep, he sat up, swung his feet from the cot, pulled on his worn boots, and moved stealthily to the tent flap.

Willie was still snoring as Spence stepped outside and looked up to find the piney woods dark. But with the distant glow of a large cook fire mingling with the narrow gray light of dawn rimming the eastern sky, he guessed it to be between five and six o'clock.

"Did you sleep well, Chaplain?" a voice spoke in the darkness.

David recognized the voice, faced the dark figure, and chuckled lightly. "Yes, Captain, I slept very well . . . after dealing with Private Marshall's snoring awhile."

Captain Foster smiled and gestured toward the smoky fire. "My troopers are roasting a side of beef. I'm sure they will share it with you." He chuckled and went on pleasantly. "As you probably know, most of the food is . . . is purchased from local farmers."

David frowned at that but remained silent.

As they came out of the trees into a narrow clearing, David saw a skewered side of beef on a spit, browning over a smoky, crackling fire about ten feet behind a two-horse wagon, surrounded by lounging Federal cavalrymen, each holding a tin plate and bayonet and impatiently waiting.

"Captain, would you allow a prayer and a brief sermon after breakfast?" David asked quietly.

"Yes, I will," Foster answered, smiling broadly. "After all, today is Sunday."

The tall chaplain shook his head thoughtfully. "Oh, today is Sunday—Palm Sunday."

The pickets about twenty or so got to their feet and stood stiffly silent as the captain pulled a tin plate from the wagon bed, handed it to the chaplain, and gestured toward the roasting beef.

David spoke quietly. "Captain, if you don't mind, I prefer your soldiers go first."

Foster chuckled. "Well, Chaplain, if that's what you prefer, they can go first—I'll go last."

*

I hope Willie is awake, David mused as he approached the tent, a tin plate carefully balanced in his right hand.

A sudden, cool morning breeze unfurled a banner hanging just above the tent. He paused, looked up, and saw a First Pennsylvania Cavalry banner. "First Pennsylvania," he muttered. *I've heard of them, but where?* he asked himself.

"Dad-gum it!" Willie exclaimed, frustration in his voice.

David ducked inside to find him sitting on the cot, struggling to get his foot in the cavalry boot. He looked questioningly at the private. "What's the problem?"

William reddened a little, looked at David, looked down at the tall boot, and said dispiritedly, "I've been trying to pull this Union boot on. But with this stiff leg, I can't reach my foot."

David Spence smiled and responded in his unassuming tone. "All right then, you eat this meat before it's too cold and I'll help with the boot."

Eagerly, Willie Marshall took the tin plate, paused, and mumbled, "I'm hoping this ain't hoss meat."

"No." Spence shook his head briefly and smiled again. "That's beef—that's prime beef."

A minute later the plate was empty.

As David took the tin plate and turned to the map table, the rustle of approaching footfalls reached his ears.

Captain Foster thrust his head through the tent slit. "We'll be breaking camp in a few minutes," he said hastily. "I have your mare and buggy outside." He held out a pair of trousers and smiled. "Give these to the private." He cut his gaze to Willie and chuckled. "They may not be the color he prefers, but Union blue is all we have."

And William Marshall, half-smiling, nodded. "Thank you, kindly captain. I reckon it to be all right. I 'spect Confederate gray will be out of style before long."

"Are we still prisoners?" David stopped abruptly. The captain had disappeared.

The sun was up but an early morning fog still lingered in the Virginia pines as the chaplain ducked outside. Again, he glanced at the banner hanging limp. *I remember now*, he told himself. *It was in the newspapers. The First Pennsylvania Cavalry lost over half their men in the charge at Cedar Mountain that hot August day. I wonder if Captain Foster was there*, he mused.

In his slightly oversized Union trousers and a crutch under his left arm, Willie hobbled out into the rising sun, a wide smile splitting his narrow face. "With these here boots, I'm thinking, I can make do with just one crutch," he announced proudly.

David Spence smiled and nodded. "Well, hopefully you'll be able to discard both in a few days. Wait in the buggy while I go over there to determine our status." He gestured toward the Union captain standing at the trail with a widespread map in his gauntleted hands. He seemed to be conferring seriously with two young lieutenants.

On long-striding legs, David moved hurriedly toward the three officers still engrossed in the map.

Suddenly, the swift thud of galloping hooves reached their ears. As one, the three officers turned and saw a Federal courier astraddle a lathered bay horse splashing up from the south.

The rider jerked the big jaded gelding to a sliding stop and snapped a sharp salute. He reached under his tunic, drew out a yellow flimsy, and ran his dark eyes across the three officers. "Important orders for Captain Foster," he said hurriedly.

"I'm Foster," the captain responded immediately, returned the salute, and extended a gauntleted hand.

The courier, a young sergeant, leaned from the snorting animal, handed him the flimsy, issued another sharp salute, pulled the mud-spattered gelding about, and spurred him down the trail.

Foster read the order. It was from General Grant's headquarters. It was short. "It's over, it's over!" he shouted. "General Grant's orders are to cease-fire and all pickets move with dispatch to the village of New Store and escort him to Appomattox Courthouse. General Lee has agreed to surrender there this afternoon."

Immediately, the two lieutenants began scanning the smudged map for New Store village. "Here it is!" the short, heavyset, lieutenant exclaimed excitedly, stabbing a stubby finger at the map. "It seems to be about seven, eight miles from Appomattox."

The tall, slender captain looked pleased as the lieutenants rushed into the trees. He raised his dark eyes, noticed the chaplain, put on a wide smile, and drew off a gauntleted glove. He took David's right hand and shook it vigorously. "Well, Chaplain, this is the day I've waited for."

Foster continued pumping his hand and David smiled. "Well, Captain, this is the day I've prayed for. What better day to put an end to war than Palm Sunday?"

Foster's countenance turned serious. He released the chaplain's hand and spoke softly. "We've prayed four long years for this day."

"Captain, will we remain—?"

"Oh, I'm sure that will not be a problem." the dark-haired captain answered the unfinished question. "You'll be able to tell your grandchildren you were a prisoner of war for about . . . about three hours," he said pleasantly, smiling broadly. "Well, Chaplain Spence, since the war has ended in Virginia, what are your plans for the future? Will you continue to be a herald of the Gospel?"

David was surprised. He saw a wide toothy smile splitting Foster's sharp countenance and hesitated a long moment, not sure how to answer the question. "Well," he finally responded, "I doubt I'm destined to become a minister. After I escort Private Marshall to the Blue Ridge, I'll go to my uncle's farm in the Shenandoah Valley, live peaceably, and raise a few cattle . . . maybe some horses. That's good country for livestock."

Foster chuckled. "Indeed, Chaplain, I'm beginning to envy you."

Then the clop of trotting hooves caught their attention. They turned and saw Sergeant Woods, astride a bay mare, emerge from the pines with a big chestnut stallion in tow. He reined the mare, saluted clumsily, and reported in his deep, husky voice. "Sir, we're all packed up and ready to move out, except for the tents."

Foster started to speak, but the ruddy-faced sergeant, smiling proudly, went on. "I got a wagon on the way to load the tents."

"That's fine, Sergeant." Captain Foster nodded. "Is there anything else?"

Woods cleared his throat noisily, his hand moving to his red beard. "Well, sir, there is one more." He left the sentence unfinished and shot a frowning under-brow glance at the big chaplain. He moved the hand from his beard to his blue jacket and drew out a revolver. Woods handed the weapon, butt first, to Foster, shot another frowning glance at David, and spurred the mare back into the pines.

David grimaced. The sergeant had found the revolver. *Will Captain Foster continue to hold us captive?* he wondered.

The captain stuffed the weapon in his tailored coat pocket, turned to David, and smiled. "Oh . . . one final thing," the captain added politely. "You may need this." He pulled the revolver from his coat pocket and handed it to Spence, his face turning serious. "With all the chaos of a dissolving army, there's no telling what you'll encounter before you reach the mountains."

"This weapon—" David started apologetically.

Captain Foster was nodding. "There's no need to explain. I saw the bloodstained slicker."

It was about ten minutes later when a two-horse wagon drawn by a couple of scrawny mules rumbled out from the trees and rattled to a halt before the tents. Six bluecoats piled out as Sergeant Woods reined his gelding in beside the wagon and dismounted.

Efficiently, the cavalrymen pulled down the banner, struck the tents, loaded them onto the wagon, and rattled away.

Somewhere within the piney grove, a bugler sounded the call and twenty-seven troopers trotted their horses out from the trees, their First Pennsylvania Calvary banners waving in a light breeze.

The slender captain swung gracefully aboard his impatient stallion and smiled down at David. "God be with you, Chaplain," he intoned sincerely. A waving salute and he was quickly gone.

David climbed in the buggy, and Willie reined the mare onto the trail at the rear of the Federal cavalry, finally in motion and moving at a fast trot toward New Store village some five miles away.

A few quiet minutes and David shifted on the seat and looked back at the buggy box. He lifted a fat haversack and smiled. "Well, William, it seems the captain has restocked our food supply."

Private Marshall shot the chaplain a sideways glance and grinned. "I reckon that captain's got a heart after all."

David smiled again. "Yes, William, I reckon he has."

They both laughed.

*

Fifteen miles southwest of the village and Sunday night was turning into Monday morning as David guided the mare across a gurgling little stream into a dewy field. He reined in the mare, turned bleary eyes to Willie, and said softly, "We'll camp here until dawn, get some rest, and let Nicie graze until dawn."

"I was hoping we'd be stopping soon," Willie drawled. "This old mare's plumb tuckered out."

David looked at him and smiled tiredly. "I believe at High Bridge you said Nicie was 'tuckered out.' But seemingly indefatigable, she keeps plugging along."

Unable to process *indefatigable*, Willie decided to put on a crooked smile. "She's a good old mare all right. I'm thinking you said when we left Richmond, Nicie might last no more'n three or four days."

With that, they both laughed again.

CHAPTER 15

—SWORDS INTO PLOWSHARES—

IN THE FIRST light of dawn, the mare, rested and fed, was now moving briskly along a winding trail, seemingly untouched by the debris of war.

As the day drew on toward noon, David opened his Bible and began leafing through the pages. He stopped at Isaiah, nudged Willie lightly, and said gently, "Listen to this, William:

> And He shall judge among the nations, and rebuke
>   many people:
> and they shall beat their swords into plowshares,
> and their spears into pruning hooks:
> nation shall not lift up sword against nation;
> neither shall they learn war any more.

David flipped to Psalms and read on:

> Come; behold the works of the LORD,
> what desolation he hath made in the earth.
> He maketh wars to cease unto the end of the earth;
> he breaketh the bow, and cutteth the spear in sunder;
> he burneth the chariot in the fire.
> Be still, and know that I am God:
> I will be exalted among the heathen;
> I will be exalted in the earth.

"You reckon," Willie inquired wonderingly, "we'll be seeing anymore wars at all?"

"Well, William, the Bible tells us there will always be wars and rumors—"

The buggy came out from the trees, and David's ears caught the sound of rushing water. He looked up and saw a swollen, fast-flowing, rock-lashed creek just ahead.

"Stop!" he called, urgency in his voice.

Willie jerked the lines, but it was too late. The buggy's momentum pushed Nicie down the steep, muddy slope. The mare plunged into the rain-swollen creek. A violent jolt and the buggy tilted. The right rear wheel disappeared in the murky water.

David righted himself. He glanced at Willie—now draped over the dashboard, gasping for air—reached out a big hand, grasped a slender arm, and pulled him upright. "Willie," he asked gently, "are you injured?"

And Willie, still struggling to regain his breath, finally gasped, "Naw . . . don't . . . don't reckon I am," the disheveled lad said haltingly. "What you reckon happened to the buggy?"

"A broken axle, I suspect." David Spence sighed and turned to look for his Bible. "I don't see my Bible!" he exclaimed worriedly. "Do you see it?"

"There it is," Willie answered croakily, pointing to the flooded floorboard.

David swept up the black water-soaked Bible, drew it across his sullied blouse, placed it reverently on the worn leather seat, and turned his attention to the mare, still standing in fast-flowing water up to her belly. "Well, Nicie seems to be all right. If we lighten the buggy," David went on thoughtfully, "I believe the mare can tow it across."

"Uh—but—" Willie Marshall started, stuttering. "But you well know," he reminded, "I can't swim a lick."

Spence climbed down into the rushing stream and raised his gaze to the slender lad. He was annoyed but covered it with a little smile. "Now, William, you know the water is only waist-deep. I'm sure I can carry you across."

Willie was not convinced. He raised his thin eyebrows and frowned. "That water's flowing mighty fast."

"You'll have to trust me," David insisted, trying to be patient with the frightened lad. "You have no other choice."

And Will Marshall, still a bit apprehensive, looked down at gushing water, looked at Spence, and nodded slightly. "I reckon you can carry me," Willie muttered, none too certain, forced a crooked little grin, and slithered across the worn seat.

David slung the gangly lad across a wide shoulder. And struggling against the swift flowing current, he managed to navigate on past the confused mare to the far side of the swollen creek, about thirty feet away.

He deposited Willie against a tall poplar tree, plunged back into the creek, and waded out to the mare. He caressed her forehead and mumbled soothingly. "Now, Nicie, towing this broken-down buggy across the creek will be a difficult task, but I'll give you all the help I can." He turned from the mare and moved carefully through the rushing stream to the rear of the buggy. He reached into the murky water, grasped the rusting cross-spring, raised the tilted buggy a foot or so, and shouted, "Giddyap, Nicie." The mare sprang forward, and struggling to hold on, David quickly covered the thirty feet to the shore. Gasping for breath, he called hoarsely, "Whoa, Nicie," and the buggy came to a sudden stop.

As the soaked, exhausted chaplain staggered over to Willie and dropped to the ground, Nicie turned her head and looked back. The mare's countenance appeared to show a touch of satisfaction, Will Marshall thought.

Two or three minutes passed. Finally, David sucked a deep breath and mumbled, "That was easier than I expected. Well, William," he went on seriously; "it seems, in addition to the wheel, we've lost your crutches and the haversack."

Willie jerked his head around. "We've done lost our haversack and vittles!" He exclaimed dispiritedly. Are you saying . . . they're all gone?"

"I'm afraid so," Spence replied in a low voice, nodding slightly. He scrambled to his feet, stroked his stubble chin awhile, looked at Willie, and smiled reassuringly. "Well, William, it could have been worse," he offered softly. "The good news is, we still have the Bible and the saddle and Nicie seems to be—"

"Do ye need a bit o' help?" a distant, deep voice called.

Almost simultaneously, David and Willie turned their eyes and saw three men on the far bank of the swollen creek.

Obviously in charge, the huge yellow-bearded man with a saber attached to his elephantine girth cupped his big hands at his mouth and called again. "Might'n we come across t' help?"

Spence swept the three men with skeptical eyes. Off to the left of the big man stood a raggedy, barefoot, long-legged figure leaning on a long-barreled rifle. He seemed to be young; about Willie's age, David guessed. And off to the right, squatting on his heels and tossing small stones into the swollen creek, he saw a round-shouldered, bandy-legged man wearing dirty, sagging trousers, supported by a rope belt. Those men, he thought, could be dangerous.

Willie turned his sharp eyes from the three men to David. "I'm thinking them three might be up to no good," he drawled.

David nodded. And on long, water-soaked legs he moved to the edge of the rushing creek, cupped a hand at his mouth, and called in a resonant voice. "Thank you for the generous offer gentlemen, but everything is in good order. After a few minutes' rest, we'll saddle the mare and continue our journey." He paused briefly, waved a hand, and called again, sincerity in his voice. "May God bless you and keep you safe as you travel homeward."

With some trepidation, David turned and strode unhurriedly to the mare and stripped off the harness. With measured steps he moved to the buggy, he lifted the saddle from the buggy box, cast an under-brow glance toward the far side of the muddy creek, and saw the three men—still there and still watching.

We might need that revolver after all, Spence thought. He propped the saddle against the tilted buggy, pulled the slicker wrapped revolver from beneath the seat, and without looking back, moved to the mare.

CHAPTER 16

—ELSIE—

TWILIGHT WAS STRETCHING dark tentacles across the meandering trail, and except for the methodical, soft clop of Nicie's hooves, all was quiet as Willie guided her through a grove of scrub pines.

Now striding about a dozen yards ahead, David noticed a pale of smoke hanging above the treetops a hundred yards or so away. He raised a hand, stopped, and gestured. "There's a house off to the left just beyond that finger of trees. Maybe we can persuade the owners to allow us a night's rest."

The slender lad reined the mare and put a little smile on his narrow face. "Well." He nodded lightly and drawled, "I reckon it won't hurt to ask."

David struck out on a serpentine animal path that led through a grove of leafy oaks. "Watch out for those low-hanging branches," the weary chaplain warned. Somewhere ahead he heard the distant howl of a hound. That was all he heard. He stopped and squinted back into the growing darkness. Willie and the mare had disappeared. And hastily, he retraced his steps along the twisting tree-roofed path.

What could have happened? David worried silently. *Maybe those three men—* He saw William Marshall just beyond the mare, prostrate on the dappled ground with both hands clasping his head, and the thought was gone.

Spence pulled Nicie aside, knelt before the moaning lad, and said softly, concern in his voice, "Move your hands so I can—" He saw blood flowing between Willie's fingers onto the back of his hands and went silent.

The dazed lad's confused eyes fluttered open. "What . . . what's going on? What happened?" he whispered pathetically.

"Lie still," David, said, forcing his voice calm. He grasped Willie's arms and pulled his blood-soaked hands from his head. In the dappled moonlight he saw a bleeding three-inch gash atop William Marshall's tousled head, running front to back.

Spence rose to his feet and pulled off his tunic. He knelt, gently wiped away the blood, and examined the wound. "I believe you struck a low branch," he said quietly. "Well," he went on, trying to sound optimistic, "it doesn't seem to be a deep cut. I think your head will be all right when I get the bleeding stopped. I'll use my tunic as a temporary bandage until—" He paused and glanced through the thin grove, at the dark buildings. "Maybe someone at that house will help." He turned back, folded the tunic, gently placed it on Willie's head, and knotted the sleeves under his chin.

Several minutes had passed before the dazed lad, assisted by David's firm hand, and was able to rise to his feet and wobble over to the mare. Carefully, Spence lifted him into the saddle, put foot to stirrup, swung up behind the thin lad, and heeled Nicie down the path.

As they turned on a narrow track and approached the gray two-story clapboard house, David saw lamplight glowing dimly through a front window and spilling onto the front porch. He pulled rein, slid back over the mare's haunches to the ground, and said quietly, "Wait here while I talk to the owner." He turned and strode briskly along a worn path toward the front porch. At the steps, in the corners of his eyes, he glimpsed movement off toward the barn. He stopped, turned, and saw a dim bobbing light, its yellow glow falling on a slender barefoot figure. "A woman," he mumbled as the light flashed across a long dark skirt.

Suddenly aware of the horse standing in the front yard, silhouetted darkly in the dim moon glow, the girl stopped and stood silent for a long moment. "Who . . . who's there?" she finally managed in a weak, frightened voice.

Willie started to answer, but David, now moving briskly toward the girl, explained calmly. "We're Confederates . . . former Confederates on our way to the Blue Ridge Mountains. The private needs treatment.

While riding through that grove back there, his head struck a low-hanging tree branch."

"Stop where you are! Don't come any closer!" the girl's high voice warned. "I have a derringer pistol and I know how to use it." She raised the lantern high enough for Spence to see.

In the dim glow, he noticed the little pistol in the right hand of a slender sun-browned girl with braided long blond hair. David estimated her age to be about seventeen or eighteen.

"Parson Coleman's done come by and told us the war was ended in these parts. He's already warned us a bunch of renegades and roving scallywags might be showing up," she went on hurriedly. "My papa says for me to carry a loaded gun anytime I come out of the house. He's in the barn with our biting dog. He's already fed the mules and I reckon he's got his long-barreled shotgun pointed at your head right now."

"Yes. Well, I certainly understand your cautiousness," David responded softly. "I'll move back far enough for you to bring your lantern over to the mare and examine the young man's head."

With the exception of a light snort from Nicie, there was silence for a few seconds.

Finally, the petite girl spoke up cautiously, "I'll take a look if you move back a goodly ways, but I ain't making promises."

David strode a dozen paces beyond the mare, turned on a heel, and asked hurriedly but in a friendly tone, "Is this far enough?"

"It's too dark. I can't see you from here, but you sound like you're far enough," the girl responded, caution still in her tone. The lantern's yellow glow moved to the mare and its dim light fell across Willie. The slender girl regarded him with raised brows. In the dim glow, she was able to see a trickle of blood oozing down his right cheek. Then she noticed the blue trousers and thought he might be Federal. *But Federal or not, he needs help*, the girl decided as she looked up into Willie's narrow face and saw a thin smile.

The slender girl turned her eyes to the big figure shrouded in night shadows and spoke calmly. "I guess it'll be all right to move the boy inside. We'll take care of him as best we can."

The fear in her voice seems to be gone, David thought as he strode into the dim yellow glow.

Willie drawled softly, "I'm thanking you for taking us in."

She strained a light smile. "Well, it's just being the Christian thing to do."

"We are very grateful for your generous hospitality," David added sincerely. "My name is David Spence." He gestured to Willie. "And this young private is William Marshall."

The girl nodded. "I'm Elsie Rogers. You might as well take the boy to the porch while I get my milk bucket. I left it out yonder a ways when I took notice of your horse." She gestured toward the large, dark, unpainted barn and William Marshall thought, *I shore wish she'd stop calling me boy.*

With Willie in his arms, Spence strode to the porch. "Are you able to stand?" he asked softly as he mounted the two rickety steps.

Willie blinked. "I'm still a mite wobbly, but I reckon—"

"I see a chair," David said hurriedly and eased the lad into the large, weathered, ladder-backed chair. He turned, rapped the door lightly, and waited impatiently. Ten, maybe fifteen seconds passed. He heard hesitant footsteps.

A dim light under the door and a frightened voice came from inside: "Who's there?"

"I'm a Confederate chaplain," he answered softly.

A long pause, and finally the door creaked inward. In the flickering glow of her lamp, David saw a tall, rail-thin woman with an ivory tucking comb holding her long brown, gray-streaked hair in place. She was in her late forties, maybe a little older, he guessed.

She lifted the lamp and squinted at him for several seconds, frowning worriedly. "What . . . what do you want from us?" the woman asked hesitantly.

In the dim light, David saw fear in her eyes. "Your daughter—"

The girl's strained voice rose from the darkness. "It's all right, Mama. I invited them in." She brushed past Spence and continued. "The boy hurt his head and needs some doctoring, and I thought it was the Godly thing to do."

With lingering suspicion, her mother drew a deep breath and observed the tall chaplain for a long moment. Finally, she nodded. And her silence became, Elsie knew, an indication of consent.

The woman gestured. "Give me the milk bucket and show these gentlemen into the front bedroom. I'll go heat some water while the stove's still hot."

David carried William Marshall into the bedroom, Elsie lighting the way. He sat Willie on the bedside, bent down, and gruntingly pulled off the thin lad's tall boots.

As David set the boots aside, Elsie placed the smoky coal oil lamp on a small table and moved quickly to the bed. Carefully, she removed the tunic from Willie's head, tossed it in a corner, and examined the dirt-infested wound. "I think," Elsie said calmly, "I'll need the scissors to cut his hair to the scalp and some lye soap to . . . to wash his head before I bandage—"

Somewhere a baby began to cry.

Elsie turned abruptly and left the room.

"Was that a crying baby I heard?" Willie asked unsurely.

David sighed. "Well, it seems Elsie has a brother . . . or sister."

About fifteen minutes later Elsie returned to the dim, lamp-lit room, and Willie's eyes followed the blurred figure with a large towel draped over her arm as she carried a big washbasin about half-filled with steaming water across to a small table beside the narrow bed.

Elsie flung the towel across her shoulder and pulled a dripping cloth from the bowl. She squeezed it with sturdy hands, turned to David, and dimpled a smile. "Mr. Spence, move the lamp a little closer. The boy's hair is matted with . . . with drying blood and—" Deciding not to humiliate Willie, she stopped and began lightly dabbing the grimy wound. She dropped the blood spotted cloth in the bowl, glanced at Willie, smiled tenderly and spoke softly. "There, I'll get the scissors and a bandage. I think we might have a little turpentine. They say it's good for cuts and such. Do you need anything else?"

"Yes'm. If you don't mind, ma'am," he answered, half-smiling, "I'd surely admire to get a drink of water."

Another tender smile and she was gone.

An hour later Willie was sound asleep, his bandaged head resting on a white feather-stuffed pillow.

David rose from the rickety, uncomfortable chair and caught the tantalizing odor of frying ham wafting from the kitchen, and thoughts of home flashed into his mind. He glanced at the sleeping lad, moved quietly out the door, and followed the odor to its source.

He walked through the open doorway into the kitchen and saw Elsie's mother bending over a smoky cook stove.

With the instinct only a woman seems to have, she sensed his presence and turned from the stove, cut her dark eyes to the tall, wide-shouldered man, and said kindly, "My name is Mary—Mary Jamison. Pull out a chair and sit to sup. We've done had our supper but thought you and the boy might be hungry. How'd you like some potatoes from the root cellar and a slice of left over ham meat Pastor Coleman brought in for the funeral?"

While rocking the baby near the door to the side porch, Elsie looked up and half-smiled. "I expect he'll be coming along tomorrow. He gets quite a few hams and chickens from church members, for their tithes mostly. And he just might bring us another salt-cured ham," she allowed.

"Well, I hope we are not a burden," David said, his tone courteous.

"It ain't much, but I reckon it's a bit better than what you've been eating lately," Widow Jamison's voice rose apologetically as she gathered her tattered apron to insulate her hand. She opened the hot firebox and dropped a stick of split oak in a bed of glowing coals, raising a shower of sparks. She turned from the stove, placed a hand on the back of a cane-bottomed chair, and half-smiled. "Have a seat here and sip the milk while I finish setting the table."

David nodded and started to speak, but she brought her gaze back to him and went on. "The bread ought to be about done by now." She hurried to the stove, insulated her hand again, and opened the oven door. And in the hot haze, Mary deftly pulled out a large pan of brown-crusted corn bread.

A thoughtful silence and the big, shirtless chaplain took a sip from the tall greenish glass. He turned inquiring eyes on Elsie and spoke cautiously. "Your mother mentioned a funeral. Did a family member die recently?"

"Yes." She nodded slightly and responded softly, quick tears flooding her brown eyes. "It was my husband, Walter. He was in General Stuart's cavalry and came home on horse furlough about eighteen months ago. He stayed about a week before he found a suitable riding horse." Through her tears she smiled down at the sleeping child and went on in a voice so low, she seemed to be talking to herself. "Walter left the trenches at Petersburg about six weeks ago and came home with a bad cough. He took to his bed with a fever and went to be with the Lord last week. A good Christian man he was."

David pursed his lips thoughtfully. "Are you the baby's—?"

"She's mine . . . and Walter's," Elsie answered his unfinished question, wiped away streaming tears, and flashed a weak smile. "Her name is Rose Rogers. She'll be a year old next month."

Still unsteady on his feet, Willie hobbled in, an anticipatory grin splitting his thin face. "It seems like I got a whiff of frying ham and figured . . ." His drawling voice trailed off when he saw Elsie's mother carefully approaching the table, a well-loaded plate of fried ham in her right hand and a bowl of potatoes in her left.

Abruptly standing, Spence pulled out a chair and motioned to Willie. He saw Mary Jamison glance at Willie's grimy hands and grimace. "If you don't mind, ma'am," he spoke up hastily, "William and I would like to clean up a little."

"By all means, Mr. Spence." Mary nodded and inclined her head toward a small table in the rear corner of the kitchen topped by a big white basin "After you wash your hands and thank God for the food, you can go ahead and eat while it's still hot," she went on firmly, placing the plates on the table as the big chaplain and Willie moved toward the little table.

Although David was hungry, he forced himself to eat slowly, but Willie, sitting across from him, exercised no such restraint on his ravenous appetite. He gave the lad a reproving glance but to no avail. Willie was shoveling potatoes into his mouth, his brown eyes firmly fixed on the plate.

David Spence's plate was about half-empty when he glanced at Willie, smiled pleasantly at Mary, and leaned back in the chair. "That was a good meal, very good indeed." He swallowed the last of his warm milk, pulled a large index finger across his tatty mustache, and went on, lowering his voice slightly. "William and I wish to express sincere appreciation for your hospitality. And Pastor, uh, Coleman for the ham," David added smilingly.

And William Marshall, still chewing, managed a substantial confirming nod.

Spence turned to Elsie's mother and asked calmly, "When is your husband coming in from the barn?"

Mary's eyes opened wide in incomprehension. Confused, she glanced at her daughter.

"I told them Papa was in the barn with the hound and a gun because I was afraid they might be roving scallywags," Elsie explained uncomfortably, flashing a glance at David.

Mary Jamison nodded and turned her sad eyes back to David. "My husband, Jessie, was killed in that big battle up in Pennsylvania. It was at a place called Gettysburg, I'm thinking. We didn't get to bury him, but Pastor Coleman, good man that he is, went ahead and put up a marker for him beside Walter's grave."

Elsie frowned for several seconds, her brown eyes raking David's filthy trousers and coming to rest on his exposed underwear. "Mama, would it be all right if we give Mr. Spence one of Papa's shirts? It would make him look more . . ." She searched for words. "He would look a bit more presentable."

Widow Jamison pursed her lips, furrowed her brow, and measured him with her eyes. "Well, Jessie might have been a little heaver, but I think it'll fit well enough." Still eyeing David, she half-smiled. "Elsie, go up to the attic and pull some of your Papa's Sunday clothes outta that old trunk. Mr. Spence seems to be a decent young man and would do well with them." As her daughter turned to leave, she went on. "And, Elsie, maybe you ought to bring a couple of blankets. It'll be a little chilly in the barn loft."

As her daughter strode aggressively away, Mary turned to the disheveled chaplain and explained apologetically. "It wouldn't be proper for men . . . strangers to stay in the house overnight with widowed women. You well know how people will talk."

"I understand," David said knowingly. "The barn will be satisfactory."

Willie smiled. "After sleeping on the ground and dozing in that old buggy, I reckon the barn to be liken a . . . a fine hotel room." Then he frowned. "What you reckon we oughtta do about that biting dog out there in the barn?"

Mary Jamison smiled at that. "Oh, that old hound won't be a problem. Rover's bark is bigger than his bite. He's just a hunting dog— rabbits mostly."

"But your daughter said—" He stopped short and put on a thin, knowing smile.

CHAPTER 17

—ROVING SCALLYWAGS—

IN THE GRAY light of dawn, a noise, possibly a barnyard rooster, he thought, had startled Willie out of a sound, dreamless sleep. A bit befogged, he closed his eyes, trying to gather his thoughts. He shivered in the unseasonable cold air filtering through the barn's wide cracks and pulled the thin blanket around his neck. Gingerly he ran his fingers across the bandage, yawned, and turned his eyes toward David's blanket, ensconced in the dark shadows near the wall.

"What time do you reckon—?" The question died on his lips. David Spence was not there. Will Marshall struggled to his feet and brushed clinging hay from his wrinkled blue trousers.

From somewhere beneath the loft, David's voice rang out. "I'm saddling the mare. I'll come up and help you down the ladder after Nicie's fed and watered."

As Willie kicked the blanket aside, cackling hens caught his attention. On booted feet, he bent forward to avoid low roof rafters, hobbled over to the sagging double-doors, and put an eye to the gap. And peering down on the front yard, he saw Widow Jamison standing in dawn's dim glow near the porch steps with a gray shawl draped over her shoulders. While holding cracked corn in her gathered apron with her left hand, she was busily scattering it to a flitting flock of demonic hens and a big squawking rooster with her right. And Beulah Marshall's son smiled. "Just like my ma," he muttered,

Suddenly, Mary Jamison tensed and jerked her head up.

Something has caught her attention, Willie thought, raising his eyes from the widow to the distant trees. Half-hidden under the trees at the fringe of the pasture, he saw three shadowy figures astride their animals. And the smile on Will Marshall's narrow face was gone.

They seemed to be watching the house, waiting.

It just might be them men we saw at that creek. They might turn out to be roving scalawags after all. "I ought to get the Colt," he muttered as he limped back to the blanket. He sat down, hurriedly unrolled the slicker, pulled out the weapon, and spun the cylinder. "Already loaded and already capped," he mumbled.

With the revolver in his right hand, he slithered across the hay-covered floor to the double-doors. He flattened his stomach against the loft floor and pushed the right door open an inch or two with the long revolver barrel. Willie propped on his elbows and waited.

Time moved forward at a snail's pace, it seemed. Finally, after three or four minutes, he ventured another look. The three men were still there. The rising sun had pushed the shadows back and he could see them clearly.

With their animals standing head to head, they were gesturing and pointing. *They seem to be arguing or planning or both*, Willie thought. *'Taint no doubt about it now. They're the same ones. I'll warn Chaplain Spence*, he decided. "Chaplain Spence! Chaplain Spence!" Willie called in a lowered tone. There was no response. "He must've already led Nicie out to the watering trough," William Marshall mumbled to himself. "Well," he mumbled on, "I'm hoping them three men won't be making trouble. I ought to stay outta sight till I'm sure," he figured and peeped through the narrow opening again. He saw the young man on a smallish gray mule pull rein and heel the bony animal back into the trees.

The heavy man on a big spotted horse and the bandy-legged man on a sorrel mare looked into the woods a minute or so. Finally, in unison, the two men turned their animals and put them into a slow walk through the tender greening grass toward the gray clapboard house, some two hundred yards away.

Willie's heartbeat quickened. He cast a glance down to the front yard and saw Widow Jamison on the porch step, holding her gathered apron with her left hand and shading her eyes from the rising sun with her right. The chickens were still fluttering about her feet. She didn't notice. She was watching the approaching figures. Finally, she turned and hurried across the porch.

Go on inside and bolt the door, Willie called silently. And then, with the porch roof blocking his view, he thought she might've gone inside. He breathed a soft sigh of relief and turned his eyes back to the two men, still moving their horses at a walk and only a hundred or so yards away. The rising sun flashed on the heavy man's saber clutched firmly in a big hand, unsheathed and lying ominously across the saddle. Willie's heart climbed another beat or two.

About thirty yards from the house the two men pulled their horses in. And William Marshall, with sick nausea rising into his throat, watched the huge, yellow-bearded interloper surveying the landscape, pointing and gesturing. And the slim round-shouldered man was nodding. It was obvious to Willie now. They had to be scalawags—or worse.

Suddenly, the men kicked their horses into a lope.

Still with a hand on the door latch and at the edge of panic, Mary Jamison shoved the door open, rushed inside and slammed it behind her. She reached a hasty hand to the lock and groped for the key. No key. "Elsie! Elsie, get the shotgun," Mary called urgently, fear in her voice.

Upstairs, in her bedroom, pinning a diaper on the toddler, Elsie heard her mother's urgent call and pondered momentarily. The shotgun! It's in the kitchen! She snatched the kicking child from the bed and moved swiftly across the room toward the open door and on to the steep staircase leading to the kitchen. With Rose firmly in her arms, she hurried down the steep, creaking stairs and laid the sobbing child in her crib. Now at the edge of panic, Elsie rushed to the big iron stove. She paused, reached across the woodbox to the corner and pulled out a double-barreled shotgun—already loaded and capped, she hoped.

Mary Jamison heard the heavy tread of footsteps on the porch and froze momentarily. Frantically, she grabbed a ladder-back chair and dragged it to the front door. Suddenly, as Mary struggled to prop it under the door latch, a loud crash of splintering wood and the door leaped from its hinges, sending the slender widow to the floor. A scream cut short by a saber stab in her back and the fifty-two-year-old widow was dead.

Elsie hesitated. Finally, with the scream still lingering in her ears, she took a deep breath, advanced cautiously toward the parlor and came into the first rays of sunlight slanting through the window. Tensely, she thumbed the left hammer, but her small, nervous thumb was unable to bring it to full cock. *Where is the intruder?* she wondered, still struggling to force the hammer. She parted the curtains with the shotgun barrels and cast a glance out the window.

The clumping of heavy boots in the hallway and Elsie swung the half-cocked weapon. The long barrels struck the glowing coal oil lamp and, with the crackling of shattered glass, sent it to the floor. Fire from the wick flashed in flowing oil and rapidly engulfed the thin curtains.

Now in the doorway with his bloody saber raised, the big man saw the climbing fire, saw a wavering, long-barreled shotgun pointed in his direction and paused, but only for five or six seconds.

The growing smoke brought tears to Elsie's eyes and clouded her vision. With all the force she could muster, she flung the heavy weapon toward the big figure and turned to run.

The heavy-bearded man pared the shotgun with his saber. He raised a long arm to shield his wide face from the searing heat and shuffled around the spreading flames to follow her into the kitchen.

With the saddled mare in tow, David rounded the barn into the front yard. He stopped and stared unbelievingly. "My Lord!" he exclaimed. Before him he saw a spreading fire and boiling smoke rising from the house. A movement—more sensed than seen. He cut his eyes to find a round-shouldered man, now afoot and approaching cautiously, a long-barreled Remington revolver in his right hand.

Surprised by David's sudden appearance, the bandy-legged renegade, his hand shaking violently, paused, took aim at the big white-shirted man about a dozen strides away, and squeezed the trigger. The weapon leaped in his hand and powder smoke jetted from its barrel. A short snort from the mare and she dropped to the ground, blood squirting from her head and legs pawing skyward.

The loft doors flew open and ricocheted against the barn.

The balding rope-belted man's anxious eyes darted to the barn and spotted Willie raising his revolver. Frantically, the man fired the Remington again and plowed a lead ball into a rough pine board about four inches above William Marshall's protruding head.

David started toward the slender, wide-eyed man when, somewhere behind him, the sound of exploding powder reached his ears and he felt the ripple of air as a thirty-two-caliber lead ball passed over his left shoulder.

About eight strides before him, a jagged hole appeared in the round-shouldered man's chest and a surprised look came upon his face. With bewilderment in his eyes, he lowered his long-barreled revolver, looked down, saw blood flooding from the jagged hole and spreading a crimson stain across his sullied blouse.

Mesmerized, David Spence watched the slender, bandy-legged man stagger forward and saw the dangling revolver slip slowly from his fingers and splash into a muddy puddle. The dying man extended a bony hand toward the big, white-shirted man and tried to speak, but all David was able to hear was a gurgling moan. The young, rope-belted man sucked a deep breath. His eyes dulled. He fell into the mud facedown and stone-dead.

With bitter bile in his throat, David rushed on past the blood-soaked body to the front porch.

The twin doors were still creaking on rust-infested hinges as Willie Marshall relaxed his trigger finger. In the acrid haze of powder smoke, he lowered the weapon and swiped a hand across his sweaty brow. He shifted his gaze back to the house and saw David rush across the porch and disappear in a cloud of gray smoke.

Somewhere, a dog yapped, and Willie turned his eyes to see Rover running at rabbit-catching speed toward the house. The thin lad mumbled. "That dog's heading for the kitchen. I need to push the door open a bit more." Still on his stomach, he reached out and gave the left door a light push, and it squeaked open far enough for him to see the side porch. And then he saw Elsie, with Rose in her arms, rush down the porch steps, and he saw her stumble in the high grass and fall to the ground.

At that moment, the big intruder staggered out from the kitchen, coughing and swiping his watery, blinking eyes with a dirty sleeve. He paused on the little porch, cleared his vision, and put a maniacal little grin on his face.

With back hair bristling and mouth drawn back in a warning snarl, Rover took a protective stance as Elsie rose on her knees and jerked the little derringer from her sullied apron patch pocket.

William Marshall thumbed the long-barreled revolver to full cock, propped his elbow against the loft floor, and aligned the sights on the heavy man's wide chest. His lips tightened. Suddenly, the little derringer popped. And in the corner of an eye, he saw a stream of smoke leap from the short barrel and saw the big man drop to his knees and tumble down the steps, the bloody saber flying from his hand and stabbing into the ground a couple of feet to Elsie's left.

"That a girl," Willie muttered on a deep sigh, thumbed the hammer back to half cock, and lowered the revolver.

Cautiously, the flop-eared hound stole over to the rotund man, now on the ground with a missing left eye and a big foot resting on the bottom step. After three or four sniffs and a contemptuous tug at a limp trouser leg, Rover sauntered back to Elsie, tail whipping.

The flames were licking through the windows. The walls were beginning to crumble as David, with the widow's limp body in his arms, rushed out of the billowing smoke. Still coughing and gasping for breath, he staggered across the yard to the shed.

Somehow, Willie had managed to make his way down the ladder from the loft and limp out to Elsie and Rose. He gathered the crying, mud-splattered child in his arms and turned inquiring eyes to Elsie. Still dazed, she was slowly getting to her feet.

"Baby Rose," Willie said softly, "seems to be . . . a bit scared. What about you?"

Elsie raised her teary eyes, saw David enter the shed with her mother in his arms, and asked Willie haltingly, "Is Mama—?" Elsie didn't finish the question. She already knew the answer.

*

It was a few minutes past noon when David hitched Widow Jamison's big ugly mules to the dilapidated two-horse wagon. He climbed aboard, gathered up the lines, slapped the reluctant animals forward, and guided the wagon on past the smoldering rubble into the grassy field. He pulled the mules to a stop beside the two bodies, now partly covered with worn-out saddle blankets. As the big, soot-grimed chaplain stepped down from the wagon, he spotted a distant rider on a tall gray horse jogging up the narrow road toward the smoking remains of the Jamison house. Somewhat apprehensive, he stood beside the wagon and watched the approaching figure; a man wearing a stovepipe hat and a tight blue suit. As he drew closer, David Spence thought, *That must be Pastor Coleman.*

Somewhat tentatively, the man reined his pale horse, a deep frown creasing his narrow brow. He drew a long-fingered hand across his stoic, bearded face, cleared his throat, and queried worriedly, a slight rasp in his voice. "What happened here?"

David opened his mouth to answer but the man went on. "On my way up here I saw some smoke and figured Elsie and Widow Jamison to be burning brush. Are they—?"

David was shaking his head slowly. "Elsie's mother is . . . dead." He sighed gloomily.

"Dead!" the tall, bearded pastor echoed, his dark eyes widening. "Was . . . was she burned up?"

"No."

Pastor Coleman frowned. "No? Then how—?"

"She was murdered," David answered solemnly. "But except for the grief, Elsie and the child seem to be all right."

"But . . . who would do that?" The long-boned man asked, somewhat befuddled.

Spence gestured, forced his voice calm, and said softly, "That big intruder just beyond the wagon is the murderer. The other man attempted to kill me."

The long-boned pastor stood in the stirrups and stretched his neck to see over the wagon bed.

David went on. "I'm on my way to bury those two bodies in that field . . . read scripture over their graves." He gestured and continued frowningly. "That big one is too heavy for me to carry. I'd appreciate your help."

The tall man looked down at his tight, fairly new blue suit. "Well, I . . ." He hesitated, turned his eyes, saw the big, white-shirted man's furrowed brow, and explained apologetically. "I could have been here three hours ago, but being he's a member of my church, I thought to stop by Samuel Bradford's place for a short visit. But old Sam, being a long talker, kept me a while longer than I anticipated. He seemed to be mighty upset about somebody stealing his spotted horse last night."

The long-boned pastor clumsily dismounted.

A forced smile and David said, extending his hand, "You are Pastor Coleman, I believe. I'm David Spence, a former Confederate chaplain," he intoned in a low voice and took Coleman's long-fingered hand briefly.

The tall, lean forty-year-old man, claiming thirty, nodded, released the big hand, scratched his right ear, turned his pale eyes toward the barn, and asked frowningly, "Is Widow Jamison . . . her body in the shed?"

David nodded.

A long pause and Reverend Coleman went on. "After I help load the bodies, I'll go talk to Elsie, Widow Rogers, about funeral arrangements. I expect, you being a *former* chaplain, she might ask you to participate."

David nodded again, taking notice of Coleman's emphases on *former*. "Yes. I would consider it an honor," he responded, his tone friendly. "She's in the harness shed with her mother's body. Oh, and there's a spotted horse in one of the stalls. It probably belongs to Mr. Bradford."

The preacher turned and pointed. "Did that dead horse belong to one of those men?"

"No." David shook his head slowly and frowned. "That's my mare. After I bury these two bodies, I'll unhitch the mules and use them to drag the mare into the pasture." He sighed and went on. "I must hurry or the day will be well gone before I get to the mare. It'll take quite a bit of shoveling to bury her."

"I'd be willing to help, but Elsie might need—" Coleman stopped and sighed deeply.

David Spence's mouth tightened slightly. "Yes. Yes, I understand. Anyway, one shovel is all she has."

CHAPTER 18

—SHADOW OF DEATH—

THE NEXT DAY, in a little white church, Ellie's mother lay in a homemade pine coffin topped by two flickering candles: one at each end and a bunch of yellow wild flowers in the middle.

William Marshall, with a fresh bandage encasing his head and Rose in his lap, was sitting on a front pew. And Elsie, at his side in a borrowed black mourning dress, was dabbing at her teary eyes with a white lace-fringed handkerchief. The black dress was a bit too large and too long for her slender frame, but the owner, a Godly widow named Nancy Callahan, who had gained the reputation of being among the top seamstress and needlework artist in the neighborhood, knowing it wouldn't fit, brought along a ball of black thread and stitched the hem up about five inches or so.

Willie glanced at the stoic pastor sitting stiffly in a high-backed chair just to the left of the pulpit. William J. Marshall found Coleman, with jaw clinched and brow knitted, his venomous, pale, unblinking eyes locked upon him. *He's jealous*, William suddenly realized. He looked at Elsie, still daubing at her eyes, and thought, *I doubt she knows that preacher's sweet on her. I reckon that's why he's visiting and bringing in all them vittles.* At that moment Willie came to realize he was a bit jealous as well.

After allowing David John 3:16, which he managed without reading scripture, Pastor Coleman got to his feet, stiffened his back, and stoically strode to the pulpit.

He cleared his throat noisily and extolled the rewards of heaven and the wages of sin. And then he lit into a long, tongue-lashing hellfire-and-brimstone sermon—interposed with several long pulpit pauses—that seemed to bring condemnation upon every sin known to man and a few that most folks hadn't yet contemplated. He had totally ignored the devout Christian widow in the pine coffin before him, David Spence realized.

As the lanky pastor droned on, Willie stole a glance over his shoulder. All thirty-seven members seemed to be frowning.

And David—sitting in the tall, uncomfortable ladder-backed chair behind the big pulpit—was mentally preparing for the graveside service.

Finally, Pastor Coleman finished the ranting sermon, sucked a deep breath, and intoned, "Let us all bow our heads in prayer?"

*

Late that afternoon, on the hilltop beside a newly dug grave, David's short heartfelt sermon emphasizing the many attributes of Widow Mary Jamison ended with the Psalm 23:

> Yea, though I walk through the valley of the shadow
>   of death,
> I will fear no evil: for Thou art with me;
> Thy rod and Thy staff they comfort me.
> Thou preparest a table before me in the presence of
>   mine enemies:
> Thou anointest my head with oil; my cup runneth over.
> Surely goodness and mercy shall follow me all the days
>   of my life:
> and I will dwell in the house of the Lord forever.

"Amen." As the four gravediggers—all church members who seemed to have a knack for shoveling—took up the ropes to lower the coffin, David removed the yellow flowers, handed them to Elsie, and whispered gently, "I'll stay until they fill the grave."

She nodded, turned, and reverently placed the flowers at the rough-cut cross atop her husband's mounded, red-clay grave.

Pastor Coleman, his black stovepipe hat still clasped firmly in his right hand—probably to avoid handshakes—was making his way through the gathering toward the wagon.

With Rose dozing in his arms, Willie was sitting on the tailgate, when he took notice of the approaching, disjointed figure. Reluctantly, he got to his feet and drew himself up slightly.

With a narrow, forced smile splitting his dark whiskers, the long-nosed pastor reached out for Rose. "I'll take the child now," he said, a touch of sarcasm in his voice.

And seeing the long-fingered outstretched hands, Rose screamed and flung her little arms around Willie's slender neck.

As if touching a hot stove, Coleman jerked his hands back.

Willie had to smile.

With a furtive glance at the congregants, now trickling down the hillside, the gangly parson spun on a heel and hurried toward Elsie. He found the sniffing girl gazing hypnotically at the yellow flowers. He grasped her arm with a proprietary hand, raised her up, and guided her down the long slope toward the barn and the pile of smoldering rubble with Widow Jamison's protruding iron-clad cook stove still standing and still intact.

Coleman glanced over his shoulder. He saw Willie, with Rose in his arms, trailing behind and asked abruptly in a low tone, "Elsie, may I have a few words with you privately?"

Before she could answer, he pulled her aside. She opened her mouth to protest, but he was nervously pulling at his ratty whiskers and still talking in a voice so low that Willie failed to understand his faltering tone.

With raised brows, Elsie was regarding the preacher apprehensively, Willie noticed. And as he slowly walked on past, he heard her say hesitantly, "Well, Pastor Coleman, I . . . I appreciate the offer. I'll have to ponder over it before I decide."

I wonder what she'll be pondering over, William Marshall pondered. And then his attention turned to Rose. She had begun to squirm and fret. "I know, you're hungry," he said softly, patting her back as he entered the harness shed. "And, Rose, I 'spect you need a diaper change," Willie added.

As she began to cry again, Elsie rushed into the shed. And with an expression Willie was unable to read, clouding her pale, tear-stained face, she took Rose and drew her close. "What are we to do?" she cried.

"I reckon you can—" Willie started. But with the sudden realization that no response was expected and he had none to give, he reluctantly held his tongue. A long moment searching for words and he decided to change the subject. "Well, I'd better go milk the cow before Mr. Spence gets here to clear out the root cellar."

Although anxious to know her discussion, Willie knew he would have to wait. As he entered the barn, he talked to himself almost audibly. *I'm beginning to believe, I might love her some. Could be pity, though*, Will Marshall thought on with a deep sigh of confusion.

That night, the soot-infested former Confederates were back in the loft, trying to get comfortable on small piles of hay. After twisting and turning awhile, Willie rose on an elbow and drawled worriedly. "I'm thinking, with the fix Elsie's in, that preacher's trying to get her to marry him."

David thought a long moment. "Well, maybe he's just trying to be helpful." His response held little conviction.

Willie lay awake, debating himself. Finally he heard Spence's heavy breathing, rose quietly, and cautiously climbed down the ladder. He hobbled out into the starry night on up the slope to the family plot and flopped down beside Walter's grave. In the weak glow of a russet half-moon he sat, still debating himself. *Maybe I can talk Elsie into going with us to the Blue Ridge. Maybe Ma will take her and Rose in—but maybe not.*

CHAPTER 19

—THE DECISION—

ABOUT AN HOUR before dawn William J. Marshall, only half-awake, rose from the dew-dampened grass, yawned, and stood in silence, listening to the faint baying of some dogs that had treed a hapless animal in the distant woods, he guessed. He gazed down the hill. All was darkness except a few glowing embers from the smoldering remains of the house.

At the barn, a dim, flickering light appeared and then suddenly the light disappeared. And Willie, confused momentarily, came fully awake and scolded himself silently. *I reckon I might be a bit addled. That's got to be Elsie going in the barn to milk the cow.*

Down the slope a dog barked. It was a low, short, friendly sort of bark. *It's Rover, announcing his arrival*, Willie figured.

And peering in the dim moon glow, William Marshall saw a tail wagging, tongue-lolling hound approaching slowly. He chuckled lightly and said to the dog, "Rover, I reckon you decided not to join in the chase and come along to lead me down this hillside. Shouldn't come up here in the first place," he muttered while stroking the dog's floppy ears. "Well, Rover," he went on with a light gesture, "I 'spect we oughtta get going."

The hound turned and trotted away.

"Beat-ness thing I ever did see," Willie muttered again. "That hound seems to know what I'm saying."

As Willie approached the barn's tall double-doors, he meditated a long moment. *Maybe I ought to wait till Elsie comes out? Maybe I ought to climb back in the loft and wait for daylight.* He didn't have to decide; the creaking barn door made the decision for him.

Elsie stepped out into the darkness with a two-gallon bucket in one hand and a flickering old lantern in the other. She saw the dark figure and stopped, quick surprise on her face. "Oh—" the young widow broke off, raised the lantern, and looked at him quizzically.

Willie blushed. A long pause and he cleared his throat. Finally, he said huskily, "I'm hoping you'll—" He meant to continue with "pardon me," but she cut in.

"Will, I've been pondering all night about my predicament. I'm hoping you and Chaplain Spence might be willing to help me make a serious decision."

"I reckon we will as best we can," Willie murmured none too certainly. "I 'spect I know what you're getting yourself into. Maybe you ought to talk with him before we begin deciding."

Rose was crying again, and Elsie glanced toward the harness shed. "I'll tend to Rose and wait in the shed till Mr. Spence climbs down from the loft," she said hastily. "Comes daylight, I'll gather eggs from the hen house for breakfast. We'll talk about it then." She hurried away, the dim lantern light bobbing as she went.

"We'll talk about what?" David's calm voice asked. And still brushing hay from his trousers, he stepped out from the barn.

"Well, I ain't sure, but I'm figuring it might be about that preacher," Willie remarked feebly. "I reckon it's what she's planning—" He went silent then, unable to finish the sentence.

A deep frown furrowed David's wide brow. Finally he nodded and spoke thoughtfully. "Well, we'll discuss her options, but Elsie will have to make the final decision concerning her future."

Willie opened his mouth to speak, but having nothing to add, he decided to remain silent.

*

About half an hour after daybreak, Elsie had a smoky little cook fire crackling under Widow Jamison's big iron skillet. She forked out a small hunk of popping tallow-colored side meat, efficiently cracked an egg into the grease-coated skillet and tossed the shell onto the growing pile. "Eight ought to be enough," she murmured. "I'll have to kill a laying hen for supper," she decided.

With the mules in tow, David rounded the barn.

And with the Jersey cow tethered to a lead rope, her bell tinkling in cadence with her stride, Willie shuffled along behind.

Without looking up, Elsie said, "Eggs will be ready in a few minutes. You might as well turn the animals out to pasture before breakfast," she went on.

As Willie passed, she looked up and said in a friendly tone, "It looks like we'll have to kill a laying hen for our next meal."

He forced the cow to a halt, twisted his face into a crooked grin, and said confidently, "I'll kill the chicken and pluck out the feathers. I killed quite a few before I went off to the war." He glanced at the chickens, now scratching in the front yard, and went on. "I'll have to shoot one though unless I wait till they go to roost."

Elsie nodded. "Shoot one then, but be sure it's a plump one."

He half-smiled and led the cow on toward the pasture gate, thinking, *I 'spect she's starting to like me a bit.*

After breakfast, while washing the singed tin plates, Elsie decided to reveal the conversation with Pastor Coleman and turned her brown eyes to David and Willie, now lounging uncomfortably on a narrow, rough-cut bench. "Well, it seems like—" She struggled to say the words. "I might have to marry Reverent Coleman after all," she finally managed. "Unbeknownst to me, he's been loaning Mama money for about two years. He said she signed a paper giving him our property if it ain't paid back come June. He told me if I'd agree to marry him, he'd burn Mama's signed note and build me a new house."

"Maybe you—" David began.

"That's downright awful," Willie put in hastily. "That preacher ought to be courting a woman nearer his own age, not taking advantage a young girl. Leastways, that's the way I'm seeing it."

"Have you seen the note?" David asked thoughtfully.

Elsie Rogers frowned. "Not yet, but I'm pretty sure he has one. He'll be bringing it in the morning when he comes by for my answer. He says he's owed two hundred dollars, more or less."

"Surely, you ain't planning to marry that turkey-necked old man," William Marshall spoke up sternly. His voice, David thought, seemed to carry a tone of jealousy.

Elsie looked up sharply, fixed him with flaring brown eyes, and snapped, "I ain't decided . . . yet." After a long thoughtful pause, she shrugged and continued in a low tone. "I know Pastor Coleman ain't perfect, but he's a Godly man."

Then David noticed a brooding look in her brown eyes and opened his mouth to speak.

"Well, I can't think of any other choice," Elsie continued, turning to a low dusty shelf, trying to force the thought from her mind. She pulled out a crooked horseshoe nail and moved to the rear wall. With the thought still lingering, she went on, a hint of desperation in her voice. "Here I am with nowhere to live, a baby to care for, and nary a dollar, excepting that jar of money Mama hid away. But I doubt it's worth the paper it's printed on."

Frowningly, Elsie scanned the dirty floor. After a few seconds, she sighed, bent down, forced the nail into a crack, and pried out a short, rough-cut board. "This is where Mama stowed about a hundred dollars of what she called rainy day money." She reached in the opening, pulled out a bluish wax-sealed quart jar, and raised it into the light. "It's Confederate," Elsie almost whispered and flung the jar back into the opening.

As she stomped the board back in place, William Marshall blurted, "Well, you don't have to marry that . . . old man. You could hitch your mules and go with us to the Blue Ridge."

"But I—"

"My ma's got a big old house and would be proud to take you and Rose in for a spell."

She looked at Willie and frowned. "I appreciate the offer, but I don't want to be a burden on your Mama . . . or anyone else."

"Do you have any relatives in the area?" David asked in a low, thoughtful voice.

"No. I might have an uncle somewhere in California though," Elsie muttered with a mixture of sorrow and grief. "That is, if he's still alive. Papa said his brother, Robert, struck out for California in forty-nine when he heard about that gold rush. We never got a single word from him after that."

David shook his head solemnly. "Well, it seems we can be of little, if any help. But if you wish, we'll stay with you and Rose until tomorrow morning."

"Well, maybe till you've decided," Willie Amended.

A troubled expression crossed her face. It lingered a brief moment before she replaced it with a forced smile. "You've been a great help, both of you." She nodded and widened her smile. "When you leave, I insist you take the wagon and mules."

"But the mules—" David began.

The disheveled girl shook her head. "After tomorrow I won't need them. If I refuse to marry Pastor Coleman, he'll take the animals and the farm. And if I do marry him, he'll just keep on preaching 'cause anyone with half an eye can see, there ain't a drop of farming blood in him."

"You're right about that," Willie hissed, barely louder than a whisper. "He ain't got a drop of preaching blood neither as far as I can tell."

There was intonation in Willie's voice that disturbed David. He looked at him disapprovingly and remained silent.

*

The rising sun had climbed above the horizon and the day was warm, unseasonably warm, when Elsie climbed out of the watering trough and slipped into the oversized pleated calico dress. It was the dress widow Callahan had thought to bring along with the mourning clothes now washed and hanging in the sun to dry.

Well, before the Pastor arrives, I'll have to decide—one way or the other, she thought as she walked slowly toward the barn.

As if drawn by a magnet force, Elsie's eyes turned to the charred remains of the house. Suddenly, the frown turned into a smile when she saw Willie standing before her mother's big cook stove. He was frying eggs, she supposed. Sometime before dawn he had cleared away the debris attached to the stovepipe and had gray smoke flowing skyward.

Will Marshall looked up, saw Elsie, put on his crooked grin, waved a hand, and turned back to the hot, smoky stove.

Elsie's smile faded. *Well, I sure hope he didn't see me, bathing naked in the watering trough.* She looked back, saw the trough, and muttered. "No. I doubt he could see me from there."

Now in the barn, David Spence sighed deeply as he viewed the old canvas. *Well, this ragged canvas is of little use as it is*, he thought. I'll have to double it to cover the wagon partly.

*

It was nearing noon. For over an hour, Willie had been limping back and forth, his sharp eyes fully focused on the narrow road. Aided somewhat by a crooked stick, he had traced a path in the drying ground. In midstride he squinted into the sun and caught sight of two horses topping a distant rise. He stopped and shaded his eyes with his free hand. "Two riders," he muttered, gazing up the narrow road. *One seems to be that preacher. But who's the man on that little gray?* he wondered.

"It seems Pastor Coleman is bringing a guest," David said matter-of-factly at Willie's back.

With quick surprise, the thin lad whirled on the stick. "I didn't figure . . ." his voice trailed away.

David pulled his blue eyes from the two distant figures and turned them to see Elsie Rogers, with Rose in her arms, step out from the shed. From where he stood he could easily see the growing concern in her face. He felt a choking knot climbing into his throat. And then a deep wave of pity swept over him. *With your guidance Lord*, Spence prayed silently, *I will do all I can to protect Elsie and her child.*

Still gazing at the approaching figures, Willie drawled worriedly, "Who you reckon that big man on that gray to be?"

David brought his attention back to the anxious lad and said quietly, "He's probably the owner of that spotted horse. Pastor Coleman said his name is Sam Bradford: a member of his church."

Will Marshall creased a frown and sighed. "I surely hope he ain't coming along to be a witness of some sort."

"Well," David Spence responded thoughtfully, "I pray Elsie will be able to solve her problems satisfactorily and we can be on our way, hopefully this afternoon."

With his eyes locked on the two men, now reining their horses at the front yard hitching post, Willie responded belatedly, "I surely hope we can."

With a thin brown folder protruding from his coat pocket, the long-legged pastor swung from the tall mare and strode over to the bulky man on the little gray. He opened the folder and pulled out a yellowish paper.

"Chaplain, what do you reckon that paper might be?" Willy asked wonderingly. "It don't look to be some sort of agreement paper."

"I'm not sure either, but I believe it's a map," David answered quietly as he watched the pastor unfold the yellow paper and raise it up for the man on the gray to see.

They talked awhile, nodding, pointing, and gesturing. The pastor was talking and pointing. The man on the bony gray was nodding and gesturing. They conversed for five or six minutes. Finally Coleman folded the paper and pushed it back in his coat pocket.

The big man pulled his foot from the stirrup, swung it over the horse's thin haunches, and gruntingly dismounted. At sixty-two years of age, he was a heavy, round-faced man with a full head of graying hair.

As the two men approached, walking at a leisurely pace, David and Willie moved over to the shed door.

"Hello, Mr. Bradford," Elsie said in a weak but friendly voice. "Come on in the shed and we'll talk. I guess you came by to get your horse."

"Yes, I did—" he acknowledged in his deep voice. He pulled off his wide-brimmed straw-hat, ducked through the low doorway, and followed her inside. "But I came by mainly to offer my condolences. A tragedy, a terrible tragedy," he almost whispered.

And Pastor Coleman, already on the bench, cleared his throat pretentiously. "Yes, indeed," he put in, trying to sound sympathetic. "It's a tragedy of the worst kind, but we must pull up our bootstraps, hold our chin high, and walk bravely into the future."

Taken aback by that, David suppressed his anger, fixed the long-nosed pastor with a level gaze, and spoke up boldly, "I believe, before we begin that unknowing journey into the future, we must take the Lord's hand and be resolute in our faith."

Under dark, hooded brows, Coleman looked up, frowned, and remained silent.

It was then, from where he stood, David saw a fast throbbing pulse in his long neck.

Samuel Bradford coughed lightly. His sharp, intelligent eyes flittered across their solemn faces and stopped on the young widow. "Now mind you, Elsie," he said gallantly, "you know . . . being a long-time neighbor for thirty-odd years or thereabouts, I ain't one to be meddling in other folks' business. On the way over, me and the good Pastor got into a serious talk about you and baby Rose."

"This should be a private discussion," Coleman spoke up brusquely. "These two strangers shouldn't be involved."

"No," Elsie retorted firmly, shaking her head. "What has to be said will be said here and said now."

"I believe we are all Christians"—Bradford glanced at Coleman—"and have Elsie's best interest at heart."

"I agree," Pastor Coleman blurted. "Elsie and the child's best interest is . . . is the arrangement she and I discussed yesterday."

Startled by that, David looked at him, his temper rising.

He started to speak but Elsie responded quickly, a hint of sarcasm in her tone. "Well, Parson, that's not my only option." She glanced at Will.

His face reddened.

Bradford smiled tolerantly. "Elsie, you know I've been trying to buy that piece of bottomland from your mama for quite a spell. I figure that good bottomland to measure out to eight, maybe nine acres." He glanced at Coleman and saw him nodding, a half smile creasing his thin face.

"Thirteen—it measures thirteen acres," Elsie corrected quickly.

"Anyhow," Bradford went on, "the good Pastor Coleman says I might get it for what you owe him. It's about two hundred Union dollars, he says."

A sharp look, followed by a fragile smile and, imperceptibly, Elsie shook her head. "Now, Mr. Bradford," she questioned firmly, shaking an admonishing finger before his big purple-veined nose, "being a good Christian man, you wouldn't be out to cheat a poor, widowed orphan, would you?"

"Certainly not," Sam Bradford responded in a voice that carried a touch of trepidation. He cast an anxious eye toward Coleman and went on in a lowered tone. "I was planning to leave an acre or two for you to raise a few cattle." Bradford lit his big-bowled pipe, drew smoke, and cocked his gray head.

Elsie studied him suspiciously. Finally, she decided Old Sam had his trading face on and held back a smile. "Still, Mr. Bradford," the young widow said sternly, "I'm sure that bottomland alone to be worth round four hundred Federal dollars. Come to think on it, that could've been Confederate money Mama borrowed."

Samuel forced a solemn look and puffed more smoke. After four or five significant puffs he withdrew the pipestem, shook his gray head, and scratched his bulbous nose. "Well, young lady, cash money is hard to come by these days."

Elsie figured it was time to play her trump card—and she did. "Now, Mr. Bradford, rumor has it that you sold some Federals two horses and three head of cattle for a goodly sum."

And somewhat taken aback by that, Sam Bradford frowned awhile. After a thoughtful half minute or so, he chuckled and stabbed the pipestem at her. "All right, young lady, you're a better trader than your papa ever was—God rest his soul. I'll offer four hundred dollars—cash money—for your property and not a cent more."

She dimpled a smile, thrust out her slender hand and said sincerely, "God bless you, Mr. Bradford." She flashed a sharp under-brow glance at the frowning preacher and went on. "If it's convenient for you, I'll be coming by your house this afternoon about five o'clock."

Samuel released her hand and chuckled again. "You seem to be in a hurry. I'll get my horse and be there in an hour or so."

He turned to Preacher Coleman and administered a friendly slap to his high shoulder, issued a wide, toothy smile and said smoothly, "Well, Pastor, you might as well ride along with me for your portion. And, Pastor, don't forget to bring Widow Jamison's note." He cut knowing eyes to the tall former chaplain and smiled.

David acknowledged with shallow nod.

As they walked out, the stoic preacher looked down at Willie with malevolence in his cold, pale eyes.

And Willie glanced up with a smile of triumph.

As the two men walked away, David Spence turned to the young widow and nodded. "Well, Elsie, when all appears lost, the Lord comes to the rescue."

"Yes." She nodded back, tears flowing down her cheeks.

Sam Bradford and Pastor Coleman were scarcely out of sight when they began stocking the wagon with supplies for the journey. It would be a three-day journey, more or less, Willie surmised after a careful survey of Elsie's tall, ugly mules. With a salt-cured ham, a coop with three laying hens, a few miscellaneous items, and two bushels of shucked corn—one for the animals and one for grinding at a mill on the way—they rumbled away.

Silently sobbing, Elsie looked back from the wagon to see the barn, the charred remains of the house, and the protruding cook stove standing as a headstone over a grave of the past.

*

It was only a day or two later when speculation was set afoot and spread throughout the county concerning the fire and the murder of Widow Jamison. Some said it had to be revenging Federals; a few said it might have been drunken Confederate deserters. Finally, the majority decided it had to be scalawags from that new state called West Virginia. But all seemed to be in agreement that Widow Mary Jamison was, with the exception a few jealous runner-ups, a good cook and a devout Christian.

Part Three
UNTO THE HILLS

I will lift up mine eyes unto the hills, from whence cometh my help.

—Psalms 121:1

CHAPTER 20

—FOOTHILL COUNTRY—

ON THE THIRD DAY, with sixty-two weary miles behind them, they reached the Blue Ridge foothills. As the dull, gray afternoon wore slowly away, they forded the Roanoke River and struck out on the winding road toward the little town of Edgewood, some twenty-two miles away.

The dark shadow of approaching dusk was creeping across the undulating foothills as they rattled southwestward along the rutted road. Spence reined in the slow-moving mules, looked into the growing shadows, and saw a narrow grassy valley stretching off toward the haze-covered mountains.

"Looks like good grazing," he spoke up tiredly. "We'll camp here and let the animals graze overnight."

Followed by Elsie's Jersey cow on a lead rope and Rover trotting along behind, David swung the old wagon from the narrow road. He pulled lines in a treelined field, turned to Willie, and smiled. "Well, William, this should be our last camp before we reach your farm."

Willie smiled back. "I'm hoping this to be our last camp. I'm guessing we've got around fifteen miles to go. Maybe if we move on a while before daybreak, we'll be home before nightfall sets in."

"Pull the wagon over yonder by that little creek," Elsie spoke up, tapped David's shoulder, and pointed. "I need to milk the cow and stake her out to graze before it gets too dark."

"Oh, I didn't notice the creek," Spence responded smilingly and slapped the reluctant mules forward.

In the dim moon glow Elsie milked the cow and David hobbled the mules in the thick grass near the low creek bank.

*

It was shortly after noon when the old wagon drawn by two exhausted mules rumbled across long-neglected planking on the dilapidated covered bridge spanning Crooked Creek. And beyond the bridge, about fifty yards or so, the road forked. Willie pulled lines and turned the wagon on the right fork. "That road goes on to Edgewood," he announced, waving a hand back toward the fork as the wagon rattled into a copse of oak trees.

Along the fringe of the road a montage of daises and black-eyed Susans were in full bloom. And deep within the woods, laurel lay in the shadows like a dark-green blanket. The trees gave way to an open valley of tall verdant grass. A split-rail fence snaked its way around the pasture and followed the contour of a low hill up the valley toward Chestnut Mountain, standing like a fortress, with towers of huge gray stone thrusting heavenward. On the eastern side of the mountain, multiple shades of green, highlighted by a dappling of flowering redbud and white dogwood in the warming days of spring, had advanced halfway up the blue-hazed mountain.

As the slow-moving wagon approached the farm gate, Willie spotted a wisp of smoke rising lazily from a hidden house and dispersing in a light breeze above the tall trees. At the gate Willie pulled the wagon to a chain-jangling stop, nudged David, and pointed off to the right. "You see that smoke? That's our house off behind them trees."

Ellie rose up to see over David's wide shoulder. "Keep an eye on Rose and I'll open the gate," she said pleasantly, turned, and moved hurriedly to the rear of the wagon.

William Marshall spoke excitedly. "We'll be home in about ten minutes, I 'spect."

"Well," David chuckled lightly, "I'm looking forward to meeting your mother and baptizing you in . . . in Crooked Creek."

Willie raised a thin eyebrow and nodded thoughtfully as he watched Elsie force the sagging gate open. He cracked the long rawhide whip above the stubborn mules. A twitch of an ear was the only noticeable response. Willie sighed deeply and cracked the whip again. As the wagon rolled slowly through the open gate, he muttered, "Them mules seem to be a bit hard of hearing."

"And so are you," Spence added with a wry grin as Elsie climbed aboard.

In the pasture, a gazing cow raised her head with casual interest as the old two-horse wagon rumbled past and on up the gentle treelined slope toward the house: a large white-washed two-story building with fieldstone chimneys on each end and a single-story hip-roofed porch spanning the front.

A mild "Whoa" and William Marshall reined the mules in near the front steps where a portly middle-aged woman stood in glaring sunlight, her eyes shaded by a big gray poke bonnet.

The heavy woman recognized Willie now busily looping the lines around the break handle. She waddled out to the wagon, screeching. "William! You're home at last. You're home at last," she repeated as the slender lad climbed clumsily from the wagon.

They embraced and the woman was still kissing Willie's sunken cheeks as David, with a tired grunt, clambered from the mud-spattered wagon. Suddenly calm, the woman looked over Willie's shoulder and saw the tall, smiling man.

He doffed his hat, presented a shallow nod, and said in a soft, sincere voice, "I'm David Spence. It's a pleasure Mrs. Marshall, a pleasure indeed. I've looked forward to meeting you for some time. You fit William's description—"

Will chuckled. "This here's Aunt Nora, Ma's sister."

Somewhat embarrassed, David nodded and remained silent.

Willie glanced at the house and asked, "Is Ma at home?"

Nora's smile faded. Her hand dropped to her gray apron and her face turned serious. There was a long pause. "She's up at the church," Willie's aunt finally managed in a lowered tone. "It's about Pastor Haskell. He passed on to heaven Sunday afternoon shortly after church service. Bad heart, I heard."

"Pastor Haskell's dead!" Willie cried. "I was wanting . . ." His voice trailed off.

Aunt Nora shook her head slowly. "Your mama seems mighty broke up about him dying all of a sudden like he did. Lilly went with her to the funeral. I thought she might be able to calm Beulah down a bit."

Willie turned to David and almost whispered, "Lilly is Aunt Nora's daughter and my cousin."

With Rose in her arms, Elsie emerged from behind the wagon.

Will Marshall's aunt gestured. "Who's that with the baby?" There was surprise in her voice.

"Oh, that's Elsie Rogers and her little girl, Rose," Willie spoke up softly. "They'll be staying with us for a spell."

Elsie threw her shoulders back, hitched Rose up a bit, forced a thin smile, and strode resolutely toward the watching trio, the smile still on her face as she pulled up. "I'm Elsie. My baby's name is—"

"For goodness's sakes," Nora said in her high voice. "William's already told me who you are." She chuckled. "Give me that baby. Any fool can see you're worn to a frazzle." *That girl's got spunk*, Willie's aunt thought, looking into Elsie's sharp brown eyes as she took Rose into her bulky arms.

The clatter of shod hooves came on a light breeze, and they turned to see a yellow-spoke buggy drawn by a fast-trotting bay horse top the slope. The girl reined in the snorting mare behind the wagon and a well-dressed middle-aged woman with dark hair and laced with random strands of gray stepped down from the black-lacquered rig. And William Marshall, moving as fast as his stiff leg would allow, rushed to greet his mother.

Finally, after another episode of hugging and kissing, Widow Marshall turned her glowing countenance upon David, extended a silk-clad hand, and raised her big, tear-filled eyes. She was somewhat taller and much thinner than her older sister, David noted as he smilingly took her hand and quietly introduced himself.

And after introducing Elsie and Rose, still comfortably secured in Nora's big arms, they moved toward the house.

As they approached the porch steps, David looked back. He saw Nora's well-proportioned sixteen-year-old daughter trudging along and kicking dirt with her shiny black shoes, a sour look on her face. She's jealous, he realized when he turned his head and saw her mother cross the porch with Rose in her arms.

David stopped.

Lilly caught up.

He grasped her arm lightly and smiled widely. "Your mother is very proud of you. She was just telling me about you taking your widowed aunt to the pastor's funeral. I would say there are very few young ladies your age could be trusted with that responsibility."

As they topped the steps, Lilly was smiling.

They entered Beulah Marshall's wide hallway to find her deploying the newcomers to the two upstairs bedrooms. Assigned to share a room with Willie, she assured David the arrangement would be temporary. After the fall, harvest construction would begin on a large bedroom in the attic, now used for storage.

David dwelt on that, but only for a moment. He saw Lilly pulling Rose from Nora's reluctant arms and smiled.

CHAPTER 21

—A PERSUASIVE WAY—

A THIN BEAM of sunlight made its way between the drapes and found David's face. He struggled out of a deep, dreamless sleep and blinked in the bright glare. He moved his head from the down-stuffed pillow into the shadows and asked himself, *What is the time? It seems as if I've just fallen asleep.* He rose quickly from the narrow bed, scratched his disheveled head, and looked across to Willie's rumpled empty bed. He got to his feet, walked across to the window, parted the curtains, looked out, and squinted in the bright sunlight. *About nine o'clock,* David guessed as he turned back to pull his trousers from a wall peg. He dressed hurriedly, hustled to the door, flung it open, saw Elsie topping the stairs, and stopped.

She smiled brightly. "Oh, there you are, Chaplain. Widow Marshall sent me up to 'roust you outta bed.' We've kept your ham and eggs warm for over an hour." She swung her slender body about, grasped the handrail, and on a quick, light tread, descended the stairs. She stopped in the hallway and looked back, a near smile on her face. "She's waiting in the parlor," Elsie almost whispered, flashing another little smile. "And she wants to see you—privately."

David Spence frowned.

"She seems to be a bit put out," Elsie went on hurriedly. "You'd better hurry with your breakfast and go on into the parlor."

About ten minutes later he was knocking lightly on the big stained oak parlor door.

"Come on in," Widow Marshall said in her strong, authoritative, no-nonsense voice.

And David, with a little hesitation, pushed the heavy parlor door open, entered the large room, and stepped on a well-worn pale-blue carpet stretching across a polished oak floor to a soot-stained brick fireplace in the far wall.

He found Widow Marshall in a wide, slat-backed, pillow-cushioned rocking chair before the lace-curtained window, bent over a big black Bible. She closed the Bible, placed it on a small round table, and swung her sharp brown eyes to the tall man.

She doesn't seem to be put out, he thought as the widow gestured toward a dark-blue, heavy-legged, horsehair-stuffed sofa. "Sit down. I hear you're a Confederate chaplain." Widow Marshall didn't bother with preliminaries.

"Yes. I *was* a chaplain." David corrected, nodded, and opened his mouth to continue.

"I guess ye know about Pastor Haskell passing away . . . away to heaven," Beulah Marshall said haltingly.

David nodded again, his face turning serious. "Yes. Willie—William has mentioned him a number of times. He said Pastor Haskell, in addition to his pastoral duties, taught children three days a week—about fifteen, I believe he said."

"Last count was twenty-two," Willie's mother corrected, daubing at her eyes with a little white handkerchief.

"I'm sure it will be difficult to replace Pastor Haskell," David said softly, respect in his voice.

A long appraising look and Beulah Marshall managed a thin smile. "William says ye might be going off to the Shenandoah Valley in a day or so."

Suddenly, realizing her motive, he responded cautiously. "Yes. Well, I'll probably leave on the next stage."

"I thought, with the approval of the deacons, ye might be willing to pastor our church for a week or so till, Lord willing, we find a schooled preacher."

David sighed, shook his head slightly, and smiled. "Well, I consider the offer an honor, but I'm determined to return to my uncle's farm in time for spring planting."

She pursed her lips, flashed him an appraising under-brow glance, and nodded slowly. "Yes, I understand. But being thu schoolhouse ought to be finished and a teacher in place when fall comes on, I thought ye, being the good Christian ye are, would be willing to take over thu preaching . . . for a couple of weeks."

David heard a touch of reproach in her tone. Willie's mother, it seemed, was not accustomed to being disagreed with. "Well, I don't know what to say," he responded defensively and paused thoughtfully for a few seconds. "You say 'a couple of weeks'?"

She shrugged lightly. "Well, offhand, I'd say upward of two weeks. It could be a mite longer though," Widow Marshall added thoughtfully with a slow nod.

David leaned forward, his eyebrows lifting. "Well, it seems you have backed me into an untenable position. I'll stay for two Sunday services"—he rose from the sofa, reached out, and grasped her languid hand, a little smile creasing his wide, sun-browned face—"providing the deacons agree."

"Oh," Widow Marshall laughed lightly, "there's no need to fret about that."

Spence chuckled. "With your persuasive way, I'm sure they will agree."

*

About an hour later David thoughtfully strolled out into the warming midmorning sunlight and made his way through the tall grass toward Widow Marshall's red barn. He soon reached a worn wagon track and paused a moment, when off to his right he noticed chimney smoke hanging above a grove of tall trees. And in the deep shadows he saw a large log house. It's probably for farmhands or sharecroppers, David thought as the rattle of turning wheels and the fast beat of hooves reached his ears. He swung about and saw a black-lacquered yellow-spoke buggy jostling toward him. It was Willie's mother.

She lashed the beast into a fast trot over uneven ground, her poke bonnet going askew. "Whoa," she ordered, drawing the anxious mare to a stop.

And holding back a smile, David creased his brow. "Well now, you seem to be in a hurry," he said politely.

She smiled at that, repositioned her poke bonnet, and chuckled lightly. "Well, I guess I'm just a reckless, sinful old woman."

David Spence creased a thin grin. "You're far from old. Why, you're as spry as a spring chicken."

She chuckled again. "It seems ye will have to kneel at the altar rail and confess to being a sinner before ye get into your first sermon. Climb in," she ordered with a smile. "There's a gray gelding I want ye to see, if Nathan ain't yet turned him out to pasture."

As the buggy rattled on toward the big barn, Widow Marshall glanced at David and said thoughtfully. "I have t' say, that gray don't look like much, but there's more t' him than meets the eye."

"Well, I'm not buying. I'm evaluating," he responded smilingly.

As she reined the mare in near the barn's entrance bay a big long-boned man with a pitchfork across her broad shoulder ambled out from the barn into the sunlight. He was tall—the tallest man David had ever seen.

"That's Nora's husband, Nathan," Beulah informed him softly behind her gloved hand.

The big, wide-faced man speared the pitchfork into the ground and four long strides carried him to the buggy. He doffed his wide-brimmed, sweat-stained straw-hat and pulled a big red handkerchief from the back pocket of his bib overalls. With a friendly smile tugging at his lips, he wiped his beaded brow and stuffed the handkerchief back in his pocket.

"Well," he boomed in a weighty voice that matched his size, "I reckon you t' be Spence, thu man that come in on thu wagon." He thrust out a big hand, attached to a long, heavy arm, and announced proudly, "I'm Nathan McBride, Nora's husband. Word is, you're a preacher of sorts."

David grasped the capacious, calloused hand and nodded. "Well, Nathan, I believe you have that right. I will be a preacher of sorts. Sunday morning, I'll be preaching my first sermon and I'm somewhat . . . apprehensive."

The big man's sun-browned face reddened. He drew his hand back and cast a guilty glance at Widow Marshall. "I won't a-meanin' t' be disrespectful," Nathan almost whispered. "Sometimes my words get a bit tangled."

David chuckled. "There's no need to apologize, Mr. McBride. I manage to get words tangled quite often. I pray they will be clear and concise Sunday morning."

Widow Marshall took over, her tone a little impatient. "Nathan, have ye turned thu gray out to pasture yet?"

"Naw," Nathan replied, "Jake's still in his stall." He adjusted his wide-brimmed hat and half-smiled. "I was 'bout ready t' milk that Jersey cow that came in with thu wagon."

"Come on, Pastor Spence," the widow ordered with polite authority. She rose up and was on the ground before Nathan's long striding feet rounded the buggy to help her down.

"Jake's in thu first stall off to thu left," Nathan called as David rushed to catch up.

She's right, David thought as he viewed the gelding. *This animal is ugly.* With mild resistance from the horse David forced the big gray's mouth open, examined his teeth, and nodded. "He seems to be about four, maybe five years old."

Widow Marshall wagged her head slightly. "Nathan says Jake's a fairly good saddle horse but gets mighty skittish when trying to be harnessed. I thought ye, being a preacher, would need a reliable riding animal for your pastoral rounds and such."

"But," David admitted, "I haven't funds to pay for the gelding."

She frowned. "Ye don't understand. There will be no charge for the horse nor the saddle. I have two Morgan mares for heavy pulling and my bay for the buggy," she went on, her frown fading.

Spence shook his head thoughtfully. "But you could sell your gelding for a fair price."

Beulah Marshall pursed her lips and gave him a long glare. "Ye know and I know, I won't be able to get anywhere near what this ugly animal's worth. Besides that," she went on hurriedly, passion in her voice, "being the devout Christian you are, I'm sure you'll take good care of the gray."

David stroked his chin and eyed the big ugly horse awhile.

"Well," he said thoughtfully, "if it's all right with you, I'll just borrow the gray until I leave for the valley."

"Till ye leave for the valley," she responded with a shallow nod and smiled unashamedly.

*

After the midday meal, while Elsie clattered about the kitchen, David wax-sealed a letter, pushed the cane-bottomed chair back from the table, and rose to his feet. With a quick breath, he extinguished the candle, sighed, and slipped the letter into an inner coat pocket. Hurriedly he crossed the hallway to the parlor, found the oak door ajar, and thrust his head into the room. His eyes came to rest on Beulah Marshall sitting placidly in her big rocker before the window, busily mending a gray shirt.

He nodded slightly and smiled. "I'm going into town to post a letter to my uncle, informing him that I'll be delayed a couple of weeks, more or less."

She bit off a dangling thread, raised her dark eyes, and smiled. "Take the buggy and be gone with ye then, and be kind enough to pick up my mail."

There seems to be a little Irish in her voice, he thought. Then he grinned. "I think I'll ride Jake. We need to get acquainted. And I'll stop by the church." He raised a brow and forced a thin smile. "Where is the church?"

Beulah Marshall chuckled lightly. "It's in a clump of trees about quarter mile this side of Oscar Stanley's blacksmith shop. Ye can't miss it."

He started to leave, then turned back and smiled. "Where will I find the post office?"

She chuckled again. "Ye can't miss it either. Edward Covington, a member of our church, just put up a big sign announcing his hardware store, as if we don't where 'tis. You'll find the post office inside. And while you're there," she went on good-naturedly, "ye might as well buy yourself a Sunday suit at Watkins's clothier. It's two doors beyond the hardware store."

"But," David protested, "I can't afford—"

Beulah Marshall raised a hand. "No need for concern. I'm giving my tithe to pay for the suit." She leaned forward in her chair and extended a yellow folded paper. "Give Henry Watkins this note, and he'll put it on my account. I'll be catching up on my tithing next month." David started to speak, but she went on firmly. "No need to argue with me, young man. What's said's said and what's done's done." Widow Marshall threw him a quick smile.

"Well, maybe—" He started, but she had turned back to her stitching.

CHAPTER 22

—EDGEWOOD—

THE TALL GRAY without encouragement moved swiftly along the road toward Edgewood. And David was smiling. "Beulah Marshall was right," he told the gelding. "There's more to you than meets the eye."

He trotted the horse past the blacksmith shop and on down a shallow slope to the town's dust-ridden Main Street. He pulled rein at the hitch rail before a weather-beaten two-story building. On the porch roof above the entrance he saw a large sign embossed with

COVINGTON'S HARDWARE
AND
DRY GOODS STORE

David dismounted, tethered the gray to the hitch rail, stepped on the boardwalk, and entered through the open doorway. A momentary pause and his eyes adjusted. Behind a worn wood counter, he saw a middle-aged man propped on his elbows, a humorless smile splitting his thin lips. He strode over to the counter, smiled, and pulled a letter from his coat pocket. Edward Covington, the storeowner as well as postmaster, David assumed, fit the description Widow Marshall had conveyed—a bit more detailed than he thought necessary.

"Hello, Mr. Covington. I'm David Spence," he said with a smile. "Would you mail this letter?"

"Howdy, Parson Spence," Covington responded, lifting his bony elbows from the worn counter. He adjusted his wire-rimmed spectacles and went on. "I heard you'd be taking the good Reverend Haskell's place for a spell."

David nodded.

The dour-faced man took the letter, held it at arm's length, squinted through his little spectacles, nodded slightly, and said frowningly, "Um, seems to be a letter to Staunton. No relatives in the state asylum up there, I hope."

David chuckled lightly. "Not yet . . . that I know of."

Covington coughed. "I'll post the letter right away. The next stage out will be Saturday round noontime. Could be a mite late though." He moved from behind the counter and strode briskly toward the post office at the rear.

David quick stepped around a pickle barrel and went on unnoticed past two old men seated on battered pine-slatted chairs, playing checkers by a tall potbelly stove standing cold in the middle of the floor. Near the stove were two empty benches mutilated with notches carved by farmers during the cold winter months as they discussed mules, horses, next year's crops, and other matters that seemed important at the moment.

"Looks like I done gotcha this time," the old graybeard announced triumphantly, and slipped his king into blocking position.

"Dad-gum it, Rob." The bald man tilted to his left and spit into a gallon bucket, filled with tobacco-stained sand. "Every dog gets au bone now an' agin. Go ahead an' set 'um up agin."

As David hurried on, he saw a half door with an adjacent counter separating the little post office from the store.

The postmaster pushed through the swinging half door, dropped the letter into a canvas bag, pulled his spectacles from an inside coat pocket, and perched them on his sharp nose. He turned to a tall, slotted box on the back wall and pulled out a couple of letters.

"I'll take—"

"I reckon you'll want to deliver the Widow Marshall's mail," Edward Covington cut in, lifting a brow and waving the letters he had already removed from the M slot.

"Thank you," David said cheerfully as he took the three letters. "I'll make sure she gets them." Half-smiling, he looked through Covington's wire rimmed spectacles at his magnified pale-blue eyes. "I look forward to seeing you in church," he added.

Covington pushed his spectacles up from the end of his nose. "Can I help you with anything else?" he offered quickly, trying to change the subject.

David forced a thin smile and answered evenly. "Not now." He stuffed the letters in his coat pocket and started to leave. He stopped, turned back, and went on, his tone serious now. "After I inspect the church I'll probably need a few items. I'm sure you allow churches discounts . . . significant discounts."

The postmaster opened his mouth to speak but changed his mind when he saw David's cocked brow. Without conscious thought, he adjusted his spectacles.

A brief wave followed by a small smile and David strode heavily toward the door. He noticed the two men silently gazing at the worn checkerboard and decided to linger a few minutes.

"Looks like I've done gotcha in a bind," the bearded checker player announced proudly.

"Now ye lookee here au minute, Rob," the slender, bald man responded firmly, his arthritic finger resting unsurely on a black chip. "I still got au move or two afore ye can start yo braggin'."

David coughed lightly.

The two men looked up sourly.

He smiled at them and said in a pulpit voice, "I'm David Spence. I apologize for interrupting you gentlemen, but I would like a moment of your valuable time to invite you to the Sunday service at the local church."

The bald man, with his finger still on the black chip, leaned left and spit a brown stream of tobacco juice into the bucket partly. "A-needin' au bigger bucket," he muttered and turned his pale eyes back to the checkerboard.

The bearded, long-jawed man smiled, thrust a big hand toward David, and started to rise. His knee struck the wobbly table, sending the checkerboard to the floor, scattering black and red chips across the room.

He didn't seem to notice. He was still smiling and his hand was still outstretched. "I'm Rob—Robert Doyle. I ain't au member but I was at thu church a while back t' hear Pastor Haskell preach. I 'spect I'll be visitin' this coming Sunday t' hear your sermon fur comparison."

David chuckled. "Well, Mr. Doyle, it seems you are setting the standard rather high for a pastor's first sermon."

"Well, young fellow," the slender, bald man—grinning through yellow, decaying teeth—spoke up in a drawling voice. "Ye ain't got much t' worry 'bout if'n you stick t' thu scriptures an' don't get too fancy . . . an' too loud. I've been in a bunch of churches—some too fancy an' some too loud."

Spence chuckled again and dropped a big hand on the man's narrow shoulder. "That's good advice. I'll keep it in mind as I prepare my sermon. I suppose you'll come with Mr. Doyle."

"I jus' might," the man responded grudgingly with an uncertain nod. He decided to spit again—and he did.

David smiled. "All right, gentlemen, I look forward to seeing you Sunday morning—both of you."

About twenty minutes later, Pastor Spence, with a large, brown, string-tied, paper-wrapped bundle tucked under his arm, exited Watkins's clothier and squinted in the sudden sunlight. His eyes adjusted. He untied the reins, swung aboard, scotched the bundle against the saddle, and nudged the big gray horse up the street.

CHAPTER 23

—STRANGE AND MYSTERIOUS WAYS—

The young minister trotted the gelding on past the town sign standing across the road from Stanley's blacksmith and wheelwright shop, rode on about three hundred yards, and headed the gray horse into a grove of tall oaks. At a hitch post beside the church steps, he reined in the big gelding, dismounted, looped the reins around the post, and viewed the whitewashed building. It was a small church, much smaller than he anticipated. But with a bell tower standing at the front entrance, topped by a small white cross, it seemed to be the standard design of most country churches.

David climbed the steps, hesitated a moment, sucked a deep breath, pulled the weathered door open, and stepped inside. Off to the right he saw a dangling bell rope, looked up into the belfry, and fought off the sudden urge to ring the bell.

He smiled at the thought as he walked slowly down the center aisle, counting pews left and right as he went. David reached the front pews, swung about, and gauged them with his eyes. "I believe each pew should seat six or seven adults," he muttered as he paused to calculate. *I believe we can squeeze in about seventy or eighty adults*, Spence figured. *But how many will attend the service?* David wondered as he stepped behind the pulpit and surveyed the room with sharp, encompassing eyes. Near the left side of the sanctuary he saw a big black potbelly stove with its protruding pipe rising about six feet and then turning to disappear in a smutty brick chimney. And off to the right, just beyond the podium, he noticed a small pump organ and smiled. Standing there, in his mind's eye, he visualized men, women, and children pouring into the church and filling the pews and, accompanied by the blaring organ, a choir singing a melodious hymn.

David hurried to the organ, grasped the pump handle, and pumped. A low whistle from the organ stopped him. No pressure. "Something's broken," he sighed in disappointment, staring at the organ. Finally, he went to his knees, searching for the problem. *I'll need more light*, he told himself as he gazed into the dusty dimness.

A door slammed. Distant footfalls blending with a low giggle and a drawling voice echoed in the empty church. "Mr. Spence."

It was William Marshall.

David climbed to his feet and brushed the dust from his trousers, and Willie went on. "We—Elsie and me—are on our way to town and decided to stop by the church. I didn't figure you to be here."

"Yes. I decided to take a look as well," David said seriously, moving to the center aisle. "It seems the organ is out of order."

Willie chuckled. "That old organ was broke down before I went off to fight them bluecoats. I figured it to be fixed by now."

"It seems the bellows have collapsed," David assumed, his voice low. "Well, what about the organist?" he asked thoughtfully.

Willie shook his head slowly. "Ms. Wilson was our organ player till she went off to Twin Oaks about a month before I left for the army. She married a traveling hoss trader, I heard."

"Well, what about the choir?" Spence was anxious to know.

William Marshall responded thoughtfully. "I recollect that most of the time there was four women, counting Ma, Aunt Nora, and four men, including me, last I was here." He shrugged. "You'll have to ask Ma. She dropped out but might know what's going on."

"I'm willing to join the choir," Elsie volunteered smilingly. "I sang in Pastor—in our choir." She couldn't bring herself to say "Coleman's."

Half-listening, David nodded. A brief pause and he responded, his voice low, his tone soft. "Thank you, Elsie. I'm sure your voice will be needed . . . sorely needed."

He cut his sharp eyes to Willie and creased a thin smile.

"William, do you know anyone nearby that has an upright piano?"

Willie frowned thoughtfully for a few seconds. He was suddenly enlightened, a wide smile crossing his narrow face. He looked at David, a discernible twinkle in his eyes. "Well, I reckon, the only one I know about belongs to Aunt Nora, but I doubt you'd be able to pry it away from her. She's mighty particular about it."

"So . . . your aunt Nora plays the piano."

Willie chuckled. "She can't play a lick. She bought it for her daughter, Lilly, but she can't play a lick neither." He shrugged and changed the subject. "We're on our way to town to see Dr. Dickerson. That is, if he's sober. We figured he might advise me about my knee problem. He was a surgeon in the army till drinking hard liquor caught up to him."

Elsie spoke up. "It's getting late. We need to hurry on."

David clasped Willie's arm and smiled. "If you return home early enough, we'll pay Aunt Nora a visit. Maybe we can persuade her to loan the church her piano until the organ is repaired."

Willie turned to go. "Don't reckon it'll do much good, unless we find a'body to play it," he called over his shoulder.

"Well," the big pastor called after them, "I'll trust the Lord to send us a pianist. And I'll pray for you and Elsie."

Elsie turned her head, smiled, and threw him a kiss, and arm in arm, they hurried away.

David Spence turned to the altar rail, knelt, and prayed silently.

*

It was nearing four o'clock when Willie reined the mare in just beyond Murphy's restaurant.

At the corner of the restaurant they noticed a little sign lettered in fading black, hanging slightly askew.

J. B. DICKERSON
DOCTOR AND DENTIST

On the sign, below the words, an arrow pointed up the outside stairs toward the second floor.

"Looks like the doctor's sign is about to fall down," Willie drawled, as he hobbled from the buggy and paused on the steep steps, his left hand gripping the rail.

"I hope it don't fall on somebody's head," Elsie added frowningly.

"Well," Willie chuckled as they climbed, "if it does, there's a doctor just up these steps."

They topped the stairs, and he pushed the creaking door open. The doctor was in. He was asleep on a narrow sofa.

"Do you think we ought to wake him?" Elsie whispered.

William half-nodded and half-whispered. "Well, I reckon—"

The portly man bolted upright and snorted. "Oh, patients . . . I was just resting awhile. Late-night visits . . ." Dr. Dickerson's voice trailed away as he stumbled to his feet. The short, stout man with a full head of curly white hair faced Elsie, his watery eyes raking her. Finally he asked, his voice low and gentle, "Well, how can I help you, dear lady?"

His pale eyes, she thought, seemed to be undressing her. Now somewhat uncomfortable, Elsie forced a smile and pointed to Willie. "He's the patient."

The doctor turned to Willie and squinted. "Well, I'll be doggone!" he exclaimed. "It's Will Marshall, back from the war already. Good to see you, Will." He smiled and extended a soft hand. "What's your problem?" he asked as Willie took the hand.

"It's my left knee. I got myself hit with Federal shellfire down at Five Forks. I thought I just might let you take a look at it. That Union captain, a doctor hisself, thought it could be a sliver from a Federal shell under my kneecap. He said a surgeon might be able to cut it out and I might be able to bend my leg."

"A Union captain, you say. Were you captured . . . or was he captured?" Dickerson said softly.

William Marshall smiled. "Well, you could rightly say I was captured, if being in Federal hands for about three hours counts."

The heavy doctor chuckled and motioned toward the adjacent room. "Go in there, remove your trousers, and I'll examine your knee." He turned back to Elsie, took her hand, and said gently, "Have a seat. The examination will take about fifteen or twenty minutes."

Thirty minutes passed and Elsie, becoming restless, rose to her feet. From beyond the closed door the sound of muted voices reached her ears, but the words were inaudible. And then she heard sudden laughter. With growing curiosity, she crossed the room and put an ear to the door. The laughter stopped, chairs scraped, and the sudden tread of approaching footfalls came to her. On hurrying feet she raced back to the chair, sat down, and grabbed up a newspaper. At that moment the door squeaked and Dr. Dickerson entered, followed by Willie, still tucking his shirttail into his trousers.

She pretended to read on for a few seconds. Finally she raised her eyes from the paper and saw Willie's solemn face. "What did he say about your knee?"

"Well, it seems William will have to go to Lynchburg," the doctor understated in a professional voice. "I'm not skilled enough to handle that type of surgery, but I'm well acquainted with a good surgeon up there." He turned to Willie and went on. "If you're willing to go, I'll telegraph Dr. Price for an appointment, providing the telegraph wire is still up."

"Might be we can wait awhile," Willie drawled in a low tone.

Dickerson spoke firmly. "I suggest you see him soon—the sooner, the better."

William Marshall cast a barely discernible glance at the young widow and responded unsurely. "Lynchburg is a ways off. But if I'm gonna get it done; the sooner, the better . . . I reckon." He sighed deeply and forced a weak smile.

"I'll let you know as soon as I hear from Dr. Price," Dickerson said pleasantly as he escorted them to the door. "And we'll . . . settle your bill then."

Willie managed a shallow nod, his narrow face flushing.

They moved carefully down the outside stairs and climbed into the buggy. Willie pulled the whip and urged the mare into a fast trot. And then, for no apparent reason, he laughed.

Elsie looked at him quizzically and asked, some frustration in her voice. "Why in the world are you—?"

"Oh, it's just that—" He laughed again, and she knew he was teasing her. "I didn't know you could read upside down newspapers."

"Did I—?" Elsie stopped. Then she smiled. "Well, I have talents you don't know about."

They both laughed.

Two or three minutes passed. Willie cleared his throat. "I . . . I hope you'll be going with me to Lynchburg," he said hesitantly.

She cut her brown eyes to him, cocked her head, and smiled. "Now, William, you know it wouldn't be proper for a widowed woman with a baby to travel with you and stay overnight. It looks like, whether you like it or not, we'll have to get married."

Surprised, William Marshall jerked the mare to a stop, dropped the lines, pulled Elsie close, smiled, and said passionately, "Well, I ain't kissed a pretty girl today. I 'spect it might as well be you. It's what my pa called a slobber-swapping kiss." And to her surprise, he did.

*

Off to the west the orange sun was settling behind the Blue Ridge, with only a quarter of its surface showing.

Now in a front-porch high-backed rocker, David watched it slowly disappear, with only a pink and purple glow remaining as moonlight enveloped the valley. *I'll wait another five minutes*, he thought. *The McBrides retire early and they may be upset if we arrive unexpectedly—and late.*

The door squeaked open and Widow Marshall, her petticoats rustling, stepped out and said worriedly, "I wonder what old Dr. Dickerson thought about William's leg." A short pause and she went on in a worried voice. "They ought t' be back—"

The rumble of fast-turning wheels and Spence spoke up. "Here they come now."

The rig lurched out from the trees into the moon glow and climbed the shallow slope toward the house. As the buggy topped the hill, Widow Marshall smiled broadly. "Well, I do declare," she murmured when she saw Elsie and Willie, sitting hip to hip, arms linked.

As the buggy turned into the yard, they went down the steps and waited anxiously as Willie reined the hard-breathing mare to a snorting stop.

The buggy was rocking on its springs as Elsie's feet touched the ground. "Where's Rose?" she asked as she rounded the buggy.

"Now, don't ye be worrying about the baby," Beulah said gently, grasping the young widow's arm lightly. "She's in the parlor on a pallet, sound asleep."

Willie climbed down, looked at his mother, put on a wide smile, and said, "I asked Elsie to go with me to Lynchburg when Dr. Dickerson sets up a time to get my knee fixed. She said it wouldn't be fitting for an unwed girl to go. I reckon I'll have to marry her."

"Well, I declare!" Widow Marshall exclaimed. "I was hoping ye might—" She failed to finish. With tears flowing, she embraced her son and her future daughter-in-law, and a round of congratulatory hugs and kisses erupted.

Finally they calmed and Willie grasped David's hand. "Pastor," he asked quietly, "do you want to go—?"

"Yes. I'll go with you to stable the mare," Spence answered knowingly.

They climbed in the buggy. And Willie, still smiling, headed the bay mare toward the barn and Aunt Nora's big log house.

*

The next morning, while still at the breakfast table, they heard the distinct rumble of wagon wheels mingling with a light jangle of trace chains.

"Nathan's on his way to finish plowing that big field down by the creek," Willie drawled.

"Well," Widow Marshall added with a complementary smile,

"You have t' give it to Nathan McBride. He's a hard worker."

David, with a hasty "Excuse me," pushed his chair back, got to his feet, and looked out the kitchen window. After a few seconds he turned back and smiled. "We may not have a pianist for service tomorrow, but we will have a piano temporarily."

As they crowded before the window to look, Willie sniggered and said slowly, "When we left last night, I didn't think Aunt Nora would be willing to turn loose of her piano. Our new preacher seems to have a winning way about him."

And David Spence, grasping the slender lad's arm, said comfortably, "It's not me, William. You must realize, sometimes the Lord works in strange and mysterious ways."

And with the exception of baby Rose, they all nodded in agreement.

The big pastor moved quickly across the kitchen, paused at the door, and smiled. "I'll saddle Jake and follow Nathan. He'll require help to carry the piano in the church." With that, he hurried away.

CHAPTER 24

—HEAVEN AND EARTH—

DAWN'S WEAK LIGHT, creeping through the second floor window, found David climbing into his new store-bought black trousers. He slipped into the frock-tail coat and turned to the little oval mirror. While busily adjusting the matching tie around the stiff collar, he heard William Marshall chuckling. Surprised, the black-clad pastor whirled and saw Willie propped on an elbow. "Well, William, I didn't expect you to be awake this early," he said smilingly.

"Ain't you a sight?" Willie chuckled lightly.

"I hope I didn't wake you." The black-clad pastor's voice was low, his tone apologetic.

"Oh, I just woke up early to be the first one to see you in your new getup. It's about as pretty as a new silver dollar."

David laughed, his teeth flashing white in the dim light. "I hope that was a complement." His smile morphed into a frown. "William, would you arrive at church a little early? I need someone to introduce me to the congregation."

Willie smiled briefly. "I'd be glad to, but I'd be willing to bet Ma's gonna be thereabouts an hour early to do the introducing. She's done made arrangement for Ellie, Rose, and me to ride in Aunt Nora's carriage. That's the way she is, sorta bossy-like."

Half-smiling, David gathered several sheets of pale yellow paper from a small side table, slipped them into an inner coat pocket, and pulled out his watch.

"Chaplain, uh, Pastor Spence, I believe you're a bit nervous," Willie observed, grinning.

"No." David smiled wanly. "I'm not nervous . . . I'm petrified."

As David turned to leave, Willie scratched his tousled head and forced a low chuckle, trying to decipher *petrified*.

David clambered down the stairs and moved hurriedly along the hallway toward the kitchen. As he passed the parlor door, a voice rang out. "Pastor Spence, would you step in here for a minute?" He stopped, turned back, paused in the doorway, and saw Widow Marshall, attired in her heavily bustled, hoop skirted pale-yellow dress, uncomfortably seated in a big rocker. *Willie was right*, he thought. *His mother is already dressed for the church service.*

With lips pursed, she ran her sharp eyes over him for a few seconds, nodding as she did. "Well now," Beulah Marshall commented approvingly, "ain't you a sight for sore eyes? It's going to be a rainy day," she predicted. "To keep your new Sunday suit dry, it might be best that ye leave the gray here and ride with me. Nathan ought to have the buggy out here in about . . ." She paused to glance at the mantle clock. "He should be along in about thirty minutes or so."

"That's very thoughtful," David said cheerfully and smiled. "I consider it an honor to escort you to church."

"Well, Preacher, get yourself on in the kitchen," Widow Marshall ordered in a friendly way. "Elsie's already fixed breakfast." As he turned to leave she went on warmly, in a lowered voice. "There ain't a lazy bone to be found in that girl."

"Yes." David smiled brightly. "I've noticed that as well."

*

It was almost an hour before the eleven o'clock service when David guided the trotting mare from the treelined lane into the wide, grassy churchyard. And the steady rain, David noticed, had turned into a misty drizzle. Surprised, he found buggies and wagons surrounding the little white church. Out beyond the churchyard at the fringe of the woods, he spotted a row of saddled horses standing at the long hitch rail, nibbling wet tree leaves, and warding off flies with swishing tails.

"Are they always this early?" David asked the widow quietly, as he reined in the mare at the steps.

Beulah laughed shortly while adjusting and pinning her Sunday bonnet. "Not that I know of," she finally answered. "Curiosity seems to have a strange effect on folks round these parts."

"I'll help you inside, then park the buggy over there," he said softly, pointing.

"Goodness gracious, Pastor Spence, you're treating me like an old lady. I can make my way inside." She stepped down sprightly, looked up at him, and nodded disdainfully.

A wide smile crawled across David's face. "Oh, I forgot." He nodded back, still smiling. "You're as spry as a spring chicken."

"Now, get on with ye, Preacher," she said hastily, her Irish bubbling up again. "I'll be waiting by the door for ye to escort me to my pew seat, with a slight bit of dignity about ye."

"Indeed, Your Majesty," David intoned smilingly. "I'm depending on you to introduce me to the congregation before I seat you." With that he touched up the mare.

Beulah Marshall, the black-clad preacher came to realize as she introduced him to the congregation, knew all the members' names, including their children and their dogs as well as several members' cats. But David, to his dismay, could remember only a few.

Several minutes before eleven o'clock, David was still at the door greeting parishioners and a bevy of visitors. He glanced over his shoulder. The church, he saw, was crowded—virtually overflowing.

Too late, he noticed the dangling bell rope and thought, *We have no designated bell ringers*. He grinned. *Well, it doesn't matter now. The church is almost full. I'll need a few volunteer bell ringers*, he decided.

Dawdlers were still trickling in as he escorted Widow Marshall to the pillow-cushioned space beside the aisle, on a third row pew, seemingly reserved for her.

He moved across the low podium to the piney pulpit. And except for a few muffled coughs and shuffling feet, the church was suddenly silent.

With an encompassing glance at the crowded room, David saw the anticipatory look in the congregants' eyes. His throat tightened. His mind went blank. He swallowed hard, pulled the yellow notes from his coat pocket, and laid them on the pulpit, trying to think.

"As you know," he started feebly, "this is my first service as a minister. And by now you probably know, I served as a Confederate chaplain. I realize it will be impossible to replace Pastor Haskell, so I'll follow a gentleman's advice I heard yesterday at Mr. Covington's store. The man advised me to stick to the Bible and not get too fancy nor too loud." David flashed a glance at Covington—sitting proudly on the front row with a wide smile on his narrow face—laughed lightly, and shook his head. "I agree with that man's first suggestion, but his definition of 'too loud' may be somewhat different from mine."

That enticed a few light chuckles.

The black-clad pastor smiled and went on forcefully. "I believe the scriptures should be loud and be clearly understood."

At that moment, Rover, unabashed, trotted through the open doorway on down the aisle and flopped at Elsie's feet.

Elsie blushed.

The congregation laughed.

And David, with some hesitation, introduced the hound. "And last but not least, I have the profound pleasure to introduce another addition to our choir—Rover." The congregation laughed again. And to his surprise, some rose to their feet and clapped.

He raised a hand, his equanimity fully restored. "I would be remiss if I failed to thank Nora McBride for loaning the church her piano until the organ is repaired. Maybe, with the Lord's help, we'll soon find a pianist. But in the meantime the choir, with a couple of new additions, will be satisfactory." He gestured and glanced at the choir, their worn songbooks at the ready position.

"And now, they will begin the service with a song you will probably hear quite often—'Amazing Grace.'"

David strode to the waiting choir and slipped in beside Willie, and with his strong baritone voice leading, they sang,

> Amazing grace! How sweet the sound,
> that saved a wretch like me!
> I once was lost but now am found,
> was blind, but now I see . . .

After the last stanza, he hurried back to the pulpit and opened his mother's black, pencil-marked Bible. With difficulty, he managed to hold his emotion in check as he read the short prayer. It was his mother's swirling script in the margin. A prayer, as a child, he had heard her quote many times.

Trying to hold back tears, David breathed a low "Amen." He raised his glistening eyes, swept the crowded room for a few seconds, cleared his throat, and said in a clear, sincere voice, "Since this is my first sermon, I believe it appropriate that I start at the beginning." He opened his Bible again and read,

> In the beginning God created the heaven and the earth.
> And the earth was without form, and void;
> and darkness was upon the face of the deep.
> And the Spirit of God moved upon the face of the waters.
> And God said, 'let there be light': and there was light.

CHAPTER 25

—LYLE DOOLIN—

ROUND EIGHT O'CLOCK the next morning, a big straw hatted lad, in dirty, ragged bib overalls, climbed the steps to Widow Marshall's side porch. Four strides carried Lyle to the kitchen door. He raised a big grimy hand and knocked heavily.

That's Nathan, Beulah thought as she placed a plate in a big tin dishpan. Another loud banging and she called impatiently, "Hold on, I'm on my way. No need t' break the door down," she murmured, drying her hands with her apron, as she hurried to the door.

Widow Marshall pulled the door open to find a tall, round-faced, dull-eyed lad with a long fishing pole across his shoulder. She forced a smile. "Hello, Lyle, It's been quite a spell since ye've paid us a visit."

"Heard Will's done cum on back t' home," Lyle drawled. "Ma's done said, 'I might jus' come on down an' get Will t' take me a-fishin' . . . fur a spell. I got my fishin' pole an' come on. I ain't 'eat yet though. Ol' Mud ain't 'eat neither."

"Come on in, Lyle," the widow said in a friendly tone. "I'll fry a couple of eggs for you and toss a hunk of biscuit bread to your dog."

"Oh, I'm reckonin' two eggs might jus' be anuff," the big lad suggested firmly as he tromped into Beulah's warm kitchen.

"Well, two it is then," she agreed, holding back a smile as she opened the firebox and dropped a good sized chunk of split oak in the glowing embers.

"Maybe you ought to—" Beulah started to say. "Take off your shoes." But looking down, she found him barefooted. "Have a seat at the table." She gestured, resisting the urge to glance at his mud-caked feet. "I'll have your eggs ready in two or three minutes."

As Lyle stuffed the last bite in his mouth, a terrible ruckus set in somewhere outside. Dogs were barking, growling, yapping, and finally moaning. Now a male voice was yelling. "Let go, Rover! Let go, Rover!" And then there was silence.

Smiling and shaking his head, Willie clomped into the kitchen. "Rover and Mud's done had a disagreement of some sort." He chuckled lightly. With a drawling "Howdy, Lyle," he gave the puzzled lad a friendly slap on the shoulder, pulled out a chair, sat down, and chuckled again. "It seems like them dogs had a little scuffle to see which one was top dog."

Perplexed, Lyle moaned, "Ol' Mud ain't hurt none, is he?"

William Marshall looked into his tear filled eyes, reached across the table, and patted the heavy lad's big hand. "Old Mud didn't get a scratch that I could see. He was a bit disrespected, I reckon you might say. Rover ain't a killing dog, except rabbits and such."

Lyle brightened. "If'n Ol' Mud ain't hurt none, we can jus' take our fishin' poles an' go on t' Crooked Creek an' catch up some fish, like we done afore ye went off t' fight thu war. Can't we . . . can't we Will?" Lyle was smiling and climbing to his mud-infested feet.

"Well, I reckon . . ." Willie's voice trailed off.

A hidden nudge at her son's back and Widow Marshall said hurriedly, "I'm sure William is anxious to go fishing with you."

Willie frowned, then forced a little smile and pushed his chair back. "I'll get my fishing pole and we'll be on our way."

At the hall door he stopped, turned back, and smiled again. "My ma might be willing to fix some leftover ham biscuits to take along with us." He was chuckling as he hobbled down the hallway.

*

As the big lad and Will Marshall strolled down the path, followed by two friendly hounds, Widow Marshall called with motherly solicitude, "William, ye be home by suppertime and have Lyle well on his way up Chestnut Mountain. No need for him t' be traipsing up there after dark."

Willie waved a brief parting gesture, turned to Lyle, and smiled. "We'll go by the barn to get the hoe and dig up some bait worms."

"Can I do thu diggin'?" the big lad asked excitedly. "I'm mighty good at diggin'."

"I'd be honored for you to do the digging," William responded in a friendly voice. "I 'spect you might just be the best digger in the whole county."

"I jus' might be." Lyle grinned. "I shore am glad ye done got yo'self on back from thu . . . thu fightin'."

Willie smiled, laid a slender arm across the retarded lad's stooped shoulder, and said softly, "Me too."

The heavy lad looked up, saw a dangling rope attached to a bell atop a skinny pole, and said excitedly, "Thu las' time we went a-fishin' ye let me ring thu bell when dinnertime comes along."

"Well, Lyle"—Willie smiled—"I don't reckon you ought to ring it now. It's a good while till dinnertime."

Lyle's wide brow creased as they walked on. After a minute or so he drawled, "How'd ye come by thu stiff leg, Will?"

"I got hit by Federal shellfire down at Five Forks," Willie answered quietly.

"I might jus' go get a shotgun an' my brothers. We'll jus' go along wif you t' get that Fed'rul man that shot up yo' leg."

Willie chuckled. "I surely appreciate the offer, Lyle. I surely do. But I doubt we'd be able to find him. Anyhow, I 'spect I'll be getting it fixed before long."

They strolled on toward the big red barn. Willie glanced up the slope at Aunt Nora's log house and saw Lilly busily sweeping the wide front porch.

Lilly spotted her cousin and Lyle, the long fishing poles across their shoulders. She dropped the broom, leaped from the porch, and raced down the hillside.

"I wish I could run like Lilly," Willie Marshall said wistfully as they watched the girl glide swiftly down the grassy slope.

"I reckon that gal t' be yo' cousin," Lyle drawled unsurely.

Willie nodded. "Her name is Lilly McBride." *She's filled out far beyond her age*, he thought but said, "She's grown quite a bit since last you saw her."

"I reckon so," Lyle Doolin put in, smiling crookedly.

As Lilly drew near the grinning lads, she slowed to a walk. "Looks like you're going fishing," she said, breathing deeply.

Willie chuckled. "How'd you know?"

Her sun-browned face reddened. She forced a brief laugh and asked, "Are you going up to Mr. Washburn's mill pond or down to Crooked Creek?"

"I reckon we'll be going to the creek and fish for trout," William answered, creasing his narrow brow. "Ma says Mr. Washburn gets a mite touchy these days about letting folks fish in his pond. Worries they might leave the pasture gate open. Could be his age, I reckon."

"I surely would like to go with you next time you go fishing in Crooked Creek," the girl said eagerly, her hand moving to her apron pocket. "I'm making a collection of these." She pulled out her hand and opened it slowly, exposing a smooth, round multicolored stone.

"Well, I declare!" Willie exclaimed, taking the stone from her outstretched hand. "Well, I declare," he repeated softly as he held it up into the bright sunlight. "I 'spect there might be some more where this one came from."

"Can I hole hit fur a spell?" Lyle begged excitedly, stretching out a big hand. "It shore is au purty rock," the heavy lad marveled as he fondled the smooth, blue-greenish little stone. "I shore would like t' keep it fur my purty thing box? My ma got me a box t' keep my purty things in. I push it under my bed t' pull out an' take a look at my purty things when I'm a-feelin' au mite poorly."

Willie frowned.

"Oh, you can have that one," Lilly said. "I have two left and planning to get some more when I go down to the creek."

"I reckon we ought to get going," Willie sighed, squinting into the bright sunlight. "I'm getting a little thirsty. We'll stop by the well for a drink of water before we dig up the worms. We need to hurry so we can be at the creek before the day's half-gone. Hot as it is, it'll be hard to catch trout after noontime," Willie thought to add.

Lilly McBride started to leave but stopped as William Marshall went on. "Lilly, I 'spect we'll be going fishing again soon. We'll stop by for you to go along if you've a mind to."

The shapely girl smiled and turned up the low slope.

As Willie drew up a bucket from the well, he glanced at the barn. He noticed Elsie's wagon and two ugly mules harnessed and hitched.

"Looks like Pastor Spence and Nathan might be fixing too haul that old organ up to Twin Oaks," he guessed.

"Ain't that a tree of some sort?" Lyle Doolin asked.

Willie saw puzzlement in his dull gray eyes, stifled a laugh, replaced it with a smile, and shook his head. "Twin Oaks is a town. It's about twenty miles off to the southwest." He pointed toward the blue-hazed mountains. "Lyle," he thought to mention, "it might be proper for us to help load that organ."

"I'd be a-willin' t' help." The big lad nodded and broke into another crooked grin. "My brother, Zack, says, if'n I was t' try, I might lift up a hoss."

"I reckon you could lift a horse." Willie chuckled and lightly slapped Lyle's heavy arm. "I just reckon you could."

Nathan and the pastor, with ease, it seemed to the watching lads, carried the organ from the barn, hoisted it into the wagon, and roped all four legs to the sideboards. From the oak-planked wagon seat, David issued a good-bye wave, and Nathan McBride lashed the tall mules into a fast trot.

The wagon rattled across Widow Marshall's lush pasture, turned on the narrow lane, and headed for Crooked Creek Bridge, the Mountain Road, and Twin Oaks, some twenty miles away.

CHAPTER 26

—THE MOUNTAINEERS—

THE DYING RAYS from the setting sun found the exhausted mules struggling up the narrow, winding road. Afoot now and breathing hard, the two men were flagging as well.

Nathan grumbled through his deep breathing. "I guess I shoulda hitched Beulah's matched Morgan mares to her big wagon 'stead of these wore-down mules pullin' this beat-up rig."

"Well," Spence said, trying to sound positive, "I believe mules are more surefooted on mountain roads."

"'Pends on how steep . . ." McBride's mumbling voice faded away as they trudged on. About ten minutes later Nathan sighed tiredly. "Dark's a-comin' on an' I 'spect this t' be good a place as any t' spend thu night."

Spence nodded.

"I'll jus' pull thu wagon crosswise," Nathan muttered, slipped the lines from his shoulder, and moved to the middle of the rocky road. And still muttering, he reined the ugly mules across to a bushy bank. "Don't reckon there's t' be heavy traffic a-comin' this away 'fore daylight." Nathan chuckled mirthlessly and went on. "I see au washed out space up ahead. 'Fore it gets too dark, I'll see if'n I can find a little kindlin' wood t' heat up a pot of coffee."

"All right, Nathan. I'll take care of the mules," David agreed softly as the big man handed him the lines and turned to go.

Pastor Spence unbit the mules and moved to the wagon for the feed bags.

. "Lord A'mighty! I'm snake-bit!" A voice cried frantically. "Pastor Spence, you'd better get up here quick."

Without hesitation, David rounded the wagon and called as he ran up the rough road. "Open your pocket knife."

In the growing darkness, Spence's eyes caught the big man sitting in the rough, dusty road about ten yards ahead with his big hands clinching his left leg, just below his knee.

David kneeled beside Nathan, grasped a big, high-top shoe, pulled it off, and ordered hurriedly, "Roll to your right. I need to reach in your back pocket for the handkerchief." There was deep concern in his urgent voice.

McBride gruntingly rolled his big body onto his right hip. "Where is the knife?" David asked as he jerked the red handkerchief from a back pocket.

"I dropped it t' hold m'leg," the big man answered, apprehension in his tone.

With quick efficiency, David selected a substantial kindling stick, slipped the big red handkerchief around Nathan McBride's heavy leg above the kneecap, and knotted it to the stick. "I'll twist it tight too slow the blood flow before . . ." His voice trailed away.

"Do what ye have t' do, Pastor," the big man mumbled weakly. "Maybe au bit of prayin' might help."

David nodded. "The prayer began when I heard you calling."

In the dark shadow of the mountain, the big pastor frantically ran his hand over the rough ground, searching for the knife. After fifteen or twenty seconds, it seemed much longer, he discovered the large folding knife under Nathan's right leg.

"Can you flair a match?" Spence asked, trying to speak calmly, as the sharp knife slit the sullied trouser leg. "I'll need light to find the snakebite. I didn't think to bring the lantern from the wagon."

"What . . . what you plan t' do?" McBride almost whispered as he probed in his overall chest pocket.

"I have to cut into the wound and suck out the poison as soon as possible. Flare the match and hold it above your leg . . . and keep still. This will be a little painful," he went on, the poised blade reflecting in the dim glow from the flickering match.

"Go on an' do what you got t' do," Nathan muttered. The knife blade pierced his leg. He groaned.

A minute later David was swiping a sleeve across his bloody mouth. "I hope," he said softly, "I removed enough venom to—"

Nathan McBride forced a weak smile and almost whispered, "You've done yo' best. We'll jus' put it all in thu Lord's hands."

"He's gonna be dead befo' daylight comes," a calm voice drawled from the roadside bushes.

Startled, David rose quickly. He saw a tall, dark figure appear out of the night shadows into a dim sliver of moon glow. Then he noticed the dark shape of a long-barreled weapon resting in the crook of his left arm.

"'Taint no doubt 'bout it, I reckon him t' be dead come sunup," the dark figure drawled again.

"I'm the pastor at the Edgewood Church," David said worriedly. "I need your help to carry Nathan to the wagon."

"No need," the man responded, caustically, "He'll be—"

"If I get him to a doctor soon, his chance for—" David stopped, glanced at Nathan, and continued. "A doctor might enhance his chance for a full recovery."

"Don't be takin' kindly 'bout them town doctors nor lowland parsons neither," the mountain man drawled firmly.

The bushes rustled, and David turned to see another dark figure appear. In the dappled darkness he seemed thinner and a little shorter than his companion. *His left arm is missing*, he thought, squinting in the dimness.

A mirthless little chuckle came from the taller man as he turned to the approaching figure and said, contempt in his drawling voice, "That big'un over thar's done got bit by au timber rattler, thu parson says. He's askin' me t' help get thu big lowlander loaded on that thar wagon."

"With this here stove-up arm," the thin figure responded in a weak voice, "I ain't gonna be a-helpin' none."

It was then that David was able to see the young man's left arm bent across his body and buttoned in a homespun shirt. "Have you hurt your arm?" he asked, forcing a friendly tone.

"'Taint nothing much . . . jus' fell off'n a big ol' rock a ways back," the young man muttered. "I reckon it t' be healed 'fore long."

In the dappled dimness David moved closer. He saw pain in the young mountaineer's face, looked down, and saw a crooked arm. He gestured and spoke softly. "Your arm is broken. If I can persuade your companion to help carry Mr. McBride to the wagon, you can ride with us down to Edgewood. Your arm needs attention soon—very soon."

Without a word, the taller figure thrust his long-barreled weapon in the younger man's right hand, moved to Nathan, stopped, and motioned to David.

And without hesitation the pastor rushed over to help.

"We'll be unloadin' that piano 'fore I help get this big ol' lowlander in thu wagon," the tall man demanded in his slow drawl.

David protested. "But . . . that organ belongs—"

"Let him have thu old organ," Nathan muttered painfully. "Just get me on down this mountain t' thu doctor."

With some difficulty, David and the mountain man managed to half-carry and half-drag McBride to the wagon.

"Jus' put him down here, Preacher," the tall figure ordered, breathing hard. "I done changed my thinkin' on thu organ. You can jus' get in an' push it up a ways t' make room fur this lowlander."

Hurriedly, David climbed in the wagon bed, untied the organ, and pushed it against the oak-planked seat.

Several minutes later, with Nathan's big, tousled head cushioned on his lap, Pastor Spence was seated in the wagon bed and the tall mountain man was lashing the mules into a fast trot.

As the wagon jostled down the rough, winding Mountain Road, David called to the tall figure on the planked seat. "I believe it would be wise to light the lantern. It's on a sideboard hook to your left."

There was no response. But a few seconds later a match flared just beyond the organ, and albeit it rather weak, the yellow light from the lantern sent its flickering yellow glow along the left side of the old wagon bed to the thin figure standing at the rear wheel, gripping the tall brake handle with his right hand.

The wagon had rattled down the rough road a half mile or so, when the tall mountaineer called, concern in his deep drawl. "Parson, we's comin' t' thu steep part. I 'spect you oughtta take thu braking 'fore thu wagon runs them mules off'n thu mountainside."

In the flickering lantern light, David looked up to see the younger man struggling to keep his balance while forcing the long brake handle with his right hand. That frayed brake rope must have broken. Spence suspected as the old wagon, picking up speed and pressing the tall mules into a fast gallop, was swinging the sharp turns down the rough road.

Suddenly, aware of the looming disaster, David grabbed the sideboard and struggled to his feet. He saw the lantern swinging wildly on its hook and the organ sliding to the left. "Sit down and hold on," the big pastor ordered as he grasped the tall handle with his right hand and the mountain man's upper arm with his left.

Dangerously near the cusp of a deep ravine, the shredded brake rope was flapping, and fast-turning wagon wheels were showering dirt and debris. He saw the lantern fly from the wagon and bounce down the steep, rocky slope, leaving a fiery trail in its wake. David's heart leaped. With all the force at his disposal, the big preacher, praying silently, locked the rear wheels and the wagon slowed. The galloping mules drew back into a fast trot and finally a brisk walk.

And Pastor David Spence, still braking, breathed a deep sigh of relief. He turned his face heavenward and cried, "Thank you, Lord!" He looked down to find the young mountaineer drawn up into the fetal position, his right hand gripping a heavy organ leg. David cut his eyes to McBride and found him on his back, still mumbling a fervent prayer.

In deep darkness the wagon reached the base of the mountain and rattled on down a long, shallow slope. About three hundred yards ahead, they spotted the yellow glow of lamplight emitting from a second-story window.

"We's comin' up on thu gristmill a ways down thar," the tall mountaineer informed them in a heavy backwoods drawl.

"We need to hurry on to Edgewood," David reminded.

The tall figure on the planked seat shrugged. "Ain't no time fur that," he said harshly, fingering the weapon propped at his side.

At the mill he pulled lines and Spence was on the ground as the rumbling wheels stopped rolling.

"Stop!" the tall mountain man ordered loudly as David, striding swiftly, came abreast the mules.

With the distinct click of a cocking hammer, the pastor slowed momentarily, looked over his shoulder, saw the dark figure raising his weapon, and braced for a lead ball. And praying silently, he picked up the pace and hurried on to the little porch. He climbed the steps and pounded the door vigorously. No answer. David pounded again and called, "open up! We need help."

"Hold yo' hosses . . . I'm on m'way," a voice, carrying some irritation, responded from beyond the door. "You're makin' enough racket t' wake thu dead." The shuffle of approaching feet and a flicker of yellow light under the door and the voice called hesitantly. "Who . . . Who's out thar?"

"I'm the pastor at Edgewood Church," David's strained voice sounded from the porch. "We're in dire need of help."

From somewhere inside another muffled voice quavered. "Let 'um come on in, George. I done heard 'bout thu new parson."

A bolt rasped. The door squeaked inward and David saw a heavy, round-shouldered man standing in the dim light of his coal oil lamp. The man, in his late fifties, lifted the lamp and squinted at the black-clad preacher for several seconds. Finally he shrugged lightly and said cautiously, "Mr. Washburn's saying, you might as well come on in."

With the clomping of heavy footfalls behind him, David stepped inside, followed by the tall mountaineer gripping his Kentucky musket. And with the long barrel pressing his broad back, David spoke up hastily, trying to ignore the prodding weapon. "I'm David Spence. We have a snake bitten man and a lad with a broken arm in that wagon." He gestured. "Can we bring them inside?" he asked, forcing his voice calm. "They'll need attention while I go for the doctor."

"You can bring 'um on in," a voice croaked from the stairs, "but that long gun's gonna be outside."

David cut his eyes to the stairs and found himself looking into the double barrels of a shotgun. It was in the knurled hands of an older man in a pale nightshirt standing darkly on the third step.

"Ye with thu long gun," the old man threatened, waving his weapon slightly, "jus' back on out that door or I'll be a-fixin' t' fill thu room with buckshot in 'bout half a minute."

The pressure left David's back. He turned his head sharply and sighed deeply. The tall mountain man was gone.

"Parson," the old man squawked, "get that snake bit man an' thu boy on in here . . . an' be on your way fur Dr. Dickson afore it's too late. You might as well take my fast hoss."

With a heartfelt "Thank you," Spence turned to leave.

"I'll be a-helpin' thu parson if need be," George offered in a friendly tone.

"Well, I'll need your help," David responded earnestly, turning back. "Mr. McBride is too heavy for one man to carry."

"Ye a-meanin' Nathan McBride," The old man croaked from the stairs and propped the heavy double-hammered shotgun against the staircase wall.

David nodded.

While scratching his ratty whiskers, the gray-bearded miller said thoughtfully, "Nathan might be a bit heavy t' lug up these steps. I'll be a-bringin' down au blanket or two t' make up a pallet. Well," he jerked his head up and rasped, "stop thu dilly-dallin' an' get 'um on in here."

"I done got thu snake bit lowlander," the tall mountain man's drawling voice sounded from the narrow porch.

Surprised, David swung about. And before him, in the fading rays from George's smoky lamp, he saw Nathan McBride, standing there, favoring his left leg, with a big arm drooping heavily across the mountaineer's shoulders.

"Might need a bit o' help t' get this here big ol' lowlander inside," the mountain man drawled.

David rushed to help.

The old miller croaked. "George, you go on up an' bring down au blanket fur Mr. McBride." As George crossed to the stairs, the miller spoke up again. "An' George, find a old sheet that's lately washed t' strip up fur bindin' his leg an' thu boy's arm. An' one more thing, George, I'm a-needin' au match t' light thu lantern before you take thu lamp upstairs an' leave us in thu dark." He gestured toward the dusty, unlit lantern hanging from a rough-cut joist. The stocky man pulled out a match, moved over to the scrawny old man, and smiled. "I guess I'm forgettin' yore nightshirt ain't got pockets."

Washburn reached up, gruntingly pulled the lantern from a rusty nail, flared the match, and with a gnarled, wavering hand, put the flickering flame to the wick.

"Where should we put him?" David asked hurriedly, backing in from the porch with his long arms around McBride's thick body, struggling to get him inside.

"Put Nathan on them cornsacks over thar," the miller croaked, swinging the lantern to light the way. "I 'spect George t' be down with a blanket soon."

"I think I might be feelin' a bit better now," McBride sighed as they sat him on the heavy, corn-filled sacks. "Parson, I'm thinkin' you suckin' out that poison might've helped . . . a bit."

"Maybe so, but I'm sure prayer was more helpful," David responded and turned to the old miller standing about three strides away. "I'm sorry," he said softly, "I don't know your name."

"Jonathan—Jonathan Washburn be my name, but a-knowin' you t' be thu new preacher, I didn't get your'n neither."

"I'm David Spence," he retorted hurriedly and turned back to Nathan. "Mr. Washburn," he continued, pulling McBride's slit trouser-leg aside, "bring the lantern a little closer. I need to take another look at Nathan's leg before I go for the doctor."

Washburn raised the lantern. The glow brightened. "Needs t' be cleaned up a bit," he observed, looking over David's wide shoulder at Nathan's big leg. "'Pears t' me them cut marks t' be mighty fer apart t' be a snakebite. Nathan," he rasped, "did ya' hear that snake rattle afore it struck you?"

"Well, I . . . I didn't exactly hear thu rattler rattle," McBride answered thoughtfully. "But I heard bushes shakin' when I stepped in t' get au kindlin' stick. Anyhow," he went on, frustration in his voice, "I'm bit. I reckon' that ought t' be plain fur anybody t' see."

"Before I go for the doctor, we'll clean the wound and take a closer look," David said gently. "I pray it's not as serious as we thought." He turned his eyes to Washburn. "I'll need—"

In the weak, yellow glow flickering across the room, he glimpsed a figure coming in from the little porch. It was the younger mountaineer with the rifled musket in his right hand.

Unnoticed, the tall mountain man had managed to sidle back to the doorway. There was a blur of movement, too quick to see in the weak lantern glow, and the long-barreled weapon was in the older mountaineer's firm grasp.

The hammer clicked.

They froze—all of them.

Now descending the stairs with a folded blanket under his left arm and the wavering coal oil lamp in his right hand, George Simpson paused. His glance fell on the propped shotgun at his feet. He cut his frightened eyes back to the musket. *That long barrel*, the stocky man calculated, *might be pointing in my direction.*

David Spence caught his eye, shook his head slightly, and mouthed a silent no.

"We ain't waitin' fur ye t' doctor on thu lowlander 'fore ye get t' my brother's arm," the tall man drawled menacingly, sweeping the long musket barrel across to the stairs.

David stepped forward, and as he did, the deadly musket tracked him. "There's no need to threaten us with that weapon," he said, forcing his voice calm. "I'll try to align the bone and splint your brother's arm as soon as we take—"

"Let them others take care of thu big lowlander," the sadistic long-legged man sneered, eyes bright as he played his game of intimidation. "I'm pickin' ye t' be fixin' my brother's arm an' I 'spect ye t' be a-doin' it right now."

David Spence's heart was pounding. He put a grim smile on his wide face and forced his voice calm. "When you stop pointing that weapon at me, I'll do what I can for your brother's arm." The musket barrel settled slowly. David nodded, his heart dropping a few beats as he turned toward the stubby man standing on the steps. "George," he said huskily," I'll need a couple of boards about a foot long."

George frowned and said slowly, "I reckon we might be able to cut up a bed slat. I reckon thu saw's out in thu barn," he went on thoughtfully and stole a glance at the tall mountain man. "I doubt I'd be allowed to go get it."

"You jus' tell my brother where 'tis," the tall man demanded, cutting his darting eyes back to David. "He'll be a-gittin' it befo' you know he's gone." He snorted a short, mirthless chuckle.

"Well, I ain't quite sure where thu saw might be," George offered frowningly. With a sudden urge to scratch his head, he laid the blanket across the wobbly stair rail and, still trying to remember, scratched in his graying hair.

Disdainfully spitting, the mountain man sneered, his eyes cold. "Well, if'n ye 'specting t' live a while longer, ye'll jus' have t' go on out an' help' Zack find it."

Surprised by his brother's threatening comment, Zack motioned to George and said softly, "Let's git a-goin'. 'Taint nothin' wrong with my legs. 'Taint no need t' be scared of Josh neither. He gets a bit showy when he's got a gun in his hands an' our oldest brother, Harley, is outta sight."

Somewhat embarrassed, Joshua stood silent as his brother and George Simpson headed for the door. Finally, the older mountaineer cleared his throat. "Now, Zack, you'd jus' better not . . ." His voice trailed away when he saw the door closing behind his young brother.

*

About an hour later Zack was upstairs in Mr. Washburn's small bedroom, sitting in the cane-bottomed chair gritting his teeth, his long face contorted in pain as David's strong hand, gripping the young mountaineer's left wrist, stretched his long arm. Zack wanted to groan, but with sheer willpower, he remained silent.

"All right, George, the bones seem to be aligned," David said hastily. "I'll hold his wrist while you wrap the bandage tightly from his elbow to my hand. Wrap two layers and keep it tight. I'll hold the splints in place while you wrap the second layer."

George Simpson wrapped the remaining three feet of sheet bandage and knotted it firmly. "Well, Zack," David assured in a soothing tone, "with the Lord's help, your arm will be healed in about a month. All we need now is a sling. George would you—?"

Simpson chuckled and answered the unfinished question. "I've done got it cut an' ready." He turned to Washburn's narrow bed and brought forth a yellowish strip from the mutilated sheet. He handed it to David, scratched his head, and smiled broadly. "I'm thankin' your doctorin' might be as good as Dr. Dickerson's. Maybe a mite better."

David sighed tiredly. "Well, George, it's not a profession I would aspire to, but when confronting desperate situations, even a country preacher is occasionally forced to resort to desperate measures."

While trying to decipher David's last remark, George scratched in his hair again.

As they descended the creaky stairs, the old miller's quavering voice met them. "I'm a-believin', an' I'm a-sayin', that thar ain't no snakebite. I've done been round au long time an' I know au snakebite when I see one."

"If 'twas a rattler bite," the tall mountaineer put in from his position near the entrance door, "I reckoned he'd be dead by now."

"That horse liniment might be thu reason that leg ain't swolled up much," Washburn speculated around his cob pipestem, nodding.

David strode over from the stairs to Nathan, still sitting on the cornsacks, a bandage neatly wrapped around his left leg. He laid a sympathetic hand on McBride's thick shoulder. "Is your leg very painful?" he asked in a low voice.

"It seems t' be a mite better since Mr. Washburn dabbed on that horse medicine," Nathan almost whispered. "I'm beginning t' think it won't no snake at all. It coulda been au stick of some sort." He motioned David closer and whispered in his ear. "I've been a-feared of snakes all my born days."

Pastor Spence smiled and whispered back. "And so have I." Still smiling, David turned to the old miller. "Mr. Washburn, I congratulate you. Indeed, you managed to treat Nathan's wound skillfully . . . very skillfully."

Somewhat embarrassed, the miller grunted, shook his balding head, and said, tone low, "Well, it won't much at all. I been a-treatin' livestock fur nigh on t' fifty-some-odd years."

"Saw thu light," a low, unsure drawling voice came from the open door. "It wuz a-shinin' through thu door, an' I come on in far some drinkin' water, if'n ye got any."

"Lyle!" Zack blurted, moving over to the heavy lad, "you shoulda got yourself on home before now. Ma had Josh an' me t' go out a-looking fur you."

"Didn't come on 'cause I had t' wait fur Mud," Lyle Doolin drawled earnestly. "I reckon he jus' went off fur a while a-chasin' after a rabbit or some critter." The heavy lad brightened and went on. "Me an' Will's done caught us up a bunch o' trout down in Crooked Creek. I got more'n Will. He said I might jus' be thu best at catchin' up fish in thu county." Lyle stepped inside and held up a string of medium size speckled trout.

"We'll be a-gittin' on home now." Joshua Doolin sighed impatiently. With the rifled musket in the crook of his arm, he took Lyle's elbow, guided him to the door, and paused. He glanced over his shoulder at Zack and gestured the long barrel slightly.

Zack hesitated, flashed David a puzzled glance, shrugged, and hurried out into the dim moonlight.

A loud "Giddyap!" followed by the sharp crack of a whip and the dull rumble of iron-rimmed wheels came from outside.

David hurried to the door, Mr. Washburn following slowly, his cob pipestem clenched firmly between decaying yellow teeth. They looked out into the dim moon glow and saw the wagon turning up the Mountain Road.

"Now, that jus' beats all," the old miller muttered in a querulous voice, shaking his head and stabbing his long pipestem at the open door. As the wagon disappeared and the rattle of iron-rimmed wheels died away, he stabbed the pipestem again and croaked on. "Them Doolin rascals ought t' be hided with au buggy whip. Them ungrateful—" He started to curse but looked at the big preacher and changed his mind.

"Well," the disappointed pastor said, his dark-clad shoulders sagging, "I'll have to go up Chestnut Mountain and visit their mother. Maybe I can persuade her to make them aware of the dire consequences Zack and Joshua will face." He paused a few seconds, nodded, and went on calmly. "Mr. Washburn, I believe the Lord has blessed us in a way we do not yet know. He may not reveal the results for a while, but eventually, I'm sure He will. In Matthew the Bible says,

> Ye have heard that it hath been said,
> Thou shalt love thy neighbour, and hate thine enemy.
> But I say unto you, Love your enemies,
> bless them that curse you, do good to them that hate you,
> and pray for them that despitefully use you.

"I 'spect it might be . . ." The old miller's weak voice trailed off and he began puffing hard at his unlit cob pipe.

David grasped a thin arm, a little smile creasing his mouth. "Well, Mr. Washburn, it seems we'll have to borrow your fast horse after all."

CHAPTER 27

—THE LABORERS ARE FEW—

JULY 22 TURNED out to be another hot, dry day. It was approaching nine o'clock that Saturday morning and Pastor Spence, aboard Widow Marshall's black-lacquered buggy, was trotting the bay mare up the dust-ridden slope.

As the rig topped the hill and drew near the blacksmith shop, David noticed Oscar Stanley—a tall, muscular man with calloused hands and a soot-streaked face—standing across the road from the shop, admiring a small wooden sign.

It seems another newborn baby or someone has moved into town since last week, David thought as he viewed the crudely burned lettering:

EDGEWOOD POPULATION — 498

He pulled the bay to a dusty stop, touched the brim of his black low-crown hat, and smiled. "Well, Mr. Stanley, it seems like we've had a slight population increase."

The gregarious blacksmith chuckled comfortably. "Maybe I'm jumpin' ahead some. Figured I'd go ahead an' add that young lady that's comin' in today for thu teachin' job." Oscar Stanley spit a good-sized stream of tobacco juice beyond the sign and drew a big finger across his heavily mustached mouth. "I didn't vote t' get her, though." A frown furrowed his wide, soot-stained brow. "I figured it t' be a waste of hard-earned money t' bring in au hifalutin' female that's jus' outta school an' ain't taught none, but Rufus Joyce, thu chairman, politicked the other town councilmen t' out vote me." He shook his head, forced a humorless smile, and gestured toward the sign. "Anyhow, she's officially counted now."

Twenty-six years before forge and anvil had thickened Stanley's arms, the right somewhat more than the left, Parson Spence noticed.

David smiled again, cocked his head slightly, and said evenly, "I might be wrong, but the first time I came this way, I thought that sign was directly across from your shop door."

The big smithy shook his head again, chuckling. "Well, Parson," he said in a low tone of confidentiality, "I've been movin' it fur nigh onto six months an' it looks like you're t' be thu first one that's took notice. Some of thu councilmen thought thu town ought t' be a-growing. So when I add a number t' thu sign, I move it out five strides, more or less."

And trying to hold back a smile, David raised a brow and forced his voice serious. "Do you move it forward about five strides when someone moves away or dies?"

Stanley chuckled again. "Don't figure much on that. I jus' leave off a number next time au new body shows up. Anyhow . . . It all evens out in thu end."

The young pastor nodded slightly and forced his countenance serious. "Maybe you should pray about that." With a friendly "Good-bye, Mr. Stanley," he raised the lines to go, but the blacksmith's big hand grasped his arm firmly.

"Just a minute, Pastor. I done got them three crosses made up fur you. Took a mite more time than I figured t' beat them silver dollars into crosses, though." The big man released David's arm, pulled his leather apron aside, probed in a sagging trouser pocket, and brought forth three small crosses attached to dainty silver necklaces.

"The necklaces, Mr. Stanley? Did you—?"

"Saw them necklaces at Covington's hardware," the smithy interposed with pride. "I jus' figured, since my daughter would be gettin' one, I'd make a contribution."

Smilingly, David fondled the crosses. "I'll tell the girls," he said softly, turned his eyes back to the blacksmith, and chuckled. "I see you engraved their initials in them as well. I'm sure your daughter will be pleased. I'll present them to the girls tomorrow, after the first hymn. And don't forget to be there early. You're still the bell ringer," he added. A friendly wave and he put the mare into a fast trot.

*

A foot hard against the brake lever brought Widow Marshall's black yellow-spoke buggy to a skidding stop in front of Draper's livery stable.

Fredrick Draper, now leaning against the unpainted wall in a ladder-backed chair, his straw-hat shading his face, was jolted out of his nap and found himself engulfed in a cloud of reddish foothill dust. Draper scrambled to his feet, coughed some, and waved his wide-brimmed straw-hat vigorously, trying to clear the air. "What's goin' on here?" he spluttered as the dust settled around him.

Finally, taking notice, the squatty man recognized the black-garbed, wide-shouldered minister and his anger quickly subsided. "Oh . . . oh it's you, Preacher." His tone sounded somewhat disapproving, David thought, as Draper beat the dust from his trousers with his wide-brimmed hat.

"Heard you're meeting the stage t' pick up that new teacher that's coming in today. Word has it that she's boarding with Widow Marshall." While adjusting his big sullied hat, Fred Draper went on. "I'm reckoning, come fall, you'll be glad not t' have them young'uns underfoot."

"Well, I believe the children will receive a much better education with a full-time teacher rather than two hours, three days a week with an untrained preacher," David responded thoughtfully.

The heavy man ruminated a few seconds. "You reckon that school building t' be finished up before thu schooling begins come fall?"

David started to answer.

Draper went on. "Word is, you won't be getting thu windows afore winter sets in."

Spence responded in his best ministerial voice. "Well, I believe, with the Lord's help and enough willing townsfolk, we'll finish before fall—well before then." He stepped down from the buggy and sighed deeply. "The town council had to order the windows from Twin Oaks. Well"—he sighed again and went on—"I expect it'll be two, maybe three weeks before they'll be ready. Sorry about the dust," he continued apologetically. "I came in somewhat faster than intended." He gestured toward Widow Marshall's black-lacquered buggy. "What's the charge to stable the mare for about four hours and grease those axles? I heard them squeaking."

"Well, reckon a Union dollar ought t' be enough," Draper responded quietly, a touch of guilt in his tone. After a brief pause he put on an impish little grin. "I reckon you'll be having one of them hide-blistering sermons at service tomorrow."

The big pastor frowned briefly. "Yes, indeed. I have a title for the sermon." He smiled and quoted,

The harvest is plentiful, but the laborers are few.

"I'll fork down thu hay," Draper spoke up hurriedly, started to walk away, stopped, turned back, and half-smiled. "I might be helping on thu building if I'm able t' find thu time."

David smiled broadly. "God bless you, Mr. Draper. That would be a fine Christian gesture if you can spare a few hours of your valuable time." He pulled two coins from his pocket and placed them in the portly man's outstretched pudgy hand. A momentary pause and the young pastor went on cheerfully. "Have a blest day, Mr. Draper. I hope you will escort your family to church tomorrow to witness the presentation of April's cross." As David turned up the dusty street, Fredrick Draper emitted a noncommittal grunt.

The rattle of an approaching wagon reached David's ears. He looked back and saw a small one-horse wagon drawn by a swayback mule pull in at the west side of the livery stable. He shook his head and frowned as the tall, thin, heavy-bearded, balding man drew the modified wagon to a creaking stop. *Well, that must be Thomas Harris*, David thought. *I didn't realize he would come down from Chestnut Mountain with his whiskey wagon today. How will I explain it to the new teacher when she sees a clump of men gathered at that wagon—sipping whiskey?* He glanced at the mountaineer. *Well, maybe I can persuade him to park his wagon somewhere else.*

As the long-boned man stiffly climbed down from the planked seat, Spence put a white, toothy smile on his face and turned back toward the whiskey wagon.

The tall, angular man in the dirty, patched trousers, trying to ignore the approaching man in the minister's garb, stroked the numbness from his posterior with both long-fingered hands. Efficiently, he dropped the tailboard and withdrew four wood dowels from lard-greased rack runners, two from the bottom and two from the top. Cautiously, he gruntingly slipped the top thirty-gallon barrel to the rear of the wagon bed. The mountain man blew dust from a rusting tin cup and thrust it under the dripping barrel spigot. He turned the handle, drained a half cup or so, gulped a significant, appreciative swallow, and coughed lightly as the corn whiskey hit his stomach. *This just might be my best batch*, Thomas Harris told himself, as he usually did, when he felt the flush and tingling sensation of the strong liquid defusing through his bloodstream. He hung the cup on the spigot handle, removed his straw-packed pewter jugs from the wagon bed, and placed them, within easy reach, under the wagon.

T. J. Harris was open for business.

He straightened, gruntingly put a hand to his side, faced the man in the black frock coat, and grinned slightly, exposing tobacco-stained teeth. "I reckon I ain't young as I use t' be." Still holding his little grin, Harris drawled on. "Well, ye being au preacher an' all, I ain't thinkin' ye t' be stoppin' t' get a sip of my prime corn whiskey."

The big pastor, ignoring Harris's attempt at levity, nodded toward the wagon. "Mr. Harris, I'm . . . we are expecting a lady schoolteacher to arrive about noon. I'm afraid if she sees your wagon—men sipping whiskey in the street—she'll get a negative impression."

Harris pushed a long, grimy hand under his dirty shirt and scratched awhile. Finally, he rested a bony haunch on the edge of the tailboard and probed his free hand in a sullied patch pocket, fished out a twist of tobacco and bit off a sizable chunk. "We-ell, Preacher," T. J. Harris responded frowningly, "I'm reckoning she'll be a-gettin' used t' it. I paid half au dollar t' park my wagon an' ain't movin' it, teacher or no teacher." The mountain man eyed David sourly, turned his head, and contemptuously spit a stream of tobacco juice on a wagon wheel.

David forced a thin smile. "I understand your position, Mr. Harris. It was rude of me to interfere. I apologize. Yes, indeed, you paid hard-earned money to rent this space and I shouldn't ask you to move." An under-brow glance at Harris's long face and David saw a thoughtful frown.

The mountain man masticated at his chaw for a few seconds. Finally he maneuvered the big chaw to his other cheek, managed a respectable spit, and changed the subject. "Parson," he almost whispered, "thar's a thing I've been a-thankin' on fur quite a spell. I reckon I ought t' tell a'body. Ye, bein' a parson an' all, seem t' be thu most likely t' not tell who 'twas." He nodded toward the blue-hazed mountains. "Them Doolin boys up thar might jus' have m'hide if'n they knowed who's done spread it about."

"Have your hide!" David spoke louder than intended and Thomas J. Harris glanced across to Draper, still dozing in his chair.

"I'm a-thinkin' an' I'm a-sayin', them Doolin boys air be mighty rough. Mighty rough," he repeated slowly while scratching under his battered straw-hat. "Lyle, thu youngest—'bout seventeen, I reckon him t' be—is gentle as au kitten, but just might be a bit feebleminded. He's thu one thu sheriff put in jail fur stealin' ol' man Washburn's cow an' calf."

"Yes." David nodded. "I met Lyle and two of his brothers a month or so ago. Do you think they will be a problem?"

A significant headshake followed a mirthless chuckle and Harris went on cautiously. "Them ornery boys might be out t' make more trouble than ye can shake a stick at." He glanced at Draper, still dozing in his chair, and went on in a lowered voice. "Word is, they'll be coming fur that boy afore court day. It'll be 'bout time thu pie judging an' hoss racing commences, I heard. Mighty quick t' get their dander up, they air." The slender mountaineer took a deep breath. "I tell ya fur sure, them Doolin's 'ull be comin' down from Chestnut Mountun. I reckon them t' be bringin' long-barreled rifles an' six-shot pistols stuffed in their breeches—loaded an' primed." With tobacco juice drooling from the corners of his mouth into his graying whiskers, TJ glanced at the shotgun barrel protruding from his whiskey wagon. He decided to spit again—and he did.

David was thoughtfully silent for a few seconds. Finally, he nodded, and said seriously, "I'll alert Sheriff Baxter."

Harris raised his bushy brows and paled noticeably. "Ye ain't gonna be tellin' him who toll 'bout it, air ye? It could be my hide if'n ye did."

There was fear in his voice, David realized. "I assure you, Mr. Harris," he responded convincingly, "in that regard your identity will not be revealed by me."

And hesitating momentarily, T. J. Harris breathed a deep sigh of relief. "Now, if'n it won't fur thu oldest one named Harley," he ventured thoughtfully, "I ain't a-believin' them others might not be too bad. He's thu one that jined up with thu Federals in late sixty-four, I'm a-thinkin'." He leaned forward, spit in the dust, and drawled on. "I'd say he won't gone no more'n six months. 'Twas 'bout two weeks after Generul Lee's done give hisself up, till he's done come back a-wearin' a blue uniform of some sort. He brought a fancy-lookin' paper an' sayin' he wus capt'n of thu regulators."

"Regulators," Pastor Spence echoed. "I've never heard—"

"Me neither," Thomas Jefferson Harris cut in, nodded, and drawled on. "It was Harley an' his brother—name bein' Joshua—that rode up t' my place on a big black hoss an' showed me a paper—which they knowed I couldn't read—an' said t' me, 'Yo' house is in thu new state called West Virginie an' you gotta pay us au whiskey tax.' I said back t' them, 'I ain't no more'n two miles close t' West Virginie an' ain't got money t' pay a tax. If'n I did, I wouldn't be a-payin' a tax on my prime whiskey know how.' An' Harley said back t' me, pointin' his finger, 'If'n you ain't a-plannin' t' pay a tax, we'll have t' break up yo' still an' take all yo' prime corn whiskey. We might have t' take that big ol' hog a-rootin' fur chestnuts over thar.'"

"They took your hog!" David exclaimed, frowning.

TJ half-smiled and scratched under his sullied shirt again. "Naw, don't reckon he did. When Harley found Joel—my oldest boy in thu window pointin' my shotgun, they pulled rein an' rode off sayin', 'Ye ain't seen thu last of us.' And I ain't, I'm thinkin'." Harris slipped his hand from beneath his shirt and pulled at his scraggly, tobacco-stained whiskers thoughtfully. "Well, somebody outta thrash them thar boys half t' death with a barrel stave. I 'spect one of these days Harley Doolin 'ull be gettin' his comeuppance," he finally blurted.

Harris could not define comeuppance, but thought it might impress the parson.

And holding back a smile, David changed the subject. "Maybe next week, on the way into town, you will bring Joel and stop by the church. I would like to meet a lad with an Old Testament name."

"Oh, his name didn't come from thu Ol' Testament," TJ retorted firmly, hiding a smile. "It comes from his uncle, my wife's brother. He got hung 'bout two years back fur stealing a hoss an' wagon, I heard."

David frowned and said softly, "I'm sorry about that. The judge seems to have administered harsh penalty for theft of a horse and wagon."

"Oh, folks up thur don't be a-caring much fur lowland courts," Thomas submitted, nodding toward the blue-hazed mountains. "I'd say he got what's called mountun justice. In our neck of thu woods we settles our own troubles. Ol' Jim Farlin, thu owner, figured poor Ol' Joel oughtta be hung 'cause he went an' sold thu load of whiskey that was on his wagon fur ten dollars—hard cash money." Harris paused a moment, spit out his chaw, and went on. "They figured it won't no way a man that's already been hung could take revenge, so they took a vote an' strung him up on thu ol' oak hangin' tree, it's called. Ol' Jim Farlin—thu undecided rascal he is—decided t' change his vote, but it didn't count 'cause poor Ol' Joel was ready well hung."

David frowned at that and said softly, "Well, Mr. Harris, I must go. I'm a little late."

"I 'spect you ain't a-knowin' much 'bout us folks up thar." TJ chuckled, nodding toward the blue-hazed mountains. "A hardy, thrifty lot, we are." A slight headshake and he chuckled again. "But we can be a mite stubborn at times."

As David walked away, Harris smiled, shook his head again, and mumbled. "Well, once in a while, we might jus' come up with a tall tale or two."

*

David Spence stepped up on the boardwalk, buttoned his clerical collar, struck out at a brisk pace, and walked on past Murphy's restaurant. He touched his hat brim and strained a smile at John Williams, a member of the church, quickly stepping past with a guilty look upon his bearded face.

He's heading for Harris's whiskey wagon, David surmised. *There you go, judging again*, he scolded himself silently. Just past the newspaper office he stopped and pulled out his watch.

"What does yo' watcha say, Parson?" a deep voice inquired.

David raised his eyes from the watch, noticed three men lounging on the porch bench by the door and tried to smile. He paused to open the watch cover. "Well, according to my watch, it's nine minutes before ten." As he snapped the cover shut, distant thunder rumbled. He glanced toward the blue mountain heights and said in a friendly voice, "It looks like rain clouds off to the west."

In unison, the three men leaned forward and craned their necks to observe the dark clouds scudding over the Blue Ridge. "Yep, it show does." The big, raw-boned man, sitting on the near end, who seemed to be the principal spokesman, agreed. "It show has been a long dry spell," he drawled on. For emphasis, the wide farmer spat a long arc of brown tobacco juice between gapped teeth and wiped his mouth with the back of a big, hairy hand. "Thu ground's so hard, I can't dig out my 'tatoes. I reckon—" He started again, but David had walked several paces beyond the trio.

"That parson seems t' have a bit of a limp. Wonder how he come by it?" the big spokesman drawled on as they watched David cross the dusty street toward the large two-story redbrick courthouse and hurry on past a Revolutionary War cannon anchored on the lawn.

"It looks like he might be goin' 'round back to thu sheriff's office," the heavy man offered. "Wonder why a parson might be goin' in thar?"

"Could be"—the tall, slack-jawed man at his elbow chuckled and slapped the big man's knee—"he might be a-goin' t' bail one of his church members outta jail." The three men laughed halfheartedly as the dark-suited pastor turned the corner and disappeared.

Chapter 28

—THE DEPUTY—

Sam Baxter's sorrel horse was not at the hitch rail, David noticed as he approached the steps. "I hope he's in," he muttered, found the door open, and stepped inside. Before him, in the small office, stood a large, scarred desk topped by a pair of big-booted feet. Behind the desk, half-hidden by a widespread newspaper, sat a tall, slender young man.

The paper lowered slightly and Roy Taylor frowned across the cluttered desk at the black-suited preacher. "Oh, it's you, Pastor Spence." Deputy Taylor's frown evolved into a weak grin. He folded the paper and swatted at a fly ineffectively."

"Roy, is Sheriff—?"

Taylor interrupted. "Sheriff Baxter's out of town. His sorrel went lame and he left round daylight on a rented mare." Roy Taylor dropped his big-booted feet heavily to the floor and went on. "He said he was heading for his brother's place over near Draper's Meadow. I reckon he's going t' get that half-Arabian stallion he had shipped by rail from somewhere in Tennessee. I reckon him t' be back Monday or Tuesday."

David, only half-hearing the deputy, muttered, "If I had known he was going up there, I would have asked him to stop by Twin Oaks to determine the status of the windows. Rushed them somewhat."

"I'd be glad t' help you," Taylor offered rather tartly.

David nodded and forced a narrow smile. "Yes. I came by to visit a young prisoner. His name is Lyle—Lyle Doolin."

The deputy pulled a desk drawer open and drew out his holstered long-barreled revolver. He tossed it carelessly on the battered desk, reached back in the drawer, withdrew a large key ring, and chuckled mirthlessly. "I consider that big Doolin boy t' be addle-headed. You won't get a bit of sense outta him." He shook his head and forced another chuckle.

The young pastor placed a firm hand on the deputy's shoulder and nodded. "Well, Roy, I believe we're all addled, retarded to some degree, some slightly more than others. It's a matter of perspective, would you say?"

Taylor frowned and reflected on that a few seconds, pulling at his right ear. "Well, I'd say that big Doolin boy's touched more'n most," he finally answered. "He's in cell three. And, Pastor, be sure t' lock thu door when you leave," the tall, slender deputy went on in an authoritative tone as he handed David the key.

And David Spence, detecting a touch of arrogance in Roy's voice, frowned and said nothing.

At cell three he looked between the bars and saw a large, round-faced lad sitting on the floor in the shadows, looking back at him. *He seems to be older, much older than seventeen years*, David said to himself. Then he remembered seeing the big lad at Widow Marshall's barn about two months ago, but not at close range.

"Hello, Lyle," Pastor Spence smiled as he unlocked the door. With rusty hinges squeaking, he pulled it open, entered the dingy, smelly little cell, closed the door behind him, and introduced himself in a quiet voice. "I'm David Spence, a friend of Will Marshall. If it's all right, I'll visit for a few minutes."

The heavy boy failed to respond. He was still staring at the black-clad visitor frowningly. As David drew closer, Lyle leaned forward slightly and light from the high, narrow window fell across his battered face.

"What happened to your face?" David asked, forcing his voice calm as he gazed at the purple bruises and swollen cheeks.

And still frowning at David, the big lad remained silent.

David saw confusion blended with fear in his eyes and drew a deep breath, struggling to control his emotion. Finally he managed a thin smile and said, forcing his voice calm, "I need to talk to Deputy Taylor. I'll be back in a few minutes."

With long, heavy strides David moved hastily to the office. He flung the door open and found the tall deputy with his big feet back on the desk and a widespread newspaper in his hands.

"Did you mistreat that boy?" he bellowed, tearing the paper from the deputy's hands.

The lean deputy paled. "Well—I—I—" he stuttered, toppling the chair as he leaped to his feet. "You . . . you don't understand, Pastor. Let me explain?"

David looked into a pair of darting gray eyes and paused. *You're acting more like a blooming idiot than a preacher*, he scolded himself silently, sighed deeply, and apologized. "I'm sorry, Roy. You said the boy gave you trouble and I assumed—well, under any circumstance, I should never lose my temper."

Deputy Taylor forced a thin smile. "I reckon I should've explained when you came in, but I figured . . ." The deputy's voice trailed off. A long, silent moment fell between them.

Finally Taylor shrugged and continued. "Well, that dumb boy is mighty strong. When I opened the cell door to hand him his supper, he charged out, calling for his mama. It was all I could do to cuff him and drag him back inside. After I went to close the cell door, he started banging his head against the bars and calling for his mama and brothers. I finally got his hands cuffed to his bunk and padded it with pillows and a couple of blankets." Roy hesitated.

The deputy shook his head slightly, forced a weak chuckle, and continued. "This morning when I carried in his breakfast, he seemed to have forgotten thu whole thing. I reckon it takes about a man and a half to handle that boy when he gets all riled up."

David extended his hand and apologized again with some reservation. "I'm sorry, Roy. I misjudged you."

The deputy chuckled, grasped David's hand, and said through a cocky little grin, "Well, as the Bible says, we are all sinners and fall short of God's glory."

"Yes." The tall pastor smiled back at him and added, "I believe I've just proven, God does not exempt preachers." He released Taylor's languid hand and they fell silent for a few seconds.

On the surface Roy's explanation sounds plausible, David told himself. But he looked deep into the deputy's darting gray eyes and found them unreadable—*There's something about him that bothers me*. The pastor admonished himself again. *Judge not that ye be not judged*, he quoted silently. "Well," he sighed, "I hope Lyle's bruises heal before his brothers come down from Chestnut Mountain."

Roy chuckled sardonically. "We ain't worried 'bout them at all. We figured they'd be coming 'bout Wednesday or Thursday. I figured, and the sheriff agreed, that we might need another deputy. We've done hired a new man named Johnny Akers and made plans for dealing with them Doolin boys. I've already put Johnny, untrained as he is, out at Crooked Creek to keep watch." He paused and stroked his clean-shaven chin.

He seems a bit nervous, David thought as the long-legged young man went on.

"Don't think they'll be making more trouble than we can handle." There was little conviction in his voice. Finally the deputy half-smiled and said smoothly, "I've been thinkin' some about visiting your church."

David corrected, his tone friendly. "Well, Roy, it's not my church. It's God's church. I'll look forward to seeing you there soon . . . very soon."

Behind them the floor squeaked and Roy looked past David. He saw the tall, heavy lad standing in the doorway, a confused look on his bruised face. "Get back in your cell!" the deputy blurted and took a step toward Lyle.

David's firm hand grasped his arm and brought him up short. "I'll take care of Lyle," he said evenly, released Roy's long arm, and turned to the frowning boy. He creased his mouth into a friendly smile and said softly, "Let's go back to your room. We'll talk about your mother, your brothers, and your dog."

The heavy boy retreated several steps, his dull eyes studying the big black-garbed man. Finally, a wide smile came upon his broad face. "I reckon you t' be that parson I seed at Will's red barn, ain't ya'? It wuz when we went t' dig up them fishin' worms, ain't it?"

David opened his mouth to answer but Lyle went on. "Ye's gonna be a-bringin' my ma an' my ol' dog named Mud. I reckon ye might be a-takin' me on home, ain't ya'?" Lyle was smiling. "My ma says, parsons help them that's done got hisself in a bit o' trouble," he said excitedly.

Spence gently grasping the big lad's elbow nodded again and forced a smile. "I'll see if I can get you out of trouble," he said softly as he guided the bulky lad back into cell three and closed the barred door behind them.

CHAPTER 29

—A PASSING STORM—

ABOUT TWENTY MINUTES later David pulled a newspaper from the stack by the *Weekly Bugle* office and dropped two coins in a tin cup. Next door, he entered Murphy's restaurant, drew out a ladder-backed chair, seated himself at a small table near the window, and began reading the front page of yesterday's paper with four-day-old news:

> Lyle Doolin, a young man from Chestnut Mountain
>   jailed
> for stealing Jonathon Washburn's cow and calf.
> Trial scheduled for next Friday—
> providing Judge Waters sobers up and shows up.

As David folded the paper, the restaurant door creaked open. He looked up and saw a man enter. It was Shaun O'Leary, a gregarious, heavy man with thick, wavy gray hair. He was dressed in a black, bespoke suite with a silk handkerchief protruding from the ruffled cuff of his left sleeve.

O'Leary ordered coffee, noticed David, and smiled as the heavy woman poured. And the big lawyer, with a steaming white mug in his right hand, carefully walked across the room toward the pastor.

As the massive man passed before a sunlit window, David saw reflecting light from a diamond-studded cravat pin. *Lawyer O'Leary seems to be dressed for a visit to the White House or some major event.* He smiled at the thought.

"May I have the good pleasure to sit with ye, Pastor Spence?" O'Leary asked with a shibboleth of Irish in a booming voice that filled the room. Without waiting for an answer, he carefully placed the overflowing mug on the table and extended a big hand.

David stood, and the lawyer's huge, long-fingered hand engulfed his. "Glad to have your company, Mr. O'Leary," he replied belatedly and motioned toward the empty chair.

"It looks as if we're t' get a wee bit of rain," O'Leary intoned as he smoothed his swallowtail coat and seated himself heavily. "Davie, 'tis a full cup of Mary Murphy's coffee ye need."

Spence shook his head and responded quietly. "I only have a few minutes until the stage arrives if it's on schedule."

"Well, Davie, m'lad, It's by great good fortune we meet this day." The lawyer paused, slurped a long, noisy swig of steaming brew from his big mug, and went on. "There's a thing of importance I need to discuss with ye."

David's brow creased inquisitively. "Well"—he half-smiled—"with my pastoral duties and helping with construction of the school, I've been rather busy."

"You may not have noticed, but I have slipped in to hear your services several times. Sat on a back pew and found a mite too much fire and brimstone in your sermons. Singed my feet, it did." The heavy lawyer laughed loudly, paused a moment, and then went on, his tone turning serious. "I stopped by Sheriff Baxter's office Tuesday morning to interview the Doolin lad. I feel trouble brewing. My desire is to have it settled before it comes to a boil."

As David started to say he had just visited Lyle, the lawyer went on. "'Tis ye that came into my mind that could help settle this matter once and for all."

"But I—"

"Well, now, Davie," the lawyer cut in, "my thought was that ye take a sack of Beulah Marshall's fine corn up to Mr. Washburn's gristmill . . . or maybe pay him a pastoral visit. A stubborn man, he is, but ye have a persuasive manner about ye that would be difficult to resist. 'Tis a matter of justice I'm looking for. If this matter goes to court I'll be defending the lad. 'Twill be my last court case. I'm approaching sixty-five years of age and have a mind to retire to my wee farm in two or three months."

Wee farm indeed, well over three hundred acres, David thought as Shaun O'Leary went on.

"Well, lad, the truth of it is, I've decided to employ an assistant. Would ye be interested in the position? There is a quality about ye that tells me ye are the lad for the position."

"Well, Mr. O'Leary—" David started.

The lawyer raised a thick eyebrow. "Pastoral work, I heard, doesn't pay a living wage and there's little prospect for advancement, I suspect. You may be able to work toward your law degree and make a go of it after I retire. You'll be studying under the best lawyer in the county, and that's no boast. Of course," he chuckled, "I have to admit to being the only lawyer in the county." He slapped the table with the palm of his big hand and concluded with "So there 'tis, m'lad."

Surprised by the heavy lawyer's offer, David paused a thoughtful moment before he replied. "I . . . I'm honored and grateful for your offer, Mr. O'Leary. Would you allow me a few days to think about it? No!" he exclaimed. "I cannot accept your generous offer. I've suddenly realized . . . I'm already rich."

"Already rich!" the lawyer echoed, baffled by the comment.

The chair protested with a low squeak as David straightened and smiled ruefully. "Yes, but not as the world defines riches."

A friendly pat on a black-clad arm and O'Leary took over. "Yes, yes. I well I understand Davie, m'lad. The Lord is your employer and ye have dedicated your life to his work. My thought was that you could assist me on weekdays and attend to your church affairs on Saturday and Sunday."

David pulled his watch from a fob pocket, opened the lid, and observed the time. It was ten twenty.

With mischief in his eyes, the lawyer chuckled. "Ah, it looks as if ye might well be expecting to meet someone. Someone aboard that noon coach, I wager. That young schoolteacher, I'm thinking."

Spence nodded slightly. "The young lady's name is Martha— Martha Kelly. All I know is, she graduated from a female college."

"Well now." O'Leary smiled broadly, the mischief still in his eyes. "If ye are looking for a young lass with that Irish name, she could very well be a likely prospect."

David chuckled mirthlessly, shaking his head. "I seriously doubt it. That is, if you are speaking of marriage." He paused for a thoughtful moment. "Well, as you probably know, it's difficult to find an eligible young lady who would be suitable for . . . willing to be a country preacher's wife."

"Well, lad, I'll be wishing ye all the luck in the world. Yes, indeed. All the luck in the world," O'Leary repeated pleasantly, thrusting out his big hand.

Suddenly the wind quickened and a dust devil swirled down the street. Lightning flashed and thunder boomed, rattling the restaurant windows. Boiling pillows of dark clouds rolled over the mountains and large drops of rain stirred the dusty street for a moment. The clouds opened. The downpour pelting the tin roof discouraged further conversation, and the restaurant patrons watched silently as the street turned into a river of red mud.

Finally, Shaun O'Leary held his empty mug up and said in a voice that easily carried over the roar of the storm. "A bit thirsty I am. I think I will sip another cup of Mary's fine coffee. It would pleasure me to serve ye one as well."

David shook his head. "No, thank you," he almost shouted. "I have to leave in a few minutes."

The passing storm was subsiding as the lawyer returned. He paused, sipped his coffee, and looked through the rain-streaked window at the muddy street. After four or five significant sips Shaun O'Leary sat down, pulled a lace-fringed silk handkerchief from his sleeve, and wiped his sweaty hands.

The rain petered out and the sun slowly returned. And resisting the urge to consult his watch again, David said, forcing his voice casual, "I must hurry to hitch the mare before the coach arrives."

As the lawyer rose to his feet and took the younger man's hand, his face turned serious. "You must visit Mr. Washburn before next week is well gone."

David nodded and responded in a low voice. "Yes, I will, but I'll need your prayers."

O'Leary put a big hand on David's black-clad arm and looked into his blue eyes. "Well then, I'll be saying, good day and good luck."

Chapter 30

—THE TEACHER—

"Thankfully, Mr. Draper left the buggy in the stable bay," David Spence muttered as he backed the mare between the shafts. He buckled the leather straps, hitched the trace chains, and climbed in the buggy. He turned the mare up the muddy street on past three soaked horses tethered to a hitch rail and a parked two-horse wagon. He chuckled quietly when he saw the three farmers sloshing across the street with their overalls hiked above their shoe tops. They kicked their muddy brogans against a bottom step, climbed on the boardwalk, and assumed their position on a bench in front of the telegraph office, too observe the arrival of the noon coach, David figured.

He reined the mare across the street from the telegraph office, swung the buggy around, and pulled close to the boardwalk.

Unless it was delayed by the storm, the coach should arrive soon, David thought. Then he muttered, "That Mountain Road could be dangerous. I pray the passengers are safe."

As if reading his mind, the raw-boned farmer, ensconced on the bench about five or six paces away, spit a stream of tobacco juice in the mud and said loudly, "I hope that thar coach got down thu Mountun Road afore thu rain mudded it up." He paused, shaved another slice of popular onto the growing pile between his muddy shoes, and drawled on. "Some folks have been stove-up right bad a-comin' down that mountunside, when it gets all mudded up, liken it is."

And his two companions, as they usually did, nodded in agreement.

David pulled the newspaper from his coat pocket and pretended to read. After several minutes he raised his worried eyes and looked over the paper toward the courthouse. He saw two farm wagons and a buggy splashing their way through the mud, but the stagecoach was nowhere to be seen.

It appeared the neighborhood had somehow caught wind of the teacher's arrival when a wagon pulled up in front of the barber shop and a dozen or so noisy children spilled onto the boardwalk. And six women, with the help of the driver—a short, stooped, old man—stepped down.

As the women approached the bench, the three farmers, with some hesitation, reluctantly rose to their feet, bowed lightly, frowned some, and stepped aside.

A syncopated nod and the women took custody of the bench.

And behind his newspaper, David Spence smiled.

After twenty minutes of nervous anticipation, he heard the crack of a whip followed by a yell and a growing rumble of heavy wheels. Then suddenly, spraying muddy streams from its wheels, the coach lurched around the courthouse and splashed up the street. Expertly, the driver guided the four lathered horses alongside the boardwalk and, with ruthless force, pulled them to a snorting stop.

David stepped down onto the boardwalk, adjusted his dark coat, and hurried past the snorting, mud-spattered horses to the coach. He stopped and waited impatiently as the stocky man wrapped the lines around the whip socket and clambered from the high seat.

The short, bulky driver pulled out the step-down, opened the coach door, and announced authoritatively. "Now you children make room for the passengers." And the children paid little, if any, noticeable attention as he helped an elderly woman down. A tall thin woman in her forties was next, with a rotund man in a wrinkled black suit following—her husband, David guessed but changed his mind when he saw the short man turn right on the boardwalk and the tall woman turn left. Finally, a slender, young woman gathered her lightly bustled pale-yellow skirts. As she decorously descended from the coach, David Spence caught his breath. He saw a young lady with a striking heart-shaped face, unblemished olive complexion, and slightly pursed lips.

Somewhat surprised by the gaggle of noisy children, she paused momentarily, quickly regained her composure, smiled broadly, and waved a white-gloved hand. The slender teacher raised her eyes, saw

David's wide smile, and flashed even white teeth in response, which brought his heartbeat into a fast gallop.

He looked deep within her sparkling blue-green eyes flecked with gold and lost the ability to speak for a moment.

David finally found his voice. "You . . . you are Ms. Kelly . . . aren't you?" he stumbled huskily.

She looked at him quizzically, nodding lightly. And Martha Kelly, deciding not to tell him she was the girl at the piano when he visited the school in April, smiled and took his outstretched hand. *Not now*, she thought. *Not now.*

"My name is David Spence, a local pastor. We . . . the search committee reserved lodging for you at Beulah Marshall's farm until you can find a suitable location in town. She's prepared a large downstairs room for you."

He was amazed that a woman could travel through dust and mud yet look so fresh and clean. Smilingly, he took the young teacher's cape, escorted her through the milling throng of boisterous children and on past the adult onlookers, who seemed to be sizing the teacher. The men were smiling. The women were frowning. And Roy Taylor, leaning a shoulder against a corner post, seemed to be eyeing the teacher lasciviously, David suspected.

Still on the boardwalk, the tall pastor helped the young lady in the buggy and hurried back for her luggage. He waited a minute or so. Finally he saw the stocky driver unleash her portmanteau from the boot and toss it carelessly onto the boardwalk.

"Take care," David called. "You almost struck one of these children."

"Didn't see them," the driver apologized halfheartedly, a grim little smile on his face.

The tall black-suited minister nodded, gathered up Martha's luggage, plowed through the mud to the buggy, and strapped it to the box behind the seat. With a faint whiff of lilac perfume in his nostrils, he climbed up beside the young teacher, gathered the lines, clucked to the mare, and turned the buggy down the street.

He was pleasantly surprised as the buggy passed the livery stable. The whiskey wagon had disappeared. *Harris is probably hiding behind the stable until we pass*, he thought and smiled inward as they swayed along the muddy road.

"How far is the Marshall's house from town?" Martha asked as the buggy splashed on past the blacksmith shop and town sign.

He cut his eyes to her and flashed a smile. "Well, that depends on the location of the town sign."

She frowned and turned her blue-green eyes upon the pastor.

Then he saw the confused frown and decided to enlighten her. He did and she laughed melodiously as the buggy rattled on through the clinging red foothill mud. They passed the lane to the church and David pointed to the steeple, barely visible above the trees. "That's the local church," he said, trying not to sound prideful.

Martha turned to see but a tall leafy oak blocked her view. She sighed and settled back on the leather seat. "Well," she said and nodded, voice low, "I'm looking forward to the service tomorrow."

There was a long, thoughtful pause.

Finally, she turned her blue-green eyes on him again and flashed an incandescent smile "That is the church you pastor, isn't it?"

David chuckled. "Yes. I'm the pastor . . . temporarily."

"Temporarily," Martha echoed, her smile morphing into a frown.

"Well," he explained cordially, "I was on my way to my uncle's farm near the Shenandoah Valley when Pastor Haskell passed away. Mrs. Marshall persuaded me to pastor the church for a couple of weeks, more or less, while the search committee searches for a schooled replacement." David paused and smiled at her. "It seems they're not searching and I'm still waiting."

The teacher turned her big blue-green eyes on him again and smiled brightly. "I believe you'll be preaching in that church a long, long time."

He heard sincerity in her voice and chuckled lightly. "Well, possibly. If I'm able to find a talented pianist that would probably encourage me to stay a while longer."

With a pursed, confident smile, Martha looked into his eyes and said, "I believe you've found one. I may not be as talented as you would prefer, but nevertheless . . . a pianist."

"Praise the Lord!" Pastor David Spence exclaimed loudly. "This is the moment I've prayed for."

*

About twenty minutes later the buggy rattled out from the trees and on up the low slope to Widow Marshall's large two-story house. The brief summer downpour in town had dwindled to a mild shower by the time it reached the Marshall farm, Spence noticed.

"My room is upstairs," he said, pointing. Then the tall pastor scolded himself silently. *You sound like a young schoolboy.*

"Well"—she pursed her lips, looked at him and nodded slightly, a little smile tugging at the corners of her mouth—"a minister in the house will be . . . comforting."

Martha's smile widened slightly, David thought, flashing her with an under-brow glance.

The buggy rattled across Widow Marshall's wide front yard, and surprisingly, they saw a dozen or so hitched buggies along the edge of the yard and a bevy of saddled horses tethered among the trees. As the buggy drew closer to the house, they saw adults crowding the porch and spilling down the steps to the trampled lawn.

And children seemed to be everywhere, running to and fro like a flock of flitting barnyard chickens after cracked corn.

David reined in the bay, and immediately, they found the buggy surrounded by a gaggle of children and half dozen or so young men that David was sure he had seen in town, ogling the teacher. He glanced at the saddled horses and saw a few with heaving, mud-spattered flanks. *They had galloped along back pathways to arrive ahead of the buggy,* he suspected.

A tall, slender rider pulled his big roan in beside the exhausted animals and threw a long, big-booted leg across the horse's haunches, and with fluid efficiency, Deputy Roy Taylor dismounted. With a polished badge on his blue shirt, a pale-yellow kerchief neatly tied around his neck and a long-barreled revolver in a wide-belted holster, hanging low on his right hip, he was dressed to impress the young ladies. And impress, he did.

Widow Marshall waded through the parting crowd, her sharp brown eyes gauging the teacher as she went. At the buggy, she put on a wide smile, stretched out a welcoming hand, and said loudly, "Well, Pastor. It looks like we got the pick of the litter."

As Martha released the widow's hand, David vaulted from the buggy. "Ms. Kelly," he explained as he rounded a mud-caked rear wheel, "I'm sure Mrs. Marshall meant that as a complement."

Martha took his big outstretched hand and stepped gracefully to the ground. "I know," she responded softly, raised her chin a bit, and looked up at David's wide face, a coy little smile tugging at her lips. "I was born on a farm near Winchester."

Beulah Marshall grasped the young teacher's arm and marched through the milling crowd, toward the front porch. "I decided t' have a little welcoming party," she explained and emitted a low chuckle. "Well, that's what it started out t' be, but it sorta turned into a celebration . . . including a barn dance. I thought that might liven up the party a bit. I hope ye don't mind," the Widow went on and Martha detected excitement in her Irish brogue.

Martha Kelly's blue-green eyes scanned the crowd and stopped on three men in overalls—sitting on the floor with gangly legs dangling from the high porch—busily tuning their fiddles. As she approached the steps, she turned her eyes back to Willie's mother. "I'm looking forward to hearing the violins," she said, a touch of excitement rising in her voice.

Widow Marshall grunted, cupped a hand at her mouth, and spoke in a lowered tone. "I think it best that you call them instruments fiddles. *Violins* sound a mite uppity round here."

And holding back a chuckle, the young teacher smiled. "I'll keep that in mind."

Just then, near the far end of the wide porch, a banjo struck up a tune, plunking a lively ditty that seemed somewhat familiar, but as hard as Martha tried, the words would not come to her. Then the fiddles joined in, and prematurely, the barn dance broke out on Widow Marshall's front porch.

About thirty minutes later a deep bullfrog voice boomed. "Now calm yo'selves, I got some important things t' say." And old Rufus Joyce, the town council chairman, managed, with a few exceptions, to silence the crowd. He lowered his voice a notch and announced with profoundness, "Before we get on with thu celebrating, Widow . . . uh, Mrs. Marshall has asked me t' make known, there ain't gonna be no tomfoolery an' no hard liquor allowed. Ain't allowin' no unmarried mouth kissin' neither," he added belatedly.

And with that, a low groan rippled through the crowd.

Unruffled, Rufus took the top porch step to introduce the teacher, ensconced within a knot of young men, introducing herself. And Roy

Taylor, now standing at her side, had pushed through the crowd to the inner circle, David noticed.

"Come on up here, young lady," the booming voice rang out again. "Come on up here so's we all can get a good look at our paid teacher."

The crowd parted, and with a deep blush in her cheeks, Martha moved toward the steps. And David, somewhat surprised by his boldness, stepped out hurriedly and took her arm. As he guided her to the porch, she cut her blue-green eyes to him and smiled a quiet thank you.

A brief introduction and the chairman, always eager to seize the opportunity, rambled on. And citing no specifics, he praised the ability of the council, under his leadership, to get things done. But as far as anyone knew, they had not lifted a finger to get anything done. After a few minutes he was talking to himself.

"And so—" Old Rufus Joyce caught the aroma of fried chicken and looked up, still talking. "And so, in closing . . ." His deep voice trailed away.

Now under the widespread oak on planked makeshift tables, Widow Marshall's ham, fried chicken, buttermilk biscuits, and a variety of desserts—prepared by the best cooks in the neighborhood—had overwhelmed Rufus Joyce's long-winded pontificating.

"Toss them chicken bones in this pan," Elsie ordered tiredly as she placed a big tin pan against the big oak. "They could be death to dogs," she added.

Twenty minutes later, the pan was full and the feast was over.

With the fiddlers fiddling and the banjo player plunking, the guests were marching toward the big red barn. As they walked along with the rhythm of flowing music, the church choir, led by Pastor David Spence's rich baritone voice, put words to the music:

> Come, we that love the Lord, and let our joys be known.
> Join In a song with sweet accord, and thus surround
>   the throne,
> Thus surround the throne, And thus surround the
>   throne.
> We're marching to Zion, Beautiful, beautiful Zion;
> we're marching upward to Zion, the beautiful city of
>   God . . .

CHAPTER 31

—THE BELL TOLLS—

EXCEPT FOR THE lingering fog girding the base of Chestnut Mountain, Sunday, it seemed, would turn out to be a comfortable, cloudless day.

Now, Beulah Marshall, knowing Martha Kelly would be playing the piano and Lilly awarded a hand-hammered cross, had made detailed arrangements for transportation to the overflowing church service. In cahoots with her sister, Nora, and an occasional parley with Pastor Spence, the widow decided timing for their arrival would be a major factor. The pastor, as usual, would rein Jake at the church an hour or so before service, and Nora's crowded carriage followed by Willie, reluctantly riding a saddled plow horse, would be unloading at the steps about ten thirty. Widow Marshall and Lilly would arrive precisely two minutes before the service and saunter down the aisle in cadence with the tolling bell. The timing seemed to be perfect—but for one minor flaw.

*

At his station under the bell rope, Oscar Stanley, the bell ringer, waited for eleven o'clock and the presentation of the hand-hammered crosses to three girls, including his daughter, Sarah.

And slouched against the wall beside him, stood Fred Draper, a close friend for twenty-some-odd years. Both men were heavy and both were friendly, but except the red rose in their lapels, that's where the similarity ended. Stanley was a tall, heavily muscled, hardworking man. Draper was short, fat, and lazy.

They were swapping congratulations when Oscar pulled the turnip watch from his vest pocket. "It ought t' be—" He looked at the watch. His wide face paled. He put the watch to his ear. "It's stopped!" he exclaimed. "What does your watch say, Fred?"

Hastily, Draper grasped a silver chain dangling from his portliness and pulled out his watch. "It's dead on eleven, but—"

The blacksmith jerked the rope and the bell tolled. He kept pulling and the bell kept ringing.

Fred Draper spoke up loudly. "I reckon my watch t' be about five minutes fast."

The bell rang on. Oscar Stanley had failed to hear the comment.

As the peal of the church bell faded, Widow Marshall's black, yellow-spoke buggy appeared, coming licitly-split from the trees to the wide yard with Lilly gripping the lines and the widow flailing the mare unmercifully while holding her wide, flowery, go-to-meeting Sunday bonnet on her head.

It was a sight to behold. But except for a couple of children peering out an open window, no one saw. The parishioners were busily thumbing in their songbook to page 42. And then, after standing two long months, gathering dust, Nora McBride's upright piano came to life.

Pastor David Spence, surprised by Ms. Martha Kelly's ability at the keyboard, smiled broadly as the choir chimed in:

> Rock of ages, cleft for me, let me hide myself in Thee;
> Let the water and the blood, From Thy wounded side
>   which flowed,
> Be of sin the double cure, Save from wrath and make
>   me pure . . .

And the congregation, now well into the second stanza, paid scant attention as the frustrated widow, with Lilly trailing behind, huffed down the center aisle toward her third-row seat.

While singing the last stanza, David ventured a glance toward the piano and the young pianist, clad in a light-blue dress. He glanced again and met her smiling blue-green eyes and his big baritone voice faded away. Good Lord! *That's the girl I saw at the piano in that school near Farmville,* he suddenly realized. *I believe she recognized me when she arrived. Why didn't she tell me?* he wondered as the choir, a tad confused, sang on and ended with

> Rock of ages, cleft for me,
> let me hide myself in Thee.

And the young pastor, still a bit discombobulated, moved slowly to the pulpit, gathered up three small neatly wrapped packages, and motioned to the girls sitting anxiously beside their proud parents on the front row. As he moved past the pulpit, the girls, bedecked in their best Sunday dresses, rose and walked shyly to the podium.

David cleared his throat and ran his eyes across the girls' parents, on to the piano and Ms. Martha Kelly's big blue-green eyes looking back at him.

He cleared his throat again, looked down at the girls, smiled, raised his eyes to the congregation, and announced sincerely, "These three girls, with encouragement from their parents, have managed to read the New Testament within two months and—"

The clapping, interposed with a number of cheers and some whistling, broke out and went on for well over a minute before the big pastor could resume the presentation.

"And on behalf of members of the church," David finally announced in a pulpit voice, "I consider it an honor to present these gifts to April Draper, Lilly McBride, and Sarah Stanley." As he handed the anxious girls their little packages, he went on in a lowered tone. "I pray each of you will be blessed by your gift forever."

Lilly turned to leave and David said quietly, "Open the presents for the congregation to see." He looked over to the girls' smiling parents and motioned them forward.

They rose slowly with some bewilderment and shuffled in behind the girls, now busily ripping paper and opening their little boxes.

"Hold your necklace high for all to see and then have a parent fasten it around your neck," David advised in a muted voice. He motioned to the choir and they rose to their feet, hymnals at the ready position.

*

The sun was high in the sky and the parishioners were well into the final hymn when the old mule pulled the creaking whiskey wagon past the blacksmith shop and on toward the treelined lane, leading to the church.

Slumped on the wagon seat with lines slack in his hands and chin lolling on his chest, Thomas Jefferson Harris seemed dead to the world around him as the clear sound of a piano accompanied by the congregation singing "Amazing Grace" floated through the open windows. The swayback mule twitched his ears and, with the gentle slosh of liquid libation in the bottom barrel, plodded slowly homeward as Pastor Spence's resonant voice rose in perfect vibrato on the last stanza: "When we've been there ten thousand years, bright shining as the sun, we've no less days to sing God's praise than when we'd first begun."

CHAPTER 32

—ANY MAN'S LIFE—

IT WAS MONDAY and the sun was well above the trees when David guided the mare across the covered bridge, turned the buggy on the narrow Mountain Road, and trotted Beulah Marshall's bay upstream toward Washburn's gristmill.

About thirty minutes later the tall preacher, with a prayer on his lips, reined the snorting horse at the mill, climbed down, and cast an encompassing glance at the weathered two-story log building chinked with gray clay from the creek bed. He saw a leaky millrace mounted high on the overshot mill and rushing water tumbling on a tall slow-turning wheel.

David shouldered a heavy grass sack, climbed the steps, paused at the doorway and squinted in the mill's dusty dimness.

"Come on in," the dim figure called as he reached up and pulled the end of a long wooden lever. A cogged gear disengaged from the shaft. The tall splashing wheel and the rumbling millstone gradually slowed, stopped, and went silent.

"Find a place t' put your corn over there," the chubby man said tartly, nodding toward a row of full sacks lining the wall. "I'll tag it soon's I get this sack of cornmeal weighed."

David's eyes adjusted to the dimness as the stubby man hoisted a sack on the cradle. "Hello, George," the tall pastor said good-humoredly. "This seems to be a busy day."

George chuckled mirthlessly as he adjusted the weights. "I'd say, thu milling business sorta comes and goes." He shook his graying head and chuckled again. "This here seems t' be one of them comin' days."

Pastor Spence smiled thinly. "Well, if you are too busy, Mrs. Marshall's corn can wait a day or two." The man started to respond, but David went on. "I would like to speak with Mr. Washburn, if he's available."

George Simpson's wide brow creased. "He's up there," he said in a low, confidential voice, raising his brown eyes toward the ceiling. "He ain't admitting it, but I can see it in his face. He's been mighty poorly fur more'n a week now."

"Have you urged him to see Dr. Dickerson?" David asked softly, concern in his voice.

The short, heavy man shrugged helplessly. "I tried that . . . more'n once . . . didn't work. He's a good man but stubborn as a balky Tennessee mule."

"Parson, is that you I'm a-hearin' down thar?" Jonathan Washburn's weak voice quavered down the stairs.

"Yes. Can I come up for a short visit?" David answered just loud enough for him to hear.

"Come on up. I was kinda expectin' you t' be passin' this away after a while."

Before David topped the stairs he could hear the miller's heavy breathing. He entered the small room across from the staircase and found Mr. Washburn in a narrow bed propped against a large feather-stuffed pillow, puffing smoke from a cob pipe.

David took the withered hand and spoke in a low sympathetic tone. "I'm sorry you're not feeling well, Mr. Washburn."

"I was feelin' right pert till I got a pain in m'chest 'bout a week ago, reckon it was." The miller gestured his pipestem toward a small cane-bottomed chair, puffed more smoke, and went on thoughtfully. "Gettin' old, I reckon."

"Oh, you're not so old." Spence tried to sound encouraging. "You will probably have many good years ahead if you take care of yourself. But as you well know, only God knows the span of any man's life." He sat down and the wobbly chair protested.

"Well"—Jonathan Washburn paused to pull a wrinkled yellow flimsy from beneath the pillow—"I wrote this here paper, as best I could, t' tell who'll be a-gettin' my belongin's."

He paused again, sucked a weak puff from his cob pipe, and almost whispered. "Would ye be a-willin' t' pin yo' name on this here paper an' take it on t' Lawyer O'Leary fur safekeepin' till I've done passed on t' heaven?" he went on weakly, extending the yellow flimsy in a withered, shaky hand. "Two or three town people's a-tryin' t' buy me out lately fur no more'n half what my place t' be worth. Thought I'd jus' make up au paper t' say who gets what."

David smiled tolerantly, took the flimsy from the shriveled hand, and said softly, "I'll sign your will and take it to Lawyer O'Leary, if you give me permission to send Dr. Dickerson up here."

Washburn scratched in his ragged gray whiskers awhile. Plainly he hadn't counted on David's suggestion that he see a doctor. Finally he responded reluctantly. "W-ell, w-ell—don't reckon it'll hurt none. Ain't a-thinkin' it t' help much neither," he mumbled.

The black-garbed preacher coughed lightly and spoke up softly. "Well, Mr. Washburn, there's an important matter we need to discuss before I leave."

The miller opened his mouth to speak but David went on. "It concerns the Doolin lad. He's in jail, charged with stealing your cow and calf."

"Charged," Washburn croaked, flourishing his cob pipe. "He's done admitted t' takin' them animals. Ain't no doubt 'bout that. 'Sides, he went an' left thu gate open an' let all my livestock out. George will swear t' that."

"Did George see him open the gate?" David asked gently.

Washburn was scratching in his whiskers again. "Didn't see him but found thu bell cow an' calf t' be missing when he went out t' round up them two mares an' thu other milk cow."

Spence shrugged and spoke as soothingly as he could. "Well, it is possible someone else left the gate open. The animals may have wandered away before the boy found them, and not knowing the owner, he could have led the cow, with the calf following, up to his home. You probably know he's somewhat retarded."

"Air ye a-sayin', he's crazy?" Washburn shook his head slowly and frowned. "Well, I shore didn't know him t' be crazy. I figured him t' be a bit addled, though."

"I have heard from a reliable source," David informed him seriously, "that Lyle's brothers will, more than likely, come down from Chestnut Mountain before court day and attempt to break him out of jail."

Jonathan Washburn nodded thoughtfully while shakily thumbing a fresh load of tobacco in his cob pipe. He flared a match on the bedpost, lit up, and puffed weakly. A few thoughtful seconds and he nodded again, pulled the pipestem from his thin bluish lips, and mumbled. "I 'spect they might jus' do that. An' they'll have t' be a-comin' by this a-way t' get t' town."

"Mr. Washburn," David Spence offered quietly, placing a big hand on the old man's bony shoulder, "we may be able to avoid this disaster if you decide not to press charges."

Still incredulous, the old man shook his disheveled, balding gray head. "They've done ready been pressed. Ye can't jus' go on an' unpress a thing that's already been pressed, can ye?"

David half-smiled. "Well, if you agree, I'll consult Lawyer O'Leary. He'll be representing the lad if it goes to court." David sighed and went on calmly. "If there is a trial, you and George will probably have to testify."

The miller reflectively sucked on a while. Finally he pulled the stem from his thin bluish lips and drawled weakly, "It ain't fit fur a'body t' get off from bein' jailed after stealin' a man's livestock. Well, I reckon I'll have t' study on that awhile. Come on back in two or three days. After I get my doctorin' done with, I 'spect I'll be decided by then. But I ain't forgettin' two of them ornery Doolin boys a-comin' in here with that thar long-barreled gun au while back." His quavering voice had lowered to a whisper.

"But Lyle wasn't—" David stopped abruptly, sighed, rose to his feet, and nodded, knowing it would be useless to press the old man. "Well," he said politely, "I'll keep you in my prayers and see you in a couple of days, Lord willing."

As the pastor descended the creaky stairs, he noticed George Simpson standing by the open door and looking up, a worried frown creasing his wide brow. David started to speak but saw George with a thick finger at his tight lips and remained silent.

A swift motion toward the doorway and the stumpy man stepped out onto the narrow porch. And David, slightly puzzled, followed him out into the bright sunlight.

"I reckon you might already know, Mr. Washburn's been forgettin' things fur a while," George almost whispered. "I figured I oughtta be a-tellin' you about him leaving that pasture gate open hisself more often than not," he went on in a tone of confidentiality.

The tall pastor scratched his ear thoughtfully for several seconds. "Well, after observing his condition, I think it would be wise to avoid the issue until after Dr. Dickerson's visit," David suggested, his voice low.

Simpson nodded lightly. "I 'spect you might be right about that. Ain't no need t' get him all riled up."

"Hopefully, I'll be able to rush the doctor out here tomorrow morning." David sighed as he stepped down from the little porch. He climbed in the buggy. With a wave, followed by a friendly smile, he reined the mare on the Mountain Road and put her in a fast trot toward the Marshall farm.

*

Early the next day, at a small table in Murphy's restaurant, slowly sipping coffee, David waited for the doctor. "He always comes by round eight o'clock for breakfast and a cup or two of coffee before going up to his office," Edna Murphy had told him. Eight o'clock came and went, but the doctor had failed to appear.

Now sipping from his third cup, David was becoming impatient. He drew out his watch, opened the cover, and checked the time. It was eight thirty-six.

"More coffee?" the heavy woman asked in her low, almost manly voice.

David turned, raised his eyes, and smiled up at the heavy woman with a big steaming coffeepot, firmly grasped in the folds of her gathered snow-white apron. She was about sixty, maybe a little older, he guessed. "You have good coffee, but three cups is my limit. It seems Dr.—"

"Glory be. He's coming in the door now," Edna Murphy said, her deep voice rising.

"I'll have the usual," the chubby doctor ordered in a reticent voice while eyeing David sourly.

The big preacher rose to his feet, faced the doctor, smiled amiably, extended his wide hand, and said cordially, "Sit with me for breakfast. I've been sipping Edna's good coffee while waiting for your arrival."

The doctor, expecting a sermon, reluctantly shook David's hand, forced a weak smile, and gruntingly lowered his big body into the chair across from the pastor. "Are you ailing?" Dickerson asked frowningly, knowing he wasn't.

"No," David answered softly. "I'm concerned about Mr. Washburn's—"

The portly doctor was shaking his head. "Mr. Washburn is . . . He's dead."

"He's dead!" Spence echoed, deep surprise in his voice.

Dr. Dickerson nodded somberly. "George got me out of bed about four o'clock this morning. When I arrived at the mill, I found him on the floor near his bed—already dead."

"I . . . well, I believe," David said softly, "Mr. Washburn realized he was near death when I visited him yesterday. He gave me a scribbled will for Lawyer O'Leary."

The heavy doctor drummed his fingers on the table and thoughtfully eyed David as Edna Murphy smilingly placed a steaming cup of coffee before him.

"Be back with the ham and eggs in a minute or two," she said quietly, raising her sharp blue eyes to David. Her smile widened and she went on. "Parson, about the coffee, I doubt you t' be changing ya mind." She saw him shaking his head, turned, and hurried away.

A noisy slurp from his cup and Dickerson frowned. "Could you . . . would it be too presumptuous to ask who will inherit Mr. Washburn's property?" he asked hesitantly.

A flicker of anger crossed Pastor Spence's wide face. "No," he answered, forcing his voice calm. "It would be highly unethical to reveal the contents of his will. And I'm sure, it would be unethical to reveal the witness's signature."

"Well, well, Pastor," the big doctor stumbled, "I had for some time, uh . . . been discussing with him that a friend and myself might be interested in purchasing his property."

David got to his feet. "You'll probably know in a few days," he said calmly. "I'm on my way to deliver Mr. Washburn's will to Lawyer O'Leary."

*

About twenty minutes later David knocked lightly at the door, and the lawyer's weighty voice boomed. "Come on in. Well, Davie, m'lad, 'tis good t' see you once again," O'Leary boomed on from behind his big cluttered desk as Spence came into the office. Gruntingly, he rose to his feet, stretched a big arm over a stack of papers, took David's hand firmly, and shook it vigorously.

David Spence forced a little smile. "It's good to see you as well, Mr. O'Leary, but I bring sad news." He paused to pull the yellow scribbled will from an inner pocket. "Yesterday Mr. Washburn asked me to bring you his will."

"Well, I'll file it," the lawyer said as he took the wrinkled flimsy and stepped out from his desk.

"I regret to tell you." David sighed sadly. "Dr. Dickerson found him dead early this morning."

O'Leary stopped. "How did he die?" he asked softly while looking down at Washburn's scribbled script.

"Probably heart failure," David sighed. "Yesterday, when I visited him he seemed fragile . . . very fragile."

Still perusing the yellow flimsy, Shaun O'Leary moved back to his tall, worn chair. "Well, looks t' be George Simpson I'll be dealing with on behalf of the Doolin lad," he said seriously.

David spoke confidently. "Well, I doubt you'll have a problem with George."

O'Leary responded thoughtfully. "Well then, it might do well for me to rush this affair up a bit. May be I can bail the Doolin lad before court day."

Spence nodded. "If George agrees to drop the charges, I'm sure I can find someone to post bail."

"Good, good. I'll be riding out about noontide to converse with him," the lawyer said with a light shake of his big head.

CHAPTER 33

—CONFRONTATION—

THE WARM MORNING sun was just above the eastern horizon when Deputy Johnny Akers reined his spotted mare in the shade of a Hickory tree and swung easily from the old Grimsley saddle.

"Just wasting time," he complained to the mare while looking through the bushes at the covered bridge. "Now that Lyle was already bonded out till court day, there's no need for Sheriff Baxter sending me out here to watch for them Doolin boys. Being court day's tomorrow, it just don't make sense at all. It just don't make sense at all," he repeated, still looking through the bushes. *Well, being only two weeks a deputy, I reckon the sheriff and Roy might be planning to keep me outta the ruckus, if one comes along. Could be, they're thinking the Doolin boys ain't got the word yet*, the young fair-haired deputy thought.

Impatiently, he watched a bevy of riders flowing out from the bridge, including half dozen or so females riding sidesaddle, their colorful calico dust aprons parading along in the bright sunlight. And round ten o'clock, he saw, rumbling out from the shadows of the covered bridge, a heavily loaded Conestoga wagon drawn by four large draft horses.

Another hour passed and the mare, growing restless, began snorting and pawing the ground. With a firm hand gripping the bridle, Johnny said quietly, "I know. I'm a bit restless myself." He glanced at the shrinking shadows. "It looks to be near noontime," he muttered. Then he thought, *I'll keep watch another half hour or so before I ride back into town. If I'm here much longer, I won't be able to get in on the race. I sure wish I had a watch*, he thought on.

The distant rumble of fast-turning wheels and echoing beat of shod hooves brought his eyes back to the bridge. With bated breath, Johnny Akers hurriedly looped the reins around the mare's spotted neck and watched—and waited.

Suddenly, a big black stallion drawing a one-horse wagon bolted out from the covered bridge into the bright sunlight.

And immediately, Akers recognized the men, two seated and one standing behind them—his rifle butt at his hip—struggling to stay upright.

Johnny could feel his heart pounding as he vaulted aboard the mare and pressed her into a long, hard gallop up the dusty road. At breakneck speed, he topped the knoll and galloped the lathered spotted mare down the slope to Main Street and on past the courthouse. He pulled the jaded animal to a snorting stop at the hitch rail, tossed the reins aside, and bolted from the saddle. With bated breath he raced into the sheriff's office, now crowded with eight nervous men—a couple armed with long-barreled rifles and the rest with antiquated shotguns.

"Them Doolin boys are coming," Johnny croaked anxiously. "They're armed to thu teeth and coming on fast," he added hoarsely.

"Ned," Sheriff Baxter ordered hurriedly, gesturing, "you and Randy climb up and take position behind Covington's big sign. And hurry up." As the two nervous men rushed toward the door Baxter called, "Hold your fire till you see one of them Doolin boys raising his rifle." He sighed. "Don't need unnecessary shooting."

*

David had cantered the big gelding down the treelined lane from the church, reined him on the road, and headed toward Edgewood, when he heard the rattle of approaching wheels. He turned in the saddle and squinted down the slope. About fifty yards away, he spotted a one-horse wagon drawn by a tiring black stallion coming up the long slope in a slow trot. "It's the Doolin boys," he muttered and jerked the surprised horse crosswise.

And with the rutted road blocked by the big gray gelding, Harley Doolin's long arms drew lines viciously. The ribbed bit bowed the stallion's neck and the wagon jerked to a dusty stop.

David found three cocked rifles pointing at his wide chest and forced a thin smile. Cautiously he swung down and led Jake on past the jaded stallion to the wagon. He saw the weapon's long barrels slowly sagging. And still trying to hold his smile, the big pastor released a pent-up breath and looked up at their frowning sun-browned faces. "I guess you're heading to town," he said in a friendly voice, gesturing. "And I suppose you're planning to race the big stallion, maybe participate in the target-shooting contest."

Harley shook his head and chuckled contemptuously. "We're a-heading fur town, but don't reckon we'll be contesting none. Now, Parson"—he waved his rifle menacingly—"you'll be a-getting that ugly hoss outta thu way or I'm gonna blow his brains clean out."

David held up a hand and warned firmly, "If you go into town brandishing those rifles, I fear you will not come out alive. The sheriff's awaiting your arrival with his deputies and over half dozen fully armed, deputized citizens."

"We've done been dishonored by locking our youngest brother up in jail," Harley responded hotly. "Ain't no way we can stand fur that."

"But I thought you knew," David said softly, "he's no longer in jail. He's bailed out and with Will at the Marshall farm."

"What's *bailed* meaning?" Joshua asked confusedly.

David started to answer, but Harley spoke up sarcastically. "It's meaning he's jus' outta jail till he goes t' court. That's being tomorrow, I'm a-thankin'."

"Yes. He will have to appear in court tomorrow," the tall pastor explained calmly, "but it's just a formality. I'm sure the charges against Lyle will be voided—dropped—and he will be released."

"Are ye a-saying old man Washburn's gonna let Lyle off'n thu hook?" Harley asked suspiciously.

David shook his head slowly and spoke softly. "Mr. Washburn is dead. His helper, George Simpson, inherited the property and has agreed to drop the charges."

"Parson," Zack Doolin said thoughtfully, "ye reckon it might be safe fur us t' go into town an' join in on thu shooting. My arms done got healed up an' I'm a mighty good shooter, with a rifled musket, that is." He turned his eyes on Harley and half-smiled. "And my oldest brother keeps a-saying his black stallion's thu fastest critter in these parts. I 'spect he might just want t' be proving it."

Pastor Spence nodded. "Well, since you haven't broken any law *yet* and your brothers agree to follow my instructions, I should be able to persuade Sheriff Baxter to disband the deputized citizens and allow you to join in the . . . festivities."

Harley spoke up forcefully. "It jus' ain't no way I'm giving up my rifle."

"Me neither," Joshua chimed in. "I ain't trusting them lowlanders no how . . . 'cept you, Preacher. I ain't taking you t' be one o' them outright lowlanders," he explained.

David nodded, half-smiling. "Would you agree to let me keep your cartridges and dole them out just before the shooting contest?"

The Doolins huddled in the wagon, mumbling in argument for two, maybe three minutes.

Finally Joshua turned to David and asked frowningly, "What do ye reckon *dole* might be?"

Pastor Spence coughed to cover a smile. "Basically, it means I'll hand out your cartridges as you need them."

"Reckon I ain't—" Harley started.

"I'm trusting thu parson," Zack spoke up boldly. "He's done fixed my arm an' we ought t' be obliged fur that."

The Doolins huddled again.

A short parley and Zack turned in the wagon. He looked down at the black-clad pastor and smiled. "We're agreeing t' have ye hold on t' our cartridges whilst we get in on thu shooting part. That is, if'n ye'd be agreeing t' let Harley ride in thu race an' . . . an' us come by thu Marshall place t' see our youngest brother."

A smile crawled across David's wide face. "I think I can arrange for you to enter the target shooting. And if the stallion has rested enough, maybe Harley can enter him in the race." A glance at the jaded horse and he went on. "I'm sure Will Marshall and his mother will welcome you with open arms." He turned his eyes on Zack and smiled. "I need to borrow your rifle for a while."

Zack opened his mouth to complain, but the big pastor explained, "I'll tie my handkerchief to the rifle and hold it up as I ride about ten or fifteen yards ahead of the wagon to the sheriff's office. And Harley, you and Joshua—to avoid encountering a nervous trigger finger—leave your weapons in the wagon bed while I go inside to converse with Sheriff Baxter."

The Doolins exchanged glances. Zack mouthed "Converse" but said nothing.

*

Cautiously, with his white handkerchief waving in a light breeze and the one-horse wagon trailing behind, the black-clad pastor trotted the big gelding down the dusty street.

David noticed movement of shadows and glanced up. He saw two bobbing hats protruding above Edward Covington's big sign and two long rifles seemingly pointing down at the approaching wagon.

He whirled Jake and galloped back to the wagon. He saw Harley and Joshua reaching down for their rifles and reined the gelding in close to block the view from the roof, he hoped.

"Leave those weapons on the floor," David Spence ordered forcefully, turning his eyes back to the sign. The rifles that had been pointed at the wagon only a few seconds ago were now gone.

As the wagon slowly passed the courthouse, Pastor Spence spotted the sheriff standing on the porch before his office with his Winchester cradled in his left arm and, likewise armed, the two deputies, Akers at his right and Taylor at his left.

Still holding the long-barreled rifled musket in his right hand, David swung down from the gelding. He saw a little smile tugging at Baxter's thick lips and gestured toward the wagon. "Sheriff, if you agree, the Doolin boys would like to participate in the horse race and shooting contest. I have custody of their cartridges."

Baxter's smile widened. He shouldered the Winchester, stepped down, strolled over to the wagon, and spoke up without rancor. "You boys made the right decision. Being in the street and outgunned, I'm sure you'd be dead by now." He turned and put a hand on David's arm. "You ought to thank Pastor Spence for saving your hides. Climb down and make sure those rifles are uncapped," Sheriff Baxter went on, his tone turning serious."

Harley's big stallion tossed his head and pawed at the ground. "My hoss looks t' need feed an' water," he drawled sullenly.

David nodded slightly and looked the sheriff in the eye. "I believe you can trust the Doolins to turn the wagon back to the livery stable and unhitch the stallion for water and fodder."

"Well," Baxter responded thoughtfully, "it will be all right if you go with them and hold onto their cartridges."

Followed by a few handshakes and several arm slaps, some of the deputized men melted away. But several, David noticed as he mounted the tall horse, were now ensconced firmly on the porch bench, hoping to pick up a tidbit of repeatable information.

CHAPTER 34

—THE RACE—

ZACK DOOLIN AND Pastor Spence were standing in the stable bay watching the gray gelding nip at a small pile of hay.

"Parson, you figure on racing that tall hoss?" Zack drawled frowningly.

David chuckled and cocked his head. "Well, Beulah Marshall said, there's more to that animal than meets the eye. I believe she's right about that, but the race up to the gristmill and back would require a much lighter rider." He cut his eyes to the lanky lad. "Yes, indeed. A rider about your weight. And Zack, I assure you, speed will not be the winning factor in this race. It will be endurance."

"What ye reckon *endurance* might be?" Zack Doolin queried, brow creased.

David chuckled again, laid a long arm across his shoulders, and said pleasantly, "Well, I define endurance as how far you can run and how quick you arrive at your destination."

Still puzzled, Zack Doolin forced a narrow smile and said cautiously, "Well, I ain't figuring that gray hoss t' beat out Harley's black." He glanced at the tall gelding. His smile widened and he added softly, "But I'd shore like t' try."

David drew out his watch, opened the cover, and checked the time. "The race is scheduled to start in about twenty minutes. We need to water Jake and be at the starting line well before then." He nodded toward Harley, standing outside at the water trough, holding his black stallion's reins. "Maybe you should tell your brother to saddle his horse soon if he intends to enter the race."

Zeke laughed. "I'm a-thinking you saw that saddle in our wagon on thu way t' town."

Pastor David Spence smiled, pulled the reluctant horse's head up, and led him out to the watering trough. About five minutes later, with stirrups adjusted and Zeke in the saddle, David led the gelding down Main Street toward the courthouse. "You see that man with the red band around his arm? You'll have to sign up for the race over there." He pointed, and Zack took notice of a round-shouldered little man seated rather importantly at a small rickety table just beyond the courthouse lawn.

Zack swung down and shouldered his way through the growing crowd to the table. Without a word, the diminutive man handed him a pencil stub and Zack noticed six signatures and several x marks as he licked the leaded end of the short pencil. And slowly, very slowly he printed his name.

"It looks like we're gonna have t' have two rows at thu starting line." Zack heard the skinny man at the table tell a heavy, older man standing at his elbow. "It bein' hot like 'tis, I didn't 'spect t' have a dozen sign up."

The older man chuckled. "Well, I reckon it could be 'cause Widow Marshall's putting up another Jersey heifer agin this year—fur thu winner."

A sour look and the man at the table handed Zack a slip of paper. "Reckon you t' be in thu second row," he said sullenly. "And be sure t' grab up a yellow ribbon at thu mill porch." Still sullen, he went on. "If'n you don't you'll be disqualified fur shortcutting. Had that happen couple years back, it was," the little man mumbled, cut his gaze back to the older man, and resumed their conversation.

"Well, Earnest, I'm reckoning, 'taint much chance of a'body winning that heifer, 'cepting Roy's stallion."

Zack made his way through the noisy crowd to David and glanced at the little slip of paper. "I got number nine," he informed the pastor. "It looks like we might have t' be in thu second row."

"Do you know which row the roan is in?" David asked thoughtfully, scratching his left ear.

"Naw," Zack responded, shook his head slightly, and half-smiled. "'Fore we find out, I 'spect we're gonna have t' wait till we get ourselves lined up."

David nodded and chuckled lightly. "Well, at that distance, I doubt it matters."

Zack's smile widened. "Well, it ain't thu roan I'm thinking about. I 'spect I'll be keeping a sharp eye on Harley's black."

*

Eleven participants, two riding bareback and one on a stubborn mule, reined their animals into position as best they could. The big mule, fighting the bit, ran in a circle, scattering nearby animals until finally the long-legged rider slacked the reins and the mule galloped wildly away.

Harley's black stallion jerked his head against the firm rein, snorting, sidling.

Johnny Akers reined hard and pulled his left foot from the stirrup just before the black collided with his spotted mare.

"Get that stallion lined up!" Earl Carson yelled.

"I reckon that mare t' be in season!" Harley yelled back.

"Thu rules don't say nothing 'bout mares in season," Earl retorted firmly. "I'm reminding," he yelled again, "if you don't come back with a yellow ribbon, you ain't winning. This race is nigh onto a five-mile run up to thu gristmill an' five back. Is yawl ready?" He thrust his weapon skyward and waited, the heavy pistol wavering, until some semblance of order was established, and the animals' heads pointed basically in the right direction.

A loud *blam!* and the blast from his big horse pistol reverberated throughout the town. The startled animals bolted, and a cloud of acrid powder smoke momentarily blinded Earl and quite a few nearby spectators.

Startled, Zack got the gelding going a fraction of a second late and found himself near the rear. And with clods of dirt from shod hooves filling the air, he finally regained his composure and reined Jake a bit outside to avoid the flying dusty debris. He gave the eager gelding the reins and slowly closed on the pack. The young mountaineer glanced past the galloping horses and found the big roan in the lead by at least six lengths, pulling away.

Roy's roan gained the "Blacksmith Shop" with well over a ten-length lead, passed the town sign, and galloped on down the long slope, effortless, it seemed to Zack.

Somewhat strung out, the dust-ridden horses pounded across the bridge and entered the turn at the Mountain Road. About two lengths ahead and off to his left, Zack saw out of the corner of his eye a large mare cut to the inside and lose her footing. He jerked hard, barely avoided the falling animal, and felt Jake slip slightly. His heart leaped. He relaxed the reins, and momentum carried the big gelding in a slightly wider arc than he anticipated. "Stay to thu outside," Zack advised the horse. "Might be we can make up a bit of ground on thu curvy parts."

The gelding was now fourth and closing fast, but Zack Doolin, remembering David's advice, pulled reins and slowed the eager horse, now galloping up the Mountain Road toward the gristmill.

"Got a ways t' go yet," he muttered, dragging a sleeve across his blinking, sweat-filled eyes.

Now about a dozen lengths ahead of the pack and two lengths behind Harley's black, Roy's big roan managed somehow to cling to the inside of the hard road as he rounded a sharp curve into a grove of oak trees. The big roan emerged from the trees, his flying hooves disgorging huge clods of sod, and galloped on toward the mill.

Pounding out from the curve, Zack was surprised when he found himself only six lengths back. "Might've gained a bit on that turn," he informed Jake.

After meeting Roy's stallion, already galloping back down the road, Johnny Akers's dust-covered mare reached the mill less than four lengths ahead of Jake to find Harley Doolin dismounted and lifting his black stallion's right foreleg.

"Done throwed au shoe," Harley spit out as Deputy Akers reined his mare to the porch and grabbed a strip of yellow cloth.

As Akers spurred his tiring spotted mare back on the Mountain Road, Zack pulled reins and Jake shied away from the porch. The sudden shift of momentum almost flung him from the saddle, but with quick agility, the young mountaineer grabbed the saddle pommel, righted himself, tightened the reins, and guided the gelding back to the porch.

"We're losing ground," he muttered as he leaned from the saddle and swiped up a dangling yellow ribbon.

With a wave to Harley, still holding the stallion's right foreleg, he heeled the ugly gelding back onto the road and on downstream toward the covered bridge.

"Thu sharp turn t' thu bridge is under a mile ahead," Zack informed Jake as he pulled within two lengths of Johnny's fading mare. "We need t' catch that roan after thu bridge, if'n we're gonna catch him at all."

Johnny's spotted mare was tiring noticeably and the gray gelding pulled ahead as they came out of the bend and clattered across the bridge. And pounded on toward the upslope, Roy's big roan, to Zack's dismay, was leading by more than a dozen lengths.

The gelding, breathing hard, topped the hill and galloped on past the blacksmith shop. He gave Jake his head and the gray surged forward. Zack could see the distance closing, but not quickly enough to outdistance the stallion before he reached the finish line, he suspected. As they pounded down the slope toward the town, he felt the gray lengthen his stride, gaining momentum. Now audibly sucking air into burning lungs, the gray gelding, galloping for all he was worth, passed the "Livery Stable." As faint yells from the crowd reached Zack's ears, he shouted to the horse. "Get a-going, Jake!" He slapped the reins against the gelding's withers and clamped his knees against heaving flanks. On by the yelling crowd, Jake galloped. "About one length now," Zack mumbled, trying to wipe sweat-congealed dust from his blurry eyes.

A hundred yards to go and Roy was furiously lashing his stallion, but Jake had nosed past the roan's rump, creeping closer.

"Run! Run!" Zack urged the gelding, standing in the stirrups. They passed the finish line almost even, and Zack thought—or perhaps hoped—Jake might have nosed out the stallion.

The judges didn't seem sure either. The four men looked at each other, gestured, and then clumped together in heated consultation.

Suddenly pandemonium set in as twenty or more spectators rushed into the dusty street to voice their opinion.

Zack swung down from the exhausted, hard-breathing gelding.

David took the reins with one hand, his arm with the other, and nodded smilingly. "Great race, Zack."

A wide smile crossed Zack Doolin's long, dust-streaked face.

With David's big hand clasping his arm and the heaving gelding in tow, they made their way through the milling crowd to Beulah Marshall's black-lacquered yellow-spoke buggy.

Now sitting primly on the leather seat, Beulah was vigorously fanning her face and conversing with neighbors. As they drew close, she turned her big brown eyes on them and smiled, still fanning. "From here it looked like Jake was slightly ahead at the finish." There seemed to be a mixture of pride and excitement in her voice.

After consulting for two, maybe three minutes, accompanied by animated gestures, interposed with an occasional elbow pull and head shake, the stern-faced judges pushed though the spectators and climbed onto the boardwalk.

Carson, the spokesman, cleared his throat with profoundness and spoke up. "Well, it looks like we done got us a situation on our hands. Some's a-sayin' it was a dead heat, an' some's a-sayin' thu gray gelding won by a whisker."

"Well," Sheriff Baxter responded thoughtfully, knocking ashes from his pipe, "I suggest the judge with the best angle make the decision."

"I'm the owner of the gelding," Beulah Marshall called, rising from the buggy seat and adjusting her flowery bonnet. "I'm in agreement with that."

"I was gettin' t' that," Earl Carson spoke up again, somewhat put out. "We've done decided." He indicated the men crowding his back and they nodded solemnly. "I was standing by thu finish line," he went on, glancing over his shoulder. The men nodded again and Carson said firmly, holding his index fingers about two inches apart, "I'm a-saying, an' they're agreeing, that gray gelding was out front 'bout this much."

And the crowd, well, they appeared about equally divided; some cheered, others cursed, and several, showing profound disapproval, threw their battered hats to the ground. No doubt, their reaction depended upon whether they had bet on Roy's stallion or the gelding.

The spectators finally wandered away, some laughing, some shaking their heads, and several still cursing under their breaths and retrieving their dust-ridden hats.

"Congratulations," Roy muttered reluctantly, taking David's outstretched hand lightly.

The big pastor smiled and responded diplomatically. "Well, we were fortunate this time, but I wouldn't expect Jake to win many races against your stallion."

CHAPTER 35

—THE SHOOTERS—

AROUND FIVE O'CLOCK buggies, riders, and spectators were flowing into the wide pasture behind the livery stable to see three men—each with a rough-hewn, tapered board and folded paper targets—proudly striding, with measured steps, toward a grove of piney trees, counting as they went.

"I figure this t' be nigh on sixty yards," the tall, skinny middle-aged man spoke up, conviction in his high voice.

"I'd say yo' long legs done carried ye a mite too far, maybe three yards too far," the heavy man argued, looking back at the stable.

The balding, round-shouldered man intervened. "Ain't no use us disputin' 'bout it . . . might's well split thu difference."

And they did.

Now standing at the corner of the stable with a big straw-hat in his hand, Earl Carson announced loudly, "All shooters got t' stop by t' draw out a number from my hat an' drop in a Union half dollar before you can target shoot t' win thu ten dollars hard money. Ain't no young'uns nor scatterguns allowed," he added forcefully as the participants, with their assortment of rifles, rushed forward.

Carson ordered loudly. "Now yawl jus' line up an' wait your turn t' draw out a number. Ain't no need t' be pushing an' shoving," he went on in a lowered voice.

At the watering trough, while Jake slurped enthusiastically, Zack Doolin cast a glance at his long-barreled rifled musket propped at the end of the trough. He turned to David and grinned. "After thu shooting's done with, I figure on winning thu ten dollars."

David Spence chuckled. "I believe you will have strong competition." He pushed Jake aside, reached behind the saddle to unbuckle his saddlebag, and went on. "Willie . . . Will Marshall is a crack shot." He pulled out three cartridges, paused briefly to hand them to the mountain lad, and chuckled again. "I might get involved as well if I can persuade him to loan me his Enfield."

Zack reflected on that a moment. Then he sniggered. "I ain't figuring a parson to be a good shooter."

The black-clad pastor sighed. "Well, you may be right about that. I haven't fired a rifle in about three years."

In his customary gate, Willie rounded the corner of the stable, his old Enfield rifle clutched firmly in his right hand. "I 'spect we ought to get ourselves in line for the shooting contest," he said with some urgency.

"Since his brothers have decided not to participate, you and Zack go ahead and draw the numbers," David suggested. "I'll tie Jake to the hitch rail before it's too crowded."

"Ain't you gonna get in on thu shooting?" Zack asked, his voice carrying a touch of disappointment.

"I'm willing to pay Mr. Carson for your number," Willie put in. "I just might allow you to use my Enfield when your number's called out," he added smilingly.

David smiled back. "Well, well, I'm persuaded." He paused to pull out three half-dollar coins. While forcing the coins in Will's sagging trouser pocket, he went on, "I'll pay the entry fees."

Willie opened his mouth to complain, but the big pastor was leading the gelding away.

As they approached the slow-moving line of shooters, Zeke drawled softly. "I ain't heard about fees afore. What's that meaning, Will?"

"Ain't quite sure myself," Willie almost whispered, "But I'm reckoning it to be paying money for . . . things."

"Well," Zeke mumbled as they shuffled forward, "I sorta figured it that a-way myself. I'm a-thankin' on gettin' thu new teacher t' give me a bit more learning come fall."

As he dropped the three silver coins in Carson's sullied straw-hat and pulled out three small strips of folded paper, Willie chuckled softly.

"I've been thanking awhile on that myself. I'm reckoning it to be proper to wait till the parson comes back before we look to see what our numbers might be." Will Marshall cut his eyes to the livery stable and saw the big pastor round the corner. He threw up a long arm and waved.

David waved back.

"He's seen us and hurrying this a-way," Willie announced.

"You reckoning Parson Spence t' be a good shooter?" Zeke Doolin asked and went on before Willie could answer. "I'd be hating t' see him get . . . get dishonored."

"Take a look at them old half-blind men," William chuckled. "I'd be mighty fooled if half of them, with their old worn-down guns, could hit the side of that stable."

Zack shook his head slowly and disagreed mildly. "Not counting my brothers, I'm seeing three old mountain men. That I'm a-knowing t' be good shooters."

Now, in front of the growing crowd at the crooked flour-marked line, Earl Carson's high voice called from atop his bony old mare. "We done got fifteen shooters signed up. As yawl can well see, we got three numbered targets set up 'bout sixty yards off fur shooting from this here line." Earl paused to pull out a sheet of wrinkled paper and perch his little spectacles at the end of his sharp nose. "Thu rule is, thu shooters that got numbers one, two an' three gets thu first shot at their numbered target. After they're done shooting, I'll be calling out numbers four, five, an' six t' step up fur thu next shots. All thu others gonna be lined up an' ready fur me t' call out their numbers. Thu three shooters that gets a shot closest t' thu center of them black crosses gets to be in thu shoot-off." Carson sucked a deep breath and announced proudly, "Sheriff Baxter's done agreed t' do thu judging."

David unfolded his little paper strip and chuckled. He saw Willie smiling and asked, "What number did you draw?"

Still smiling, Will Marshall answered. "I got number three."

"Well, doggone!" Zack exclaimed. "That's beating me. I got number thirteen."

Pastor Spence chuckled again. "It seems you both beat me. I have number fifteen."

With his crooked little grin on, Will Marshall eyed David and drawled, "Looks like you're to be the last shooter, Pastor." With that he hobbled out, took a stance at the white line, and faced target three.

Proficiently, he bit off the end a cartridge, rammed it down the barrel, thumbed the hammer to half cock, capped the nipple, and waited for the two fumbling shooters at his right to load their long-barreled weapons.

"Wait fur them three that'll be marking thu target's t' get outta thu way before ye start a-cocking your rifles," Carson warned and gestured toward the three figures standing beside the targets. He cupped his hands at his mouth and yelled. "Best yawl get oughtta thu way now. We're 'bout ready t' start thu shooting!"

He reined the mare, looked down at the three anxious shooters, and creased a thin smile. He raised his voice, almost high enough for all to hear and stated the obvious. "Thu ones that ain't able t' put a hole in thu target ain't gonna find his number on it." Carson turned his bony horse, raised a hand above his head, and cleared his throat. "Now when I drop my hand, yawl can go on an' shoot."

Willie firmly held the Enfield at the hollow of his shoulder and thumbed the hammer to full cock.

A wide flourish and Earl Carson swung his long arm downward. Three rapid cracks of exploding black powder disturbed the grazing cattle in the adjacent pasture and caused Carson's mare to flinch, followed by a short disapproving snort.

In a haze of powder smoke, Will Marshall lowered his rifle and squinted to focus on the man rushing out to target three. The man marked the bullet hole, but at that distance, Willie found it difficult to see. *It looks to be marked a bit to the right, but it might be close enough to make the shoot-off,* he thought. *I'll have to tell Pastor Spence this Enfield pulls a mite to the right,* he decided.

"Numbers four, five, and six, step up t' take your shots," Carson almost shouted, a touch of irritation in his high voice. He lowered his voice and continued. "Now, if yawl don't be a-hurrying up, it'll be nighttime afore all thu shooting's done with."

*

The setting sun was just above the mountains when the final shooters moved to the line. And standing there, his blue eyes gauging target three, out of the corner of an eye, David glimpsed a figure at the adjacent position and turned his head. Somewhat surprised, he saw Roy

Taylor adjusting the sight on his Spencer lever-action repeating rifle. And beyond him at the number one position stood Zack, looking back, a big smile splitting his lean face.

"Parson, with that old Enfield, I 'spect you'll be wasting shot and powder," Roy said, his tone carrying a touch of sarcasm.

He put on his cocky grin and fondly caressed the Spencer.

And David, forcing a half smile, responded calmly, "Well, I'm sure, with your reputation as a crack shot, you will do well."

Carson raised his hand and David thumbed the hammer to full cock. Then he remembered Willie's words: "This old Enfield pulls a mite to the right."

Omitting his wide flourish, Earl Carson swung his arm downward, and the loud crack of rifle fire had little, if any, effect on the grazing cattle, but Carson's horse managed another snort.

Before the powder smoke cleared, Earl was trotting his old mare out to the targets. He glanced over his shoulder, saw the surging crowd, and heeled the bony animal into a slow lope.

At the targets, Carson gruntingly swung from the horse and turned to see Sheriff Baxter galloping his short-coupled stallion on past the hurrying crowd.

Sam Baxter reined his anxious horse to a snorting stop before the targets and gruntingly dismounted.

And Earl, waiting nearby, seemed to be frowning. "Them onlookers are mighty keen t' see who thu winners for thu shoot-off might be," he said to the sheriff. "I'm thinking, there's some betting going on."

Baxter chuckled lightly, strolled over to the target, and responded with a thin smile. "Yes, I'm sure there is, but that's not unusual." He stopped at target one and pulled a six-inch wood ruler from an inside coat pocket.

Carson stepped out, trying to hold back the anxious crowd. His effort was laudable, but the result, the big sheriff could easily see, was a total failure.

As the crowd surged on past the frustrated straw hatted man, Baxter thrust out his ruler and shouted angrily, "You might as well back off a ways. I ain't measuring the bullet holes till you do."

"Now yawl done heard thu sheriff," Carson added firmly, cleared his throat, and went on croakily. "Do what he's a-saying so we can get thu shoot-off done with before dark sets in."

Reluctantly, the murmuring crowd shuffled back, but only five or six yards.

While searching his pockets Sam Baxter muttered, "Well, I thought I brought a pencil. Earl," he asked quietly, leaning close to the rawboned straw hatted man, "do you have a pencil?"

Earl Carson nodded and drew a pencil stub from his coat pocket. "I got one, but it's needing a bit of trimming." He reached in a big patch pocket and pulled out a large folding knife. "Won't take more'n a minute," he went on.

Less than a minute later the sheriff was standing with Carson at target one and saying, "I'll hold the measuring stick in place while you mark it at the closest bullet hole."

"It looks t' be a bit under two inches," Carson guessed.

"Write down number thirteen," Baxter said, squinting at the scrawled number just above the hole. "Let's move on to target two," he went on hurriedly.

Carson licked the leaded end of his pencil and scribbled in his little pad.

At target number two, Sam Baxter shook his graying head and laughed lightly. "It looks to be only one good shooter in this bunch."

Earl bent forward to see. "Seems t' be a mite lessen a inch, low an' a bit t' thu right," he muttered, raised his voice, and went on. "I'm a-thinking that shooter, whoever he might be, is winning thu ten-dollar piece of money. What number do ye see?"

Sam Baxter squinted. "It's number fourteen."

"Number fourteen," Carson murmured thoughtfully, cleared his throat again and scribbled as they moved on to target number three. Suddenly, he brightened. "I'm reckoning that t' be Deputy Taylor's number. Thu crack shot he is . . . I figured him t' be in thu running for thu ten-dollar prize money."

The big sheriff gestured and said evenly, "Maybe so, but we'll know for sure in a minute or two."

"Well, looks t' be a draw," Earl estimated, his pale magnified eyes peering through his little spectacles at the two bullet holes, about an inch from the intersecting lines—one above the other and almost overlapping. "I'm a-believing them two's done made thu shoot-off," he went on, conviction in his tone.

"Yes. I'm sure they have." Baxter smiled, moved closer to read the numbers, and raised a hand to shade his eyes from the setting sun. "The top hole is number fifteen and bottom hole is"—he tilted his head slightly—"number three."

As they turned to announce the three finalists, the crowd surged forward.

Earl Carson cleared his throat noisily, pulled a blank yellow paper from an inside coat pocket, adjusted his spectacles, and announced with some dignity, "Me an' our good sheriff—who'll be running for re-election, come November—has done measured them close bullet holes an' come up with thu three numbers that'll be in thu shoot-off t' win that new minted ten-dollar piece. I 'spect yawl—"

"Shut your mouth an' say who's gonna be shooting," a deep, querulous voice bellowed. And the anxious crowd seemed to agree.

Unabashed, Earl coughed a little and went on. "When you're a-hearing your number called, step out an' move on back t' thu shooting line whilst Joe puts up a new gunshot target." He cleared his throat again, adjusted his little spectacles, squinted at the little pad, and announced with vigor. "Thu three best contested shooters air number three, number fourteen, an' number fifteen."

Willie turned to David and smiled. "Well, Reverend, looks like my old Enfield's done put us both in the shoot-off."

David chuckled. "I expected you to do well, but after three years without firing a shot, I thought I might have been a . . . a little rusty."

Earl reined his bony mare at the mutilated line and motioned the three participants forward. Somewhat hoarse now, he croakily announced: "Rules agreed to by thu town council—of which I'm au longtime member—decided t' allow three shots apiece for thu shoot-off." Earl coughed a little, lowered his voice and went on. "Thu one that drawed out thu short straw t' be thu first shooter is Will Marshall, whose mama's known t' be a pillow of thu county an' a ways beyond," he said, conviction in his tone.

The anxious crowd clapped politely and Carson decided to continue. "Thu second shooter, thu one I figured t' be in thu shoot-off from thu beginning, is Deputy Roy Taylor." And in unison with several hidden hoots, a smattering of claps rose from the crowd. "And now thu last shooter," Earl croaked on, "that come into our hill country a while back an' took on thu preaching job after Pastor Haskell passed on—bless his sweet soul—is gonna be thu good Pastor Spence."

Another round of tired claps, and Carson pulled his bony horse aside as Willie hobbled up to the trampled line. Efficiently, he rammed in a charge, thumbed the hammer to half cock, and pressed a percussion cap to the nipple.

"Ye got three shots, Will," Earl said, just loud enough for him to hear. "Just go on an' start your shooting."

As Willie lifted the rifle to his shoulder the crowd went silent—silent enough for some to hear the click of the cocking hammer.

William Marshall squeezed the trigger and sent a lead ball to the target sixty yards away, more or less. Efficiently he reloaded and fired again. And within a span of two minutes, Willie had fired three shots and Joe was before the target marking holes.

With a confident smile on his face and the Spencer at his hip, Deputy Taylor strode forward, tipped his wide-brimmed hat, executed a shallow bow, and levered a bullet into the chamber.

"Now, Roy," Carson warned, "don't ye be a-raising that new rifle till Joe gets done marking thu holes. A bit slow, Joe is," he muttered.

Finally, Joe moved aside.

The tall, slender deputy put the rifle to his shoulder, and instantly, it seemed, the distinct crack of a Spencer lever-action rifle filled the air. With the rifle still at his shoulder Roy smoothly levered in another fifty-six-caliber bullet, fired again, and with equal action, he plunged the third bullet into the target, some sixty yards away.

"It's already loaded and already capped," Willie said smilingly as he thrust the Enfield into David's big hands. "And don't forget, it pulls a mite to the right. Ain't allowing you to dishonor my old Enfield," he added, his smile widening.

David strode to the scattered line and moved to raise the half-cocked rifle.

"Wait!" yelled Earl croakily. "Joe ain't outta thu way yet."

Without comment, David lowered the Enfield.

A minute later Joe was well out of the way, and Earl Carson was croaking in a voice that few could hear and no one could understand.

Finally, Sheriff Baxter stepped forward and took over. He nodded and smiled at Spence. "Go ahead, Pastor, fire away."

David aligned the rifle sights on the intersecting lines, and then, to compensate for the pull to the right, he swung too aim left about an inch. He put on a thin smile, moved the sights back to the intersecting lines, squeezed the trigger and the Enfield plunged a fifty-seven-caliber, lead ball into the target, dead on the horizontal line, but about an inch to the right of the vertical line.

After David's third shot, Joe hurried out, pulled down the paper target, and rushed to meet Carson's trotting horse followed raggedly by the tiring crowd.

About halfway to the stable, Joe Miller, breathing hard, stopped and waited for Earl to pull his mare in and dismount.

Gruntingly, Carson swung down and turned to Miller, who seemed to be smiling through his walrus mustache, but he wasn't sure. Carson pointed at the ground and croaked. "Lay thu target out Joe so's we can see who thu winner might be."

"Well," Joe said, "I'm 'ready a-knowing thu winner." His smile widened enough to be noticeable. "It ain't hard t' see."

Carson bristled. "Joe, jus' stop your bragging an' lay it out, will ye?"

"Ain't no need t' ruffle your feathers," Miller muttered as he spread the paper target on the ground before Carson's big feet.

Earl Carson pushed his spectacles up from the end of his nose and leaned forward. He straightened, nodded, turned his magnified eyes to Miller, and croaked apologetically. "You're right, Joe. It ain't hard t' see." He noticed the sheriff off to his left and motioned him forward.

Sam Baxter closed the six strides between them and Carson croaked again. "Sheriff, I reckon ye might's well go on an' give out thu ten-dollar prize money."

Baxter nodded, looked down at the target, and nodded again. He pulled a silver coin from his vest pocket, held it above his graying head, and turned to face the muttering crowd. "The winner of this year's shoot-off"—he paused for effect—"is William J. Marshall."

And the crowd cheered. Some seemed to be cheering because Willie won, but some seemed to be cheering because Deputy Roy Taylor lost.

Sam motioned Will forward, took his hand, held it up, and announced in his big, deep voice, "Well, there's no doubting we've got some mighty good shooters in these parts, but I'm proud to proclaim Will Marshall as the top shooter in the county." And smiling widely, the big sheriff placed the coin in Willie's hand. As the crowd clapped politely, he nudged William with his elbow and went on just above a whisper. "Say something, Will."

Willie's face reddened. "Well—well—I'm thinking yawl," he stuttered, turned, and hurried toward the livery stable.

At the edge of the dwindling crowd, he saw David, stopped, and started to speak, but Pastor Spence took his hand, smiled, and said sincerely, "Congratulations, William. Although Deputy Taylor is a proficient marksman, I was not surprised that you won."

Willie smiled. "I'm reckoning you might've won if you hand-a pulled off to the right. Now, Pastor Spence, I'm thinking you done that on purpose. I told you that Enfield pulls a mite to the right."

"Now, William," David Spence chuckled, "as you well know, country preachers are prone to make mistakes . . . occasionally."

Part Four

A TIME TO DIE

To every thing there is a season, and a time to every
   purpose under the heaven:
A time to be born, and a time to die; a time to plant, and
   a time to pluck up that which is planted . . .

—Ecclesiastes 3:1–2

Chapter 36

—LILLY—

On Tuesday morning, the twenty-second day in August, they were sitting on the creek bank holding their fishing poles with dangling baited lines in the gurgling, fast-flowing stream.

"Will!" Lyle called excitedly. "I've done hooked up au big'un."

"Hold on, Lyle," Willie responded calmly. "Don't be jerking too hard or you'll break the line. The creek ain't too deep along here. I'll wade on out to get it." Hastily, Will Marshall rolled up his trouser legs and moved carefully in the knee-deep creek. "I'm seeing a big catfish," he called over his shoulder.

As Willie grasped the line and lifted the writhing fish from the water, Lyle announced proudly, "it show is au big'un. Will, ye a-reckonin' that t' be thu biggest ol' catfish that might've been lately caught up in Crooked Creek?"

"It just might be, Lyle. It surely could be," Willie said, grinning as he climbed onto the creek bank. "Whilst you string the catfish"—he gestured vaguely—"I'll go on up there where Lilly's gathering the rocks and get out the ham biscuits. We might as well eat in the shade of that willow tree. I'm getting a bit hungry."

Lyle nodded his large head and his wide mouth creased a crooked little grin. "I reckon I done come t' be a mite hungry m'self."

And Lilly, standing in the fast-flowing creek, with her skirts hiked just above her knees, looked up. She saw William Marshall approaching and moved cautiously across the stony creek to the sandbar. She gathered her shoes with a free hand and hurried across to the bushy bank.

Lilly stepped through the bushes, flashed Willie a little smile, and said teasingly, "I guess you quit fishing to get some of them ham biscuits."

He chuckled. "I'm about as hungry as them old dogs." He gestured toward the two dogs lying comfortably in the shade of a poplar tree. "After we eat, I'll be going on home. I promised to hoe weeds out of the garden while Ma and Elsie string green beans."

"But . . . but so far I ain't found but two colored rocks," Lilly complained disappointedly, slipping a hand in her apron patch pocket.

Willie opened the half-gallon bucket, issued a significant sigh, and smiled thinly. "Well, a promise is a promise."

Lyle sauntered up, a big smile splitting his wide, ruddy face. "Look a-here, Lilly. I done caught up a big ol' catfish," he announced again, holding the catfish at shoulder level.

She forced a grin. "It's a real nice fish, Lyle."

"You had better tie that fish in the creek or it won't be fit to eat by the time you get home," Will Marshall advised weightily.

Five minutes later they were sitting on a log, in the dappled shade of the willow tree. While Willie distributed the ham biscuits, Lyle was devouring them with the rapidity of a starving hound. He handed Lyle a biscuit and chuckled. "Looks like you've got the last one. Ma packed in about a dozen. She's trying to fatten me up a bit but didn't count on you eating like you do."

Still chewing, Lyle nodded and tried to grin. He swallowed hard, turned his pale eyes on Lilly, and saw the dangling cross, and a wide smile crawled across his ruddy face. "My ma's got one o' them crosses. It's au big wood cross settin' atop our big ol' fireplace." He reached out a big hand, grasped her little hand-hammered cross, and pulled it close to his face.

"Don't pull it," Lilly warned worriedly. "You might break the necklace. If you like, I'll take it off and let you hold it awhile."

"Don't—" Willie began.

"Can . . . can I put thu purdy little ol' cross 'round m'neck?" Lyle asked, fidgeting excitedly.

"Well, I guess you can wear it, but just for a few minutes," she responded hesitantly, flashing a glance at Willie. She saw him frowning and went on. "My papa's gonna be mighty upset if something happens to my necklace."

With dull eyes locked on the little necklace, the big lad's mind had failed to process her warning.

Lily loosened the clasp, fastened the necklace around his bulky neck, and forced a wan smile.

"Well," Willie sighed patiently, "I reckon it to be a pretty little cross for a female. I ain't gonna be caught dead wearing one, though," he added, casting an under-brow glance at Lyle. There was no reaction that Will Marshall could see.

The big lad fondled the little cross awhile.

Finally, after four or five minutes, Willie rose to his feet and sighed lightly. "I reckon we ought to get on our way home before it gets too late to get the hoeing done. Lyle, you might as well give back Lilly's necklace before we go."

"I'll be a-taken it on home t' show my ma," he responded, nodding his head and smiling. "I'm thinkin' she might jus' be a-likin' t' see it afore I'm bringin' it on back."

Willie frowned. "But, Lyle, you ought to . . ." His voice trailed off when he saw the big, round-shouldered lad climbing to his feet.

Without a word, Lyle swung the fishing pole across his round shoulder, pulled the catfish from the creek, and walked away, still smiling.

"I want my necklace," Lilly pleaded, "please, get—"

William grasped her arm firmly and almost whispered. "Don't worry, I'll be going on up to visit him in a few days and get it back."

"But Papa's gonna throw a fit if he sees my necklace gone," Lilly grumbled frowningly. After a brief pause, she frowned again and added, "I surely hope Lyle will be willing to give it back."

*

Silently, Lilly trudged along with Willie toward the Marshall farm. Suddenly, a thought and she smiled inwardly. *April ain't wearing her cross, except on Sundays. I'll stop by her house for a visit and borrow her necklace.* "I've been thinking for a while about visiting April Draper," she said in a casual voice, looked up at Willie, and smiled. "I think, while I'm out, I might as well walk on up to her house. It ain't more'n half a mile."

Will Marshall turned, smiled at her, and said teasingly, "You better be on home before dark sets in or your pa might give you a good switching."

Lilly McBride grinned. "My mama does the switching in our house if need be."

Willie pulled a sleeve across his sweat-beaded brow. "It'll be mighty hot to be hoeing—" In the corners of his eyes, he detected movement within the hillside trees.

Suddenly a horseman materialized, reined onto a little game path, and turned down the weedy slope.

Lilly saw the roan, raised a hand too shade her brown eyes, and squinted in the bright sunlight. "It looks to be Deputy Taylor. I wonder what he's doing up there."

Willie shrugged and they walked on.

A few minutes later, about fifty yards ahead, they saw Roy Taylor rein his big roan onto the road. He pulled the stallion to face them and hooked a booted leg around the saddle pommel.

Willie and Lilly exchanged glances and picked up the pace.

As they approached the deputy, he put a cocky grin on his sharp face, tipped his wide-brimmed hat, and said knowingly, "I saw you two and that crazy Doolin boy fishing in thu creek a while ago. It wouldn't surprise me none if he turns up in jail again, right soon." He chuckled contemptuously and went on, his sharp eyes locked on Lilly. "I doubt he'll be able to find his way home."

A flicker of anger crossed Willie's face and he retorted hotly. "Lyle ain't smart, but he ain't as dumb as you're thinking he is."

Roy failed to respond. His mind was elsewhere, Will Marshall could easily see. Another cocky grin crawled across Roy's face, exposing even white teeth. He nodded slightly. "Lilly, you sure are light on your feet. I noticed you at the teacher's party, whirling around at thu barn dance, all dressed up and looking well-nigh courting age."

Lilly saw his lustful eyes sweeping her and she blushed hotly. A momentary pause and she spoke up boldly. "Now, Roy Taylor, anybody with half an eye can well see, I'm going on sixteen and already reached courting age. And I reckon, I've been courting age for . . . for quit a spell."

Another cocky grin split Taylor's long face. "Yep, after a closer look, I reckon you have." The lean deputy touched the wide brim of his black hat, chuckled lightly, whirled the roan, and galloped away.

"That bigheaded bas—" Willie looked at Lilly and decided not to finish.

She smiled at him. "Well, Roy seems to be a bit arrogant, but he sure is handsome."

Will Marshall frowned, grunted, and hobbled on ahead.

CHAPTER 37

—MURDER—

IT WAS ABOUT four o'clock the next afternoon and Beulah Marshall was sitting placidly in her overstuffed rocker before the lace-curtained window.

Fast-moving footfalls in the hall and the parlor door flew open. Nora burst in, her face pale and her red-rimmed eyes flowing tears.

"What—?" The widow started, her knitting needle poised in midair.

"Lordamercy," Nora McBride moaned. "Lilly went down to the creek early this morning t' get some more shiny rocks and ain't got home yet."

"Now, Nora, it's more'n three hours till dark," Beulah responded soothingly, getting to her feet and embracing her sobbing sister. "She'll probably be home well before then."

Color rose in Nora's face. She was not convinced. Still crying, she shook her head. "Lilly said she'd be home about noontime."

"Why don't you get Nathan to take the mare and ride down to see about her?" Beulah asked softly.

"He's gone to the back pasture too drive in the livestock," Nora whimpered. "With them animals spread all over the pasture, he might not get home before dark sets in."

"Land sakes, Nora!" the widow exclaimed firmly, trying to hide her concern. "Ye know how young girls are. She's probably lost track of time. Pastor Spence has Jake tied out back and upstairs working on his sermon, I think. If need be, I'll have him ride down to the creek and fetch Lilly."

Nora nodded in her tear-soaked handkerchief.

With the light rustle of layered petticoats, Widow Marshall swept past her heavy sister. At the parlor door she stopped short, swung about and her wide hoopskirts, gathering momentum, followed. She tried to smile and force confidence in her strong voice. "I'm sure Pastor Spence will be bringing Lilly back before dark." Beulah Marshall turned and hurried along the hallway to the stairs. She hiked her wide skirts and maneuvered them up to the second floor and found the bedroom door open. Her sharp eyes fell on David sitting behind a little table and rapidly scratching a pencil stub across a yellowish sheet of paper.

"Pastor Spence," she interrupted hastily, a troubled tone in her voice, "Nora's downstairs. It might be nothing to it at all, but she's worrying about Lilly."

David rose quickly from the uncomfortable chair and crossed to her. "What has happened to Lilly?" he asked. And Beulah heard deep concern in his low voice.

She sighed. "Nothing . . . nothing, I hope. But I think it would please Nora if you would ride on down to Crooked Creek. Lilly might still be collecting them little rocks."

The pastor turned to leave and Beulah followed him to the stairs.

"You'll need William to show you where she gathers up them little rocks," she suggested firmly as he hurried down the stairs. He stopped, looked back and she went on. "He's at the barn, I think."

David rushed out the kitchen door and saw Willie, walking, in his stiff-legged gait, up the path toward the porch. The big pastor stepped down and hurried to meet him.

William Marshall grinned and started to speak. But seeing the pastor's frowning brow, the grin was suddenly gone.

David gestured toward the gray gelding standing in the shade of a tall maple and said seriously, "Ride with me down to Crooked Creek. Your aunt Nora is concerned about Lilly."

*

About twenty minutes later, riding double, David trotted the gelding out from the covered bridge.

Willie pointed. "She's been getting them little rocks a ways downstream." As the pastor pulled reins and heeled Jake into a fast canter, Willie tightened his grip around the big pastor's waist and went on. "When we get there, you'll be seeing a big willow and a sandbar on this side of the creek." Neither David nor Willie uttered a word as they rode on.

About five minutes later a weeping willow came into view and David pointed. "Is that the tree?" he asked anxiously.

"That's it. But with the creek-side bushes, we ain't gonna be able to see the sandbar from here," Willie Marshall acknowledged.

The tall pastor reined the gray down the steep roadside bank to the gurgling, fast-flowing stream and reined him in under the drooping willow tree branches.

Willie slipped back over the gelding's gray haunches to the ground, cupped a hand at his mouth, and called loudly, "Lilly!" The gurgling, fast-flowing water was all they heard. With David close behind, he hobbled over to the creek bank, parted the bushes, and exclaimed, "Footprints! She must be just past that big overhanging bush," Willie went on as he pushed through the low bushes.

"Wait!" David's troubled voice stopped him. "There's something odd about those footprints."

William Marshall swallowed. "What you reckoning might be looking odd?" he asked, bewilderment in his voice.

"I'm not sure myself," David sighed as they moved on past the low bushes. "But let's not disturb the prints until we find Lilly."

"There she—" The words died on Willie's lips. Off to his left, facedown in the gurgling water, he saw Lilly McBride. She was wedged against a large protruding rock, her skirts billowing and her long, dark hair flowing in the stream. Shocked, they froze momentarily and then rushed across the sandbar.

And David, now several strides ahead of the hobbling lad, plunged into the creek, and gathered the lifeless girl in his arms. He crossed the sandbar, gently laid the limp body on a grassy patch, and pulled the torn bodice over her exposed breast.

As Pastor Spence bowed his head to pray, Willie dropped to his knees and grasped Lilly's cold, limp hand, tears flowing down his cheeks.

David prayed a minute or two, raised his teary eyes, saw the purple marks on Lilly's slender neck, and wiped away the tears. He turned to Willie and spoke softly. "William, ride Jake to town. Find Sheriff Baxter and tell him Lilly's dead, maybe murdered. And tell him to bring a wagon to transport—" His scratchy voice faltered.

"I reckon we ought to tell—" Willie started weakly.

Before he could finish David interrupted firmly, "No. Don't tell anyone until Sheriff Baxter gets here to investigate."

Will Marshall climbed to his feet and looked down at the lifeless girl despondently. Fighting to hold back tears, he turned, gathered the reins, put a big high-top boot in the stirrup, swung into the saddle, and lashed the tall horse up the steep hill.

For a few seconds, David watched Jake galloping away, then sighed deeply, pulled off his frock coat. and prayerfully spread it over the lifeless body. After meditating a minute or two, he turned his thoughts back to the footprints in the sandbar. *I doubt they are important, but I'll take another look before dusk*, he decided.

At the sandbar he squatted on his heels for a minute or so, gazing at the receding little shoeprints. He turned his eyes to Willie's and his shoeprints, about three or four strides to his left and frowned. "That's it," he mumbled. "Lily's footprints are not evenly spaced nor indicate movement through the sand." And then he noticed fine lines in the sand. *Her shoes should be nearby*, he thought as he brushed past the protruding bush.

David stopped, his eyes scanning the sandbar. Off to his right, about ten strides away, he saw a little shoe lying crookedly at the edge of the fast-flowing creek. "Only one shoe," he muttered confusedly, pulled at his left ear, and went thoughtfully silent.

Several minutes passed. Suddenly, he snapped his fingers, his mind galloping. "She didn't make those footprints," he muttered. "Whoever killed her swept the sandbar with a bushy branch to remove his prints and pressed her shoes in the sand as he backed away from Lilly, probably on his knees. When the murderer had crossed the sandbar to the creek bank, he tossed the shoes back toward the body." *But why would anyone go to all that trouble to cover his tracks?* the pastor mused as he turned his eyes back to the coat-covered body.

*

The sun had settled low in the western sky and pushed lengthened shadows from roadside trees to Crooked Creek, when David Spence heard the fast clop of shod hooves intermingled with the rattle of Sam Baxter's rented one-horse wagon.

As the sheriff pulled the bony mare to a stop on the road, Willie reined the surefooted gelding down the steep hill, slipped from the saddle, and explained apologetically. "I'm sorry it took so long. The sheriff couldn't tame his new stallion to harness. He had to hire that wagon and bony mare from Mr. Stanley and left Deputy Taylor a note. I reckon he'll be coming along soon."

The big sheriff stumbled down the steep, weedy hill, stopped alongside the body, and reverently doffed his battered slouch hat. After a few seconds he bent down and pulled aside the pastor's black coat, exposing Lilly's pale face and her purple-marked neck and studied the body a long minute. "Well," he sighed solemnly, shaking his big graying head slowly, "there's no doubt, somebody strangled this girl. Where'd you find the body?"

David pointed. "We found her in the creek just beyond the sandbar, lodged against a large rock."

"Well then, let's take a look," the sheriff muttered and abruptly turned toward the creek.

The pastor's big hand grasped his sleeve. "Wait," he cautioned firmly, "I believe you should take a close look at the footprints before we walk onto the sandbar."

"The footprints? Well, we—"

Galloping hoof beats stopped Baxter.

As one, they turned to see Roy Taylor spurring his big roan horse from the Mountain Road down the steep hill.

Viciously, he pulled the double-bitted bridle and brought the stallion to a sliding stop. And Roy, with a long leg already crossing the horse's haunches, swung down and doffed his wide-brimmed hat. He looked down at Lilly's pale face, sighed and, shook his head slowly. "It's a pity that young girl had to drown," he muttered.

David responded sadly. "No. She didn't drown. She was murdered."

"Lilly murdered!" Taylor exclaimed loudly. "Why would anyone kill her? Had to be crazy," he went on, shaking his head.

Sam Baxter pulled out his big-bowled pipe, flared a match with his thumbnail, lit up, and puffed smoke. After sucking several significant puffs, he pulled the crooked stem from his wide mouth, bent forward, and pulled the coat gently to cover Lillie's face. He nodded somberly and sighed deeply. "Well, let's examine the murder scene. Better be careful where you walk. Pastor Spence thinks the footprints might be helpful."

As they started single file, Roy rushed forward, came abreast the sheriff, and moved to pass.

"Hold up, Roy," Baxter ordered firmly. "Your big boots might disturb the evidence, if there is any. I'll take the lead."

Falling back to the sheriff's side, Roy Taylor apologized. "Sorry about that, Sheriff. I had my mind on that poor helpless girl and . . . reckon I got a bit over anxious."

Drawing vigorously at his pipe, Baxter nodded and mumbled around the stem. "I understand, Roy. I'm anxious as well."

A few minutes later the heavy sheriff was squatting on his heels, staring at the footprints. He pulled the pipestem from his mouth. "Pastor"—he nodded—"I believe you're right about these prints. It looks like the murderer staged it to look like she drowned."

Roy spoke up. "I'm believing it was Lyle Doolin that murdered Lilly. He goes barefoot all summer. And knowing the tracks would lead to him, he had to cover them."

"But Lyle ain't smart enough to—" Willie started.

"Hmm . . . that's a possibility." Baxter pecked his big-bowled pipe against a creek-side rock, grunted, rose up, and stuffed the pipe in a sagging coat pocket. "Looks like, after the funeral, I'll have to ride up to the Doolin's place and ask a few questions—serious questions."

"I think we oughtta strike while the iron's hot," Deputy Taylor put in passionately, too passionately, David thought.

The sheriff shook his head thoughtfully. "No. We'll wait. A few days won't matter. I'll consult her family first."

CHAPTER 38

—APRIL'S CROSS—

Two DAYS LATER, at the Lilly McBride's funeral, Martha Kelly was playing the piano softly as a long line of solemn-eyed parishioners shuffled down the center aisle to view the body.

While wiping away flowing tears with a dainty white handkerchief, April Draper looked in the red-velvet-lined, oil-polished oak coffin, saw Lilly's pale-pink dress, and saw the pink rose in her hand and the silver comb in her hair. "My cross!" she cried, turned to her mother, and sobbed in her wet handkerchief. "I thought . . . I hoped Lilly would be wearing my cross."

In the crowded aisle about five paces back, with Elsie at his side, Willie heard April's sobbing comment and thought, *Lilly did borrow April's cross after all, but she wasn't wearing it when we found her. Maybe Aunt Nora knows if she was wearing it when she struck out for the creek.*

Elsie nudged him and whispered, "Lilly stopped by on her way to the creek. I'm sure she was wearing the necklace. You reckon—?"

"Later," Willie murmured, tightened the grip on Elsie's arm, and shook his head lightly. He glanced over his shoulder. In the crowded aisle he saw the sheriff and Deputy Taylor.

She nodded and they moved on toward the polished oak coffin.

*

At the graveside burial service, many parishioners and neighbors sang in mournful voices "Nearer, My God, to Thee" and "Amazing Grace."

The sparkle in Nora McBride's dark eyes was replaced by a gloomy stare. Brokenhearted, she cried, somber and bitter. Somehow Nora imagined that God had singled her out for cruel and unusual punishment, and she asked herself, *Why me, Lord? Why me? Why me, Lord?*

As Pastor Spence finished the elegy, Willie swept his eyes across the tearful crowd and found Sheriff Baxter standing beside Roy Taylor. *I need to tell the sheriff about April's cross before he goes up to question Lyle,* he decided.

David ended with a heartfelt payer and the solemn crowd began to melt away. And Willie, still watching the sheriff and Roy, leaned close to Elsie's ear. "I need to get Sheriff Baxter aside," he whispered. "I have to tell him about April's cross before he goes up Chestnut Mountain to question Lyle."

Elsie nodded and almost whispered. "Let's catch up to them and I'll find a way to get Roy away from Sheriff Baxter for a few minutes, I hope."

"How're you—?"

Already slipping through the crowd, Elsie Rogers was approaching the two men, now strolling toward their horses.

Willie saw her stumble and fall at Roy Taylor's feet. He shook his head slightly and half-smiled as the deputy reached down, grasped her arm, and raised her up. She gestured toward the church. And with Roy's big hand gripping her upper arm lightly, Elsie hoppled off toward the side door.

Now standing by his short-coupled stallion, thumbing a load of tobacco in his big pipe, the sheriff raised his sharp gray eyes and saw Will Marshall, approaching at a stiff-legged gait.

Willie opened his mouth to speak.

"I hope Elsie's leg will heal soon," Baxter said, frowning.

And Will Marshall, forcing a frown, nodded. "Oh, I'm reckoning it'll be healed up in a day or two." He turned his head, glanced over his shoulder, and went on in a low voice of confidentiality. "Elsie said Lilly was wearing April Draper's cross when she went down to the creek."

The sheriff sucked at his pipe awhile. Finally, with the pipestem still in his mouth, he spoke thoughtfully. "I'm not sure that will be helpful. But you ought to keep it under your hat for now."

Willie nodded. "I will. But the day before she died," he almost whispered, "Lyle was at the creek with Lilly and me. He took Lilly's necklace on home to show his mama."

Baxter pulled the pipestem from his wide mouth and questioned in a low tone. "Are the necklaces identical?"

Willie nodded again. "They're mostly alike, excepting their initials being scratched on the backside of the crosses. I'm thinking the necklace might've fell in the creek whilst the killer was choking Lilly. I reckon the water to be about two feet deep where she—" Will Marshall could not finish.

The sheriff raised his sharp, wide-set eyes to Will and spoke in a lowered voice. "I'll be going up to visit the Doolins in the morning. I'll ride by the creek on the way. And, Will, I believe, since you are well acquainted with Lyle, it would be helpful if you go with me." Sam Baxter looked over Willie's shoulder, saw Roy approaching, and went on in a low tone. "Meet me at the gristmill about eight o'clock tomorrow morning."

Willie nodded and swung about. And with another shallow nod, he brushed on past the deputy and hurried toward the side door.

*

With the rising sun at his back, William J. Marshall reined Jake at the gristmill. He saw his mother's buggy near the side porch and mumbled to the gelding as he dismounted. "Looks like Pastor Spence and Ms. Kelly started round daylight to get Ma's corn up here. The pastor said he might be bringing the corn an' just might bring Ms. Kelly along to see what a gristmill looks like." *Wouldn't surprise me none if they're doing some courting along the way*, he speculated. And as he climbed the steps to the narrow porch, he smiled at the thought. He stepped through the open doorway, met the teacher, and stopped.

Surprised momentarily, she jerked her head up and looked into his dark eyes questioningly. And then a sudden smile dimpled her heart-shaped face. "William, I didn't expect to see you up here."

"I'm . . . I'm too meet Sheriff Baxter round eight o'clock," Willie said haltingly. "We're going to visit the Doolins. He wants to see if they know anything about Lilly's—" He saw David approaching and stopped.

"Well, William." The tall pastor smiled. "It seems we are heading in the same direction. Your mother said you might be going with Sheriff Baxter to interview Lyle. Martha, uh, Ms. Kelly and I are going up Chestnut Mountain as well." He smiled down at the petite teacher. "She's looking for a suitable place to teach the children on weekends. And as often as possible, I'll go up there for Sunday afternoon services."

Willie smiled and nodded. "Seems like the last time I was up that away I saw a log house in the midst of some chestnut trees that looked to be empty. I reckon it to be no more'n half a mile before getting to the Doolin house."

"We'll ride—" The gristmill came to life and the rumbling grindstone silenced David momentarily. He raised his voice and continued. "We'll ride on ahead and inspect the house." He grasped Martha's arm lightly and flashed a smile at Willie and a wave to George—now busily dumping corn in the feeder—and they left.

CHAPTER 39

—THE SLY FOX—

INSIDE THE RUNDOWN log cabin, David swept his blue eyes around the room and frowned. He turned to Martha, smiled thinly, and tentatively understated, "Well, it . . . it needs some repair, but most of the timbers are chestnut and in good shape."

Martha Kelly, nodding slightly, said thoughtfully, "I think it's large enough for twenty students, maybe a few more."

Spence shook his head and chuckled. "Before we move in, maybe we should find the owner."

As they walked to the buggy, Martha flashed him with blue-green eyes and smiled. "I believe Widow Doolin, since she lives less than a mile away, can provide all the information we need."

David took her hand gently and chuckled again. "Yes. Yes, I believe she can. We'll ride up to her house and ask," he went on softly. At the buggy he pulled her close and asked cautiously, "Would you consider marrying . . . a country preacher?"

Martha flashed her incandescent smile. "Well, are there any country preachers available?"

David smiled widely and kissed her passionately. "Only one, my darling—only one," he said hoarsely.

As the buggy neared the mountaintop, David pulled the tired, snorting mare in and pointed to a shallow valley. "That's the Doolin house," he said confidently.

"Are you sure?" Martha asked wonderingly as she looked into the valley at the large log house sitting atop a low rise. "I expected to see a small cabin," she continued as David opened his mouth to answer.

"Yes, I believe that's the house." Spence smiled. "According to Mrs. Marshall's description, that must be the Doolin house."

He clucked the mare forward about twenty yards to a shallow gap and reined her down a narrow clay track snaking through a thick forest of tall chestnut trees.

After jolting on a quarter mile or so, the buggy emerged from the trees and rattled across a shallow, meandering spring-fed stream. The house was clearly visible now and David reined the mare.

The ringing echoes of an ax blade chopping wood came to them and David chuckled. "Well, I'm sure someone is home." He raised a hand to shade his eyes and went on. "Looks like Harley Doolin up near that shed."

Some seventy yards away, the ax flashed in the midmorning sun and chestnut chips flew as the tall mountain man expertly cut small branches into firewood. Harley stopped and propped his ax against the chopping block. He drew a sleeve across his sweat-beaded brow and turned his attention to the house.

As one, Martha and David shifted their focus to a thin, slightly stoop-shouldered woman in a long gray dress and a black poke bonnet shading her face, moving from a little back porch toward the shed, a wooden bucket in one hand and a gourd dipper in the other.

"That must be the Doolin boy's mother," Martha said quietly as she looked across the mare and saw the woman dip the gourd in the wooden bucket and hand it to the long-muscled mountain man.

David flicked the mare, guided her past a large hillside garden and on up the slope toward the big, log house. *I wonder what happened to Elsie's wagon and mules*, he pondered as he reined the mare. He looped the lines around the whip socket and sighed. *I'm somewhat reluctant to broach the subject*, he thought. *Well, hopefully, the Doolin boy's mother will explain*, David thought on as he rounded the buggy and reached up to help the teacher down.

Martha gathered her skirts. As she took his hand to step down, a drawling voice called. "Parson, I saw you an' thu teacher comin' up thu hillside."

David turned and saw Zeke Doolin standing on the front porch with a double-barreled shotgun across his shoulder and a wide smile splitting his narrow face. The slender, barefoot mountaineer descended the four steps and ambled down the narrow path, still smiling.

About halfway down the slope, he stopped, lowered the long-barreled shotgun, propped it against his left hip, poked both index fingers in his mouth, and whistled loudly—so loud the bay mare jerked the buggy forward. David reached for the lines, but Beulah Marshall's bay had stopped and snorted disapprovingly.

"Come on, Mud," Zeke called loudly, his cupped hands at his mouth. And the flop-eared hound, with noticeable enthusiasm, bolted from the garden patch and raced up the hillside.

Zack turned his dark eyes back to the couple, still standing beside the buggy, and shrugged, his smile morphing into a frown. "I 'spect yawl done come up here t' take back them bony mules an' that ol' wagon," he drawled cautiously. "If'n you did, Josh's done took them up creek a ways t' load up some black rocks. I'm thankin', he might still be in hollerin' distance."

Martha smiled. "No. We didn't come for that. We came to find a building, a suitable building to teach children and any willing adults unable to read and write."

Zack nodded respectfully and spoke slowly, discernible pride in his tone. "Yes, ma'am. I've done been schooled some an' able t' scratch out a bit of writin' myself. I got my learnin' from a roving preacher. It was nigh on five years back, reckon it was." A moment of silence and the slender mountaineer added thoughtfully, "'Taint no doubt, thar's a passel of young'uns here 'bouts a-needin' some schoolin' though. Myself an' Will's been thinkin' on gettin a bit more learnin' ourselves."

Martha smiled again and the young mountain man's sun-browned face turned crimson.

"Well, Zack, what about that cabin about a half mile down the Mountain Road?" David asked, saw the hound, with lolling tongue, whipping his tail against Zack's leg, and had to smile.

"Have t' ask Ma 'bout that," Zack drawled thoughtfully while stroking the anxious hound's floppy ears. "That ol' log house's been empty fur quite a spell." He shifted his sharp eyes to Martha and grinned. "I 'spect you t' be a bit worn-down, ma'am. We'd be much obliged if'n ye an' Parson Spence would be willin' t' go on in an' make yo'selves at home. I reckon Ma might be showin' up right soon. Me an' ol' Mud's goin' on down t' ketch that ol' rabbit that's been feedin' in our garden. Ol' Mud ain't gotta strong nose fur huntin' rabbits, but come nighttime, he's big on fox huntin'."

Zack shouldered his shotgun and smiled. "Ye might's well go on an, talk t' Ma whilst I hunt down that rabbit." And followed by the anxious flop-eared hound, he headed on down the path.

About five minutes later the slender teacher, followed by the big pastor, topped the steps to find Lyle standing in the doorway, a wide smile on his round face and a small wooden box tucked under his right arm.

"Howdy do, Parson. Yawl can jus' come in if'n ye want to. I'll be showin' yawl my purty thing box an' my pa's ol' turnip watch. It's what Ma give t' me. She's done toll me Pa's passed on t' heaven an' won't be needin' it no more."

David Spence forced a smile. "That would be an honor, Lyle."

"I consider it an honor as well," Martha Kelly put in smilingly as they followed the heavy lad inside.

Excitedly, Lyle opened the box, drew out the watch, and observed it a long moment. Suddenly his round face fell. "'Taint a-runnin' now," he said slowly, putting the big watch to his left ear. "I reckon it t' be 'cause I ain't wound it up fur quite a spell." And still fondling the watch, he creased a frown and went on. "Ain't found thu li'l ol' cross I'm s'pose t' give back t' Will's kin neither. I've done showed it t' my ma. I wuz thinkin' ye might be willin' t' take it on back when yawl's ready t' go."

David smiled inwardly and said patiently, "Will is on the way up to visit you. He'll probably arrive in an hour or so."

Lyle frowned again. "I 'spect he jus' might be gettin' mad at me fur losin' his kin's cross."

Martha dimpled her incandescent smile and asked softly, "Would you mind if I look in your box too?"

The big lad extended the box, smiled broadly, and drawled, "It a-bein' a mite heavy. I reckon I oughtta hole on whilst ye an' thu parson takes a look."

They peered in the box. And with feigned interest, they saw a ball of twine, a large comb, a turkey feather, a small lump of coal, a faded daguerreotype, and a little round multicolored rock.

"Well, I don't see the necklace," David said evenly, his big hand resting on Lyle's shoulder. "Maybe it's somewhere in your room."

At the back wall a door squeaked open, and a tall, thin woman in her midfifties appeared. She paused, removed her black poke bonnet, and squinted. Finally she nodded unsmilingly and said, "Howdy. From what I've been a-hearin' from m'boys, I'm thinkin' yawl t' be thu new town parson an' school mm. I'm Callie Doolin an' mighty proud t' have ye come a-callin'. Ye might as well pull out a chair t' sit a spell. I'd be offerin' ye a taste of sourwood honey if'n ye like."

David opened his mouth to speak, but she shifted her gaze to the big lad and went on softly. "Now, Lyle, ye have t' put thu box away whilst we got these kind folks a-vistin'."

"Ma, ye reckon I can be a-showin' my purty things agin after a spell?" the big lad asked, disappointment in his whiny voice. "Thu parson was a-sayin Will might be comin' 'fore long," he went on, voice still whiny.

"Jus' take the box on back t' yo' room fur now," Callie said patiently. "Later on, if'n our vistin' folks find time, I 'spect they might jus' be willin' t' take a look."

David saw a flash of disappointment cross Lyle's broad face. "Yes, indeed," he said hastily, nodding. "We are looking forward to examining your pretty things again." He smiled, glanced at Martha, and found her smiling and nodding as well.

Reluctantly, Lyle climbed the steep stairs to his room.

As his footsteps faded, Callie leaned forward and spoke in a low, confidential voice. "Pastor, I'm a-thinkin' ye might be willin' t' take thu young girl's cross on back when ye go on home. I've done slipped it outta Lyle's box an' put it in a little ol' bowl a-top thu shelf . . . over thur." She tilted her head and pointed to the rough-cut shelves on the wall above a small lampstand. "An', Parson"—Callie half-smiled—"I'm a-thinkin' ye jus' might be able t' reach it."

Her voice seems a little warmer now, David thought. And with Callie Doolin following closely, he strode heavily across the room, reached up to eye level and pulled a small yellowish bowl from the top shelf. David placed the bowl in her outstretched hands and forced another smile.

Callie nodded. "I'll be a-thankin' ye, Parson." She tilted the bowl and Lilly's little necklace fell into her cupped hand.

From outside came the fast clop of approaching hoof beats, followed by the snort of an anxious horse. And hurriedly, Callie stuffed the necklace in her apron patch pocket.

"That's probably Sheriff Baxter and Will Marshall," Spence guessed. "I believe the sheriff will be interviewing Lyle."

Widow Doolin's heart leaped. Her sharp eyes stared at him awhile. "Why's he a-comin' up here t' talk t' Lyle?" She asked, and he heard concern in her voice. "He's done been let outta jail."

David shrugged his wide shoulders and responded softly. "I know, but the sheriff is investigating the murder of a girl—Lilly McBride." He paused briefly. A deep sigh and he continued. "That necklace belonged to her."

Callie swung about and hurried to the front window. She looked out, saw three men walking briskly toward the front porch, and turned her sharp, dark eyes on David. "Who ye reckon' thu tall fellow a-wearin' thu big ol' black hat might be?" She asked anxiously. "I'm knowin' Will Marshall, but don't reckon I've seen thu big-hatted fellow afore."

"He's Roy Taylor, the sheriff's deputy," David responded, his voice low, thoughtful.

Widow Doolin nodded and opened her mouth to speak. Three light taps on the front door stopped her. She moved to the door, hesitated momentarily, and then pulled it open to find the heavy sheriff standing there, a battered slouch hat in his right hand and a big-bowled pipe in his left.

Baxter half-bowed, cleared his throat, and said respectfully, "Dear lady, I hope we're not intruding. We . . . I thought we'd stop by and talk to Lyle for a few minutes. It concerns the death of a young girl, Lilly McBride. I ain't accusing anyone yet. I believe Lyle and Will Marshall were with her at Crooked Creek last Tuesday, the day before . . . before she died."

"Now, Sheriff, ye ain't accusin' Lyle of a wrongdoin', air ye?" Callie questioned anxiously.

Sam Baxter wavered for a moment, then repeated tersely, "I ain't accusing anyone yet, but I'd like to know his whereabouts last Wednesday."

Callie sighed. "I reckon, ye a-bein' a lawman, ye might jus' come on in an' get it done with. Ye can hang yo' hat on that peg aside thu door."

She gestured vaguely. "I'll be a-gettin' him t' come on down t' talk with ye fur a spell. Don't reckon it t' be a bit o' help though," she added wryly.

As the sheriff turned to hang his hat, Roy pulled at his coat sleeve and whispered, "Don't forget to ask about that necklace."

"Hmm-m" was Baxter's only response as he hung his battered slouch hat on a wall peg. He swung about, put a thin smile on his wide face, and strode across to David and Martha, now rising from split-bottomed chairs.

He shifted the pipe to his left hand, gave Martha a shallow nod, took David's extended hand, and looked at him quizzically. "Well, Pastor," he said softly, "I didn't expect to see you . . . and Ms. Kelly up here."

"We were—"

Willie's voice cut abruptly into David's. "Sheriff, I forgot to tell you they'd gone on up here, looking for a place to teach."

At the stairs Callie's strong voice called imperiously. "Lyle! You jus' push yo' box under thu bed an' come on down. Will Marshall's done come by t' pay us a visit."

And Lyle's muted voice called back. "I'll be a-comin' on t' visit Will soon's I get m'purty-thing box stowed."

About a minute later, smiling broadly, Lyle lumbered down the creaky steps. He paused momentarily on the bottom step and frowned. He spotted Willie, regained his broad smile, and pushed his way between Sheriff Baxter and Deputy Taylor. He grasped Willie's upper arm firmly—firmly enough to bring forth a little grimace that Will Marshall tried to cover with a narrow grin. After several shoulder slaps and a couple of light arm punches, Lyle stepped back and drawled. "Howdy do, Will. I 'spect ye done come up t' visit fur a spell. Might jus' be we can be a-goin' down t' thu creek fur a bit o' fishin'. Las' time I wuz thu on-lest one t' ketch up a big ol' catfish an'—" He noticed Will Marshall's deep frown and stopped.

At that moment Sam Baxter, standing about three feet away, reached out and grasped the big lad's elbow. "Lyle," he said, his voice low, but carrying a somber tone, "I need to talk to you about Lilly, Will's cousin."

Lyle Doolin brightened. "She's thu one a-givin' me thu purty little ol' rock a while back an' seed me catch up that thur big ol' catfish." He turned his dull eyes to Willie and went on gleefully. "An' Will wuz a-sittin' on that log when she let me—"

"Let's move out to the porch," Baxter suggested calmly while hustling the lad to the front door. "We need to talk . . . privately."

As the door closed behind them, Callie noticed Roy Taylor moving stealthily up the stairs and said to herself, *I 'spect he's a-goin' up there a-huntin' fur this here necklace.* She slipped a hand in her apron pocket and thoughtfully caressed Lilly's necklace, her anxious eyes sweeping the room. They stopped on the big pastor, now seated on the worn horsehair-stuffed sofa with Martha Kelly at his side.

Resolutely, Callie strode across the room. And David, with his blue eyes fully focused on Martha, failed to see her pull up at his shoulder.

She prodded lightly.

And with the smile still lingering on his lips, he swung his head around and saw Widow Doolin frowning down at him, and the smile was quickly gone.

"Parson," she almost whispered, "I 'spect you'd jus' better be a-takin' this here little ol' necklace on back t' thu killed girl's kin." She opened her clasped hand.

David Spence gave her a shallow nod, took the necklace, and slipped it in his coat pocket.

The room went silent for a minute, maybe a bit longer.

Finally, heavy, fast-moving footfalls on the stairs and Roy Taylor appeared. And hesitating hardly a moment, he rushed out the door and thrust a necklace before the surprised sheriff's face. "I've found it!" he exclaimed. "It was in a box hidden under his bed," Roy went on, excitement in his voice, perhaps a bit more excitement than necessary.

And David, hearing Roy's loud, hasty statement, frowned, glanced at Martha, and rose from the couch. He issued a deep sigh and strode heavily across the room, his right hand moving to his coat pocket.

"I suspected that dumb—" The words died on Roy Taylor's lips when he saw the big, black-suited pastor step through the doorway with a hand-hammered cross attached to a dainty necklace dangling from his right hand.

David frowned and eyed Taylor hard. "This is Lilly's cross," he said weightily, shifting his blue eyes to Baxter. "And, Sheriff"—he sighed—"if the cross in Roy's hand is April's, I think I'm sure we will know who murdered Lilly."

Roy Taylor paled. Panic-stricken, he glanced at the sheriff and froze for a moment.

A quick move and Baxter snatched the necklace from Roy's big hand. He flipped the cross, squinted at the initials a moment, and jerked his head up. "Roy, you're—"

Taylor's heavy fist sent Sam Baxter to the porch floor. Without bothering to use the steps, he jumped to the ground and raced down the grassy slope, trying to jerk his long-barreled revolver from his low-slung holster as he ran.

And Sam Baxter, now staggering to his feet, was pawing at his holster. He saw Roy's weapon clear the holster and his pale-blue eyes rounded. A flash of fire from the deputy's revolver sent a forty-four-caliber bullet toward the porch. It sang past Baxter's head and plunged into a post off to his left. Normally, well known for accuracy, Roy would hit the target, but his hurried, offhand shot had missed by three or four inches.

The lean deputy raced on to the fence. With an encompassing glance toward the house, he holstered the long-barreled revolver and nervously untied the halter strap. He put a big foot to stirrup, swung aboard the big roan stallion, and spurred him into a fast gallop.

While stumbling down the path, Baxter raised his revolver, but before he could fire, the galloping stallion had passed the garden patch and disappeared, leaving a thin curtain of dust in his wake.

Down in the corn patch Zack heard the blast from Roy's revolver. And with the corn too high for him to see, he pointed the double-barreled shotgun skyward, thumbed back both hammers, and squeezed the triggers, filling the atmosphere with lead balls and him to the ground.

Harley came running down the hillside with his long rifled musket gripped firmly in his right hand. "What's all thu shootin' about!" he yelled to the wobbly sheriff.

Now regaining a modicum of equilibrium, the sheriff jerked the halter strap from the split-rail fence, clumsily climbed onto the nervous half-Arabian stallion, and gathered the reins. Baxter turned his head, saw the mountain man pull up just beyond the fence, and called out hurriedly, "Don't worry, Harley. No one is hurt yet."

The short-coupled horse, anxious to run, tossed his head and Sam slackened the reins. "Roy will probably head for West Virginia to hide out awhile," he murmured unsurely as the horse galloped up through the chestnut forest.

At the Mountain Road, Baxter reined the snorting animal to a walk, leaned left, and scanned the hard-packed ground. "Well, Justice, I don't see any tracks," Sam mumbled to the eager horse. "Best guess is he's heading for the border." He pulled reins and spurred the prancing stallion into a fast gallop up the Mountain Road. He mumbled to the horse again. "The state line is about a dozen or so miles away. We'll have to keep moving at a fast pace if we have any chance to overtake that stallion before he's safely across."

With amazing stamina, Justice galloped on across the mountainous terrain, but after four or five miles, Sam Baxter, realizing his short-coupled stallion was beginning to fade, reined him back into a brisk canter.

The sheriff's high-stepping horse moved on through the mountaintop spruce forest. As the thinning trees finally petered out, giving way to a low slope of scattered cedars, the sheriff told himself, *Maybe I was wrong. Roy, the sly fox he is, might've figured, I'd figure he'd head for West Virginia and galloped his roan stallion down Chestnut Mountain.*

"What's that? A horseman moving westward within those cedars," he muttered. *It's got to be Roy Taylor*, he reasoned.

With reins firmly clutched in his left hand and a cocked revolver in his right, the big sheriff raked spurs and Justice bolted down the shallow slope.

And Roy, suddenly aware of the pounding hooves behind him, twisted in the saddle. His heart leaped. Charging down upon him, trailing a cloud of sun-shot dust, he saw a galloping wild-eyed, short-coupled horse topped by the determined sheriff.

The long-boned deputy jerked out his long-barreled revolver and glanced back again. He saw the badge on Baxter's breast pocket glistening in the bright sunlight and his eyes widened. Brutally, he dug spurs into the big stallion.

With eyes fixed on Taylor's big horse, now in a fast gallop, Sam Baxter slapped the stallion's flanks lightly with the reins, and immediately, the horse responded. Now quickly gaining ground, the short-coupled horse raced on down the narrow dusty road. And the result, the big sheriff knew, was a foregone conclusion.

Roy glanced over his shoulder again and swung his revolver to target the big sheriff, but the half-Arabian had already overhauled the galloping roan stallion. With all the force he could muster, Baxter brought the long barrel of the revolver to Roy Taylor's black-hatted head. He toppled to the ground, raising a good-sized puff of dust, and the big roan galloped on.

The big sheriff reined in his lathered, hard-breathing horse. Gruntingly he slipped from the old saddle and rushed over to the lean, dust-covered deputy, now on his knees, trying to shake the cobwebs from his brain. A rivulet of blood from Roy's scalp had cut a crimson path down a grimy cheek, Baxter noticed.

"Well, I reckon I'm caught," Roy mumbled, still dazed.

The sheriff grasped his arm roughly and brought him to his feet. And without a word he tensed his grip on Taylor's upper arm and guided him to the jaded half-Arabian stallion. At the nervous horse, he spun the prisoner and pressed the revolver at his back.

Roy grunted and did not speak.

The big sheriff released Taylor's arm and, cautiously, reached his free hand behind the saddle, unbuckled the saddlebag, and pulled out a pair of handcuffs. "All right, Roy, I'm sure you know the procedure," he ordered impatiently as he pulled the revolver back and thrust the open cuffs toward the prisoner.

Taylor looked at him stonily, extended his hands, and spoke bitterly. "You ain't got authority to arrest me. We've already crossed into West Virginia."

Sam Baxter chuckled mirthlessly. "Well, Roy, that's debatable. I didn't see any border signs and no one seems available to verify where the line is, so I'm assuming we're still in Virginia." He cautiously pressed the cuffs on the deputy's wrists and nudged the revolver firmly against his ribs. "Get moving, Roy," he ordered tiredly. "It's a long, rough walk to Edgewood, especially in those high-heeled boots."

Chapter 40

—A HANGING MOOD—

THE THIRD FRIDAY in September was court day. Folks were crowding in from the surrounding countryside and beyond. Horses and mules, tethered to hitch rails, lined both sides of Main Street, many with women's colorful calico dust aprons adorning their sidesaddles.

David reined the buggy in front of the courthouse to find it filled to capacity, with the complaining overflow crowd blocking the entrance and spilling down the steps onto the stoned walkway. The men, gesturing and cursing loudly, seemed to be angrily discussing the pending fate of the prisoner. In their eyes he was already convicted, already condemned and ready to be hung, which they intended to do.

And the women, many with picnic baskets, David noticed, had segregated themselves by age and social status into small clumps at the fringe of the courtyard.

Martha Kelly turned her blue-green eyes upon David, dimpled a small smile, and said, "Well, it seems we arrived a little late."

He nodded and the buggy leaned as he stepped down. Pastor Spence swung adoring blue eyes to her, shrugged, and half-smiled. "Yes. Well, it seems we are two, maybe three hours late."

"I'll introduce myself to those ladies," the teacher gestured as David raised a helping hand.

He glanced across the courtyard and saw a gaggle of women. They seemed to be staring in their direction. He smiled. "You don't have to introduce yourself. They already know—"

"Maybe so." Martha laughed lightly. "But just to be sure, I'll reintroduce myself."

And David Spence, still smiling, watched her fluidly move across the crowded courtyard. The smile faded. He turned and shuffled along with the noisy throng. *The sheriff will be moving Roy to the courthouse in a few minutes*, Spence thought as he shuffled on shoulder to shoulder with the milling crowd.

Finally, unable to move forward, he turned his eyes to a big heavy-bearded man wearing a wide battered straw-hat and red suspenders attached to haphazardly patched trousers. "Is it always this crowded?" David asked, raising his voice just loud enough for the man to hear.

The bulky man flung a heavy elbow to make room and pulled a cob pipestem from his wide mouth. He leaned closer to David, shook his big head slowly, and said, "Don't reckon 'tis, but bein' a lawman on trial fur killin' au young gal—an' bein' Lawyer O'Leary's thu prosecutor—this is gonna be a humdinger." The big man shook his head again, thumbed his red suspenders, and raised his voice. "It shore is a pity a passel of folks might be a-missin' it." He snapped his suspenders for emphasis. "That is"—he sighed and nodded toward a ruddy-faced man with a coiled rope in his hand—"if'n it gets that fur along."

*

The growing noise at the courthouse caught Sheriff Baxter's attention. Already nervous, he turned from his battered desk and looked through the dingy window a long minute. Finally, he faced deputy Johnny Akers and said wearily, "Well, there's no way we can get Roy through that crowd in front of the courthouse. I didn't realize we would have a hanging mob on our hands."

"I reckon them knowing it's just you and me," the young deputy said thoughtfully, "we have to find a way to distract them so we can slip the prisoner out the back door and on to the basement steps."

Baxter glanced at the oval wall clock. "We only have forty minutes to come up with a plan." He paused momentarily, scratching in his gray hair. "Maybe I should ask the judge to postpone the trial till tomorrow," the sheriff went on thoughtfully. "We might be able to move Roy into the courthouse in the dead of night."

"It'll be a full moon," the young deputy reminded frowningly. "I 'spect some of them hotheads, knowing it to be postponed, might be hanging around come nighttime."

"You're probably right," Baxter acknowledged with a sour smile. "I should have taken my wife's advice a year or so ago when she wanted me to retire." He sighed deeply, turned from the desk, and strode across to the wall gun case. He pulled out a Winchester lever-action rifle and a full box of cartridges. While shoving the cartridges into the rifle, the sheriff turned worried eyes upon Deputy Akers. "One of us will have to go out there and fire a few shots over their heads if necessary."

"I . . . I'll go," Akers said after a long moment, his voice quavering. "I thought up the distracting idea, and I ought to be the one to do the distracting."

Sam Baxter shook his big head slowly, frowned, and sighed. "No. I'll go. Most of those people out there know me." He gestured. "When I step outside, you rush Taylor to the back door and wait inside until the noisy crowd is silenced or you hear rifle fire. And, Johnny," the sheriff warned firmly, taking the rangy, fair-haired young man's arm, "Roy Taylor is sly—sly and wicked." He went on, his voice carrying a tone of ambiguity. "You must stay alert, with your revolver at full cock and pointed at his back." Baxter reached down to his belted holster, pulled his revolver out about halfway, and let it drop back. He levered a cartridge into the rifle chamber, strolled ponderously to the door, turned his head, and nodded to the anxious deputy. The heavy sheriff sucked a deep breath, pulled the door open, and walked out into the bright sunlight.

With nerves tight, Johnny Akers cast a glance out the window, pulled his revolver from the holster, and spun the cylinder. He turned back to the battered desk, grasped a big key, and hurried out to cell one. Near the cell he pulled handcuffs from a wall peg and looked between the bars. He saw Roy Taylor, a black wide-brimmed hat covering his face, seemingly asleep on the narrow bunk. Akers wasn't sure. "All right, Roy," he said loudly, "it's time to go." He cleared his throat and flashed the cuffs. "Poke your hands between the bars."

Taylor chuckled under his hat. "I heard you and Baxter talking about hurrying me 'round to thu basement." He lifted the hat from his face, sat up, and went on, his eyes flinty and his tone caustic. "You're thinking, with that crowd waiting out front, you'll be rushing me along, but I ain't in a hurry to go." A sly smile crawled across Roy's lean face.

And Akers, gaining some courage, thumbed his revolver to full cock and sighed. "Roy, that mob out there seems to be in a hanging mood. You will do as I say or I'll kick you out into the street and let them have their way with you."

Somewhat surprised by Akers's rough tone, Taylor nodded briefly. "You win, Johnny. I'll go along with you." Still holding his cocky grin, he thrust his hands between the bars.

Akers cuffed Roy's wrists, rattled the key into the lock, turned it, and pulled the squeaky door open. "Come on out, Roy. You try to press me and I'll blow you to kingdom come," the young deputy warned, trying to put harsh authority in his voice.

"Now, Johnny," Roy said, his tone turning friendly, "With my hands cuffed and that mob itching to hang me, I'd have to be crazy to attempt an escape."

"You might be at that. Now move on to the back door," the deputy ordered in a raised voice, his weapon prodding Roy Taylor's back. "I 'spect the sheriff will be firing any minute now," Akers muttered.

*

Followed closely by the tall black-clad pastor, Baxter, with the rifle pointing skyward and pressed at his hip, shouldered his way through the rowdy mob. He climbed the courthouse steps and faced the angry crowd. With David at his side, the bulky sheriff raised the Winchester above his head and his booming voice rose strongly, evenly, authoritatively. "You are breaking the law and the leaders of this riot will be punished—I promise you that."

Sheriff Baxter finally came to realize, as hard as he and David tried, their threats and cajoling would have little, if any, effect on the boisterous, surging, bloodthirsty mob. Reluctantly, he lowered the rifle to his shoulder, aimed just above their bobbing heads, and pulled the trigger. A loud bang of exploding powder and the rifle bucked, sending forth a stream of pale smoke laced with sparkling bits of yellow flame. With fluid efficiency he ejected the cartridge, fired again, and kept firing as fast as he could.

Now inhaling powder smoke, the surprised mob stopped surging and slowly backed away, cursing and grumbling as they went.

*

With the crackling of rifle fire in his ears, Akers pressed the revolver firmly against Roy's ribs, flung the heavy door open, and shoved the long-legged prisoner out into the bright sunlight. And with the prodding long barrel at Taylor's back, they struck out at a trot along the back wall toward the corner, about twenty feet away.

Roy's long striding legs pulled him slightly ahead. He turned the corner, threw himself against the brick wall, and thrust out a big-booted foot.

Johnny went sprawling on the hard-packed ground, his cocked revolver flying from his hand and striking an imbedded rock, inducing exploding powder to send a forty-four-caliber bullet skyward. Akers scrambled to his knees. His wide eyes darted ahead to the revolver about six feet away, still smoking. But before he could move, Roy, with quick agility, jumped past him and scooped it up. As the cuffed hands turned the revolver on Johnny, Roy Taylor put on his cocky grin and thumbed the hammer to full cock.

And as he did, Johnny Akers, still on his knees, saw the revolver cylinder turn slightly and closed his eyes to pray. A distant crack, followed by a loud thump and Johnny's eyes blinked open. And then, they widened. "What!" he exclaimed, utterly confused. Before him, flat on his back with a jagged hole between his eyes and gushing blood flowing over his sharp countenance, he saw Roy Taylor, stone-dead. Johnny cut his wide eyes to the tree-covered hill about a hundred yards off to his left. High up on the hillside, he spotted a pale of gray smoke rising slowly above a large protruding boulder and a shadowy figure melting into the thick timber.

It was then that he realized, the rifle fire in front of the courthouse had ceased, but he could still hear the distant murmur of complaining voices. The deputy shook his head and muttered bitterly, "They don't know yet, but they're all riled up to hang a man that's already dead."

About two hours later the sheriff was standing with Deputy Akers on the big boulder and saying, "Looks like it may have come from this rock. But how anybody could shoot a man between the eyes from this distance is a mystery to me."

"Has to be a crack shot," the deputy put in, nodding.

"Yes," Baxter agreed with a light shrug. "He's a crack shot, but I doubt we'll ever know who he is."

Could've been a woman, the deputy thought but said, "Anyhow, it seems to me, justice has been served."

With that, Sheriff Baxter smiled ruefully, nodded, and drew smoke from his big-bowled pipe.

CHAPTER 41

—THE GIFTS—

IN DAWN'S WEAK light, William Marshall woke suddenly, heard the rumble of heavy wheels, and rose on an elbow, straining to see David across the room. "Well, I declare," he scolded himself, in a low voice as he got to his feet. "I keep forgetting. The parson's been camping up at the schoolhouse about a week to help get them windows in before our wedding day." *Seems like I heard a wagon*, he thought, scratching under his left arm. Willie yawned widely as he strolled toward the window. "Nathan's got the wagon out mighty early," he muttered as he parted the curtains. "I'm thanking—" He stopped and stared unbelievingly. After a long moment, he finally managed, "Well, I declare!"

At that moment Elsie, still in her nightgown, burst into the room. "Will!" she exclaimed. "My mules and wagon, they're parked out front and all spiffed up."

Willie turned from the window, a wide smile splitting his sharp countenance. "It seems like the Lord's took hold of the Doolins."

Elsie looked at him, a coy little smile tugging at her lips. "Yes, I reckon you'll be a bit closer to the Lord after you're baptized come Sunday morning."

William J. Marshall furrowed his brow. After a thoughtful moment, he nodded and murmured seriously, "I reckon, I know I'll be much closer after I'm baptized." He smiled, grasped her small hand, and went on. "And I'm gonna be mighty happy after we're married about noontime on Sunday if Preacher Nash shows up."

"I'm sure—"

Willie didn't let her finish. He pulled her close and kissed her willing lips. As they parted, he looked over her shoulder, saw the open door, and chuckled. "Ma might have a fit if she walks by and sees you in your nightgown and me in my nightshirt, kissing."

Elsie giggled. "Oh, I'm sure she would. I guess we ought to get dressed and go out to see about the mules and wagon."

"And the organ," Willie added, chuckling.

About twenty minutes later they strolled across the wide yard, hand in hand. And Elsie glowed, her brown eyes sweeping the wagon. "Well, I have to admit, this old wagon looks right smart better than when them Doolin boys stole—took it."

Willie put his right foot on the wheel hub. "I'll climb up to see about the organ," he said gruntingly as he struggled to get his stiff leg over the sideboard. "Might's well leave the organ on the wagon and stow it in the barn. I 'spect, Pastor Spence will haul it on up to Twin Oaks to get it fixed," he went on in a low voice as he grasped the handle and pumped. "Looks like—" He stopped and smiled broadly, his long-fingered hands still gripping the handle. "Elsie," he announced, "I 'spect this old organ might be already fixed. Come on up and press the keys whilst I pump." He dropped the newly hinged tailboard, extended a long arm, and pulled her into the wagon bed.

"I declare!" Elsie declared, pressing the keys and smiling up at Willie. "Them Doolin boys must've hauled this organ all the way over to Twin Oaks and had it fixed."

"Well," William Marshall spoke up thoughtfully, "Lyle's done said his brothers might be hauling black rock to the New River water tower. I heard the Virginia and Tennessee railroads switching over to coal-fired trains. That might be where they got the money to fix the organ and wagon. I 'spect it might be wedding gifts from the Doolin boys—encouraged a bit by their Mama, I'm thinking."

"Well, it's mighty Christian of them to bring . . ." Elsie's voice trailed away as a buggy rattled into the yard.

"That'll be Dr. Dickerson," Willie Marshall murmured wonderingly, his sharp eyes locked on the swaying buggy. "Seems to be in a mighty big hurry," he went on as he climbed clumsily from the wagon.

The doctor reined in the big mare and held out two yellow flimsies. "I finally received a telegram from Dr. Price. He's scheduling your surgery for early Tuesday morning. You need to be in Lynchburg by

Monday to be examined. The other telegram is for Pastor Spence. It's from Staunton. Must be from his uncle," Dickerson speculated.

Willie started to speak, but the doctor went on. "I have to be on my way. Mrs. Martin's baby is due any minute now, her seventh." With that he swung the buggy and lashed the mare into a fast trot.

William Marshall turned back to the wagon and smiled up at Elsie. "Well, looks like, since the train gets to the New River water tower round six o'clock, we might have to spend our first married night on a train to Lynchburg."

"That's fine with me," Elsie rejoined pleasantly. "Lord willing, your leg will soon be fixed and we'll be having a happy lifetime together."

A wide smile split William Marshall's narrow face. "Well, while I stable the mules, I reckon you oughtta get inside so Ma can finish pinning up the wedding dress to fit you." He chuckled. "It'll take quite a bit of sticking to get it down to your size."

"I'd surely like to have Ms. Kelly play the organ at our wedding," Elsie said meditatively, took his hand with tenderness, and stepped down.

He chuckled and pulled her close. "I doubt she'll be willing to play the organ on her wedding day."

Elsie responded quietly. "Umm, well, it was just a passing thought."

"I reckon I'll be hauling the organ on up to the church in the morning," Will Marshall drawled. "I 'spect I'll have to ask Pastor Spence to help get it inside, though." He glanced at the organ and nodded. "I reckon it's a mite heavy for me to handle."

Elsie laughed lightly. "To save time, I can handle the mules and haul the organ up there while you go along on the mare to the schoolhouse and fetch the Pastor."

Willie chuckled. "I reckon you can handle them tall mules, but there ain't no way to save time no matter what."

"Now, Will Marshall"—the young widow smiled—"you know and I know that's just a saying."

Willie smiled back and said thoughtfully, "Well, Pastor Nash might know an organ player that would be willing to come in Sunday and play, I'm thinking."

Elsie frowned and shook her head slowly. "It's much too late to get in touch with him, I'm thinking."

CHAPTER 42

—A BIT EARLY—

THE MORNING SUN had climbed above the distant trees and creeping into the valley, when a man wearing a dark long-tail coat, a tall black hat, and clerical collar rattled his dirt-splotched, rickety old buggy drawn by an indifferent horse along the treelined lane. On the torn leather seat beside him was a dog-eared, leather-bound Bible and a well-worn carpetbag.

The buggy rattled into Widow Marshall's front yard. And Reverend Henry Nash, a slender, long-legged sixty-two-year-old man, with a weak "Whoa, Kate," pulled his plodding bony chestnut mare in. He cast an encompassing glance at the big house and mumbled to the mare. "A bit early, I believe. Well, Kate, maybe we'll be in time for breakfast," he mumbled on, stepped down, and affectingly stroked the horse's neck. *Might as well go see*, he decided, lifting the tall black store-bought hat from his head. He spit in his left hand and slicked down his thinning gray hair.

Widow Marshall turned from the kitchen table, glanced out the window, and chuckled lightly as the spindly pastor pressed his black stovepipe hat on his balding head. "Well, Elsie, it looks like Pastor Nash has arrived a day earlier than expected."

At the big cook stove, Elsie flashed her quick brown eyes from the crackling ham to the window and smiled. "As my mama always said, better a day early than a day late."

Still peering out the window, Beulah Marshall grunted and spoke up again. "He's heading for the front porch and looks to be hungry as a bluetick hound. You might as well toss another slice of ham meat in that skillet." Another mild grunt and she nodded toward the hallway. "I might as well be neighborly and invite him in."

The stringy pastor climbed the steps, crossed to the door, and raised a clasped hand to knock. At that moment the door flew open. And with the clasped hand still raised, his mouth gaped in surprise when he saw Widow Marshall standing in the doorway, her dark eyes sweeping him appraisingly, and slowly moved the raised hand to his tall hat.

Finally, she nodded with dignity and forced a thin smile. "Come on in, Pastor Nash. I'm thinking, after your long ride from Twin Oaks, you might be a bit tired."

The thin pastor swept off his black hat, swung it to his bony chest, and flourished a polite bow. He looked past her and cleared his throat noisily. "A fine home you have here, madam. A fine home indeed. I apologize for arriving early," he went on in a sincere voice. "Yesterday I visited my sister Lucy. Her being a spinster and living three miles off to the south, I figured, to avoid the long journey from Twin Oaks, I'd stay overnight with her and come on a day early. I'll be spending a night in your big house if it meets your approval." He half-smiled and sniffed noticeably. "It seems like I'm smelling coffee boiling in your big kitchen."

Beulah Marshall smiled brightly. "Why, land sakes, Pastor, come on in my kitchen for some coffee. You're as welcome as flowers at springtime. And you might as well help yourself to ham meat and fresh-baked bread."

And enthusiastically, he did.

*

Shortly before noon, with the mules hitched and Elsie smiling down from the wagon, Willie gruntingly climbed on the bay mare. A smile broadened his narrow face. "I'll gallop on ahead," he said tenderly. "I'm hoping to find Pastor Spence at the schoolhouse. I 'spect we'll be back at the church by the time you get there."

Elsie Rogers laughed lightly. "With these old mules being well-rested and the wagon axles well-greased," she teased, "I just might be waiting awhile for you and Pastor Spence to show up."

Still smiling widely, Will Marshall nodded, threw her a kiss, and kicked the surprised mare into a fast gallop.

The young widow flicked the lines against the reluctant mules' haunches and the wagon rumbled away from the barn. Elsie drew near the wide yard and noticed a figure shaded by a little white lace-fringed parasol descending the front porch steps. "I think that's Teacher Kelly," Elsie muttered. "She might be planning to ride with me up to the church." The young widow sighed and half-smiled. *She's all dressed up and anxious see Pastor Spence*, Elsie thought as she guided the rumbling wagon across the yard and reined the mules at the porch steps.

"I'm somewhat anxious to play the organ," Martha Kelly said hesitantly as she thrust the parasol behind the seat.

And Elsie, with a small knowing smile stretched out a hand and helped her climb onto the seat. She lashed the mules and the old wagon jolted past Pastor Nash's hitched horse and on down the treelined lane. With the fast clop of shod hoofs and clatter of iron-rimmed wheels in their ears, they remained silent for several minutes.

Finally, as Elsie reined the mules on the Edgewood Road, Martha turned to her and smiled. "About an hour ago I spoke to Pastor Nash about music for our marriage service. He said his sister, Lucy, plays the organ in his church occasionally and might play for us. Her fee, he supposed, would be about five dollars. And since she lives alone, in addition to the fee, we will have to send someone to transport her to the church."

Elsie Rogers was thoughtfully silent for a long moment. Finally, she said cautiously, "That seems like a mighty high price for two, maybe three songs."

Martha Kelly dimpled a smile. "Yes, it is somewhat expensive, but playing the organ and traveling about three miles each way, five dollars seem to be a bargain." Martha laughed lightly. "And of course," she added, "David will be paying half the cost for the organist and half for the pastor's service as well."

"I think you're right about that," Elsie nodded, turned her big brown eyes on Martha, and smiled. Suddenly the smile turned into a frown. She hesitated, considering. "But . . . but who might be willing to fetch Pastor Nash's sister?"

Martha laughed lightly. "It seems Widow Marshall and Nora are already preparing for that. They thought it might be a nice ride, so they decided to have Nathan hitch a big Morgan mare to Nora's carriage. Mrs. Marshall is confident she can persuade Pastor Nash's sister to accept her offer."

"Well," Elsie put in smilingly, "I'm thinking it would be mighty hard for anybody to resist Beulah Marshall when she sets her mind to do a thing."

"Yes, I know" was Martha's quiet response.

Chapter 43

—THE LORD WILL PROVIDE—

WILLIE TROTTED THE horse through Edgewood and reined in near the little schoolhouse, standing in a narrow field, some twenty yards from the dusty road. He swung down, looked up, and saw the gray gelding hobbling and cropping the lush grass near the unpainted building. As he turned to loop the reins around a sapling, the big gelding raised his head and neighed. *A greeting to Ma's mare*, Willie guessed.

Followed by three stern-faced men, David rounded the corner, stopped before the little school, doffed his hat, settled onto his knees, and clasped his hands. And belatedly, as the pastor bowed his head to pray, the three trailing men dropped to their knees.

Willie issued a friendly pat to the mare's neck, turned, and started through the high grass. He glanced up again and saw four men on their knees, praying fervently. He stopped, pulled off his battered, sweat-stained hat, pressed it over his heart, closed his eyes, and mumbled a short prayer:

> Now Lord, being I ain't baptized yet, I ain't the one to
>   be asking favors.
> But I'm thinking, since I'm planning to do that
>   tomorrow about sunup,
> You might allow my praying to be a bit early. I'm hoping
>   and praying,
> You'll take care of the children and Ms. Kelly, the teacher.

"Amen." William Marshall opened his eyes on the four men still kneeling and still praying. And trying to be patient, he waited.

Finally, after a minute or so, the men stopped praying and got to their feet. The solemn congregants shook David's hand briefly, threw a parting wave to Willie, and hurried away.

Pastor Spence turned, smiled, motioned Willie forward, and said loudly, a touch of excitement in his voice, "Come, Will, take a look at the windows and go inside with me. The tables and chairs have arrived. And except for a stove, the painting, and a few minor items, the building should be completed well before school begins. The stove can wait until late October," he added.

Inside, with sharp eyes scanning, Willie strolled silently between the tables to the small, battered desk, standing near the front wall. He turned on a heel, hobbled back to David, and exclaimed, his voice echoing in the empty room, "Well, I declare. Looks like you've got tables sized to fit big folks and little children."

David chuckled and then he nodded. "Well, it wasn't my idea. Mr. Covington and Mr. Stanley decided Martha, uh, Ms. Kelly might have a few adult students, so they built three adult-size tables. And William"—David chuckled again, placing a big hand on a large table—"I believe you will fit comfortably here."

Willie nodded and smiled a little. "I reckon it just might fit after I get my leg fixed. Well, Parson," Will Marshall drawled on, "I rode on up to get you to help me get the organ in the church. Ellie's already on the way with the wagon by now."

"The wagon . . . the organ . . . I don't—" David started.

Willie smiled. "Elsie reckoned the Doolins might've brought it for a wedding gift. It was about daybreak when we saw her mules and wagon in the front yard. We found the church organ, already fixed and ready to play. That is, if we're able to find a body that's willing to play, excepting Ms. Kelly," he added in a low voice.

David grasped Willie's arm firmly and smiled widely. "Well, I'm sure the Lord will provide. We must be on our way to move the organ inside the church. It would be unwise to keep Elsie waiting."

"I reckon her to be a mite feisty myself." William J. Marshall smiled. Then he chuckled lightly.

*

At an easy cantor David and Willie were moving stirrup to stirrup along Edgewood's Main Street. As they passed the telegraph office, Will Marshall noticed the faded sign above the door. "Well, I declare!" he exclaimed, shoved a hand in his coat pocket, and pulled out a yellow flimsy. "I clear forgot about that telegram from up Staunton way." He leaned from the mare and handed the crumbled flimsy to David.

And the big pastor, anxious to see, reined Jake to a walk and ripped open the smudged yellow telegram. David raised his eyes and frowned. "This telegram was sent four days ago."

"Lines might've been down," Willie mumbled.

Spence scanned the telegram again and frowned again. "Uncle Ben is coming to the wedding. He wants me to meet him at the courthouse Saturday morning. That's today and well past morning. Uncle Ben should be here by now," he muttered worriedly. "William, you ride on to the church and I'll—" David stopped abruptly, chuckled, and gestured. "I believe that's his wagon up ahead, parked at Murphy's restaurant."

"Seems like he brought along two fine-looking horses with a touch of thoroughbred blood," Willie observed, a mischievous smile flitting across his narrow face. "Reckon they might just be wedding gifts for you and Ms. Kelly."

"That's a possibility," David responded softly as he swung down from the tall, ugly horse. He flashed a glance at the well-fed mares attached with lead lines to the tailboard, busily nibbling hay from Uncle Ben's wagon bed.

Willie pulled a foot from the stirrup and moved to dismount. He saw Spence shaking his head and settled back in the saddle.

"You ride on to the church," David said thoughtfully. "I'll take a look at the mares, find my uncle, and be there as soon as possible."

Will Marshall looked down at the wagon and frowned. "Can't rightly see how you'd know that to be your uncle's wagon."

David laughed lightly and pointed. "That yellow pillow on the seat tells me it's his wagon."

"Oh, I reckon it does. 'Taint much doubt about that now," Willie said smilingly, pulled reins, and prodded the mare into a comfortable trot.

"That looks to be Aunt Nora's carriage up ahead and coming on right pertly," Willie informed the trotting mare. At the livery stable, he reined in the snorting horse and squinted into the bright sunlight.

"'Taint no doubt. That's Aunt Nora. And looks to be Ma lashing that plow horse half to death," he informed the mare again with some exaggeration as he watched the swaying carriage.

With a quick wave, followed by a half smile from the carriage, they rumbled on past the big-footed mare, raising a goodly amount of reddish, foothill dust.

Willie creased a frown and shook his head. "Don't rightly know where they'd be going in such a hurry," he muttered and slacked the reins, and the bay mare gaited into a fast trot up the gentle slope.

*

David knotted the reins to the hitch rail and strode out to the wagon. As he approached the two horses, he smiled. "These young mares seem to be up to Uncle Ben's standards," the pastor mumbled. "They seem to be well fed, well shod, and well broken to saddle as well, I believe." He smiled again, turned to move past the wagon, glanced in the bed, and stopped. He saw two saddles, a well-used trunk, and a neatly folded canvas tent with *US* stamped on it. He chuckled. *That sidesaddle confirms Willie's prediction*, he thought as he stepped onto the boardwalk. The clatter of iron-rimmed wheels caught his attention. He grinned briefly. Then he frowned and muttered, "That's Nora's carriage." *But where is she going, and why is she hurrying that big draft horse?* David Spence wondered as he turned and entered Murphy's restaurant.

In the dimness he blinked and paused. After a long moment, Uncle Ben's familiar laughter reached David's ears and enticed several nearby customers to turn their heads.

Spence scanned the room. He found his uncle comfortably sitting at a small table across from Mrs. Murphy, cutting enthusiastically into a thick steak. Her big steaming coffeepot was near at hand, David noticed as he strode across the room, weaving his way between the small, well-worn tables.

Ben forked a good-sized, pinkish-centered chunk into his wide mouth, raised his eyes, and saw his nephew. He leaped to his feet, grinned, and tried to speak. Finally as Spence approached, he stopped chewing, swallowed hard, and grasped his nephew in a bear hug, tears filling his big dark eyes. "Davie . . . Davie, m'lad," he said huskily, "I've been missin' you . . . missin' you mightily."

"Well, I've—" With tears rolling down his cheeks David paused, wiped them away, and started again. "I—"

"Coffee's still hot," Edna Murphy's deep voice took over. "Might's well seat yourself and sip a cup while he downs that steak. Me'n your uncle's having a lively conversation about horses, cows, farming, an' such."

David shook his head and tried to smile. "Thank you, but I need to hurry. I'm expected at church in a few minutes. I saw Uncle Ben's wagon and stopped by to escort him to the Marshall's home."

"But he's only took one bite off'n his steak," the heavy woman protested, a touch of disappointment in her deep voice.

And laughing hardily, Ben reached down and put a big hand on her shoulder. "I doubt I'll be starvin' anytime soon. If you'll be kind enough t' loan me a plate an' pour another big cup of that good coffee, I'll be chewin' on that fine steak whilst we ride along to . . . to wherever my nephew's taking me."

*

Twenty minutes later, as the big wagon, with Jake and the mares in tow, trundled out from the trees into the churchyard, Benjamin Roberts turned to David and creased his wide forehead. "I'm mighty anxious t' meet up with that teacher you'll be marrying tomorrow," he said anxiously. "Ms. . . . Ms. Kelly I think her name t' be."

"Well, I'm sure—" His nephew smiled and gestured. "Well, I'm sure you will meet Martha Kelly in less than a minute."

Ben turned his head, saw the three figures standing at the side door, and asked hurriedly, "Which one of them young women's Martha Kelly?"

David Spence smiled. "She's the pretty one."

Ben laughed heartily. "Well, Davie, m'lad, with my weak eyes, I'd say they both look t' be pretty's a speckled pup."

Still laughing, Ben Roberts pulled his big, plodding horses in beside Elsie's ugly mules.

"She's the young lady in the blue dress," David finally managed.

They stepped down and Martha rushed on past the mules to Ben's big wagon.

And seeing her, Ben stroked a big steak-greased hand across his sullied shirt, put a wide smile on his face, and strode forward, right hand extended. He took her hand gently and looked at her appraisingly. "Hmm . . . Davie won't a bit overselling when he wrote me an' made mention of you."

"Well, Mr. Roberts," Martha laughed lightly, "I doubt he was overselling when he mentioned you."

Ben turned to David, chuckling. "Well, Davie, m'lad, I'm already liking this young lady," he finally managed.

David grinned proudly. "Well, Uncle Ben, I appreciate your appraisal, but I knew you would—"

"Pastor Spence," Willie's strained voice rose from the side door, "I 'spect we ought to get the organ inside and load up Aunt Nora's piano. It'll be turning dark before we can get it on home."

Spence sighed softly. "William hasn't heard that his aunt donated the piano to honor her deceased daughter, Lilly." He paused a long, thoughtful moment. Then he sighed again, forced a smile, and went on. "Well, Uncle Ben, I guess it's time we go to work. We may need your help to carry the organ inside. And afterward, while Martha plays, you can join us in a hymn, maybe two." He glanced at the low sun. "I believe we have plenty of time."

David's uncle noisily cleared his throat. Then he smiled. "Be glad to, m'lad. Be glad to."

*

As the orange sun settled behind the tall trees, Uncle Ben reined his big matched horses, followed closely by Elsie's little mule-drawn wagon, into Beulah Marshall's front yard. And shadows were spreading fast as Ben's big wagon rattled on toward the barn.

Willie reined the mules in at the front porch, turned on the wagon seat to Elsie, and said worriedly, "I don't see Aunt Nora's carriage. You reckon—?"

"Could be," Elsie interrupted, trying to sound positive, "Aunt Nora's took it on up to her house."

"Could be," Willie Marshall muttered, unconvinced. "I reckon I ought to—"

"There they are, coming out from the trees," Elsie interrupted again, excitement in her voice. "I sure hope they got that lady to play the organ."

"Was that where they were rushing off to?" Willie questioned, his voice hardly louder than a whisper.

Elsie laughed. "Oh, I thought you knew. Your mama and Aunt Nora went to get Pastor Nash's sister. She'll be playing the organ at our wedding. That is, if your mama's persuading was anywhere near what I think it to be."

"With me worrying and all, you shoulda told me before now," Will Marshall muttered rather resentfully as he clambered down from the wagon. He turned back and smiled up at her with pride. "Well, I'll be seeing if Ma's persuading still works." The resentment in his voice, Elsie noticed, had disappeared.

Aunt Nora's strong "Whoa!" and pulled lines brought the big, snorting, hard-breathing mare to a stop about four strides from Elsie's wagon.

And squinting in twilight's dim glow, Willie hobbled over to the carriage. "We've been a bit worried about yawl being home before dark sets in," he drawled, still squinting to see into the rear seat, now deeply darkened by the black canvas top.

Beulah Marshall gruntingly stepped down from the carriage, laughed lightly, and spoke up, a touch of excitement in her voice. "William, I'm mighty pleasured to introduce Ms. Lucy Nash. She's the spin . . . lady that'll be playing the organ tomorrow."

That spinster ought to be playing my well-tuned piano, Nora thought. She grunted and started to complain but changed her mind.

The woman leaned forward. Her stern face came into the moon glow, and Will caught his breath momentarily. *Looks to be cut from the same bolt of linen cloth as Pastor Nash*, he thought, gazing at the spinster.

A short pause and Willie forced a thin smile. "I'm plumb proud to meet you, Ms. Nash," he finally managed as he took a hobbling stride past his mother and belatedly thrust a greeting hand into the carriage. He grasped her languid hand lightly and went on hesitantly, "I'll . . . we'll be thanking you for coming to play at our wedding."

Nora spoke up impatiently. "I need to get Nathan to stable this old mare before he's abed." She raised the lines to slap the horse but stopped to say, "I'm getting Ms. Nash bedded down at my house for the night. I 'spect her to be a mite tired."

A confirming grunt from the backseat was all William heard the spinster say.

CHAPTER 44

—THE THRONE OF GOD—

IN THE VALLEY it was still dark, but the dim glow of dawn had brightened the mountaintop. And unable to sleep, William Marshall flung the blanket aside. He had tossed and turned throughout the night, his cluttered mind darting between the baptizing at sunrise, the wedding at noon, and the eighteen-mile journey to board the train at the New River water tower at six o'clock—or a bit later.

In the dimness he reached for his shirt and trousers draped across the foot of his narrow bed. And taking care not to roust Pastor Nash from his deep, snoring sleep, Willie swung his big feet from the bed and slipped into his clothes. He gathered up his high-top boots and moved quietly out the door. Stealthily, he descended the creaky stairs, heard the clatter of dishes, and saw a yellow shaft of lamplight spilling from the kitchen into the hallway.

I reckon that to be Elsie, he thought. She's already up early and fixing breakfast. *This being our wedding day, I might as well slip in and plant her with a big old kiss*, he decided, an anticipatory smile splitting his lean face as he treaded lightly along the dim hallway.

In the yellow glow from the kitchen, Will Marshall paused, saw the slender figure bent over the big stove, and quietly lowered the boots to the floor. He sneaked across the kitchen, pursed his lips and tapped her shoulder.

Startled, she spun around. Martha Kelly's mouth flew open, and so did his. "What—?" She started. There was quick surprise in her blue-green eyes.

"I—I—I'm—I figured you to be—" Willie stuttered, his face beet red. A pause and they both laughed.

"What's you laughing about?" Elsie's inquiring voice interrupted from the doorway.

Will whirled to face her and stuttered again. "Well—I—I was thinking—"

Martha smiled. "I think . . . well, it seems to be a case of mistaken identity."

Willie nodded significantly and breathed a deep sigh. "It shore was. There ain't no doubt about that."

"It better be a mistake," Elsie teased. "Shame on you, Will Marshall. Here it is our wedding day and you're trying to kiss the preacher's bride. Now, William"—she smiled—"daylight's coming on and you ain't had your breakfast. Folks will be flocking in before you get your baptizing clothes on."

He forced a frown. "Now Ms. Kelly, here it is, we ain't yet married and she's started giving orders."

Martha Kelly smiled and slipped an arm around Elsie's waist. "Well, it's never too early to take control. Now William," she ordered forcefully, a little smile tugging at the corners of her mouth, "have a seat and eat your breakfast before it gets cold."

With a slow headshake, Willie obediently pulled out a chair and drawled. "Well, I can't rightly figure what the country's coming to. It won't be long before women might be controlling the whole dang world."

Elsie laughed.

Martha nodded, smiled brightly, and spoke softly. "Yes. We know."

*

It was nearing full daylight. The gray light had brightened and the mist-shrouded orange sun was rimming the eastern horizon.

Noisy rumbles and boisterous laughter came from outside, and Elsie looked out the kitchen window. Buggies, wagons, a dozen or so mounted horses, and four gangly men on mules riding double were migrating into Widow Marshall's front yard. She turned to the table where Willie sat, noisily sipping black coffee, and spoke hastily. "Will, folks are already pouring in. You need to commence getting ready."

Will Marshall pushed the chair back, climbed clumsily to his feet, and looked out the window. "Why're all the folks gathering here? I figured them to mostly gather at the creek."

"Well," she laughed, "it seems the Lord works in strange and mysterious ways." *And so does Beulah Marshall*, Elsie thought but said, "I reckon they're gathering to escort you down to the creek. With folks coming in afoot, I'm glad we'll be taking the wagons."

William Marshall gulped two loud swallows from his cup, sat it on the table, turned, kissed Elsie's cheek, and said as hurriedly as his drawl would allow, "Reckon I ought to go on upstairs and put on my baptizing clothes before Pastor Spence brings his uncle's big wagon out from the barn."

As Willie turned to leave, Spence stepped in from the side porch. And Martha, busily washing dishes in Widow Marshall's big tin pan, rushed to meet him, her wet hands dripping water as she went. They kissed passionately, and Elsie quoted, "We ain't allowing no unmarried mouth kissing."

Martha had to laugh when David said, "It seems I've heard that statement before."

*

With Nora's two-seat carriage leading the way, six crowded wagons rumbled out from Widow Marshall's front yard and on down the dusty, treelined track. And trailing the rattling wagons were two rented rigs, five buggies, and over two dozen men and several women riding horseback.

It was nearing eight o'clock, and sunlight was creeping down the mountain slopes, when the wagons turned at the fork.

David rose up from the lead wagon's planked seat and sang out in a strong baritone voice that carried well beyond the rear wagon:

> Shall we gather at the river,
> where bright angel feet have trod,
> with its crystal tide forever flowing
> by the throne of God?

"Sing out! Sing out loud!" Pastor Spence bellowed. And with the addition of Irvin Hensley's harmonica, Uncle Ben's deep voice and nearby choir members, they sang on:

> Yes, we'll gather at the river,
> the beautiful, the beautiful river,
> gather with the saints at the river
> that flows by the throne of God.

As the wagons rumbled across Crooked Creek Bridge, a choir was stretching back well over three hundred yards. And their blended voices could be heard for half a mile, maybe a bit farther.

Chapter 45

—A Time to Wed—

It was several minutes after ten o'clock the next morning when Nathan McBride turned Nora's black lacquered carriage on the dusty Town Road.

"Now, Nathan, don't you be urging the horse along. That big mare will be stirring enough dust to dirty our Sunday clothes and clog up baby Rose's little lungs," Nora warned sternly while brushing Rose's pale-yellow dress with a white-gloved hand.

Rose looked up and giggled.

Nora flashed a glance back at the stoic spinster, stiffly ensconced on the rear leather seat, and went on. "Baby Rose looks like Lilly when she was about a year old."

Nathan cut his dark eyes to Rose, saw her blue eyes, her yellow hair, and grunted. "Rose ain't lookin' no ways like her. Lilly's hair was black an' her eyes brown."

"Well now," Nora said sharply, "anybody with eyes to see would notice how her smile is like Lilly's." As Nathan opened his mouth to respond, she went on. "Anyhow, while Elsie and Will are in Lynchburg, she'll be with us for about two weeks. I'm thanking, by then, you'll be seeing her smile, like I do."

He grunted again and changed the subject. "Have t' be hurryin' along. You're knowing I have t' go on back t' get Beulah an' thu brides an' get them t' church before noontime." He frowned and grumbled on. "Now you're knowing, I'm t' be standing as best man fer Will. Folks might be pokin' fun at me fer quite a spell if'n I brought them in late to their own wedding. Might jus' be pokin' fun at you too," he added, grinning slightly.

Nora bridled. And hearing no humor in his remark, she gave him a reproving look and remained silent.

As the carriage rattled across the churchyard, Nathan noticed the ugly gelding at the hitch rail and Beulah's hitched buggy parked in the shade of a large oak.

He chuckled. "Looks like thu pastor an' Will've done hurried into their Sunday clothes an' already here. It looks like Will's brought Beulah's buggy along. I reckon it to be fer you, baby Rose, an' her t' ride on home after thu wedding."

On a loud "Whoa" Nathan pulled the snorting Morgan horse in before the church steps. Gruntingly, he stepped down, forced a little smile, bowed gallantly, and raised a hand to help the black-clad spinster from the backseat.

She emitted a sour-faced grunt, hiked her dark skirts slightly, took the offered hand, and carefully stepped down. A pause to smooth her skirts and she hurried to the steps.

And not bothering to wait for Nathan, Nora, with Rose in her arms, struggled with her wide hoopskirt awhile. After several grunts and a couple of deep sighs, she finally managed to climb down from the carriage. Another sharp glance at Nathan and she waddled over to the steps.

And Nathan McBride, now back on the leather seat, was muttering to himself. "It's gonna be a long day. I promised Will I'd ride Jake an' follow them on t' thu New River water tower to bring back thu carriage." He turned the big Morgan onto the lane and went along through the trees at a fast, dusty trot, still muttering. "I'm a-thinkin' dark might set in a goodly while 'fore they board thu train an' head on out to Lynchburg."

*

It was nearing eleven o'clock. And for the third time Fred Draper reached under his frockcoat and pulled out his big silver-plated watch. He opened the lid, turned to Oscar Stanley, standing just inside the church door, and chuckled, his eyes crinkling. "I reset my watch 'bout daylight this morning. I ain't plannin' t' let it run down like you did when you was thu bell ringer a while back."

"Well, I ain't thu only one t' be making mistakes," Stanley responded, slightly put out. "If'n yore watch had been set right I wouldn't a-rung thu bell when I did—embarrassing it was."

"Didn't mean t' be a-criticizing none," Draper responded in a low, apologetic voice. He glanced at his watch. "Thu church is gettin' a bit crowded," he almost whispered. "Them Doolins done come in an' took up a whole back pew. Well, with thu sheriff and his new deputy, Johnny Akers, just across thu aisle, I don't reckon they'll be makin' trouble."

"Don't reckon they will," Oscar put in. "I 'spect their mama's done tamed them down a bit."

"You ought to be gettin' in your pew seat 'fore it's full up," Fred Draper almost whispered again. "I have t' stay back here t' ring thu bell come noontime. That'll be when thu weddings commence," he explained belatedly, knowing Stanley already knew.

Oscar hurried down the center aisle and Draper glanced at his watch again. He closed the lid, slipped it into a fob pocket, and reached for the dangling rope.

The bell tolled.

And with the exception of a crying baby and rustle of starched petticoats, the crowded sanctuary went silent.

Pastor Spence rose from a high-backed chair, moved quickly to the pulpit, and opened his mother's big Bible. He raised his eyes, saw a room filled with smiling faces, and nodded, trying to hold back joyful tears.

"Well, this is a wonderful day," he finally managed. Then he quoted, "'This is a day the Lord hath made. Let us rejoice and be glad in it.'" And a multitude of voices echoed, "This is a day the Lord hath made. Let us rejoice and be glad in it."

A hardy "Amen" and David went on calmly, "The last Sunday in April, when I introduced myself, I intended to serve as your pastor for two or three weeks and move on to my uncle's farm near the Shenandoah Valley." Without pause he took an under-brow glance at the third row pew. "But now, as I look out and see your smiling faces, I believe God, in his boundless wisdom, sent me to this place, to marry, to live in peace, and to serve as your pastor."

The congregation clapped politely.

David held up a hand and continued. "We have guests with us today. Most of you probably know Pastor Henry Nash." He turned and gestured toward the slender minister in the high-backed chair to his right and chuckled lightly. "I'll have to keep an eye on him. He will be performing two weddings this afternoon."

The parishioners laughed lightly.

Pastor Nash sat stoically, thin arms crossed.

David paused to clear his throat and flashed another glance at Uncle Ben, sitting stiffly beside Beulah Marshall's pillowed seat. "And we are honored to have Pastor Nash's sister, Lucy, at the organ today." He gestured. "And I hope each member of the church will take time to thank the Doolins for having the organ repaired."

With that, a low murmur rippled through the crowd. And all eyes, it seemed to David, swept to the back pew where the Doolins sat stiffly, clean and well dressed.

"And lastly," Pastor Spence gestured again, "I find it a great pleasure to have my uncle, Benjamin Roberts, as my best man."

Somewhat embarrassed, Ben, nodding lightly, forced a grin.

Pastor Spence shook his head and chuckled. "Uncle Ben has asked to speak for a minute or two after the service. Heaven only knows what he'll say, but I pray he will not disavow the agreement to serve as my best man in our wedding ceremony." David reached for his hymnal and went on. "Now turn in your hymnal to page thirty-two and we will begin the service with 'Amazing Grace.'"

After the last stanza, David moved behind the pulpit and began the service with a short prayer. Then he opened his big Bible, raised his blue eyes to the crowded parishioners, and spoke forcefully. "Today I'll read from Ruth, chapter two:

> And Ruth said, "Entreat me not to leave thee,
> or to return from following after thee:
> for whither thou goest, I will go;
> and where thou lodgest, I will lodge:
> thy people shall be my people and thou God my God:
> 'Where thou diest, will I die, and there will I be buried:
> the Lord do so to me, and more also,
> if ought but death part thee and me.'"

"Amen." David ended his brief sermon with a heartfelt prayer, gently closed the worn Bible, and nodded toward Uncle Ben, now with his big handkerchief at his nose, but secretly wiping tears from his ruddy cheeks.

Ben Roberts put his handkerchief away, rose slowly, moved on past Widow Marshall's comfortable pillow, and strode heavily to the low podium. He faced the anxious congregation, shoved a big hand into his coat pocket, frowned, and pulled out the empty hand. His frown deepened. He slipped a nervous hand under the coat to an inner pocked and pulled it out again—still empty. "Aw . . . It must be here somewhere," he mumbled, voice tight. Now somewhat frustrated, he searched a trouser pocket and produced a crumpled slip of paper. He read silently, lips moving slowly. Finally, he stopped reading and it occurred to him that he had never given a speech and promised himself that this would be his first and final speech.

Finally Uncle Ben lifted his head, cleared his throat, and intoned hoarsely. "Beulah Marshall's a-saying in this here note that, since she ain't able to be here till wedding time, I'm to do thu presenting." Benjamin Roberts was searching his pockets again. With several incoherent mumbles he unbuttoned his black long-tailed coat and pulled his big watch from a fob pocket. "Well, here 'tis," he said, relief in his deep voice. He stripped a large dangling key from his silver watch chain and motioned to his nephew.

Somewhat surprised, David stepped from the pulpit and faced his uncle.

With the key protruding from his big, callused fingers, Ben forced a light chuckle, thrust it toward the confused pastor, and spoke as softly as he could. "Widow Marshall says this here key is to fit thu front door of thu church parsonage." Ben paused to consult the wrinkled paper. "It's willed by good Pastor Haskell."

With that, David's eyes widened in surprise and a murmur rippled through the congregation.

David took the key and Ben Roberts went on. "Beulah Marshall said for me t' get thu sheriff t' tell how thu church got hold of Pastor Haskell's house." And still trying to keep his voice low, Ben said, "Davie, I 'spect you oughtta call on the sheriff to do thu explaining."

Pastor Spence nodded and spoke softly. "Sheriff Baxter is coming down the aisle now."

Ben Roberts sighed deeply, stepped down from the low podium, and headed for his third-row seat, pulling out his big handkerchief as he went.

In the aisle, at the third row, Baxter met Ben Roberts. *I might as well shake his hand*, the big sheriff thought. *It might win a few more votes come November.* He paused, shifted a thick, worn Bible to his left hand, took Ben's hand briefly, nodded, forced a smile, and hurried on down the aisle. He stepped onto the podium and turned to face the anxious crowd. Without conscious thought, he pulled out his big-bowled pipe and stuffed the crooked stem in his wide mouth.

"It's some kind of miracle, Pastor Spence might say." He pulled the pipestem from his mouth and chuckled. "I might be able to speak a bit plainer with the pipe in my pocket."

"As I was saying"—Sam Baxter started again while stuffing the pipe in a sagging coat pocket—"it might be a miracle that you got Pastor Haskell's house after sitting empty since mid-April. A pure miracle, I believe it was. As you might already know, Pastor Haskell's wife passed away awhile before he came from out east, some eighteen years back, to pastor our church. They didn't have any children nor other relatives that we know about. With him passing suddenly and not leaving a will and the house in town, the town council voted to auction it off.

"Now that I think about it, Pastor Haskell might've been in some pain when he brought his big Bible by my office a week or so before he passed away. He said to me, in a serious way, 'Now, Sheriff, if anything happens to me, I'll be depending on you to give my Bible to the church.'"

Baxter paused, brandished the big Bible, cleared his throat, and shook his graying head. "I didn't think about his Bible till the town council decided to auction off the pastor's house. And since I had custody of the key, I decided to go up there to find the Bible. I did. It was on his desk gathering dust and open to a handwritten page. I could see right away he had pinned his will in the Bible. With no witness signature, I figured, to make it legal, I'd take it to Lawyer O'Leary for verification. I took up some of Pastor Haskell's sermon notes to match up the handwriting. I thought it matched and so did Lawyer O'Leary. He decided, and I agreed, that I'd have to ride over to Twin Oaks and get Judge Waters's approval to be sure it's legal.

"And so—" The clumping of heavy boots stopped him.

"And so—" He started again and Fred Draper's loud voice broke in.

"Tom, thu church is full up. Looks like yawl gonna have t' stand at thu back wall if'n you're plannin' on stayin' at all."

Sam Baxter bristled, his temper flaring. He started to complain, but realizing November's election was less than two months away, he decided to force a light chuckle. He did and said hesitantly, "Bring your family on in TJ, uh, Mr. Harris. I'll wait," he added with a weak smile.

And Thomas Jefferson Harris, trying to walk softly, moved on squeaky boots along the back wall to the corner, followed by his diminutive wife and five children, two boys and three girls, all between eight and seventeen years old, Joel being the oldest and his brother Jack the youngest.

"And so," Sam sighed, "this is not only a Bible, but I'd say it's a legal document as well." He turned to David and smiled broadly. "Pastor Spence, you take custody of this Bible. And, Pastor"—he laughed lightly—"you and Ms. Kelly can move in today—that is, unless you've made plans for a wedding trip."

Pastor David Spence smiled thinly and almost whispered. "We plan to go with Will and Elsie to Lynchburg and stay until after the surgery. If it's successful, we'll go on to visit Martha's parents up near Winchester for a week or so." David chuckled and went on. "We hope you will keep our decision a secret for a couple of weeks."

*

The bell tolled.

The brides were late.

Fred Draper released the bell rope and lumbered over to the open door. "I jus' felt it in my bones Nathan was gonna be late," he mumbled, thrust his big head out, and squinted in the bright sunlight. He saw Nora's carriage emerge from the trees and mumbled on. "Well, reckon they'll be a mite late, but no more n' two or three minutes late."

Nathan reined the big Morgan mare in at the steps. He flung his bovine body from the rocking carriage and rounded the rear wheel to help Widow Marshall and her wide, multilayered skirts from the front seat. Sweating profusely, he pulled a new, store-bought black coat sleeve across his streaming brow and raised a large callused hand to help her down. And with amazing agility, she took the outstretched hand, gathered her skirts, stepped down, climbed the church steps, and rushed through the doorway. She was hurrying down the aisle to the third row pew as the brides, in their long white wedding gowns, cautiously climbed down from the buggy.

Beulah Marshall stopped at pew three, turned, and looked back through the doorway. The two brides were topping the steps, hand in hand. She smiled briefly, turned back, and motioned a white-gloved hand to Willie, now sitting stiffly on a front pew at the aisle.

He nodded. His face paled as he stumbled to his feet and cut a glance at David, now stepping down from the podium. And then he turned to see the brides, side by side, moving slowly down the aisle, their faces barely visible behind white lace veils.

The organ blared.

Willie hobbled to the left, David stepped to the right, and Pastor Nash strode stiffly to the center of the podium.

William Marshall and David Spence were smiling proudly as they watched the approaching brides. But the thin pastor stood stoically, his big Bible at the ready position.

Almost simultaneously, David and Willie stepped out before the podium to meet their brides.

Pastor Nash cleared his throat noisily. "Let us pray," he said in a high, nervous voice. He mumbled a short prayer, cleared his throat again, placed the open Bible on the pulpit, and pulled a folded yellow paper from an inner coat pocket. He gazed at the paper several seconds, sucked a deep breath, and swept his eyes across the crowded room. He half-smiled, cleared his throat again, turned his eyes to the yellow paper, and read, his voice surprisingly clear:

Dearly beloved,

for as much as all marriage is a holy estate
ordained to by God's holy ordinance to be honored by all.
Martha Kelly, do you take David Spence to be your
wedded husband,
to have, to hold and obey from this day forward,
for better, for worse, for richer, for poorer,
in sickness and in health, until death you do part,
according to God's holy ordinance?

And Martha, somewhat nervous herself, responded, "I, Martha Kelly, take thee, David, to be my wedded husband, to have, to hold and"—she looked up at David, her eyes moist, a smile on her face—"obey from this day forward, for better, for worse, for richer, for poorer, in sickness and in health until death us do part, according to God's holy ordinance."

*

About thirty minutes later David was at Nora's carriage, gently helping Martha onto the rear seat while Willie struggled to get Elsie's wide skirts onto the front seat.

As David rounded the carriage, he felt a tugging at his sleeve. He stopped, turned his head, and saw a tall, rangy, stoop-shouldered, clean-shaven man. "I don't believe—" he started. After a brief pause he recognized the man, smiled, and went on. "Well, hello, Mr. Harris. It's been a while since I've seen you. I hardly recognized you without your whiskers."

Harris put a hand to his chin and smiled through his yellow teeth.

"I don't believe you've met my wife, Martha," Pastor Spence announced, pride in his voice.

T. J. Harris's smile faded. "Don't reckon I have, Parson, 'cept one time a while back, in passin'."

David laughed shortly. "I believe it was the day I met you at—" He paused then, not wanting to embarrass Thomas. "Yes. It was the Saturday she arrived on the stagecoach."

Another pause and Tom's smile returned. "Parson, I'd be mighty proud if'n you'd spare a bit o' time t' look at m'wagon."

Spence frowned. "But Thomas, I've seen your wagon."

"Me an' Joel's done fixed it up au mite. I kinda figured ye might want t' take a look afore ye ride off."

David glanced over his shoulder at Nora's carriage, now surrounded by a gaggle of giggling women. He turned back to Tom Harris, smiled, and gestured. "Yes. Well, I'll take a look, but we have to hurry."

Harris pointed. "We got that old mule an' wagon shaded under that thu big ol' tree. Joel ull be bringin' it round fer you t' see."

He motioned to Joel, now impatiently waiting on the wagon, his mother and four squirming siblings on three rows of removable planked seats behind him.

The gangly lad lashed the bony swayback mule into a slow trot.

As the one-horse wagon approached, David smiled and said, "Well, the mule looks the same, but that wagon has been . . . reconfigured."

Harris considered the meaning of *reconfigured* for a few seconds. Finally, he said proudly, his admiring eyes scanning the approaching wagon, "It took a bit o' doin', but me an' Joel's done turned my whiskey wagon to a coal-haulin' wagon. Couldn't do much 'bout thu mule though." He wheezed a weak chuckle, shook his head, and went on. "I got right with thu Lord a while back an' give up on whiskey stillin'. Thu good Lord's done put all that black rock underfoot on my land an' I figured He's done put it thar fer me t' use. I'm throwin' in with them Doolin boys. Their vein's 'bout petered out an' we made up a deal t' go half an' half, 'round two weeks ago, reckon it was."

Half-smiling, David said hesitantly, "You . . . you're dealing with the Doolins."

TJ chuckled. "Them Doolin boys shore have growed up lately." His hand went back to his chin, unconsciously searching for his nonexistent whiskers. He cut a sideways glance at the big pastor, nodded, and went on. "I'm a-doubtin' Harley 'ull be gittin' his comeuppance after all."

David started to laugh, but seeing Thomas Jefferson Harris's serious countenance, he put a big hand on his narrow shoulder and smiled. "Well, Mr. Harris, I doubt he will. I pray you and the Doolins will be successful, very successful. And, Thomas, I look forward to seeing you and your family in church next Sunday." David shook his head lightly and smiled. "Make that Sunday after next. Pastor Nash has agreed to preach next Sunday. My wife and I will probably be at her parent's farm for a short visit."

The lean mountain man smiled. "I sorta figured that. We'll be a-comin' on anyhow though. Well, I'd better get a-goin'." He turned to the wagon and glanced at Nora's carnage. "Will Marshall looks t' be a bit anxious hisself," T. J. muttered as he climbed up beside Joel. He smiled through his yellow teeth again and spat to the other side of the wagon, and with the crack of Joel's long whip, they rumbled away.

David turned, put a wide smile on his face, and nodded his way through the crowd, shaking hands as he went. At the carriage, he climbed onto the rear seat beside Martha. And still smiling, he reached over, took her white-gloved hand, and put it to his lips. That brought forth a few cheers and handclaps from the crowd.

He felt a tugging at his long-tail coat, looked down, and saw Widow Marshall, her wide flowery hat still somewhat askew.

She almost yelled, "I need the parsonage key. Pastor Nash, bless his sweet soul, was a bit messy with his housekeeping. We . . . well, several women and myself decided to have our new parsonage cleaned up before ye get back from your wedding trip. I expect that to be two weeks, more or less," she added as David smilingly handed her the big key.

Willie frowned and spoke tartly. "We'd better hurry on to catch the train." Waiting no time, he flicked the lines against the Morgan's haunches. The carriage jerked forward and he headed the big horse down the lane, lined on both sides for about fifty yards or so with men, women, and children tossing flowers and ribbons in the path of the fast-moving carriage while singing,

> Amazing grace! How sweet thu sound,
> that saved a wretch like me! I once was lost,
> but now I'm found, was blind but now I see.
> 'Twas grace that taught my heart to fear,
> and grace my fears relieved;
> How precious did that grace appear,
> the hour I first believed?

Pastor David Spence's big baritone voice joined in and could be heard for half a mile or more, some thought, as the carriage, followed by Nathan McBride on the ugly gelding, with the faint jangle of trace chains, rolled on through the grove and disappeared.